Praise for the novels of
Emilie Richards

"Richards's writing is unpretentious and effective, and her characters burst with vitality and authenticity...."
—*Publishers Weekly* on *Prospect Street*

"Richards's ability to portray compelling characters who grapple with challenging family issues is laudable, and this well-crafted tale should score well with fans of Luanne Rice and Kristin Hannah."
—*Publishers Weekly*, starred review on *Fox River*

"Well-written, intricately plotted novel..."
—*Library Journal* on *Whiskey Island*

"A flat-out page turner... reminiscent of the early Sidney Sheldon."
—*Cleveland Plain Dealer* on *Whiskey Island*

"Richards's characterization and plotting are all on target."
—*Publishers Weekly* on *Beautiful Lies*

"A multi-layered plot, vivid descriptions and a keen sense of place and time."
—*Library Journal* on *Rising Tides*

"Intricate, seductive and a darned good read."
—*Publishers Weekly* on *Iron Lace*

"A fascinating tale of the tangled race relations and complex history of Louisiana...this is a page-turner."
—*New Orleans Times-Picayune* on *Iron Lace*

EMILIE RICHARDS

THE PARTING GLASS

MIRA®

ISBN 0-7783-2047-2

THE PARTING GLASS

Copyright © 2003 by Emilie Richards McGee.

www.MIRABooks.com

Printed in U.S.A.

ACKNOWLEDGMENTS

My thanks to fellow writers Karen Young, Diane Chamberlain and Patricia McLinn for their affectionate support and feedback during the creation of *The Parting Glass,* and to Damaris Rowland for her insights and suggestions. I'm grateful, too, for Madelyn Campbell's considerable medical expertise and her willingness to share it.

A very special thank-you to all the readers who asked me to continue the Donaghue story, and particularly those at Cleveland's Irish Cultural Festival who related their personal stories of Whiskey Island and prodded me to look into Cleveland's bootlegging past and mysterious tunnels.

Special thanks to Michael McGee, who accompanied me on two research trips to County Mayo during particularly rainy weather and almost never complained. And as always, thanks to my talented editor Leslie Wainger, who never fails to inspire and encourage.

THE PARTING GLASS

Of all the money ere I had,
I spent it in good company,
And all the harm I've ever done,
Alas was done to none but me
And all I've done for want of wit,
To memory now I can't recall
So fill to me the parting glass,
Good night and joy be with you all.

Of all the comrades ere I had,
They're sorry for my going away,
And all the sweethearts ere I had,
They wish me one more day to stay,
But since it falls unto my lot
That I should go and you should not,

I'll gently rise and softly call,
Good night and joy be with you all.

(This is a traditional Irish ballad for singing at the end of an evening, a gathering or an event. One of Ireland's most popular, it is documented as far back as the 1770s.)

prologue

1923
Castlebar, County Mayo

My dearest Patrick,

So many years and so many miles separating us, dear brother. For centuries we McSweeneys knew nothing of loneliness but everything of each other. And what else was there to know? What else is there in the end but family, land and church? The rest is like butter on bread, mere pleasure with little nourishment.

Now our family has been dumped like ship's ballast on distant shores. You in Ohio, our dear sisters in Australia, Nova Scotia and the grave. We are old, all who remain, and separated by much more than miles. We know so little of each other now. I have the new photograph that St. Brigid's made for you, and I thank you

for sending it, but what happened to the young man I
knew, so straight and tall? What happened to the priest
with fire in his gaze and vitality in his step? Has he gone
the path I've trod myself? The path that leads to only
one destination?

I cannot imagine you as an old man, dear Patrick. You
only celebrate Mass on Holy Days, hear confession but
infrequently, read for hours each day and contemplate?
What exactly do you consider now that your time is
your own, my brother? The years you have already
lived? The green island of your birth? Our dear, dear
land that McSweeneys will never work again?

Perhaps, had I married, I might find more to do with
my own time. I would have grandchildren and great-
grandchildren, and I would dandle them proudly on my
knee. Instead, with no family to succeed me, I think only
of the family from which I came, of you and Ciara and
Selma, of dear Una who was with us such a short time.
Not a one of us with offspring of our own, and a long
proud line in ashes at out feet.

I remember all, even at this final juncture of my life.
I remember songs and laughter, the fragrance of bread
baking on a stone hearth, the bleating of sheep in our
paddock. I remember a small lad tugging at my skirts,
saying his prayers with a childish lisp, cowering behind
closed doors for fear of the boogeyman on nights when
Mayo's bog land was cold and misty.

How fortunate I am to have these memories to comfort me. How fortunate are all who have had family to
cherish. This can never be taken from us, dear Patrick.
No matter the years that separate us, you and all our
loved ones are always with me.

                                        Your sister,
                                        Maura McSweeney

chapter 1

Peggy Donaghue avoided the parking lot of the Whiskey Island Saloon whenever she could, which wasn't easy since she lived directly above it. On days when there was no parking on the street, she reluctantly took the reserved spot closest to the back door and sprinted for the kitchen. She wasn't superstitious. She just didn't believe in tempting fate.

Not unless the circumstances were exceptional.

The young man standing just behind her cleared his throat. "It's real windy, Ms. D. You don't have to stay out here. Nothing's going to happen, I promise."

Peggy pulled her long chestnut hair into a temporary ponytail so it would stop whipping into her eyes. Over one shoulder she could see that Josh, tall, lanky and clearly uncomfortable, wasn't looking at her. That was understandable. Josh had just stolen his very first car. He was praying, just as Peggy was, that the owner wouldn't realize his brandnew Honda Civic was missing.

"I trust you, Josh. And I even trust them." Peggy nodded to the group of four adolescent boys who were poring over the car like melted butter on the saloon's Friday night pierogi special. "But I'll just stay here in case they need me."

"Nick was locked away in his study. When he gets like that, he doesn't know what's going on. He's not going to know." Josh's tone was less certain than his words.

"He's probably got stuff to do before he leaves town." Peggy saw a familiar figure coming up between the rows of cars. The willowy strawberry blonde was unmistakable—and related. "Uh oh, we've been nailed," she said in her best Jimmy Cagney imitation. "It's the calaboose for us now, Scarface."

Josh's pale cheeks grew red. "I gotta go. Winston's gonna make sure it gets done right and stuff. I gotta go home in case Nick notices—"

Peggy waved him away. "You go on. I'll face the music alone."

Josh looked properly grateful and took off, skirting Peggy's older sister by ducking behind the back row of cars. Plastic bags and newspaper from somebody's blown-over garbage can skittered across the lot in his wake.

Casey Donaghue Kovats came up beside Peggy and stood for a moment watching the group of adolescents tape strings of firecrackers to the back bumper of Niccolo Andreani's car. The silver Civic was parked close to the back door of the saloon so that it would be out of sight from the road.

"You're letting those kids tape fireworks to the bumper? You worked in an emergency room. You know how dangerous those things are."

"No 'Hi, how are you, isn't this a windy day'?"

"Peggy, have you lost your mind?"

"Fireworks *are* dangerous. These are firecrackers, and they're only slightly higher-tech than tin cans and old shoes."

"Megan's going to have a fit."

"I certainly hope so. We've gone to a lot of trouble." Peggy motioned to one youth, a handsome young African-American with meticulously divided cornrows and a roll of duct tape adorning one arm. "Winston, will you please reassure Casey that Nick's car won't blow up?"

Winston abandoned his supervisory post to join the two sisters. "Yo, Ms. K. Nothing gonna happen here but a little noise."

Casey still didn't look convinced. "I have great faith in your abilities, Winston, really I do, but what if—and I know this is a remote possibility—you're wrong?"

"Can't be wrong. We tried it out yesterday."

"Yesterday?" Peggy was intrigued. This was new information.

"Yeah, at some wedding. Somebody got married down at the Baptist church."

"Somebody you know?"

Winston shrugged. "Learned a lot. Like don't put balloons and firecrackers on the same bumper, unless you want a real mess."

Peggy tried not to smile. "See? I told you we were in the hands of a master."

Winston escaped back to his job as Casey rolled her eyes. "I can't believe Nick had the bad judgment to leave his car at the saloon in the first place," Casey said.

"He didn't. Josh delivered it half an hour ago. Nick doesn't know it's gone."

"Then how's he getting to the church?"

"I thought he could walk. He's only a few blocks away."

A gust of wind pushed Peggy against Casey's hip and made nonsense of that plan. The sky was growing steadily darker, and the wind was accelerating. That morning the official forecast for the spring day had been breezy, with the slight possibility of a shower. But this was Cleveland. Weather was the only guarantee. The particulars were in the hands of God.

"I'd give him my car, but I don't have a car anymore," Peggy said.

"You need to remind me you're moving halfway around the world tomorrow? Like it's not on my mind?"

Peggy ignored her. "Jon can drive Nick to the church. Will you call him and ask?"

Jon was Casey's husband of just a year and nearly always willing to lend a hand. "I guess he won't mind. At least he won't get blown off the road in this wind. Jon can take care of himself." Casey smiled. Peggy had noticed that Casey did a lot of that these days. Grinned when she had reason to, smiled mysteriously when she didn't. Marriage agreed with her.

More than two years had passed since Peggy and Casey had come home to Cleveland, lost souls looking for a place to hide. Now Peggy was the mother of a son, Casey was married to her best friend, and Megan, who ran the family saloon, was about to celebrate her own wedding.

Of course, what sounded like a trio of happily-ever-afters wasn't. Not quite. Each sister still faced considerable hurdles, but Peggy didn't want to think about her own. Not for the moment. Today was Megan's day.

"Remember the last time we stood around the parking lot like this?" Casey said, as if she knew what was going through Peggy's mind. Both Peggy's sisters had consistently read her thoughts since the day she was old enough to have any.

"We were at gunpoint," Peggy said. "And Niccolo walked by and saved us. Now he's about to marry our sister. Odd how things happen, isn't it?"

"I peeked inside. I can't believe what they've done, can you?"

"They" was the Donaghue family—and everyone in Cleveland who was related to them or wanted to be. A veritable horde of friends and family had descended that morning to scrub and decorate the saloon where Megan and Niccolo's reception would be held after the ceremony at St. Brigid's.

Peggy checked her watch. "I still have a million things to do before Kieran wakes up." The atomic clock had nothing on Peggy's toddler son for keeping life precisely on schedule.

"You're still planning to leave him upstairs with a baby-sitter?"

"He'll be happier. Everybody will be happier."

"The old place looks great. The way it did when we were kids and Mom was in charge of family wedding receptions. Megan's going to love it."

Peggy knew better. Someday Megan, their oldest sister, would look back at this day with appreciation, even nostalgia. But today she wouldn't notice a thing. If all the signs were correct, Megan was going to walk through her own wedding ceremony and reception like a newly sentenced prisoner on her way to serving a lifetime behind bars.

Casey grinned. "Okay, maybe she's going to be a little jittery, and maybe she won't notice every little detail...."

"Come on, we'll be lucky if she's only comatose. I don't understand why she and Nick didn't elope."

"She didn't want to set that kind of example."

"For who?" Peggy realized "who" the moment she asked the question. "For me? Megan was afraid if she eloped, I'd copy her someday?"

"I think that's part of it."

"Unbelievable."

"And I think Nick wanted a real wedding," Casey added, before Peggy could expound. "He wanted his kids to witness it. They take a lot of interest in this kind of thing, even though they'll never admit it."

The kids Casey referred to were a large group of teens and pre-teens, including those who were so relentlessly decorating Niccolo's car. Altogether there were more than a dozen verging-on-delinquent and occasionally endearing adolescents who were part of an organization called One Brick at a Time. Niccolo Andreani was the director, founder and jack-of-all-trades who ran it.

"So Megan's doing this wedding for everybody else?" Peggy said.

"She won't talk about it, so I'm just guessing. But you know she's been a wreck ever since she agreed to marry Nick. She adores him, so it can't be regret. I just think she hates being the center of attention. She's happiest when she's running everybody else's lives from the sidelines."

"Well, it's about time she had her day, whether she wants it or not." Peggy glanced at her watch. It was ten, and the wedding was at one. "What's on your list for the rest of the morning?"

"About a million things before I help Megan dress, including a hair appointment."

"Well, I have about a dozen more on mine. Then I have to get dressed, get Kieran set up—"

"And pack."

"I have everything ready to go. Aunt Dee came and got our suitcases early this morning, so I can clean up tonight after the reception and they won't be in the way. Megan's already advertising the apartment." Peggy tried to stave off further discussion of her impending departure. There had been dozens of such conversations, all of them fruitless, since she had announced she was moving to Ireland for a year. "Right now I'd better get busy. Because Kieran really is due to wake up—"

A gust of wind nearly lifted her off her feet, and this time it sent her smashing into Casey. Peggy's shriek was eclipsed by an earsplitting crack. For a moment she was so disoriented that the sound didn't register. Then in horror she turned her head toward the car and saw disaster swaying just above it.

"Get away from the car! Everybody! Now!" She extricated herself from her sister, and almost as one body they hurled themselves forward. "The tree—"

Winston and his crew were tough guys, but they were also survivors. Instinctively they scattered like the leaves that were raining from the big maple tree positioned just over Niccolo's new Civic. A horrifying screech, like ten giant fingernails on a heavenly blackboard, rent the air. Then, as Peggy watched in horror, the tree wobbled uncertainly and split in two.

With a thunderous roar, followed by the scream and crunch of metal, the half closer to the saloon fell on Niccolo's car, flattening the roof and hood. The other half of the tree remained awkwardly, tentatively erect. Nick's car looked like a week-old sandwich fished out of a teenager's bookbag.

Peggy did a frantic head count and assessment. The tree had fallen just slowly enough to give the kids time to get away. They looked shaken, but unharmed.

"Everybody's okay," Peggy said. She repeated it as a question and got satisfactory answers from all the kids. Winston herded them to the other end of the lot, where they shouted and pointed excitedly.

"It missed the saloon," Casey said, her voice shaky. "But, lord, Peggy, that door into the kitchen isn't going to open again until we get a crew out here. It opens out, and the tree's smack against it."

Peggy raised her voice over the intensifying wind. "Who cares about the door? What about Nick's car? How are we going to tell him, and what are he and Megan going to use on their honeymoon?"

"They—they can take mine on the trip. Jon and I can make do with one car until they get back."

"We still have to tell Nick."

"Yeah? Exactly when?"

Peggy was still trying to process this disaster. She was the most analytical of the sisters, but analysis was beyond her at the moment. "How would you like to know something like that right before you head off for your wedding?"

"Wouldn't."

"Can we keep the kids quiet?"

Casey glanced over her shoulder, and the wind whipped her hair over her eyes. "Winston can. Besides, it was probably his idea to have Josh bring the car over. He'll want to take as much time as he can owning up."

Family and friends began pouring out the front doors of the saloon.

"St. Patrick and all the saints! Better call a tree service," somebody shouted.

Another voice chimed in. "Get a wrecker."

Casey documented the obvious. "Any sane person would cancel the reception."

Peggy was trembling now, a delayed reaction that grew more ferocious as she realized just how lucky everyone had been. "You said it yourself. We have a blocked exit. Legally we have to lock our doors."

Casey put her arm around Peggy's shoulders. "That's the

good thing about the Donaghues. Not a soul who's invited to the reception will report us."

"Casey, do you think maybe we could deed this parking lot to the city and get it out of the family once and for all?"

Two hours later Megan Donaghue stared into the full-length mirror on Casey's bedroom closet door. A disgruntled woman in unadorned ivory silk gazed back at her. "I really don't know how I got talked into this. I look like a lampshade."

Casey spoke from the floor below. "You look gorgeous, and there's not one inch of frou-frou on that dress. If it were any simpler we'd call it a slip."

"I should have worn a suit. Only suits make me look like a penguin. How come you got the legs, and Peggy got all that gorgeous straight hair, and I got—" She paused. "Nothing. Not a damn thing."

"Apparently Nick thinks you have some redeeming feature, and if you don't stand completely still, I'm going to stick this needle someplace it wasn't meant to go."

Megan knew her sister and stopped wriggling. Besides, Casey had seemed unusually edgy since Megan had arrived at the house. She didn't want to take any chances. "Maybe it's just momentum. You know? Maybe we just fell into this and kept falling, and eventually he just couldn't figure out how to get out of it. Maybe he's been trying to tell me he doesn't want to marry me and I haven't been listening."

"Megan, Niccolo's been trying to get you to marry him for two years. That's what you weren't listening to. Then you finally stopped making excuses, and here you are." Casey stabbed her needle into the portion of the hem that had come unsewn.

Megan stared at her image in the mirror. She had hoped that on her wedding day, at least, a voluptuous redhead with a come-hither expression and tits would stare back at her. Real tits that filled out a bodice, tantalizing and promising. Instead she saw a short, compact body and the rectangular face that went with it. Granted, there was nothing seriously wrong with the face. The features matched well enough; the amber eyes were large, the expression forthright, and the bright red curls had been tamed into a semblance of order by Casey's own stylist.

"What does he see in me, Casey? I mean, Nick's a good-looking guy. I'm not blind. Some might even say he's gorgeous. I'm wearing a Wonderbra *and* mascara, and nobody's going to faint from passion when I walk down the aisle."

"Megan, don't ask him what he sees in you on the honeymoon, okay? Because he's supposed to be dizzy with desire, not laughing his head off."

"Why am I doing this?" Megan pushed one wayward curl into place. She had been dragged kicking and screaming to the wedding boutique and chosen the simplest dress in the place, but she had refused unequivocally to wear a veil. Instead a spray of silk orange blossoms adorned her short hair, threatening to take off for parts unknown if she continued to bob her head.

"Let's see." Casey clipped the thread and sat back staring up at her sister. "Why are you doing this? Maybe because, despite being hopelessly unworthy of love yourself, you love him?"

"Funny, Case."

"Then if it isn't love, maybe it's just good sex? Or could be you need somebody to fix the toilet when it runs—"

"I know how to fix the toilet."

"Back to sex, then."

"You don't have to be married for that."

"Then you tell me."

"I'm going through with this because Nick wasn't happy living together. He believes in love, marriage." Megan scowled at the curl and pushed it into place once last time.

"He's a romantic?"

"He was a priest." Megan took a deep breath and let it out slowly "He's still deeply religious. Living together never sat well with him. He needs vows. He needs the Church's sanction."

"So you're doing all this for him" Casey got to her feet and started toward the closet to get her own dress. "Congratulations. That makes you a martyr. The church reserves a special place in heaven for people like you."

Megan waited silently as her sister shed her shorts and T-shirt and slid into a slip and panty hose. Then Casey slid her matron-of-honor dress over her head and presented her back. "Zip this, will you?"

Megan did. The fiery copper-colored silk almost matched Casey's hair, normally a long mass of curls but today tamed in an intricate French braid woven with silk baby's breath.

The three Donaghue sisters shared red in their hair, but there was little else that physically tied them together. Peggy, with her oval face and dark amber eyes, was beautiful by anybody's standards. She had softer features than her sisters and a womanly body that had ripened even further during her pregnancy.

Casey was more interesting than pretty, but she made full use of her irregular features, bright hair and angular model's body by choosing dramatic, quirky clothing and makeup. Casey always made a splash.

Then there was Megan. Sensible, cut-the-fuss Megan who felt perfectly at home in khakis and an emerald-green polo shirt running the family saloon. Today she felt like a little girl playing dress-up. A particularly awkward little girl.

"Here's the problem," Megan said. "I'm not doing this just for Nick. I believe in marriage, too. At least theoretically."

"When we were growing up you didn't see too many happy marriages up close. You were too busy raising us to pay much attention."

"Mom and Rooney were happy at times."

"Well, sure, when he wasn't hallucinating. Then Mom died, and Rooney flipped his wig altogether and took off for parts unknown. And you were left to carry on."

"There are plenty of happy marriages in the family. Look at Aunt Deirdre and Uncle Frank."

Casey went to the dresser mirror to check her makeup. "You were too busy protecting your turf to pay much attention, Megan."

Megan supposed Casey was right. Their father, Rooney, had abandoned the family when Megan was only fourteen. She had spent the next years trying to do everything a teenager could to keep the family saloon in operation and her sisters together. And she had been scarred by her father's desertion. At first Niccolo had paid the price.

"I know I was affected by those early years," Megan said. "But I'm over the worst of that. Now I'm a big girl. I understand why Rooney left. I'm just glad to have him back—more or less back, anyway. I know he did the best he could."

Casey faced her. "If everybody *without* mental illness tried as hard as Rooney does, the world would be a pretty spectacular place."

"It's not seeing enough good marriages that scares me. It's seeing *one*. Yours," Megan said bluntly. "Lately, that's what worries me."

"What are you talking about?"

"You and Jon. I don't know how you do it. The two of you are happier together than you ever were apart. You make it look effortless."

"Jon and I were friends in high school." Casey tugged one shoulder of Megan's dress lower, then slapped her sister's hand when she tried to pull it back up. "But what does that have to do with you? You love Nick. You like Nick. What's the problem? You have what you need, don't you?"

"You make it look easy, and it's not. I don't know how to just fall into marriage the way you and Jon did. Nothing's ever easy for me, Case. I don't know about easy. I don't think Nick does, either."

"Everybody has to work at being married. Maybe Jon and I make it look easy, but I can tell you there've been a few great fights." Casey's eyes shone. "And some great make-up sex."

"What if I give it my all and it turns out I'm not good enough?" Megan turned. "You do marriage counseling sometimes, right?"

Casey, who was the brand-new director of a charitable organization that delivered social services to West Side residents, shrugged. "It's not my field of expertise."

"Is this anxiety natural?" Megan bit her lip, then remembered she was wearing lipstick. "For two cents I'd bolt for the door and just keep going."

"And what if you did? What's waiting out there that's so tempting?"

"I don't want to fail."

"What would happen if you did?"

Megan considered, but not for long. "I'd die. I can't screw this up. If I get married, I want it to last. And what if I can't figure out how to make that happen?"

Casey crossed the room and rested her hands on her sister's shoulders. "Megan, you don't have to carry the weight alone. Remember? There are two of you, and I've never known two more capable people. You'll be a roaring success. Someday you'll be kicking yourself for telling me all this."

Footsteps sounded in the hallway, and the door burst open. "Oh, Megan, you look gorgeous!" Peggy flung herself through the doorway. "Spectacular. Oh, I'm going to cry."

"You'd better not. Don't you dare."

"I've got to get dressed." Peggy headed for the closet. "I had to give the baby-sitter instructions, so I'm late. I didn't have time to get my hair done, and in this wind it wouldn't have mattered, anyway. But if I pull the top part back and fasten the fancy combs I bought in it, I'll pass. Besides, everybody's going to be looking at Megan."

"Oh, God, I'm getting married." Megan's hands flew to her cheeks. "Look, one of you do it instead, okay?"

Peggy pulled her dress from Casey's closet. It was the same simple design as Casey's, but in forest green. "I'll gladly marry Nick. Think he'll notice the difference?" She slipped off her T-shirt and let the dress slither over her arms and bodice. "I'll just tell him you changed your mind. He won't care."

"Or I could do it," Casey said. "Then he and Jon can duel for nights in my bed."

Megan thought if she took one more deep breath she would hyperventilate. "I'll live through this, right?"

"If you don't, the *Plain Dealer* will have one whopping story." Peggy presented herself to Casey to be zipped. "Any word from Rooney?" she asked Megan.

Understanding and accepting her father's illness had taken Megan a long time. At some point in the two years since he had returned to his family, she had thrown away the need for an easy diagnosis and settled for the fact that Rooney was not like other men. He had battled hard for sanity, but the years and a dependence on alcohol had taken a permanent toll.

Still, Rooney was no longer homeless, as he had been since Megan's adolescence. Every night he returned to eat dinner and sleep at Niccolo's house in Ohio City, a West Side Cleveland neighborhood. He no longer drank, and he took medication that helped him think more clearly. He was sometimes confused, but rarely confused about who his daughters were. He had missed a large chunk of their lives, but he was learning to know them again on his own terms.

"I reminded him about the wedding this morning," Megan said. "He was up early."

"What did he say?"

"Nothing that made much sense, but he didn't seem surprised, like maybe he'd remembered already. Will he get there, do you think?"

"He knows where St. Brigid's is," Peggy said. "He can find his way anywhere."

"Megan, let it be enough that he remembered, okay?" Casey said. "He remembers you. This morning he remembered you were getting married. He wants to be there, even if he doesn't quite make it. A year ago, when I married Jon, he had trouble remembering my name."

Megan knew that if they searched for and found their father, corralled him and herded him into a car, he would panic. She considered, instead, the one thing she could control. "There's still time for me to head for Botswana or the Canary Islands. I don't care which."

Peggy joined her, leaning down to kiss her sister on the cheek. She stepped back and wiped away a faint smudge of lipstick. "How about the church, instead? You don't have a passport."

"Yes, I do. I made sure of it."

"You don't have a ticket."

"There must be planes to Botswana every hour on the hour."

"From Hopkins? You'd be lucky to hop a jet to Newark."

"That would do." Megan straightened her spine. "You think I'm kidding."

"I think you're terrified," Casey said, joining them. "I never thought I'd live to see the day you owned up to it. Now, are we going to church, or do I let everybody know you're a pitiful coward?"

"That's a stupid question." Megan whirled and took one final look at herself in the mirror. Actually, the view wasn't as bad as she'd feared. She looked like...a bride. "Let's go."

Casey shrugged. "You're so darned predictable."

chapter 2

Niccolo was glad Megan hadn't chosen a formal wedding gown, because then he would have to wear a tux, and he was already afraid his seldom worn suit was going to be wringing wet by the ceremony's end. St. Brigid's wasn't particularly hot. But he was particularly nervous.

"Josh, come here a minute." He motioned to the gangly young usher who was trying to herd a string of shoving adolescents toward a pew at the front.

Josh obliged, turning over his end of the line to Tarek, another youth, who was dressed in neatly pressed slacks, a sportscoat and shining loafers. Tarek had told Niccolo that this was his first time in a Christian church, and he had made a carefully annotated list of what he should wear, right down to the conservative tie.

"Where's Winston?" Niccolo asked when Josh joined him in the narthex. "He'll help keep them in line."

Josh didn't quite meet his eyes. "Oh, he's not here yet. He had stuff to do this morning."

Winston, Josh, Tarek and all the other kids in the pew, were part of Brick. One Brick at a Time had started out as a bunch of neighborhood pre-adolescents watching Niccolo renovate an old house in Ohio City, and now it was a chartered nonprofit organization that taught basic carpentry and plumbing skills, and remodeled old houses. Home repair and remodeling were secondary to the real skills the participants learned, though: self-control, self-worth, the importance of follow-through, and community service. Brick hobbled along on a knotted shoestring, but Brick hobbled forward.

Niccolo's collar was in danger of cutting off his air supply. He pulled it away from his throat. "Can you keep them in line long enough to get them to the reception?"

"Sure, they'll do what I say," Josh promised. Niccolo didn't doubt he meant it.

Josh was Niccolo's biggest success story. Although most of the Brick kids came from safe enough homes, Josh hadn't been so lucky. He had moved in with Niccolo two years ago to avoid his father's alcoholic rages, and had blossomed immediately. For the first time in his life his grades were excellent, and his self-esteem was growing. He talked confidently about college now, and Niccolo had no doubts he would do well.

"Do you see the big guy at the end of the second pew?" Niccolo pointed through the doorway toward the front. "With black hair and the pretty woman in blue beside him?"

"Uh-huh."

"That's my brother Marco."

"He looks like you. How come he never comes to visit?"

Niccolo tried to think of a kind way to phrase the unkind truth. "My family wasn't happy when I left the priesthood. Marco's been running interference—" He saw that Josh didn't understand. "He's been trying to help the others understand that making a change was the right thing for me. Particularly my parents and the grandparents who are still alive."

"I get it. He doesn't want to alienate them by coming here while he's working on their heads."

Niccolo liked the way "alienate" had just slipped from Josh's lips. And of course Josh had understood the subtleties of his explanation. Josh was a natural psychologist.

"You've got it. But he's here today, and I'd like him to have a carnation for his lapel." Niccolo motioned to the one in Josh's. "Like yours. Will you take it up to him?"

"Sure. Cool." Josh took a boutonniere from the white florist's box beside Niccolo. "Anybody else coming? From your family, I mean?"

When Niccolo shook his head, Josh looked perplexed. "They don't like Megan?" Clearly Josh couldn't imagine such a thing, since he practically worshiped at Megan's feet.

"They wouldn't like anybody I chose. Don't worry about it. Marco's here. That's a start."

"So even good families can act crazy, huh?" Josh seemed to like that thought. He was smiling a little when he started back into the nave and up the aisle.

"What are you doing out here?"

Niccolo turned to see his best man coming through the door. Jon Kovats, Casey's husband, was dressed in a dark suit, too, only on Jon it looked perfectly natural. He was a prosecutor, with quiet, clean-cut good looks that gave crime victims faith and an unwavering gaze that gave defendants shivers down their spines.

"Aren't you supposed to be hiding somewhere with Father Brady until right before the ceremony?" Jon asked.

Niccolo hated to admit the truth, that after Jon had dropped him off at the side door, Niccolo had sneaked into the narthex for a look at the guests. He had hoped his parents would relent and attend, although he hadn't said as much to Josh.

"I was just getting some air," he said, "and checking to see if anything had to be done out here."

"Nick, you can let go of everything for a while. Let the rest of us take care of the details. That's why we signed on."

"Have you heard anything from Casey?"

"Anything?"

Niccolo tugged his collar away from his throat again. He had gone from a priest's dog collar to a working man's flannels. Ties felt unnatural. "Lately, I mean. In the last half hour?"

"Not a word. Why? She's helping Megan dress. I'm sure there hasn't been much free time." Jon frowned. "You're afraid Megan's not going to show up, aren't you?"

"It crossed my mind."

"Megan lives up to her commitments. To the point of mania, as a matter of fact. It's something the two of you have in common."

Jon knew them both too well. Niccolo couldn't stop a smile, but he sobered quickly. "She's afraid everything will change, that I'll wake up one morning and realize I made a mistake, only I'm too good a Catholic to admit it."

"Megan? She has a superhero ego. I can't believe that."

"Strong ego, yes, but she's just not sure how to go about being married. And Megan hates being unsure about anything."

"Just Megan? Or you, too?"

Niccolo thought the question was insightful, but he wasn't surprised. He and Jon had become close friends in the two years they'd known each other, and Jon was a master at uncovering secrets.

"I've never been married, but I plan to work hard at it," Niccolo said.

"Whoa there. Not too hard, or you won't have any fun. It's not a job, it's a relationship."

"She deserves the best. A hundred percent. Two hundred."

"She deserves a man who's enjoying himself."

There was a commotion at the door, and Niccolo turned. A distinguished-looking man with silver hair was helping a plump, attractive woman through the doorway. For a moment Niccolo stood absolutely still; then he turned back to Jon. He cleared his throat. "Jon, come with me, will you? I'd like you to meet my parents." He glanced at the doorway again. "And my grandfather."

Jon was a good enough friend to understand the significance of those words. He clapped his hand on Niccolo's shoulder. "Do you believe in omens?"

"I'm too Catholic not to."

Megan had refused a limousine. Didn't understand the point, didn't want the fuss, and refused to spend the money. Neither she nor Niccolo was ever going to be rich. There were better uses for their dollars.

She had refused rides with family, turned down Jon's offer to ferry her in a friend's fire-engine-red convertible, refused everything, in fact, except the simplest solution. She, Peggy and Casey would ride to the church together in Casey's car.

She just hadn't reckoned with a flat tire.

Now the sisters stood outside Casey's house and stared forlornly at the evidence.

"There's debris all over the roads from the wind. I guess I drove over something on the way back from the saloon," Casey said.

"Yeah, like a railroad spike. That tire's a pancake."

"And I sold my car," Peggy said. "I hitched a ride over here from Uncle Den."

"Charming." Megan kicked what was left of the tire, most likely doing permanent damage to her ivory pumps. "I don't suppose either of you wants to change this?"

"In this dress?" Casey looked down and shook her head. "Not a chance."

"We'll call a taxi," Peggy said.

"This isn't Manhattan. Nick will be married to somebody else by the time one gets here." Megan kicked the tire again, shoes be damned. "Maybe somebody's still left at the saloon. Casey, can you find out?"

Casey dug in her purse for her cell phone and made the call. They all stood perfectly still, waiting until she flipped it closed and shook her head. "It's a miracle. They're all on time for the wedding. Everybody but us. Jon's already there with Nick, and I'll bet his phone is off." For good measure she punched in more numbers, with no success.

"Do you know your neighbors?" Megan looked around. "You must know somebody by now."

Casey inclined her head to the left. "They're out of town." She inclined to the right. "I'm taking in their mail and papers." She nodded to the house across the street. "They're on the wrong side of one of Jon's cases and about to move to a secure location. And the house next to theirs is empty."

Megan peered around her, mind whirling. Casey and Jon had purchased one of Niccolo's Ohio City renovations. The house, a brick Colonial Revival with classical detailing, suited the busy couple perfectly, and best of all, it was only four blocks from Niccolo's house on Hunter Street.

"Okay, let's hike it, then. We'll get Charity."

Her sisters groaned. Charity, Megan's dilapidated Chevy, was renowned for its bad temper. Charity only began at "home." The joke was rarely funny.

"Got a better idea?" Megan demanded.

"Well, we'll see if Charity feels at home at Nick's. If she doesn't, maybe *your* neighbors will be more helpful than Casey's," Peggy said. "Let's march."

Megan started down the sidewalk at a fast clip. She heard her sisters behind her, but she was on a mission now. She had said she would marry Niccolo, and it was too late to call off the wedding gracefully.

They tramped in silence, three women in ballerina length silk dresses and hair whipping in the accelerating wind.

"It's going to rain," Casey said, a block from Niccolo's house. "God, I hope we get to the car before it does."

"It better not rain!" Megan marched on.

They turned down Hunter, and Megan could just see Charity at the end of the block in front of Niccolo's—her—house. "Lord, let her start."

"This really is a red-letter day. That was a prayer," Casey said. "Megan's praying."

"I'll have you know I'm in tight with the Lord. I had to be to get married in the church."

"At least temporarily. Did Father Brady faint when you joined him in the confessional?"

"Father Brady is nicer and apparently more optimistic about my soul than you are." Megan was afraid to look at her watch. They were cutting this close, and it was going to take some real time to repair all the wind damage.

The raindrops started just as they got to the car, but Charity started with the first turn of the key.

"Do you believe in omens?" she asked Peggy, who climbed in beside her.

"I'm too Irish not to."

Megan double-parked Charity at the curb, but she didn't turn off the engine. The small parking lot looked full and altogether too far away from the entrance she planned to use. St. Brigid's had a side door just past the sanctuary that led to a stairwell. One flight up there was a room where the brides usually dressed—and now she fervently wished she'd decided to use it. Once upstairs and ready, she could make her entrance through another stairwell into the narthex and eventually up the aisle to meet Niccolo and Father Brady.

Too bad she hadn't packed her hiking gear.

"We can do this." She took a deep breath. "I'll leave the key in the ignition. The neighborhood's tough enough that maybe somebody will steal her. Once they see what they're into, they'll park her somewhere nice and safe until I can find her again."

"We're still fifty yards from a door," Casey said from the back seat.

"It's only sprinkling."

Peggy wiped the foggy windshield with her fingertips. "You know what? You've lived here too long. By anybody else's standards, that's a downpour. And you hate getting wet."

"Megan," Casey said, "nobody will steal Charity, and you're going to get towed if you stay here."

Charity chose that moment to sputter and die.

"Looks like I don't have a choice, and I'd rather bail her out of the impound lot than be late for my own wedding."

"At least your ambivalence disappeared," Casey said.

Megan didn't bother to correct her. "Can you two get yourselves inside?"

Peggy had been scrounging under the seat for an umbrella. She held one out to Megan, a poor cousin of the species but still useful. "You go ahead. The weather's only going to get worse. I'll see if I can start this monster."

"I'm not walking down the aisle without you. You have to hold me up." After a lot of speculation on who should accompany her on the trip down the aisle, Megan had asked Casey and Peggy to walk just a step ahead of her, more escorts than attendants. She had a dozen male relatives who would have been happy to do the honors, but she had chosen her sisters instead. The man who should have walked with her wasn't up to the task.

Megan gauged the distance and the raindrops. "Which should I ruin? My pumps or my panty hose?"

"I brought extra panty hose." Casey was leaning over the seat now.

Megan removed her shoes and opened the door. "See you inside." She flipped open the umbrella, and in stocking feet she sprinted across the grass to her favored entrance. At the door to the stairwell, she shook like a spaniel, closing her eyes and the umbrella and letting the raindrops fly. When she opened them, her future husband was staring back at her.

"Nick!" She put a hand over her heart. "What are you doing here?"

"Checking to see if you'd deserted me at the altar."

She stared at him. The dark suit set off his wide shoulders, black hair and neatly trimmed beard. With his olive skin and Roman centurion features, he was the perfect finale to any walk down the aisle.

"You weren't supposed to see me like this."

He was smiling now. "I remember the first time we spent an evening together. Do you?"

At the moment she wasn't sure she remembered her own name. She stared at him, this gorgeous, masculine human being who wanted to share her life.

"You invited me home after a day at work," he said, "and you were exhausted. So you took a shower while I waited, and when you came into the kitchen your hair was wet. Sort of like it is now. And I was flattened by desire."

"Flattened?"

"Metaphorically. More or less the opposite of my real state, I guess."

She smiled. "I'd forgotten."

"So I have a thing about seeing you wet. And dry, for that matter. Just seeing you."

"Oh, Nick." She wanted to fall into his arms. Instead she spread her skirt, holding it out with both hands like a little girl in petticoats. "Are you sure you want to go through with this? I'm not much of a bargain."

"We never get guarantees, but I think you're a pretty safe bet."

"I'm a mess. I'm dripping, my car's probably going to be towed, and I've ripped my stockings into shreds." A hand leaped to her hair. "And I lost my damned orange blossoms."

"Good. You look perfect the way you are." He paused. "Although my mother and father will be more impressed if you put the shoes on your feet."

"They came?"

He nodded.

This time she did fall into his arms. Casey and Peggy arrived just as they finally stepped apart. "Peggy got Charity parked. We—" Casey stopped when she saw Niccolo. "Get out of here," Casey told him in mock horror. "Go wait where you're supposed to. This is bad luck."

He grinned with no contrition.

"Scoot!" Casey gave him a mock shove. "Go tell the organist to do another round of 'Jesu Joy of Man's Desiring.' Give us ten minutes."

"Five."

"Seven. Go!"

"Bye..." Megan watched him leave. Nick turned in the doorway and blew her a kiss.

"Megan!" Casey grabbed her shoulders and turned her toward the stairs.

They were ready in ten minutes, panty hose changed, hair dry enough. Megan entered the foyer flanked by her sisters. Through the door into the church she could see that Nick, Jon and Father Brady had already entered from the front. The orange blossoms had been restored—Casey had rescued and pocketed them early in their walk—and even Megan's shoes had been wiped clean. She was ready.

"Do you think Rooney made it to the church? Do you think he's here somewhere?" Megan positioned herself at the doorway. Heads were beginning to turn.

"He wanted to be," Peggy said.

The strains of Beethoven's "Joyful, Joyful We Adore Thee" sounded from the front of the church. Megan had begged the organist to step up the tempo a little so the trip to the front wouldn't take so long. Now the familiar melody sounded like the most strenuous selection in a Richard Simmons exercise video. *Sweating to the Sacred.* Clearly, after the delay, the poor woman was ready to call this gig quits.

"Okay, we're going in together. Don't walk too fast and leave me behind." Megan took a deep breath. "Let's go."

"I love you," Casey said, and Peggy echoed it.

Megan's eyes filled with tears. "Just go, okay?"

They started down the aisle. She took a step over the threshold and into the back of the church. Like one body the assembled guests rose. From the corner of her eye she saw a lone male figure step into the aisle. Then, as naturally as if he had rehearsed the scene for hours, Rooney Donaghue, shirt buttoned properly, clean shaven and smiling, came toward her and held out his arm.

chapter 3

None of the Donaghue sisters were sentimental, but despite that reputation, Peggy choked back tears during the ceremony. Megan was radiant as she joined her life with Nick's, and even though Peggy hadn't spent much of her adult life in church, the familiar rhythms of the wedding Mass touched her. But nothing touched her more than seeing her father take his rightful place at his oldest daughter's side.

That glorious glimpse into the sacred exploded the moment she opened the door into the Whiskey Island Saloon.

"Ice machine gave up the ghost." Barry, their bartender, pushed past her on his way outside. "Going for ice."

"I—"

"And the band says they need more room to set up than you gave them," he shouted over his shoulder. "So I moved tables out of their way, only now there aren't so many tables—"

"I—"

"And there's trees down all over Cleveland, so there's no

hope of getting a crew in tonight to cut it up. We roped off the area around the kitchen so nobody'll park near the piece that's still standing. But we can't even get the car towed until..." His voice trailed off as he disappeared into his car and slammed the door.

Peggy wondered exactly what she was going to tell Niccolo and Megan when it came time for them to make their getaway and Casey's car—if her tire was fixed by then—was waiting for them at the curb instead of the Honda.

"Peggy?" A strong hand ushered her all the way in. She looked up to see Charlie Ford, one of their loyal patrons. "The bakery just called. The cake's all set up, but they forgot the petty cash, or something like that."

"Petit fours. I thought maybe they had just put them in the kitchen." She was beginning to panic. This was a crowd that would expect sweets before the cake was cut.

"Said they'd be by with them shortly. Not to worry."

"Easy for you to say."

Charlie's eyes sparkled. His only son lived in New York, and the staff and patrons of the Whiskey Island Saloon were his Cleveland family. "And Greta says she's going to quit if she has to stuff one more piece of cabbage."

Greta was Megan's treasured kitchen assistant and a fabulous cook in her own right, as well as a dedicated employee. "She always says that. Anything else?"

"Kieran went down for a nap about an hour ago, and the sitter left. The baby monitor's in the kitchen with Greta."

Peggy had expected that. The sitter had other obligations, and they had agreed to this compromise, knowing how regular Kieran's nap time was. The older woman was one of the few outsiders who was willing to look after Kieran at all. How blessed it was to let someone else assume her son's care for a few hours, and how impossible that would be beginning tomorrow.

But that was the way she had wanted it.

Charlie clapped Peggy on the shoulder. "Say, have you heard the one about the Irish priest who got stopped for speeding on Euclid Avenue? See, the cop smells alcohol on the good father's breath and notices an empty wine bottle on the floor, so he knows he has to ask him about it. 'Father, have you been drinking?' he says. And the priest says, 'Just water, my son.' So the trooper picks up the bottle and holds it out in front of him. 'Then what's this, Father,' he says. The priest throws up his hands. 'Jesus, Mary and Joseph, he's done it again!'"

She groaned. "Charlie, you're the worst."

He grinned as he disappeared into the growing crowd.

Peggy went straight to the kitchen. Greta was supervising a crew of cousins and customers who were setting food on platters and taking it out to the bar for the reception. Behind her, Peggy could hear the front door opening and closing regularly, and she knew that soon enough the saloon would look the way it did on St. Patrick's Day.

"Everything going okay in here?"

Greta looked up, her moon face glowing with perspiration. "Did you know Nick's family was bringing food?"

Until she'd seen them at the church, Peggy hadn't even known Nick's family were bringing them*selves*.

Greta waved one hand behind her toward the steel counter on the far wall. "Piles of it. They dropped it off before the wedding. His mother gave me instructions, like I don't know how to heat up covered dishes? Why didn't somebody tell me? I've been cooking for a week."

"Nobody knew they were coming, Greta. I'm sorry. But I can guarantee everything you cooked will get eaten. Every single bit of it, and they'll lick their plates."

"Manicotti like you never seen. Sausages and peppers. Meatballs!" Greta grimaced. "All of it pretty good, too."

Peggy put her arms around her for a quick hug. "Soldier on, okay? The Donaghues will eat their weight in corned beef. You can count on it."

"They better!"

"No sounds from upstairs?"

"Not a peep, and I've got the monitor turned up all the way."

"Just let me know." Peggy heard the unmistakable pop of a champagne cork and sprinted back into the saloon and behind the bar. "Sam, who told you to start opening that?"

Sam Trumbull, another loyal customer, gave her a cock-eyed grin. He was a little man, with a chronic thirst and a line that could convince any stranger to buy him a drink in ten seconds flat. "Somebody put me in charge. I can't remember who."

There was just enough champagne for one good round of toasts right before the cake was cut. Before that the guests would have to settle for the excellent wines Niccolo had chosen, Barry's mixed drinks, or the best Guinness in Cleveland.

"Not another bottle," she warned. "Not until I tell you to. It's going to go flat."

"I just thought I'd check and see if the temperature was right." He held out the bottle. "Want to see?"

"One glass, Sam. That's it. Then pour the rest of it for—" She turned and pointed. "The man and woman over there. That's my aunt Deirdre and uncle Frank."

He looked disappointed, but he nodded.

The wind was rising outside, and Peggy checked the saloon clock. "I hope everybody gets here before this storm really breaks. It rains, then it stops, then it rains...."

"Cleveland spring." Sam lifted his slight shoulders.

"Well, once they're all here, it won't matter." She looked up as the door opened and Jon and Casey came in, followed by a large contingent of distant Donaghues.

Casey found her and pointed behind her, mouthing, "They're coming," enough times that Peggy understood. "The wedding party will be here pretty soon," she told Sam. "Remember, don't pop those corks until I signal. Promise?"

Casey managed to thread her way over to the bar as Peggy exited. "Where's Kieran?"

"Upstairs sleeping. The baby monitor's in the kitchen."

"You've got a lot of people here that want to help you."

"Kieran doesn't need a lot of people, Casey. He needs a quiet environment and my full attention."

"If this sojourn in Ireland doesn't work out, you know you can always come back, right? Nobody will say 'I told you so.'"

The door opened again, and this time Megan and Niccolo came through it, just behind Rooney. Behind *them* were the olive-skinned, regal members of Niccolo's family. Peggy knew they were Andreanis because they were the only people in the saloon she didn't know by name.

"Are they behaving themselves?" she asked Casey. "Nick's family?"

"Actually, they're charming. His mom's a little reserved, like she's here against her better judgment, but the rest of them are great. And can they tell stories. The trip from Pittsburgh's worth a book. Maybe the Italians and the Irish are cousins under the skin? They're going to get along with everybody."

"And how's Rooney doing?"

"He's here, isn't he? And it looks like Aunt Deirdre's corralled him. She'll make sure he's fed and happy and not given anything to drink."

Megan made her way toward her sisters. She was stopped, hugged and kissed by everybody between them.

"Other people have nice, quiet receptions," she said. "Sit down dinners. Chamber music."

As if on cue, the Celtic band —the lead singer was a second cousin on their mother's side—began to play. The noise level doubled.

"Other people don't have this much fun!" Peggy hugged her. "You doing okay?"

"We had to park down the street. Uncle Den claimed there wasn't any room in the lot, not even for the bride and groom."

Silently Peggy blessed her mother's only brother and refused to meet Casey's gaze for fear she would give away the truth. She just wondered how long it would take before someone mentioned the tree to Megan or Nick.

"Who invited all these people?" Megan shouted.

"You did!"

"Niccolo's family will think he's married into an insane asylum!"

Peggy looked past Megan to the Andreani gathering in the corner. Only they weren't in the corner anymore. They were mingling and chatting, and they looked as if they were having fun. Even Mrs. Andreani, who was holding a small black-haired girl, looked as if she were loosening up. She caught Peggy's eye and gave a slight smile.

There was a brief lull in the music, and Peggy heard Greta calling her. "Uh-oh, I'd better follow that sound. Kieran's probably up."

"What are you going to do with him?" Megan said.

"I'm going to bring him down for a while and see how he does. If he minds the noise and confusion too much, I'll take him back up. There are plenty of people who will take turns watching him." Peggy started off through the crowd, but she was stopped by her aunt Deirdre before she could get to her son.

"I can't believe you're leaving tomorrow," Deirdre said.

Peggy loved her aunt. Deirdre Grogan was Rooney's sister, and she and Frank, her husband, had raised Peggy after Peggy's mother died and Rooney left. At the same time Deirdre, who had undoubtedly wanted full custody, had been sensitive to Megan's need to have a say in her baby sister's life. So Deirdre had walked a difficult line. She was kind, patient and completely opposed to Peggy's decision to take Kieran to Ireland.

"I love that color," Peggy said, hoping to change the thrust of the conversation. Deirdre always dressed with quiet, expensive good taste. Today she wore a sage-green linen suit that set off hair that had once been the color of Casey's but had less fire in it now.

"Are you sure you won't reconsider, darling? After all, what do you know about this woman? What do any of us know? And how can we help Kieran if you're off in the middle of nowhere?"

Peggy knew that her aunt was distraught, because Deirdre never interfered. Two years ago, when Peggy informed her that she was pregnant and didn't intend to marry the father, Deirdre had asked only what she could do to assist.

"I know enough about Irene Tierney to risk the trip," Peggy said. "She's been warm and welcoming, and she's anxious to meet even a small piece of her American family. Until a couple of months ago, she didn't know we existed."

"But doesn't it all seem odd to you? She's in her eighties? And she found you on the Internet?"

"Her physician gave her a computer to amuse her and got her connected. It's something she can do from home that gives her broader interests. She's mostly housebound. And I think it's wonderful that she was so adaptable and eager, and that she found us."

"I still don't understand what she wanted."

Peggy looked toward the kitchen and saw Greta standing in the doorway, pointing toward the stairs. Peggy waved at her to let her know she'd gotten the message. She was growing frantic, the response of any mother of any species separated from her bawling youngster. "I've got to get Kieran. We can talk later."

Deirdre looked contrite. "Can I help? Would you like me to—"

"No, but thanks. Stay. Enjoy yourself. I'll be down with him in a bit."

Peggy didn't add that she planned to take her time. There were a dozen relatives who would try to corner her before the night ended and quiz her about the remarkable decision to fly thousands of miles to live in rural Ireland with a woman she'd never met. She wasn't anxious to face any of them.

Upstairs, the tiny apartment, often stuffy in late spring, had benefitted from the afternoon's wind and dark skies. Peggy knew, without opening the bedroom door, that Kieran would be staring at the sheer curtain beside his crib. Even though the window was only open an inch, the curtain would wave with each gust, and Kieran's gaze would be locked on that movement. He might even imitate it, waving his hand back and forth. When there was no curtain blowing, no clock pendulum swinging, no ceiling fan revolving overhead, she had seen him follow the slow back and forth of his own hand for as long as an hour, mesmerized and calmed by the fruitless repetition as she sat distressed beside him.

If only she could unlock the mystery that was Kieran Rowan Donaghue.

She opened the door and saw that she had been right. Kieran was awake, but he wasn't sitting up. He was lying silently, waving his hand back and forth in time to the movements of the curtain. If Kieran was capable of happiness, then he was happiest at moments like this. Happiest when he was alone, with no one asking more of him, no one expecting recognition or, worse, love. No one to distract him from the isolation he craved.

"Kieran?"

He didn't turn, but she hadn't expected him to. He heard her, though. She knew he did from the way his plump little body stiffened and his hand no longer kept rhythm. His mouth tightened, and he made a sound of distress, an animal sound. Cornered prey.

"Sweetheart, it's Mommy. How's my Kieran boy?" She moved slowly toward him. She knew better than to ask him to quickly give up his solitary world. Not so long ago the family had teased about Kieran's "sensitivity." He would be an artist, a poet, a musician, their Kieran. He was a visionary, this youngest Donaghue. He saw the world differently, experienced it at a level more visceral, more elemental, than most children.

In those happy days, before the diagnosis of autism arrived with the crocuses and early daffodils and turned a Cleveland spring into Peggy's personal nightmare.

"Kieran," she crooned. "Kie—ran."

He turned to her at last. His angelic little face registered dismay. He had a rose-petal complexion and soft auburn curls. His pale blue eyes were as bright as stars, but whatever dwelled behind them was Kieran's own secret.

"Mommy's here," she crooned. "Mommy loves you, and she's here. Mommy's not going anywhere, sweetheart. Kieran. Love."

He didn't lift his arms. He didn't smile. His body, which had been soft with sleep, stiffened into steel. Then he turned away, turned toward the open window and the waving curtain, and began to hum.

chapter 4

So far, Megan had survived. Rooney's appearance at her side had been a gift. She had never expected to walk down the aisle on her father's arm, and that small miracle had gotten her to the front, where the man she loved waited to hold her up. Niccolo's smile and Father Brady's patient prompting got her through the service.

Now, hopefully, champagne and Guinness would get her through the rest of the reception.

"My car's missing," Niccolo shouted in her ear.

For a moment she didn't understand. The Civic was nearly new. If the engine was missing, that was a bad omen.

"I think somebody took it to decorate it," he elaborated.

She felt herself turning shades of mottled pink, the curse of a redhead. After the reception, she and Niccolo were leaving for a relative's cottage on Michigan's Drummond Island. She had envisioned anonymity and absolute peace on the drive.

"We're stopping at the first car wash," she warned.

He grinned. She couldn't recall ever seeing Niccolo look happier. She wondered what she had done to deserve him, this man who had stood by her through all her doubts, fears and general neuroses.

"I'd like to outrun this storm," Niccolo said, "but I think we'll be driving right into it."

"It's raining again? Maybe we won't need a car wash."

"Pouring. I'm used to odd weather, but this takes the cake."

Casey pushed through the crowd with a full plate of food and handed it to Megan. "You haven't eaten a bite. This is fabulous. Both the Andreanis and the Donaghues outdid themselves."

Megan realized she was starving. "Nick?" But she needn't have worried. She saw that Jon was hauling him to the bar to fill his own plate. Niccolo's brother Marco was helping.

"Having fun?" Casey said.

Megan dug into the best manicotti she'd ever tasted. She wondered if Mrs. Andreani would share the recipe. It was probably too soon in their relationship to ask, considering that until just hours ago Niccolo's mother hadn't wanted to acknowledge her existence.

"Is this supposed to be fun?" Megan said.

"You're enjoying yourself, aren't you?"

A cousin with a full tray of Guinness stopped, and Megan took a pint, suffering a hug while she was at it. "How do I eat and hold this?"

"I'll hold it." Casey took the Guinness.

"I'm doing okay," Megan admitted.

"Everyone's so happy you married Nick."

Megan had never realized the Donaghue clan had such remarkable taste. "Nick tells me his car is missing?" She watched her sister's face. "Casey? I don't think I like your expression."

"What did Nick say, exactly?"

"That somebody had probably taken it away to decorate it."

"That's the kind of thing people do for weddings, right?"

"You know more than you're saying."

"There are good times and bad times to discuss surprises."

"And there are good and bad surprises." The band started

a chorus of "Cockles and Mussels," and over her head, drifts of white tulle swayed frantically when someone opened the front door. "This had better not be one of the bad ones," she continued in a louder voice. "Just tell me that whatever damage you did to the car, soap on the windows, shoes on the bumper, whatever, can be quickly dispensed with once we're out of sight."

Peggy arrived with Kieran in her arms. "What's out of sight?"

Megan's heart squeezed painfully as it always did when she saw her nephew. "Hey, kiddo."

She tried to keep her voice low, although that made it inaudible. Kieran responded badly to noise and confusion of any sort, and now, in the center of the raucous crowd, he was eyeing her as if she were a stranger, although Megan had fed and rocked and changed him as often as anyone else in the world.

Kieran had seemed perfectly normal at birth. When he was still an infant, Peggy had started medical school, and Kieran had been lovingly passed among family members who were thrilled by the chance to care for the little boy while Peggy attended classes and studied. But no matter how much time they spent with him, Kieran had never seemed to remember them.

Peggy brushed his auburn curls with her fingertips. "Try saying hi," she told Megan.

"Hi," Megan said warmly.

Kieran stared at her, his cherubic face expressionless, then he focused his gaze just behind her. Megan turned to see what had interested him and saw a reflection of the swaying tulle in the bar mirror.

"Hi," Megan repeated.

Kieran didn't look at her. He seemed hypnotized by the movement. Just as she started to change the subject, he gave a lopsided smile, then reached toward the mirror. "Hi. Hi. Hi."

Peggy looked disappointed. "Better than nothing."

"He's not quite two," Casey pointed out. "Boys don't talk as early as girls."

"But most boys know the difference between reflections

dancing in a mirror and their favorite aunts." Peggy sounded matter-of-fact. "Well, that's going to change. When you see him again, you're going to be surprised at the improvement."

Megan wanted to argue. She wanted to shake some sense into her sister. When Peggy had learned Kieran's diagnosis, she'd quit medical school, perhaps forever, divorcing herself from a lifelong dream in order to devote herself to her son. Now she was taking Kieran all the way to Ireland to live with a distant cousin the family hadn't even known about until two months ago. All so that she could somehow turn him into a "normal" child.

Unfortunately, Peggy was the only Donaghue who believed this was the right course to follow.

"He seems pretty perky, considering all the chaos in here," Casey said

Megan knew Casey was trying to divert the conversation and supposed it was just as well. Peggy's mind was made up, and all the discussion in the world wasn't going to change it.

"I think I'll see if I can get him to eat something, then I'm going to take him upstairs for some quiet time. We'll be back for cake."

Megan and Casey watched Peggy wind her way to the bar. "I still can't believe she's moving to Ireland," Megan said.

"Finish your food, Megan. The band's gearing up for some set dancing, and you'll be expected to give it a try."

Megan groaned. "You couldn't head them off?"

"They're playing for free. Remember?"

"Hand me the Guinness, would you?"

Upstairs, Peggy settled Kieran on the living room rug with a quilt and a menagerie of stuffed toys. The apartment was plain but serviceable. Best of all, the modest rent came out of her share of the saloon's profits. The Whiskey Island Saloon had been in the Donaghue family since its construction more than a century before. The three sisters were equal partners, and although nowadays Megan kept the food hot and the liquor flowing, both Peggy and Casey had pulled their share of Guinness along the way.

"Tomorrow we're going on a plane," she told her son.

He didn't look up at her words. For months, before the battery of tests that had pinpointed Kieran's problem, she had worried that his hearing was impaired. She hadn't expected autism, so she hadn't been prepared.

The day she got the diagnosis would be etched forever in her mind.

"Autistic disorder," the specialist had said matter-of-factly, as if he were diagnosing a head cold. "Moderate, we think, although that's not as easy to pinpoint as it might seem. It's really a spectrum, Miss Donaghue. Generally those who suffer with it have problems understanding the emotions of others. They have difficulties with language and conversation, and they often fixate on one subject or activity. The prognosis depends on many things. Early intervention is key, but I'll warn you, the cost, both in time and money, can be enormous."

Now Peggy dropped to the floor and sat cross-legged beside Kieran. "We'll go high in the air, right up into the clouds. And I'll be with you the whole time. Just Mommy and Kieran."

He picked at the felt eyes of a teddy bear. He never held or cuddled his toy animals. He found something to pick apart, and he could work at it for long stretches of time, only pausing to rock himself when he tired.

"Then we'll be in Ireland," she said. "And Mommy will set up a classroom for you at Cousin Irene's. We'll have toys and games, and you'll learn so much, Kieran. I know you will. And when we come back to Cleveland, you'll be able to speak and make eye contact and..."

He looked up. The living room curtain rustled and caught his attention. "Hi. Hi."

She gathered him close, although he whimpered at her touch. "You're going to have every chance I can give you," she said fiercely. "If I have to fly to Mars and back to make sure of it."

Four of the Brick kids found an untouched tray of Guinness and took it into the storeroom for their own private party.

Casey spotted them before Niccolo could and confiscated their hard-won treasure.

Marco, his wife Paula and their two young daughters staged a slide show on one of the saloon walls of photos of Niccolo as a little boy. Not to be outdone, Uncle Den enthralled a group of admirers with story after story of the three sisters as children.

"Please, God, let the toasts begin," Megan said. "I won't survive much more of this."

"Hold your head up," Peggy said. "You're only getting married once."

"Can't you get Kieran and Aunt Dee and bring them down? All of you have to be here when we cut the cake." Peggy had settled Kieran upstairs in the apartment an hour before. Now Deirdre was sitting with him and saying her goodbyes.

"Do you really think it's time?"

Niccolo joined them. "You know, if we'd ever put all these Andreanis and Donaghues in the same room, we probably would have been too scared to merge our genes. Can you believe our children will have both sets?" He shook his head.

Megan couldn't imagine a child of theirs at all. She knew Niccolo wanted children right away. She'd tentatively agreed to have them someday, but not on his timetable. Marriage itself was going to take enough trial and error.

"Will you start herding everybody to the back of the room?" she pleaded. "I don't think I'll live through much more of this."

"You're having a ball." He leaned down and kissed her, and people began to clap.

"I would like to get away sometime before dark," she said, smiling up at him.

"Don't look now, but it's been dark all afternoon."

"You know what I mean."

"I'll herd. But don't expect this to end any time soon."

"They can party until the wee hours, but you and I are leaving once the cake's been served."

"Promises, promises." He winked at Peggy before he left to begin edging people toward the wedding cake.

Megan watched as Niccolo made remarkable progress. At her suggestion, the cake had been set up in the back of the saloon. She had tried to get into the kitchen to make sure everything was ready for cutting and serving it, but she'd been outmaneuvered. There had been a conspiracy all day to keep her as far away from the kitchen as possible.

As if she would try to take over her own reception.

Casey joined them. "That time already? Will you be able to bring Kieran down now?" she asked Peggy.

"Maybe now that he's had some quiet time. I can't guarantee he'll be tantrum free."

"All two-year-olds have tantrums," Megan said. "You certainly had your share."

"You've got to get used to the idea that he's not just any two-year-old, Megan," Peggy said. "It's the only way we can help him."

Megan knew Peggy was right. At first Peggy, too, had struggled to accept her son's disability, but at last she had made the adjustment. Megan was still rooted firmly in denial. "I love him. I love you. I don't want to lose either of you."

Peggy kissed her cheek. "You won't. Now let me get him."

"And I'll help Nick," Casey said. "He's managed to get everybody moving. Which was the key to getting them into the back of the room faster, do you think? Cake or champagne?"

Megan was only yards away from Niccolo when the building began to shake. For a moment she thought the band had turned up their amplifiers to grab everyone's attention. But the sound was more freight train than feedback.

The saloon shook again. A woman screamed, and Megan registered alarm on the faces closest to her. Then, as she saw Niccolo struggling through the crowd in her direction, the building shook once more, the roar grew deafening, and the front facade of the saloon collapsed inward.

The building shook again as more screams erupted. Glassware at the bar shattered and fell to the floor, and a hole the size of a child's wading pool opened to the left of her head. Debris rained down, followed closely by water. Then both the cacophony and the tremors ceased.

"Megan!" Niccolo reached and grabbed her, wrapping his arms around her. "Are you okay?"

"What—" She realized she couldn't breathe. She struggled, but her lungs wouldn't inflate. Her legs felt like rubber bands, and she clung to him and fought for air. People were pushing past her, heading away from the destruction.

"Take it easy. It's okay." He smoothed her hair, but his hand trembled.

She caught a breath at last. "What—"

"Tornado," he said. "It sucked up part of the roof. Damn, we're idiots. Nobody was listening for tornado warnings. I—"

"Nick!" Casey reached them. "Where's Jon?"

Niccolo released Megan. "He was in the very back. I've got to see what kind of damage was done. I've got to find my family."

Megan started after him. She knew his real mission was to see if anyone had lagged behind and been caught in the collapse. The sight that greeted her nearly tore the breath from her lungs again. The roof over the front quarter of the building had fallen to seal off the entrance completely. What rubble she could see beneath it was waist-high. "Oh, God!"

Casey grabbed her. "Stay away, Megan. For Pete's sake, don't get near—"

Jon reached them. "Get in the back with everybody else. Please. It's safer."

"What if somebody—" Megan couldn't finish that thought.

"Most everybody was in the back milling around the cake. If we're lucky... Just help us get everybody else back there now. We'll do head counts. Start, would you?"

Megan knew he was right. Thick dust choked the room, and her vision was obscured. But nothing she could see indicated that anyone had been in the extreme front when the wall collapsed.

Casey was already helping people move farther toward the back. Megan saw one of the Brick kids holding his head, but he was walking unaided. One of Marco's daughters had a scratch on her cheek, but the bleeding didn't look serious. Niccolo's mother had her arm around his grandfather and was helping him walk. Megan turned to see Peggy struggling with the door to the apartment, and she remembered that Kieran was upstairs with their aunt.

As she watched, Peggy wrenched open the door, despite the crush of frantic guests, and disappeared into the stairwell. The back of the building seemed secure, but what if the second story wasn't? What if the upstairs, which camel backed the saloon, had been blown away? The apartment only ran across the back, but what if...

She stumbled forward, helping a great-uncle who seemed unable to find his way. Once she was sure he was heading in the right direction, she made it to the door and started up the stairs.

"Peggy?" She called her sister's name as she climbed. The stairs seemed secure. Above her, everything looked the way it always did. "Peggy! Aunt Dee!"

The door at the head of the stairwell was open. She made it to the top without incident and found Peggy and her aunt clasped together in a bear hug, Kieran screaming between them.

"Thank God." She joined them.

"The bedroom's wrecked," Deirdre said calmly. "The window exploded. There's glass everywhere, but Kieran and I were in here."

"Let's get downstairs. We can exit through the kitchen door. The front's a nightmare."

"No, we can't get out that way," Peggy said. "The back door's blocked."

Megan knew she wasn't thinking clearly, but now she was particularly confused. "How do you know? You came straight up here."

"A tree fell in front of the back door this morning, Megan. Right on top of Nick's car. We'd pulled his Civic out behind the kitchen door to decorate it, and that old maple toppled right onto his roof. Nobody wanted to tell you until we had to. We didn't want to spoil—"

"I guess you didn't."

"I'm sorry," Peggy said.

The loss of a car seemed inconsequential at the moment. "Nick's won't be the only car in Cleveland to suffer storm damage. Kieran's okay?"

"Just scared. We're all scared," Peggy kissed Kieran's hair. "Aunt Dee?"

Deirdre drew herself up straight. "Let's get downstairs. Did you see your uncle?"

Megan tried to remember if she had seen Uncle Frank. "I didn't, I'm sorry. But I didn't see any serious injuries." She thought of the roof sitting at the front of the saloon and what might be under it. "Nick and Jon were checking when I came upstairs."

"I think we need to go down right away." Deirdre no longer sounded calm, and Megan knew reality was setting in.

They started for the stairs. Megan went first, with Peggy and Kieran right behind her and their aunt bringing up the rear.

Niccolo was waiting at the bottom, and at the sight of them, he looked relieved. "I don't think anyone was buried in the rubble," he said in a low voice. "There's no sign anybody was that close. Some people were hit by flying debris. There's some blood and some bruises, but none of the injuries are life-threatening. We're doing a head count now."

"Nick, there's no exit." Megan stepped aside to let Peggy and her aunt by. "There's a tree blocking the kitchen door."

"Jon told me."

"Maybe it's better if we stay inside until the fire department can get to us. Outside must be as bad as in. Wires must be down, trees are down. If nobody's seriously hurt here—"

"Megan, a couple of people claim they smell gas."

She couldn't breathe again. She was angry at herself for succumbing to fear, but anger was not inflating her lungs.

"Take it easy," he said, spotting her dilemma. "Let yourself go limp. Don't think about breathing...."

She obeyed as well as she could. In a moment the light-headedness passed and air was moving again. "What's wrong with us?" she gasped. "Why didn't we have the radio on? Why didn't somebody warn us?"

He ignored her question and began to catalogue their options. "We can't get out through the front. The roof is precarious. If we start moving debris, more of it could fall, and somebody could be injured or killed."

"We put a steel door in the kitchen two years ago after that carjacking. There's no way we'll be able to break it down, not with a car and a tree in front of it."

"Are there other exits? Anything I don't know about?"

She tried to think. There were no windows on the sides of the building. "Kitchen window?"

"Too small for most of us, and blocked besides. The tree did a lot of damage."

Now she understood why no one had allowed her near the kitchen.

"We might be able to get the smaller children out that way if we have to," he continued.

Megan had often fantasized about a picture window over the side work counter. She had told herself she would put one in someday, even if the view was mediocre and she had to add bars for security. "The fire department must be on the way," she said.

"I don't think we can count on them coming quickly. I'm sure we're not the only casualty."

"There's a hole in the roof."

"No help."

"The gas won't build up, will it? Even if there's a leak, it'll dissipate."

"I'd rather not find out."

"Are the phones—"

"Dead. And so far nobody's gotten a cell phone working. The local tower might be down, or the system could be flooded with calls."

Jon arrived. "Rooney's missing."

Megan looked at Niccolo, searching his eyes. "Did you see him recently? Do you remember? The last time I saw him,

Aunt Dee had him tucked under her wing, but she was upstairs with Kieran when the tornado hit."

"He was with your uncle Frank," Jon said.

"Is Uncle Frank—"

"Fine. But he lost Rooney after the tornado."

"Were they in the front?"

"No, in the back. He should be safe, but he's disappeared."

"Anyone else missing?" Niccolo asked.

"Not that we've discovered. Unless somebody was here alone with no one to vouch for them."

Megan frantically tried to think. "Where could Rooney be?"

"Upstairs?" Jon asked.

"No, we were just up there. Maybe he's hiding. In the kitchen or behind the bar?"

"We checked."

"Storeroom?"

"Checked it."

"The cellar," Megan said. "Did anybody check the cellar?"

The cellar door was located—inefficiently—inside the kitchen pantry. The cellar itself was tiny, damp and unpleasant, and only used for storing kegs or a temporary overflow of canned goods.

"I can't imagine he'd go down there," Jon said. "Will he even remember the cellar's there? I didn't."

"It's hard to tell what he remembers. But for a long time the saloon was his life. He knows every nook and cranny."

"I'll check." Jon turned away, but Megan stopped him.

"No, let me."

"I'll come with you," Niccolo said.

"Shouldn't you and Jon stay up here and try to figure out what to do?"

"It will only take a moment."

They started through the throng of guests toward the kitchen. Megan was impressed with everyone's calm. She heard weeping, and coughing from the dust, but order had been maintained. She comforted people as best she could and promised they would know what to do shortly. When she reached the kitchen, she saw the old maple tree lying in front of the window, heavy branches like arms lifted imploringly toward the sky. Greta and another kitchen staff member were waiting for them.

"I don't know why this window's still in one piece, but it is," Greta said. "Do you want us to knock out the glass?"

"Not yet," Megan said. She couldn't imagine anyone escaping that way. Perhaps a small child would fit, but no one could know what awaited a child outside. For the moment it was better to keep everyone together. "Greta, have you been here the whole time? Since the tornado hit?"

"I ran out into the saloon right afterwards. We all did. To see what happened."

"You didn't see Rooney come in here, did you?"

"I wasn't paying attention." Greta sounded contrite, as if she should somehow have had her wits completely about her during the crisis.

Megan was fighting panic. "I smell gas," she said. "Very faint, but noticeable."

"The stove is off," Greta said. "And I blew out the pilot light. That was the first thing I checked when I came back in here."

"We'll check the furnace when we go downstairs, but it's fairly new, isn't it?" Niccolo asked.

"Last winter," Megan said.

"Then it should have a safety shutoff. That's probably not the problem."

"Let's find Rooney. One thing at a time." She put a hand on Greta's shoulder. "Hold the fort, okay?"

"We've got clean towels, and we still have water. We'll help people clean up as best we can."

Megan headed for the pantry. The cellar was so rarely used that boxes of supplies partially blocked the doorway, taking advantage of every inch of room. The saloon had always needed more storage area. Now it would need so much more than that.

"I guess he could have gotten through without moving anything. If he stepped over these, opened the door a crack and squeezed through," she said, pointing to the boxes.

"The electricity's off, so there's no light down there."

"We've always kept a couple of flashlights on a rack in the stairwell. I never go down without one. I'm afraid I'll end up in the dark if there's a power failure."

"We'll take a quick look."

"I was going to increase our property insurance," she said as he helped her shove boxes aside so the door would open wider. "I just never seemed to find the time for a consultation with our agent."

"Don't think about that now."

"When you vowed for better or worse, I bet you weren't thinking the big guy upstairs might take you up on that last part so soon."

"Megan, this is the *better* part. It's a miracle no one was killed. If the twister hit us directly, it would have taken the whole building and everyone in it. We probably caught the tip of the tail."

That wasn't lost on Megan. *Miracle* was not too strong a word, particularly if help arrived quickly and cleared an exit.

She edged in front of him. "Better let me go first. I know the layout. I can feel around for a flashlight."

"I see light down below." He stepped aside.

Megan felt a rush of gratitude. Light meant Rooney was downstairs. Now she was only afraid they might find him in a state of terror.

She felt along the wall to the rack where the flashlights were kept and found only one, snapping it on to illuminate the path. "Rooney," she called. "Don't be afraid. Nick and I are coming to get you."

She started down, shining her light just in front of her so that Niccolo could find his way, as well. Halfway there she saw her father below them, banging ineffectually on a paneled wall with his palms. He was a slight man and—she noted—paler than usual. She wondered if he really believed that his meager weight was any match for the saloon foundation.

"He must have panicked," she said so that only Niccolo would hear. She moved faster and hoped that her new husband could still see well enough to keep up. At the bottom she started toward Rooney.

"Hey, Rooney, it's okay. The fire department will get here soon. And they'll get us out. But you need to come upstairs with Nick and me. You shouldn't be alone down here."

Rooney turned to examine her. He did not look panicked. He looked, in fact, disturbed by the interruption. "Here somewhere."

She was often puzzled by her father's attempts to communicate. There had been a time when almost everything he'd said was a mystery. More recently, though, all the other changes in his life had led to clearer, more precise exchanges. They'd had real conversations where both of them were heard and understood. She was afraid this wasn't going to be one of them.

"Yes, you're here," she said. "But it would be better if you were upstairs."

He gazed at her as if she were a little girl again. "No way out."

"Maybe not this minute, but the fire department—"

"No way out there." He shook his head and pointed above him. He looked annoyed, as if Megan just didn't understand.

"No, but there will be."

He turned around and began banging his palms on the wall again. Megan imagined that prisoners pounded cell walls the same way. "Rooney, that's not going to help. Come on upstairs with me, okay?"

"Are you looking for something?" Niccolo asked him.

Megan wished Niccolo would stay out of the exchange. She was afraid Rooney was going to become even more distracted. "Nick, I—"

"Here someplace." Rooney moved down an arm's length and continued pounding.

"Megan, he's not upset. He's looking for something," Niccolo told her. "Do you know what it might be?"

"I don't think—"

"Listen..." Rooney stopped pounding a moment, then started up again.

She was growing more disturbed. She didn't like being

away from the others. Maybe someone had gotten through to the fire department. She wanted to know if help was on the way. She wanted to figure out strategy. She wanted to see to her guests. "Rooney, I don't hear anything! Please come up."

"It sounds hollow." Niccolo took her arm. "Do what he says and listen."

"So what if it's hollow? Who can tell why..." But she fell silent, aware that nothing she could say was going to turn the tide.

"What's behind there, Rooney?" Niccolo asked.

Rooney grinned. "Jail time."

Megan caught Niccolo's eye and shook her head. Niccolo was expecting too much.

"Jail time?" Niccolo asked. "Jail for who?"

Rooney was picking at a sheet of paneling now, trying to pry it loose with fingernails that weren't up to the task.

"For who?" Niccolo repeated.

Rooney stepped back, obviously frustrated. "Tools. Hammer might do."

"What will we find if we pry the panel loose?" Niccolo asked.

"Nick, please don't continue this," Megan pleaded.

"Jail time," Rooney said. He paused. "For bootleggers."

Megan faced her father, Niccolo's part in the conversation forgotten. "Bootleggers?"

Rooney smiled. "I wasn't born."

"Megan, do you know what he's talking about?" Niccolo asked.

She was ashamed. She had been so sure Rooney was just talking crazy. "When I was a little girl the grown-ups talked about tunnels down here. Not when they thought we could hear them, of course. We weren't really supposed to know. It was a family secret. But I haven't thought about that for years. I thought the tunnels were probably just a story, a Donaghue fairy tale."

"Bootleggers?" Niccolo asked.

"I don't know for sure, but if there are tunnels, maybe they were built to smuggle in bootleg whiskey during Prohibition.

There's another bar on the West Side that claims they have tunnels that lead all the way to the water."

"The Shoreway would make that impossible here."

"It wouldn't have then, because the Shoreway wasn't there in the twenties. Besides, if there are tunnels under the saloon, maybe they led out to a road on Whiskey Island where liquor was brought in from the water. I do know Cleveland had its share of rum runners. Canada's right across the lake, and Canada never bought into Prohibition."

"So if it's true, the tunnels might still be here?"

"Could be, although in what kind of shape, I don't know. If they exist, they've been walled away my whole life. I guess it depends on how sturdy they were to start with."

"Sturdy enough, I bet. If they were built for bootleggers, they wouldn't have taken any chances. Liquor was a profitable business."

"Yeah, for people like Al Capone. This is Cleveland."

"Elliot Ness came here after Prohibition to clean up the city," Niccolo said. "There must have been some business here to draw him."

Obviously he'd been listening to Jon, for whom Cleveland history was a favorite subject. "Are you thinking we might tear out this wall and see what's here?" she said.

"Rooney, does the tunnel lead outside?" Niccolo put his hand on the old man's shoulder. "Can we get out this way?"

Rooney gave a slight nod.

That was enough affirmation for Niccolo. The possibility existed. "Can you get my kids and get us some tools?" he asked Megan. "And more flashlights, if you have them?"

"The kids?"

"Do you know anybody more talented at destruction?"

She left the two men below and raced up the stairs. In the saloon, she clapped her hands to get everyone's attention. "Has anybody been able to reach the fire department?"

Nobody had. Sirens had been heard in the distance, and shouting somewhere down the block.

She explained quickly what Rooney had found and what

they planned to do. Jon and Casey had organized people into small groups. One was tearing towels into makeshift bandages to supplement the small first aid kit. Another had stationed themselves as close to the front as possible to yell for help. Another was washing and doctoring cuts and bruises. One group was making attempts to comfort and entertain the children.

Barry the bartender kept a crowbar behind the bar for security. He gave it to Winston, who headed straight for the kitchen. The other kids followed with whatever they were handed. Megan pulled a toolkit and more flashlights out of the storeroom, Greta gave Josh a mallet she used for pounding round steak. Peggy, trying to manage a struggling Kieran, volunteered to go upstairs and look in the apartment for more flashlights, but that effort was vetoed as too dangerous.

Megan promised she would come back with news the minute she knew if the tunnels existed and if they led to safety.

"They exist." Deirdre grabbed her arm as she was heading back into the kitchen. "Your father's not imagining this."

"Do you know where they lead?"

Deirdre shook her head. "We weren't supposed to know. I think my father's generation was afraid we'd find a way to get inside and someone would get hurt. Do you want me to go down and help?"

"Stay here and help Peggy with Kieran, will you?" Megan could hear her nephew wailing. The crowd, the noise and the confusion were bad enough for a normal child.

She left Casey and Jon in charge, confident they could keep chaos at bay. Downstairs, she saw the boys at work and marveled. The tornado had nothing on the Brick kids for destruction.

Someone had wanted the tunnels sealed for all time. Five minutes into the pounding and prying, that someone was thwarted.

"Step back," Niccolo commanded, and the kids did so without argument. He kicked away the last remnants of the paneling and shined his flashlight inside.

"What do you see?"

"I'm going to have to go inside to find out."

She didn't want him to go. Even if the tunnels had been safe at one time, they had been sealed off for decades. But what choice did they have? The saloon wasn't safe, either, with a quarter of the roof on the floor and gas seeping from God knew where.

"I'm coming, too," she said. "Two lights are better than one."

"Please don't," Niccolo said. "Not until I've checked it out a little."

"I'm coming."

He knew better than to argue, especially in front of the young men, who seemed entranced at the possibility of marital discord so soon after the wedding. "Okay, but step carefully."

"Really? I thought we could do an Irish jig or two on the way through." She winked at Josh. Now that the fun part was over, the kids were beginning to look uneasy. "We'll be right back," she promised. "One of you run upstairs and see if anybody's had any luck calling the fire department."

Nobody moved. "Or not," she said. She watched Niccolo step through the ersatz doorway into the tunnel. Rooney, who had stayed to watch the demolition, stepped in after him.

"Rooney," she called. "Please don't do that." Her plea was ignored. She followed, stepping into the space and shining her light all around. Niccolo and Rooney were just ahead.

She hadn't had time to think about what they might find in the little time that had passed since they found Rooney beating on the cellar wall. She'd formed a fuzzy mental image of a narrow dirt passageway filled with debris, bats and cobwebs. She had not expected a tunnel wide enough for three people to walk abreast. She hadn't expected massive, roughly-hewn ceiling beams or dirty plastered walls. She caught up to her husband and father.

"Look at this." Niccolo aimed his light to the right.

She followed the beam and saw a storage cellar similar to the one they'd just left. It was piled with boxes, and the shelves lining it held old glass canning jars, some of which were still filled with garden produce.

She whistled softly. "I had no idea. Look at this place."

"Let's keep moving."

"Where do you think it comes out?"

"It goes down from here. There are steps ahead." Niccolo shined his flashlight.

"When they built the Shoreway, they must have buried the entrance," Megan said. "We're going to find a dead end."

"No," Rooney said.

She had new respect for Rooney's grasp of their situation. She followed, trailing her flashlight along the walls.

The steps were steep, ten of them, each so narrow they had to walk single file, and the ceiling grew lower until she was stooping. They halted abruptly at a small flagstone-surfaced platform. Stones layered the wall, too. Her heart sank. Then Rooney stooped and began to jiggle a stone near the top.

She saw light.

"Nick?"

But Niccolo was already helping his father-in-law move the stone. With every inch, more light streamed into the tunnel. "Get the kids," he told her. "Then go upstairs. If the fire department isn't on its way, bring everyone down here. Tell them to be careful. But this is our way out, Megan, and we'd be fools not to take it."

chapter 5

The tunnel opened onto the hillside overlooking the Shoreway. Niccolo supposed at one time it had extended farther, but the Shoreway construction had destroyed the rest of it. Most of the entrance was walled in by dirt and even a grove of small willow trees. But there was a hole hidden by the trees that was just large enough to escape through.

"Lived here," Rooney told him after Megan disappeared back through the tunnel. "In the bad years."

At first Niccolo didn't understand; then everything fell into place, and he realized what the old man was saying. Rooney had disappeared from his daughters' lives for more than a decade. At some point in time he had probably lived in this tunnel close to the people he loved but hidden from their view. It was probably due to Rooney that the entrance had been uncovered, then sealed with stone. They could thank Rooney for this escape route.

"I saw you the night of the carjacking. Do you remember

that? And you disappeared down the hill. I thought you crossed the Shoreway. Were you living in the tunnel then, too?" Niccolo asked.

He didn't really expect an answer, and he didn't get one. Rooney's grasp of time was uneven. There were still days when he believed his wife was alive, days when he seemed surprised to find that his daughters were fully grown. Two years ago Niccolo had tracked the old man to a makeshift "den" on Whiskey Island, but now he knew where Rooney had stayed on the coldest days of that winter. He supposed that at the height of Rooney's illness it was possible he had found places to live all over the city, places where he could escape and feel secure. Niccolo just hoped those days were over.

He and Rooney worked at moving the rock out of the way until they were joined by Josh, Winston and Tarek. Megan had asked the other kids to help her bring people downstairs and through the tunnel. The boys were on an adrenaline high. This was a day they would talk about for the rest of their lives.

With the help of more strong arms, the rock rolled away easily. They worked at another, widening the space until Niccolo could squeeze through. Outside, a fine rain fell, and the skies were still dark. But the wind had died down, and the air felt fresh and clean. There was no traffic on the Shoreway, which was only yards down the hill. He motioned for Winston to join him. Winston squeezed out the hole and gazed around.

"Well this part of C-town's not looking so bad," he said.

"Can you find your way along the hillside and back up to the street? See if you can find a working telephone and report what happened at the saloon?"

"Then I gotta call my mom."

Winston wasn't such a tough guy after all. "Make that your first call, okay?" Niccolo said.

"I'll find somebody'll know what to do."

"Watch carefully for wires on the ground. Treat them like deadly snakes. Be very, very careful."

"I'll come back and let you know."

"No, don't. Go home." Niccolo paused. "If you can get there."

Winston nodded. "You think that twister did lots of damage?"

From the hillside, Niccolo couldn't tell. Nothing looked out of place, except for the fact that no traffic was moving on the Shoreway. "Tornadoes are funny. They'll take one house and leave everything else around it unharmed. It may have touched down on Lookout Avenue and no place else."

"Hey, man, I'm ghost." Winston raised his hand in good-bye and started across the hill.

"Good luck," Niccolo called.

"Got my finger on the trigger."

Niccolo, ignoring that imagery, turned and gazed up the hill. From the rear, what he could see of the saloon appeared undamaged. He was too far below the street to see anything that had happened there. He headed back into the tunnel just as Josh and Tarek led the first group of guests to the opening.

Niccolo explained how they would be exiting. "Is everybody okay to climb down to the road?" The climb wasn't steep, but some of the older guests would need to take their time, since the path would be slick from the rain, and no one had worn hiking boots to the wedding.

"Apparently they've blocked it off, because there's no traffic," he continued. "We'll gather down there as a group and walk along the road to the first exit. I'd rather do that than risk going up to the street. I don't know what the rest of Lookout looks like."

Everyone seemed in agreement. He ushered them outside, comforting and questioning each one about injuries.

For the next twenty minutes he consoled and assisted his wedding guests. Peggy came through clutching Kieran. He counted Andreanis until the last one came through. The rain had nearly halted by the time the last group arrived. Megan brought up the rear, with Casey and Jon just ahead of her. Megan didn't mince words. "Nick, the gas smell is stronger."

"Everybody's out?"

She hesitated long enough that he wasn't reassured.

"You don't know?" he said.

"Did Josh come through? Aunt Dee thought she saw him opening the door to the apartment. One of the flashlights died, and earlier he'd said he was going to look for another."

Niccolo had seen Josh come through at least twice, but he wasn't sure if the young man had gone back inside to escort more guests or gone down to the Shoreway. He tried to remember, but the afternoon had become a blur of faces and situations.

"I went to the bottom of the stairs and yelled for him before I left, just in case," Megan said. "I think he would have heard me if he was in the apartment. I'm sure he would have. He probably came through and you just don't remember."

Probably wasn't good enough. Even though Josh was fully capable of finding his way outside now, he might not understand the urgency. They had played down the gas smell, so as not to unduly scare anyone. Panic was an even worse threat.

Niccolo decided to agree, at least outwardly. "I'm sure you're right. Help the rest of the people down to the Shoreway, okay?"

"You're not going back inside, are you?"

If Megan thought he was going back in, she would insist on coming with him. Niccolo asked forgiveness for lying to her on their wedding day. "No, I'm going to see what's going on up above. I sent Winston to find a phone and call the fire department."

Megan hesitated.

"Please, go on," he assured her. "I can take care of myself."

"Shouldn't I come with you?"

"I think you should stay with our guests. Jon, will you and Casey help Megan make sure everybody gets to safety?"

Jon knew Niccolo was lying. Niccolo could see it in his eyes, but he nodded. "We'll take care of it."

"I'll join you the moment I can."

"Okay."

Niccolo watched them go. Rooney had already made the climb, and no one was left at the mouth of the tunnel. He waited until Megan's view was obscured; then he started back inside and climbed the steps up into the tunnel. "Josh?"

He tried again to remember if Josh had gone back inside. He started down the tunnel shining his flashlight on the floor just ahead of him, listening carefully. "Josh?"

He was almost at the entrance into the cellar when he heard an explosion. A split second afterward the world went black.

He awoke sometime later. Time had stopped for him, and when he opened his eyes he didn't know where he was, or even who. He was lying on his back, staring up at a poorly plastered wall. The room was dark, but a beam of light shone at the wall's bottom. He wasn't in any real pain, although he was afraid if he moved too quickly that might change. He lay still, trying to put his thoughts together.

He'd heard a noise. He thought he remembered flying through the air, but how could that be? Unless he was dead. He'd heard afterlife tales of tunnels, of moving rapidly toward a bright, healing light. But if this was the afterlife, it was highly overrated. The floor beneath his fingertips was clammy. The air he breathed was smoke filled. Despite years in the priesthood, he'd never been a big fan of the biblical version of Hell, and he discounted that possibility immediately.

"Nick?"

He heard a woman's voice in the distance. At the sound of his name, memory rushed in to fill the void. He had gone back inside the tunnel to find Josh. There had been an explosion.... He tried to sit up, but immediately his head began to throb. He decided against moving for the moment.

"Nick?" This time the voice calling him was a man's.

"Here," he croaked. "I'm here. I'm okay, I think."

He heard footsteps, quick ones, and loud enough to make his head throb harder. He realized the light that illuminated the bottom of the wall was a flashlight. *His* flashlight. He had dropped it. He felt for it until he had it in his grasp. Then he shined it on the wall, hoping to guide his rescuers.

"Here," he croaked again.

He waited. His vision was blurry, but as he stared at the wall, his eyes began to focus. Above him was an image. He struggled to focus more closely. A woman gazed down at him, an image as familiar as his own.

The footsteps drew closer, but now he paid little attention. He drew the beam along the edge of the image. Up, down, across. It was pronounced, certainly not the result of his injury. He was not looking at something that wasn't there.

The Virgin Mary was looking down at him, and she was weeping.

"Nick, my God, are you all right?"

He heard a man's voice. Jon. He was glad to put a name to it. Then he heard a woman's, and he knew the worst moment of his day wasn't over.

"Megan," he croaked. He turned his head to see a vision in white running in his direction. She fell to the ground beside him.

"Are you okay? Don't move. What happened?"

"Explosion. Gas leak. Maybe in the cellar. Fumes ignited by the—maybe the water heater. I should have thought to blow out the pilot light." He coughed.

Jon joined them. "Were you in the cellar when it blew?"

Niccolo tried to remember. "Almost. Where am I?"

"About ten yards down the tunnel."

Niccolo realized he must have been knocked off his feet by the explosion and catapulted to this place. "I should be..."

"Dead," Jon supplied. "For sure. I don't know why you aren't. It's nothing short of a miracle. Can you move your arms and legs?"

Niccolo tried. He felt bruised all over, but nothing seemed to be broken. "Josh?"

"Down below. You should have waited to find out."

"Time wasn't a friend."

"You said you were going up to the road," Megan said. "You lied to me."

"I didn't want you to worry...."

"You two settle that later. Right now, I think we need to get you out of here," Jon said. "The fire department's on its way. They'll address the leak, wherever it is, but we don't want another explosion while we're in here."

"Fire..." Inevitably, it followed explosions.

"There's not much to ignite down here. We can assume the furnace room will be a total loss."

Niccolo struggled to sit up. At the second try, and with Jon and Megan's help, he managed. The world spun, but when he opened his eyes again, the Virgin still stared down at him.

"Tell me I'm not imagining her," he said.

"Nick, you're not imagining me," Megan said.

"You're real. I know. Her." Niccolo shined his light on the wall again.

Jon and Megan turned to see what he was talking about. Niccolo watched Megan's face. He watched his bride's eyes widen. She stared at the wall, then at him. And then Megan, whose relationship with the Church was suspect at best, made the sign of the cross.

chapter 6

Cleveland's Hopkins airport was open for business, and planes were still flying. That seemed incongruous to Peggy, who only the day before had wondered if she or Cleveland would survive the tornado's devastation. Now, she stared at the ceiling in Niccolo and Megan's guest bedroom and wondered how she would feel tomorrow, when she woke up in another strange bed. This time in Ireland.

A faint rapping launched her to her feet. She opened the door a crack to see her sister's serious face.

"Phil tracked you down," Megan said softly, so not to wake Kieran. "Nice of him."

Peggy wasn't surprised at her sister's tone. Megan did not like Kieran's father, nor, for that matter, did Casey. "At least he's calling, Megan. I should have called him myself last night. There was just so much going on."

"I suppose even Phil finds it hard to ignore the fact that the saloon was struck by a tornado. We're the toast of the town. We made statewide news."

"You're supposed to be on your honeymoon." Peggy looked around for something to pull over her T-shirt so that she could take Phil's call.

"We'll go after I get the estimates for renovations. I'll have plenty of time to relax. I won't be working for months." Megan shook her head as if she was still adjusting to that thought. "Let me get you a robe. There's nobody in the kitchen. You can talk to Phil there."

Peggy checked Kieran, who was sleeping soundly, his tiny body curled in a ball. She wanted him to sleep, since their flight to Ireland was going to be trial enough. When Megan returned, she wrapped the flannel bathrobe around her and secured it; then, with a nod to her sister, she went down to the kitchen and picked up the receiver.

"Phil?"

"I was beginning to think you weren't going to speak to me."

She found a chair and tried to make herself comfortable. "Things are in chaos here, but we're all right. I'm sorry you had to hear about it from somebody else."

"The *Columbus Dispatch* had a front page article. Kieran's okay?"

"Fine. We're all lucky. Just cuts and bruises and one mild concussion. It was one of those freaky things. Lookout Avenue caught the tail of a twister. There were trees down all over the West Side, but it could have been so much worse."

"The paper says the saloon sustained the worst damage on the street?"

"Let's just say we won't be serving Guinness for a while. Luckily it's not a total loss. And since she has to close and renovate anyway, Megan's swearing she'll improve the place while she's at it."

"Megan said you're still planning to leave today."

"I am." Peggy considered her next words but decided to go ahead. "I wish you could have come to say goodbye this week, Phil. Kieran will be a whole year older by the time we get back."

"Tanya's been sick. I was afraid to leave her."

Tanya was Phil's wife. They had married six months ago, and Tanya had wasted no time getting pregnant. Peggy wondered if Kieran was the reason for her haste—and continuing morning sickness. Tanya was young and insecure. Peggy had tried to find ways to assure her that Kieran was no threat to her marriage, but the message had never been received.

"I'm sending an extra check to Ireland," Phil said, when Peggy didn't respond. "A good-size one. I know you'll need some help getting settled."

Phil was as generous as he could be with child support, and that was one area where Peggy couldn't fault him. He had little interest in Kieran, but he did take his financial responsibilities seriously. He was a fledgling architect with years of school loans to pay off, but he shared what he could.

"I appreciate it," she said. "I'm going to buy supplies for Kieran's classroom once I get there. Whatever you send will go toward that."

"How is he?"

Uncharitable responses rose to her tongue, but she overcame them. "He's the same, Phil."

"Is he talking yet?"

"He can say hi. But he'll be talking up a storm by the time I bring him home."

"I'm sorry I couldn't...you know."

She didn't know. Couldn't visit? Couldn't love his beautiful, distant son? Couldn't promise that he ever would?

"I hope you'll write him," she said. "I'll read him your letters, and I'll put your photograph in his room."

"Sure. That's a good idea. Please do that."

"Goodbye, Phil. Give Tanya my best wishes and tell her I hope she feels better soon." She hung up, suspecting that Tanya would feel better the moment Peggy and Kieran's plane took off for Shannon Airport.

"I'm making coffee." Megan stumbled into the room. "One cup or two?"

"I'll take a pot." Peggy watched her sister wander the room

trying to find her wits and the coffee filters at the same time. Megan was usually a morning person, but she'd used up a year's worth of energy yesterday, and it showed.

"Nick's still doing okay?" Peggy asked.

"His skull must be made of titanium. I woke him up all through the night like the E.R. doc told me to, until he said if I woke him up one more time he'd start divorce proceedings."

"A little edgy, huh?"

"He claims he doesn't even have a headache."

"It's really something of a miracle, huh?"

"Peggy..." Megan filled the glass pot with water. She turned off the tap and faced her sister. "I've got to tell you something. But only if you promise not to laugh."

"Any chance I can keep that promise?"

"Maybe." Megan seemed to realize she was clutching the pot of water to her chest. She turned and poured it in the coffeemaker and installed the coffee filter. "When we found Nick yesterday?"

Peggy felt her skin growing cold. She hadn't slept well, despite true exhaustion. Every time she'd closed her eyes she'd felt the house rocking the way the saloon had rocked when the twister touched down. Or she'd heard the explosion and felt the same stab of terror she'd felt when she realized Niccolo might have been caught inside.

"I was sure he was dead," Peggy said.

"I know. He should have been. He was blown ten yards or more."

"You were going to tell me something funny. I could use it."

Megan measured the coffee into the pot and flipped the switch. "It's only funny coming from me. When we found him, Peggy, I couldn't believe he was alive. Talking, too, like nothing much had happened. We told him we had to get him outside, and he sat up. Then he shined his flashlight on the wall right under where he'd landed."

Peggy was waiting for the punch line. "And?"

"There was an image there."

Peggy waited. She had no idea what her sister meant.

"I don't know how to explain it," Megan went on. "An impression of some kind, I guess. A stain? But it looks like the Virgin."

For a moment Peggy didn't understand. "Virgin?"

"Holy statues of our lady. She's facing the other wall, robed, and her arms are out like this." Megan demonstrated, as if she were welcoming guests. "And, well, here's the thing. The face has no features, not really, but where her eyes should be..." Megan looked away. "Tears. It looks like she's crying. Nick woke up, and that's what he saw."

Peggy didn't know what to say. "Well..." She frowned. "Megan, you don't think this is some sort of a miracle, do you? That doesn't sound like you."

"I think it's a coincidence, and for that matter, so does Nick. It was just, well, spooky." She shook her head. "No, that's not right. It wasn't spooky. It was lovely. Comforting, as if..." She shrugged. "For just a second there I felt like I used to when I was a little girl and we'd go to St. Brigid's as a family. Sometimes, when everything was very quiet and the candlelight flickered on the wall and you knew the organ music was about to start. In that moment, you know, that's how it felt."

Megan rarely talked about religion and never in a positive way. She'd been born a Catholic and would die one. Like all of them, she loved Father Brady, and she understood her new husband's devotion to the Church, but without Niccolo in her life she would have remained only nominally involved. She was a Holy Days Catholic, and her sisters were the same.

"You had a spiritual experience," Peggy said. "I think that's wonderful. Treasure it."

Megan seemed to shake off the moment. She opened a cupboard and got down coffee mugs. "Yes? Well, I'm not looking for another one. Not if Nick gets blown down a tunnel first. That's the real miracle. He's alive."

Peggy took her mug and held it up high. "I'll drink to that."

"What will you drink to?" Niccolo came into the room, looking sleepy-eyed but completely well.

"Your health." Peggy held out her mug, and Megan filled it.

"Then I'm going to drink to a safe trip today for you and Kieran." Niccolo crossed the room and gave Megan a bear hug before he got a mug for himself.

Peggy felt right at home. The room was lovely. Simple bird's-eye maple cabinets, white tile countertops and back-splash, capped off with rich dark red wallpaper Megan had put up last month. Niccolo's oil paintings of Tuscan villages harmonized with Megan's quirky farm animal canisters. Her sister had upholstered the kitchen table chairs with remnants of old quilts. Niccolo had crafted the table from a black walnut tree that had been cut down to make room for a neighbor's addition.

"You're sure you want to go today?" Megan asked her. "I mean, the airline will let you change your ticket, won't they?"

"Do you need me here?" Peggy said. "Be honest."

Megan looked torn, but in the end she shook her head. "There's nothing you can do. We've got inspectors coming, insurance adjusters, and later there'll be contractors. It's going to be a zoo, but at least it will give me something to do so I don't have to think about what happened."

"It's another piece of luck that Aunt Dee already had our suitcases," Peggy said. "And I guess there won't be any hurry on cleaning out what's left in the apartment...."

"We won't be renting it out for a while, that's for sure."

"A delay would be hard to explain to Irene. She's made special arrangements to have me picked up at Shannon."

"I wish we knew this woman. I wish somebody in the family had met her."

"She *is* family," Peggy said. She had expected this last-ditch effort on Megan's part to get her to reconsider, and she settled in for it.

"But what do we know about her? Her grandfather was the brother of our great-great grandfather. That's not much of a tie. And until she found us on the Internet, we didn't even know there *were* relatives on that side of the family. We were supposed to be the last of the line."

"Well, we will be soon enough." There was little that Peggy

knew about Irene Tierney, but she did know that the old woman wasn't well. She was eighty-one, had never been married and had no family in the small village of Shanmullin or in all of Ireland. She lived in the thatched cottage that had once been the home of Terence Tierney, the sisters' great-great grandfather, and sadly, her life was drawing to a close, most of it lived without knowledge of their existence.

"And I don't really understand what she wanted with us in the first place," Megan said. "Information about her father, who we never even knew existed? I don't know what we can tell her."

Peggy thought Irene's story was intriguing. In her first contact Irene had written that her mother and father had brought her to Cleveland as a small child. There had been no future for the family in Ireland, and there had been some hope there might be relatives remaining in Cleveland. They'd found none, as it turned out, and after Irene's father died just a few years later, her mother had taken her young daughter back to Ireland to eke out a living on the Tierney land. Not until four months ago, when Irene, surfing the Internet, had come across mention of Terence Tierney in a newspaper article about the Whiskey Island Saloon, did she realize the Tierney family had indeed lived on in Ohio.

"She wants to find out how her father died here," Peggy said. "That's natural. You of all people should be able to understand that. When Rooney was missing all those years, we wanted to know what had happened to him."

"I just don't understand why her own mother didn't tell her. Or how she thinks we're going to find out anything."

Peggy didn't know herself. She had done a little research at City Hall for Irene but hadn't found anything. She hoped her sisters would continue while she was in Ireland.

"It just seems like so much to take on," Megan said. "Kieran, caring for an old woman you don't know..."

Peggy didn't repeat what she'd told Megan so many times before, but it hung unspoken between them. She was determined to help her son, and that meant hours of work with

Kieran every day. Irene needed a companion, but not constant care. Going to Ireland was the only way Peggy could afford not to work at a full-time job. Irene was giving her free room and board, and with Phil's monthly check, Peggy could manage their other expenses if she lived simply. And what other way was there in rural Ireland? The arrangement was ideal, a surprising and wonderful gift.

"She's excited about having Kieran there." Peggy got to her feet. "She's never had a child in the house. She needs help, she needs family. It's an opportunity I can't afford to ignore. I've talked to her enough to know we'll get along. Trust me a little, okay?"

Megan set her coffee mug on the counter and embraced Peggy. "I love you. You know that's what this is about, right?"

Peggy hugged her back. She saw Niccolo watching them. She was glad her older sister was in such capable hands. Megan didn't realize how much she needed someone to lean on occasionally. "You'll take care of her?" she asked him.

"If she'll let me."

Peggy squeezed Megan hard, then stepped away. "Make sure you do," she counseled her sister. "And stop worrying about me. I'm going to be just fine. Kieran and I are going to be just fine."

They weren't fine, nor had Peggy really expected them to be. Kieran did not take well to changes. He didn't take well to strangers, to noise, to being shuffled from one place to another, to being tearfully hugged by family or to seeing his mother choke back tears as she said goodbye.

As it turned out—and as Peggy had feared—he didn't take well to airplanes, either. By the time their first flight landed in Boston, a hundred pairs of eyes were trained disapprovingly on her. What kind of mother was Peggy that she couldn't comfort her own child? And why didn't that beautiful baby quiet down when she took him in her arms? Why did he fight to get away from her?

She understood the censure she read on the faces of her fellow passengers. She understood the mixture of concern for that angelic-faced little boy as well as the irritation that the devil inside him was ruining their flight. She'd been prepared, but of course, she hadn't really been. Nobody could be.

They had a long wait in Boston, another strike against the trip in Kieran's baby mind. She finally got him to sleep in his stroller, and she paced the length of the airport, over and over, until she was worn out, but anything was better than hearing her son scream. When she finally had to wheel him to security and he awoke to find himself somewhere new, the screaming began again.

He would not be consoled, and she carried him on board that way, listening to the murmured reassurances of the flight attendants and their well-meaning suggestions, and knowing that none of the suggestions would help. She managed to give him the antihistamine and decongestant her pediatrician had prescribed for the journey, both to help with pressure in his ears and to help him relax, but Kieran was oblivious. The flight was full, and there was no elbow room.

She explained Kieran's problems as best she could to the friendliest of the flight attendants, and miraculously the young woman was able to find passengers willing to trade seats in order to give Peggy and Kieran a little more space. They moved to the back, where they had a row of three seats to themselves and where Kieran's screams were less audible. The extra seat comforted him a little, and two hours into the flight he stopped sobbing and took his favorite blanket. He picked at the fibers, unraveling it bit by bit, but since he was quiet, Peggy didn't care.

She fed him, she talked to him, she sang softly to him— something she usually tried not to do in public, since she couldn't carry a tune. When he slept fitfully, she slept, too. But by the time the plane landed at Shannon Airport, she felt as if she'd traveled to the ends of the earth. Kieran's little cheeks were splotchy and his eyes red from exhaustion and panic. An overseas flight was hard for any young child, but what was this like for her tiny son, who perceived the world as a frightening place and the actions of those who loved him as a morass of signals his brain couldn't process?

They waited for the others to disembark, a ritual that went faster than usual. In her distress, she wondered if the haste was due to Kieran and the frantic need of those on board to get away from him. She understood only too well, since, in her exhaustion, part of her wished for the same. When it was their turn, she gathered her carry-on and started toward the front.

Shannon Airport was well laid out and reasonably quiet. After they cleared customs, she looked around for Finn O'Malley, Irene's physician, who had promised he would drive Peggy and Kieran to the village of Shanmullin in County Mayo. Having a doctor take a full day out of his busy schedule had seemed odd enough, but Irene's warning had been odder.

"You won't get much out of Finn," she'd said in their last telephone conversation. "He's a quiet man, and he runs deep. But don't let him frighten you, Peggy. A man who's easy to know is a man with little enough inside him."

At the moment she would gladly have settled for easy. She couldn't imagine stumbling through a conversation with anyone right now, much less a difficult man. She wondered if Dr. O'Malley had been Irene's physician for many years, if he was semi-retired and able to make this trip without considering his patient load. Irene had given her very few details. Dark hair, tweed jacket, punctual.

She looked around, hoping to spot somebody who matched that description. Kieran chose that moment to fall apart. The airport was one more new environment. He was exhausted, confused and inconsolable. He wiggled to get down, and when Peggy set him on his feet, he threw himself to the un-carpeted floor and began to wail, kick and pound his fists.

Kieran in full tantrum mode was frightening to behold. The disintegration of any two-year-old affected the people around him. But Kieran's tantrums were so uncontrolled, so horrify-ingly wrenching, Peggy had learned that onlookers could seldom walk away. They hovered nearby, watching and waiting to be certain that something would be done.

Unfortunately, Peggy had learned there was nothing to do except remain calm and in control. She stayed near him, making certain he didn't hurt himself, but other than that, there was little more. Holding him made things worse. He couldn't hear her or sense her in any way when he was this upset. What tentative ties Kieran felt to her or the world dissolved in a tidal wave of emotion.

"You're going to simply let him bash his brains out?"

Peggy glanced at the stranger who had joined her, then back at her son. The man was older than she was, but still young. His hair was coal black, and in one quick look she registered austere features and censuring eyes. "I'm sorry he's disturbing you. This will end." She didn't add "soon." That was too much to hope for.

The stranger didn't depart. She could hardly blame him. Well-meaning people always gave advice, as if doing so would absolve them of guilt if the child harmed himself.

"This is Kieran Donaghue, isn't it? And you're Peggy Donaghue?"

She glanced at him again. "Dr. O'Malley?"

"Finn. Just Finn. And you've brought this screaming child to live with Irene?"

Tears sprang to Peggy's eyes. She had been in a high state of anxiety for forty-eight hours, and despite outward confidence, she'd had doubts all along that she was doing what was best for her son. Now this man, with his frigid black eyes, stiff spine and disapproving expression, reached deep inside all her fears.

"He's been in a plane for hours. He's exhausted, frustrated, distraught. He's not like this all the time."

"But often enough, I'd guess."

She stood a little straighter, although she didn't know where the energy came from. "I've explained Kieran's problems to Irene. She knows them all. She still wanted us."

"She's a gullible old woman, lonely, though she'll never

admit it, and dying. Not the best combination to make decisions, is it?"

Kieran was still flailing, and a crowd was gathering, but the strength of his tantrum was waning. Kieran, too, was exhausted from the trip and didn't have the energy to sustain a fit of this magnitude.

Peggy faced Finn. He was tall, nearly six feet, she supposed, with broad shoulders and narrow hips. She'd expected new tweed and found old herringbone, buttoned over faded jeans and a navy-blue T-shirt.

"She'll be glad to have me," she said, "and glad to have Kieran. I'm not a nurse, but I've had medical training, and I like her. I know that already. And I know she's lonely. Now she won't be anymore."

"Sometimes loneliness is better than the alternative."

"And sometimes staying out of matters that don't concern you is better than poking your nose where it doesn't belong!"

Something sparked in his eyes. "I can assure you that's not a problem of mine."

Anger died. "I know she's a good friend. She's told me. And you're worried. But you don't need to be. If this doesn't work, I'll leave. You can count on it. I just think it's worth a try. Can you be so sure it's not?"

His gaze flicked to Kieran, still kicking, still miserable. "Irene says he's autistic?"

Peggy hated the word. It reduced her son to a label, to a condition, a disorder. He was Kieran, her only child, Phil's son, Megan and Casey's nephew. He was Irish on her side and Slovak on Phil's. His father was a talented young architect, and someday his mother was going to be a doctor. He was intelligent, although she knew unlocking that part of him would be difficult. He was a beautiful little boy and would undoubtedly be a handsome man.

He was Kieran.

"He is who he is," she said. "And when this year is over, we'll know him better and all his potential."

He appeared unconvinced. "These are your bags?"

"Yes, but I have to wait for him to calm down. This is the only way I can make sure he does. I can't interfere."

"I'll take them out to my car. I can do it alone. I'll wait for you outside." Without another word he hooked the larger suitcases together, leaving her with the carry-on, and walked away.

The trip to Shanmullin was going to take hours. Peggy hoped they would all survive.

Finn O'Malley had resented making the trip to Shannon Airport. He had tried repeatedly to talk Irene out of this daft scheme to bring a stranger from the United States to care for her, but Irene was as stubborn as any Irishwoman. In her youth she'd had red hair, too, lighter than Peggy Donaghue's, but thick and straight like the young woman's. He wasn't given to stereotypes, but the myth of the stubborn redhead had some appeal. In her long lifetime Irene had resolutely refused to marry, refused to move into town as she aged, refused to hire a companion, refused to go to hospital when poor health necessitated it.

And she had refused, although her very life had depended on it, to accept the fact that Finn had given up practicing medicine. She had refused a new physician until Finn had been obliged to treat her or watch her die unaided.

Stubborn.

Now this young cousin of hers seemed to prove that Irene's contrary nature was going to be carried on in the distant family bloodlines.

"You're certain you're related to her?" he asked, as they finally neared the village.

Beside him Peggy opened her eyes and turned her head to look at him. Her eyes were unfocused and heavy-lidded from lack of sleep, but even so, he had been surprised to find such a beautiful woman waiting at the gate. "I'm sorry?"

He hadn't talked to her on the trip thus far. Thankfully the child had quieted almost from the moment they pulled out of the car park. Banging one's head against the floor would do that, Finn supposed. The boy had worn himself out, and the mother had fallen asleep nearly as quickly and slept for more than three hours.

"I said, you're certain Irene is really your cousin? It all seems tenuous to me."

"Something tells me that anything short of DNA analysis will leave you wondering." She said it with a faint smile to soften her words. She yawned and stretched, and the seat belt tightened across her breasts at the movement. Unfortunately, he was not oblivious.

"Protecting her seems to be my job, whether I choose it or not," he said, looking straight at the road ahead.

"Why is that? What's your relationship to her, other than physician?"

"She was my grandmother's best friend."

"And you're carrying on the tradition. I like that."

"She gives me no choice."

"I can see she wouldn't. Once we began discussing this arrangement, she gave *me* little choice, either. She's a tyrant, isn't she?"

He couldn't fault the way she said it. With admiration and affection. And besides, it was altogether true.

"Has Irene explained how we're related?" she said.

"She's been circumspect."

"Here's a history lesson. Back in the nineteenth century there were four Tierney brothers living in the house Irene occupies now. Two of them died. A third, Terence, emigrated to Cleveland, where another brother had gone and died before him. Terence is my ancestor. The fourth, Lorcan, traveled to England and disappeared. Everyone thought he died there."

Finn wasn't sure why he had asked. The details were too complicated and intimate, but now that she'd begun, he couldn't tell her so. "But if he *had* died there, I suppose you wouldn't be on your way to Shanmullin now. Irene wouldn't be alive."

"That's right. Lorcan was *her* ancestor. Lorcan was jailed in Liverpool. I don't know for what. By the time he made it back to Shanmullin, his family was gone. All of his brothers were dead by then, and his parents had gone to Cleveland years before to live their few remaining years with Terence's widow, who had remarried a man named Rowan Donaghue. Lorcan was poor and illiterate and didn't know how to get in touch with them or even if they were still alive. The village priest was dead, as well, and by then a good portion of Shanmullin had emigrated, too."

"Your name is Donaghue, not Tierney."

"Lena, Terence Tierney's wife, had a son by Terence, born after his death. When she married Rowan Donaghue, Rowan adopted little Terry, and they changed his name to Donaghue. They went on to have many more children, but Terry's my ancestor. So technically, my sisters and I are Donaghues by adoption, not that it matters. We all have the same great-great grandmother."

"And Irene's grandfather stayed on in Ireland and worked the land?"

"Irene says that Lorcan was in his forties by the time he came back to Ireland, tired and bitter. He married a local woman, had one son, Liam, and died years after."

"Liam is Irene's father."

"That's right."

Finn knew the rest. In the early 1920s Liam and his wife Brenna had abandoned Ireland for the United States, hoping to start a new life. Irene had been only a small child at the time and remembered little about those years. "I suppose all this somehow explains why Irene's family didn't find any Tierneys in Cleveland."

"Exactly. Lena married a Donaghue and changed her son's name. That was many years before Liam arrived in Cleveland, and apparently he never talked to the few people who might have remembered, including Lena herself, who was an old woman by then. Irene just happened to find out about us on the Internet. The *Cleveland Plain Dealer* did an article about the history of the saloon my family owns, and Terence Tierney's name was mentioned because Lena was the founder and he was her first husband."

"Odd that Irene would still be looking for relatives, don't you think?"

She combed her hair back with her fingers, a lovely, feminine gesture he hadn't been privy to in a long time. "Not really. She never married, and she has no children. We all want to feel connected, don't we? She's not well. I think the idea of wanting some part of you going on into the years is natural."

He froze, fingers gripping the steering wheel. At one time he'd understood that need himself.

Peggy looked over her shoulder at her sleeping son. "Kieran's my bid for immortality, I guess. Do you have children, Finn?"

He could not bring himself to answer casually, and that angered him. The question was simple enough. The answer was impossible.

"You'll meet my daughter Bridie," he said at last. "She visits Irene when she can." He had expected more questions, but she was surprisingly perceptive and didn't ask them.

Just in case, he changed the subject. "We're nearing the village. Sneeze and we'll have passed it before you open your eyes again."

"It's all so beautiful." Peggy's gaze was riveted outside the window.

"Yes, you Americans always seem to think so."

"And you don't?"

"There's been hardship here, the likes of which you probably can't imagine. It's only now coming back to life. Not always with the old families. With new people and holiday cottages, and people working from their homes. You see leprechauns and fairy hills, and I see people who work too hard and earn too little."

"Yet you stay? There must be a draw."

They passed through the main street of the village, lined with colorfully painted buildings nestled shoulder to shoulder. Mountains hung like stage props behind them, and the ocean sparkled in the distance. A brook ran through the center of a tiny town square. As villages went, it was picturesque and tidy. He imagined she was enthralled.

They were out in the country again before he answered. "I stay because I stay," he said.

The last kilometers were silent. He pulled into the gravel lane lined with a spotty hedgerow that ran to Irene's cottage. He risked one glance at Peggy Donaghue. She was leaning forward, and even though her son stirred behind her, she didn't turn. "Oh, look at this. This is where my sisters and I came from, Finn. And it's so glorious. How could Terence Tierney ever have left?"

"I'd suppose he was starving." He pulled up near the house and turned off the motor. "Irene will be out to greet you, count on it."

Peggy opened her door and took a step toward the thatch-roofed cottage. He was almost sorry it was so charming, with its whitewashed stones and paned windows. Finn watched as Irene opened the traditional half door, a door she'd painted brilliant blue and let no one dissuade her. He stayed in the car as the two women eyed each other. Then he shook his head as Peggy covered the distance between them at a sprint and fell into Irene's withered arms.

chapter 7

The Tierney Cottage had been remodeled in Irene's lifetime. Her mother, Brenna, had remarried several years after their return to Ireland, and Irene's stepfather had been a man of some wealth. He had purchased the land that the Tierneys had worked for centuries as tenant farmers, and more beyond it. Together he and Brenna added bedrooms and a kitchen with an inviting fireplace. And when the cottage became Irene's after their death, she added electricity, gas heat, fresh plaster and imagination.

Peggy lay in bed a week after her arrival and stared up at the beamed ceiling in the room she shared with Kieran. Not a cobweb hung there; not an inch of the ceiling was stained or peeling. The cottage was pristine. Irene might have refused a live-in companion until Peggy's arrival, but she hadn't refused household help. The day she'd realized she could no longer keep the house spotless, she hired a neighbor to come and clean each morning and lay the turf fire. In good weather Nora Parker bicycled over bumpy roads, cheerful and ready, after the exercise, to put the place to rights. She made breakfast, too, and even though it was only just seven, Peggy could already hear her bustling around the tiny kitchen.

Nora's existence was a welcome surprise. Peggy had expected to clean and cook, but Irene had explained that she could never sack dear Nora or worry her by letting Peggy take on any of her jobs. Nora brought news from the village, fresh groceries and a blithe presence that disguised the analytical soul of a military commander. No one except Nora had the same stiff standards as the mistress of the house, and the two women gleefully plotted each morning to rid Tierney Cottage of every hint of dust.

The evening had been almost warm, and Peggy had slept with the windows open. This morning a cool breeze stirred the lace curtains, but sun beamed outside the windows. The house smelled pleasantly of centuries of peat fires, an organic, earthy fragrance imbedded deeply in wood and stone. The breeze smelled of the ocean, a quarter of a mile in the distance.

Peggy wondered, as she did every morning, what her ancestors had thought upon rising each day. Had they been so worn with hunger and care that they cursed the rocky windswept promontory on which some more romantic forefather had built their home and grazed their sheep? Had they cursed the invader who had taxed them heavily and sent their food to market when they needed it to feed their children? Had they stopped, for even a moment, and felt a surge of gratitude for the beauty of their surroundings?

Finn had said she would see leprechauns and fairy hills, but the good doctor was wrong. Peggy saw reality. That didn't make her love it any less.

Kieran stirred, then came fully awake. He laughed, a sound that always thrilled her to the marrow. She didn't know at what, and she didn't care. His laughter, as rare as it was, still meant Kieran might someday find real humor in his life. A laughing child was not afraid or confused or oblivious to his surroundings.

"Kieran," she called softly. "Kieran..."

She sat up and looked over at his crib. Kieran lay on his

side, looking at her. "Kieran," she said with a big smile. "How's my little guy?"

He smiled and laughed again. Her smile widened. Then she saw that his gaze was fixed on the wall just behind her. She turned and saw sunlight reflected through the east window. It glistened and moved as the lace curtain blew.

"You like that, don't you?" she said, only a bit disappointed. "It's like liquid gold, isn't it?" She held up her hand, index and middle fingers like bunny ears. "Hip hop goes the bunny rabbit." Her little shadow bunny hopped across the wall.

Kieran screeched in excitement, and Peggy felt a surge of the same. She made the bunny hop backward. Forward, backward, a quick dip out of sight and then back up. An ear quirked, then straightened. "Here comes Peter Cottontail," she sang off key. "Hopping down the bunny trail." She couldn't think of the rest of the words. She hummed instead and made her bunny hop in rhythm.

Kieran stood and shook the bars of his crib. "Hi. Hi."

"Bunny," Peggy said. "Bun-ny."

"Hi, hi!"

She was so glad to see him happy that nothing else mattered. This was a little thing for most mothers, but with Kieran, unbridled happiness was rare enough to be treasured. She would never take any child's joy for granted again.

She rose when she tired of the bunny hopping and went to the crib. He looked up at her, then over at the wall, his bottom lip quivering.

"Yes, Mommy made the bunny hop," she said. "Kieran can make him hop, too." She lifted him from the crib and took him to her bed, propping herself on the pillows as she had before. Then she took his resistant little hand and held it up in the beam of sunlight.

"See, Kieran can make shadows, too."

He had stiffened the moment she touched him. He was still stiff, but interested. She could see his little eyes narrow in concentration.

"Kieran can make shadows, too." She took his arm by the

elbow and gently moved it back and forth, back and forth. His fist was balled, as if he was about to strike out. He watched the shadow change and cocked his head to examine it better.

"Kieran can make shadows." She pointed to the shadow of his fist. "Shadow." Then she moved his arm again. "Back and forth, back and forth."

She watched his expression. He forgot to resist, to tense, to be afraid. He was caught up in the movement. She guided his hand, but he did the work.

He tired at last, scrambling to get down, but she held on to him. "Sorry, partner, but let's do a quick change before you go scurrying off." He protested, but she was firm. In a few minutes his diaper was changed and clean overalls had replaced his pajamas. Then Peggy slipped into jeans and a fleece sweatshirt before she opened the door into the living room.

The living room was the loveliest in the house, with plastered white walls, stone floors and high ceilings. A fireplace for burning blocks of turf snuggled into one wall; mismatched windows with spectacular views of rock-strewn fields and sheep snuggled into two of the others.

"Good mouilng," she called to Nora. "What a beautiful day."

"It is that," Nora said. "And herself's having a bit of a lie-in this morning."

Peggy came to attention. Irene was usually bathed, dressed and waiting for Nora before she arrived. "She's not feeling worse, is she?"

"No worse than usual, if that's what you mean. Only tired. Hip's bothering her a bit, and she didn't sleep as well as she might have."

Peggy had made sure Irene took all her medicine before retiring, so she knew that couldn't be the problem. Irene had gladly agreed to let her take control of all health matters, and Peggy had drawn a chart to make sure every pill was taken on time.

"She may need more anti-inflammatories," Peggy said. "I'll talk to Dr. O'Malley."

"She takes a barrel of pills as it is." Nora was somewhere

in her fifties, silver-haired and thin as the rushes in Irene's meadows. She was widowed—claiming that widowhood was an improvement over what had come before—but she had three adored sons who lived in the county and six grandchildren, so she never lacked for family.

"She takes quite a few," Peggy agreed, "but not too many. Dr. O'Malley's a careful man."

"He was the best doctor in Mayo, and that's a fact. My family went to him, from granny on down. And we were all better for it."

Peggy tilted her head in question. "Was?"

"Surely you know he doesn't practice anymore?"

Peggy had a forlorn vision of a medical license suspended and wondered if Irene was in such good hands after all. "I didn't know. Why in the world?"

"I'd tell you if I had time for a cup of tea and a chat, but there's none this morning. He's on his way, and I promised Irene I'd bring her a tray in bed."

"Of course. I'm sorry. I'll ask Irene...." She looked up from fastening a snap on Kieran's shirt. "Is it okay to ask her?"

"Oh, she'll be happy to tell you, I'm sure."

"I'll make Kieran's breakfast."

"All done, and yours as well."

Peggy thanked her, and Nora gave her a warm smile. "You're not what I expected, you know."

"I'm not?"

"We only see the telly. What do we know?"

Peggy hated to think her countrymen were represented worldwide by "Survivor" and "The Simpsons." "I'm afraid if you were expecting glamour or excitement, you picked the wrong girl."

"I hoped for good manners and a warm heart and got them both."

Peggy was touched. "You and Irene are wonderful. I couldn't be luckier."

"Enough of this, I've got work to do." Nora headed for the kitchen.

Peggy joined her there as soon as she could drag Kieran away from a window overlooking the road. The window was low enough that he could see over the ledge, and the view of endless stone walls lined with wind-tortured evergreens, blackthorn and fuschia always seemed to fascinate him. She'd found him there many times in the past week and wondered exactly what he saw.

"There's porridge and bacon, and I made coffee the way you like it," Nora said, passing back and forth between the stove and the tiny refrigerator.

"I love the way you take care of me, but I worry we're too much work."

"Not at all. I'd have cooked the same, only less."

Peggy installed Kieran at the table. Before their arrival Irene had borrowed baby furniture from families in the parish, never having needed any herself. The high chair nestled perfectly against an old pine table, scrubbed in its time by generations of Tierney women.

She fixed oatmeal for her son with honey and lots of fresh, sweet milk straight from a neighbor's dairy. She was particularly careful about Kieran's diet, foregoing all sweets and processed foods, since some people felt they were a particular problem for autistic children. She cut him a thick slice of the brown soda bread Nora had brought with her that morning from the village grocery, and thought of Megan and the bread she made for lunches at the Whiskey Island Saloon, lunches her sister wouldn't be serving again until the renovation was completed.

Nora dried her hands on a tea towel. "I hear the doctor's car. I'll just go and let him in."

Peggy finished fixing breakfast for Kieran, who was beginning to whine and pound the table. "I'm almost done, kiddo," she said. "Good food for a good boy." She set the plate with bread in front of him, the same plastic plate he had used at home. He ate the bread with his fingers and ignored the spoon she set beside the bowl of oatmeal.

Peggy made a note to herself to introduce holding the

spoon during Kieran's "school time" that morning. In the meantime, she spooned oatmeal into his mouth whenever he would let her.

A piece of bread hit the floor, and she stooped to pick it up and carry it to the trash container under the sink. When she straightened, Finn was standing in the doorway.

"He loses more than he eats," Finn said.

"Does he look malnourished to you, Doctor?"

"Finn. Nora tells me you have advice for me?"

Peggy realized he was talking about the anti-inflammatories. "Not advice. I'm not that presumptuous. I did have a question, though. Irene's hip has been giving her fits."

"She refused surgery when it was an option. It's not an option now."

Peggy knew that much. She also knew Finn wanted to cut the conversation short. He was always curt with her, but by the same token, he was always warm and reassuring with Irene, a completely different man. She forgave him a lot because of that.

"Is there anything else we can do for the pain? Increase her anti-inflammatories? She won't tell you she's hurting."

His expression softened. "But I know."

"And there's nothing you can do?"

"Her medication is a careful balance. She's reached that unenviable stage when one need overshadows another, and hard choices have to be made."

Peggy felt just a glimmer of the excitement that had highlighted each moment of her brief med school career. This was what she had studied so hard for. The choices. The careful balancing of priorities. The ability to alleviate pain and change lives for the better. "I know it's difficult," she said. "Quantity vs. quality of life."

"It's rarely that simple."

"I thought you'd want to know," she said. "I'm not trying to step on your toes."

"I do, you're right. Thank you."

She studied him. During her week in Ireland she had come

to the conclusion that Finn was one of the handsomest men she'd ever meet. He was tall and lithe, but not too thin. His black hair was curly and just a little too long. She liked it that way. It gave him a brooding, Byronesque appearance that wasn't belied by the man himself. He had strong bones and dark brows sheltering eyes that took in everything but gave little in return.

The few men who had briefly shared her life—including Phil—had been stark opposites. Open, friendly faces, stores of small talk so that she didn't have to work when she was with them. She didn't like to guess thoughts or feelings. She'd never had the inclination or the leisure to try.

This man was different. Perhaps it was the relative peace of life here, the additional time for contemplation, but at odd moments she found herself wondering about Finn. He was a mystery, and for once in her life she had the time to look for solutions.

"How has the boy taken to life here?" Finn asked.

The question surprised her. Except for grilling her about her tenuous relationship to Irene, he had asked very few questions since picking her up at Shannon. "He's adjusting," Peggy said. "Finn, would you like some coffee?"

He shook his head. "You have plans to work with him yourself?"

"I've already begun. We've made a little classroom in the third bedroom. I'm starting today."

"You're qualified?"

"Who could be more qualified? Who loves him more and cares more about what happens to him?"

"Love gets in the way more often than not." He said this as if he were Moses recapping the Ten Commandments for the Israelites.

"It can." Peggy put more bread on the table in front of Kieran before she went to the slate counter to pour herself some of the coffee Finn had refused. "I know I have to be objective. But I have great materials, contacts on the Internet and a therapist I'll consult with by telephone when I need to." She waited until her cup was full before she turned. "And frankly, I'm cheap enough that I can afford myself."

He actually smiled. She had the same feeling she'd had that morning when Kieran smiled. For a moment the sun came out and life seemed filled with potential.

"You don't strike me as cheap, Miss Donaghue."

"If you're Finn, I'm Peggy. Otherwise I'll have to reconsider."

He didn't say anything for a moment. The smile was gone now, the face carefully blank. When he spoke at last, the words seemed to come from some place where he hadn't lived for a while. "I have some children's toys. Irene says you brought very few and need more. I can bring them for Kieran, if you'd like."

The last things she had expected from Finn were assistance or the depth of emotion that seemed to echo in the simple offer. For a moment she didn't know what to say. Then she nodded. "We'll be very careful with them, but, Finn, I can't guarantee—"

He lifted a hand, as if to ward off the rest of her words. "No need. I won't want them back. Give them away if there's anything left when he's finished." He turned without another word and disappeared into the living room.

She was left wondering exactly what price the man had just paid. And for what.

Irene Tierney was too thin, and it took her too long to get from one place to the other on legs that no longer seemed to do what they were told. Her hair was as white as the waves cresting at the shoreline, and her gray eyes behind thick glasses were filmed with early stage cataracts. She was bent, gnarled and blissfully young in spirit.

"It's a blessing of growing old," she told Peggy that afternoon after lunch. "You see yourself the way you were once upon a time. Not the way others see you. I'm twenty-seven. Just a bit older than you, dear."

"Do you have pictures? So I can see you that way, too?"

"I have an album as thick as your forearm, but later, when you aren't so worn out."

Peggy *was* tired. The morning hadn't gone well. She knew it would take time for Kieran to get used to the classroom and the "lessons" they were working on together. She had chosen the simplest things to start with. Holding a spoon. Stacking two blocks. Pointing to herself when she said "Where's Mommy? Here's Mommy." She had worked in the smallest increments, planning to reward him with cheese or crackers, two of his favorite foods, if any progress was made.

No progress had been made.

"It didn't go well, did it?" Irene asked. "Today, with the *bábai*."

"As well as I expected." Peggy watched Kieran's eyes droop. He looked as tired as she felt, although he hadn't yet abandoned his favorite window. "Everything takes time."

"He has gifts. I'm sure of it. I feel them in his soul when I look at him. What does he see, do you suppose, when he stares out that window?"

"I wish I knew. I wish I could step into his world and see. It would help so much."

"You know, don't you, that you can't manage this on your own?"

Peggy started to protest, but Irene shushed her. "You're patient and hardworking, but even the best teacher needs help. And it will be good for the boy to have other people interact with him."

"He's always had lots of people interacting with him. Too many. My family took charge of him, carried him everywhere, fussed over him. That's one of the reasons—" Peggy abruptly fell silent.

"I'm guessing now, but could it be you feel a tiny bit guilty about that? That so many others took care of him while you went to school and worked?"

Irene wasn't psychic. Peggy had led her to that conclusion, she supposed, with other things she'd said. From the beginning Irene had wanted to know everything about her life and that of her sisters. Irene was hungry for family and couldn't be filled up quickly enough. They had talked nonstop for a week.

"I do feel guilty," Peggy admitted. "I keep thinking that if I'd just been there all the time, he would have bonded to me. That he would need me in a way he doesn't seem to now."

"Isn't that part of his condition? Not to bond with the people who love him, at least not in the way we want him to?"

Peggy had been surprised and touched to discover all that Irene had taught herself about autism. She had done a concerted search on her beloved Internet and knew just about everything it had to teach about the disorder. "It is part of it, but I worry that I caused it."

"You and every mother of such a child."

"He needs lots of time with me now."

"That he'll get, no matter what you decide. But won't he improve quicker if you have a little help and more teaching time? A girl from the village, perhaps? Maybe one who wants to be a teacher herself someday. We could ask Nora for advice."

"I'll think about it." Peggy rose to get her son before he fell asleep on his feet. "I did have a piece of good news this morning."

"Did you?"

"Finn says he has toys for Kieran. I'm not sure what, exactly, but he says he doesn't need them anymore." She lifted Kieran, who immediately began to fuss. "I'll be right back."

"I'm not planning a holiday anytime soon."

Peggy returned after Kieran was in his crib. She'd left him thumping his hand across the bars. He would continue until he fell asleep mid-thump.

"Toys?" Irene said. "That's remarkable, you know."

"How and why?" Peggy paused. "And Nora told me this morning that Finn isn't a doctor anymore. The man's a real mystery to me."

"The stories are connected," Irene said. "Sit a moment."

Peggy did, although she was aching to get outside for a walk. She and Kieran had taken one earlier, but they hadn't gotten far. Kieran was afraid of wind, of which there was a great deal on the coast, and she'd had to bring him inside after only a few minutes.

Irene went straight to the heart of the story. "Finn lost his wife and two sons just two years ago. They drowned in a storm. Finn's sorry that *he* didn't. He's never forgiven himself."

Peggy was stunned. "That's too sad to comprehend."

"Immeasurably so, yes. Luckily his daughter wasn't with him. Bridie was older than the boys and spending the day with a friend. They found Finn near shore, nearly drowned himself. Afterward he simply gave up." Irene shrugged. "Lost interest in practicing medicine. In living, as well..."

Peggy was torn between sympathy and concern for Irene. Finn was still Irene's physician. "But he still sees at least some patients?"

"Oh, he's kept his office in town, but he claims that's only because there's not much commerce in real estate here and no one to sell it to. No, he sees only me, and only because I refuse to see anyone else. I told Finn I'd die in my bed rather than see Dr. Joseph Beck and nearly proved it. He treats me because I was his granny's best friend, and he doesn't want to answer to her in the next world. Eveleen could pinch the back of a neck just so." Irene demonstrated in the air. "It's nothing to look forward to."

Peggy was still caught up in Finn's tragedy. "That explains so much about him. He's so..." She couldn't think of a kind word.

"Difficult," Irene supplied. "Yes, he is that, our Finn. He wasn't always. He's never been easy, but in the old days he was a pleasure to know. The pleasure has gone out of it now. Lucky for him the people of Shanmullin remember the old Finn and pray he'll be back. No one understands pain better than the Irish, although there are many others who are our rivals in that curse."

"The toys must have belonged to his sons."

"I suspect so. And it won't be getting rid of them that will be the problem. No, the problem will come when he has to touch them, put them in new boxes to bring to us, remember..."

"Does having Bridie help, do you think? He must be so grateful she was spared."

"A difficult man, and a difficult father these days, I'm

afraid. He was one of the best until the drownings. But he's kept his pain locked inside and never shared it with her. She's a sweet little thing, one of my favorite people in the wide world. You'll meet her soon, I expect. She visits often."

"How old is she?"

Irene did the math. "Eleven. And if she doesn't find her father again soon, she'll be looking for him in other men soon enough, mark my words." Irene patted Peggy's hand. "Nora's planning to stay until four. It's windows today, and scrubbing the floors. Why don't you take a ride into the village? Do you some good. If Kieran wakes up, we'll be sure he's happy."

Peggy doubted her son would wake. Predictability was the way he dealt with his confusing life. The thought of biking into Shanmullin, which so far she'd only seen in passing, was tempting. Irene had told her there were bicycles in a nearby shed. Peggy was sure they were old, and just as sure they were well kept up.

"You're certain?" she said.

"Oh yes."

Peggy could feel energy returning. Fresh air and exercise were more likely to restore her than a nap. She hugged Irene. "What can I get for you in the village?"

"Now, I was hoping you'd ask. There's a list in the kitchen. You run on and have a good time. Turn right on the main road and you'll be in the village before too long. Just be sure to mark the end of the boreen in your mind so you don't get lost coming home."

Freedom. With a smile and a grateful wave, Peggy went to find the list and say goodbye to Nora.

chapter 8

Peggy calculated that she had almost two hours before Kieran woke up. She had another teaching session planned for the afternoon. More holding a spoon, more "Mommy," and a fierce coloring session with a red crayon. If there was time or patience left, she would begin teaching him to turn the pages in a cardboard picture book. So far he'd shown no interest in the stories that were read to him, but she was hoping that would change.

She found an assortment of bicycles in the shed. One, shiny green with a deep basket, looked newer than the others, and a trial run proved it was in good working order. She started up the lane, turning when she was halfway to wave at the women in the cottage, who were undoubtedly spurring her on.

After a week of gloom the day was breathtakingly lovely, just cool enough to keep her from growing overheated as she struggled up the incline that led to the main road. Wild primroses grew in the ditch, and iris made ready to burst into bloom. Hovering in the distance, she could see the Atlantic, with mist-shrouded Clare Island, and farther beyond, Croagh Patrick, the conical mountain named after the saint who was said to have fasted there. Fuschia in the hedgerow were just beginning to bloom, the scarlet flowers bobbing in the gentle wind, and a magpie roosted on the lichen-encrusted stone walls, watching her with a startling lack of concern.

On the narrow main road the few cars that passed gave her wide berth, which was lucky, because it had been some time since she'd ridden a bicycle. Megan and Casey had taught her, of course, running along beside her at breakneck speed to catch her if she fell. They had always been there to catch her, mothers well before their time, and she missed them already.

She passed Technicolor sheep grazing in fields clumped with rushes. The sheep were splotched with dye to establish ownership and gave the landscape a surprisingly whimsical touch. Farmhouses and vacation cottages dotted the undulating hills, and "famine cottages," nothing more than roofless, abandoned dry stone houses, were more plentiful than she'd expected. Some farmhouses were old, none thatched like Irene's, and she gave thanks for the stroke of good fortune that had landed her in such a picturesque setting. By all rights, Tierney Cottage should have fallen to the ground years before—and would have, if Brenna and her second husband hadn't restored it.

She was perspiring by the time she arrived at the outskirts of Shanmullin. Her legs ached, and her behind protested the narrow plastic seat. She still felt exhilarated. Playtime was a concept to introduce to Kieran, not something she indulged in herself. She reveled in it now.

The town of Shanmullin could have been a *National Geographic* cover. The main street curved in a gentle arc leading farther uphill. Buildings lined it, some white with bright trim like Tierney Cottage, more in varying shades of green, gold or blue. The signs looking over the sidewalk were half divided between "Irish," the country's original Gaelic language, and English. Some fair number of the signs advertised pubs, and the Guinness signs were a nostalgic reminder of home.

On one side of the street a dog ambled in and out between parked cars, stopping long enough to sit and scratch in a sliver of sunshine; on the other side a woman stood talking to three men in Wellingtons and woolen flat caps outside one of the pubs.

Peggy parked her bike against one of the buildings and started up the sidewalk, window shopping as she went to discover what Shanmullin had to offer. She found the church, a restaurant, even Finn's "surgery" tucked away on a side street with an air of abandonment. An hour later she came out of the grocery store, Irene's shopping list completed. She'd bought hairpins, knitting needles—because Irene was determined to make Kieran a sweater—and the latest issue of *The Irish Times*. She'd experienced good "craic," or "crack," as a bonus, not the illegal variety but the Irish version: lively conversation. The proprietor at the news agent had asked for her life story and given his own, his more colorful than hers. She thought she'd made a friend.

At the end of the sidewalk she saw the same dog she'd noticed earlier. He was floppy-eared, varying shades of red-brown, and vaguely bloodhound in appearance, a change from the multitude of Border Collies that had observed her trip to town. His long body stretched from one end of the slate walkway to the other; his head was pillowed on his paws. If a dog could look forlorn, this one did.

She approached him tentatively. She had great respect for man's best friend, and she stopped a few feet away, debating just walking around him instead of approaching.

"Hey, fellow."

He thumped his tail lethargically. He was too thin, and droopy-eyed to boot. As she stared at him, a girl in a school uniform of plaid skirt and navy sweater came out of the shop to her left and joined Peggy in the investigation. She had a cloud of white-blond hair that would undoubtedly darken someday, and delicate features distorted by a frown.

"He's been out here a week," she said, her voice rising and falling like a sad Irish ballad. "His owner died."

Peggy shook her head. "Well, that's a shame. Does he have a name?"

"Banjax. Mr. McNamara said he wasn't good for anything, but he's good for mourning Mr. McNamara, isn't he?"

"I'd say so." Peggy stared at the poor tragic beast. "Nobody's claimed him? Family doesn't want him?"

"People feed him, I guess, from the pubs at night. Crisps and things. But my father says somebody will carry him out to the country before too long, and he won't be coming back."

Peggy didn't like the sound of that. "I guess there's no organization in town to take care of homeless pets."

"Just people who take them in if they can." The girl looked up at Peggy. "You're not from Shanmullin."

"Ohio, in the United States."

"I'm Bridie O'Malley."

Finn's daughter. Peggy hadn't suspected, not only because the odds were against meeting this way, but because Bridie didn't resemble her father in the least. She was as blond as he was dark. Peggy thought she had a good idea what Finn's wife had looked like.

Peggy introduced herself. "Irene Tierney tells me you're a good friend."

"Oh, you're the American who's living at Tierney Cottage. I've heard about you."

"Your father was kind enough to give me a ride up from Shannon Airport."

"He was off work that day. I wanted to come, but I was in school."

Peggy glanced at her watch. It was only one-thirty. "You're off early today?"

"The teachers are talking to the parents this afternoon." She made another face.

Peggy smiled at her. "Are you worried? I was always worried about conferences, even if I was doing okay."

"Oh, my father won't be there. He's working in Louisburgh all day."

Peggy hadn't realized that Finn worked at anything besides

his medical practice. She should have figured that out; after all, he and his daughter had to eat, even if he refused to see patients now. She stored this question away to ask Irene.

"I want to take Banjax home," Bridie said. "I'd like to own a dog."

Peggy heard an unspoken "but" in that sentence. She supposed it had to do with Finn. He seemed like a man who wouldn't want any extra warm bodies to feed or care for. "You're worried about him. Let's think, is there anybody who might take him? Anybody you could ask?"

Bridie screwed up her face again. While the father rarely allowed thought or feeling to show in his expression, the daughter repressed nothing. "Granny 'rene!" She looked up. "You can take him home with you, Mrs. Donaghue."

Peggy was the one to grimace now. "Bridie, I don't think—"

"But Granny 'rene's dog died last year. Pickles. A little yappy dog who nipped at my ankles every time I visited. Irene didn't like him, either, but she said an old friend, even a nasty old friend, had to be protected. Well, Banjax was an old friend of Mr. McNamara's, and now he has to be protected, too. And Granny 'rene's the one who will do it."

Against her will, Peggy felt herself sinking deeper into the conspiracy. Irene wasn't well, and she was already dealing with two strangers in her house. A dog, a dog in urgent need of Prozac, at that, seemed like the ultimate imposition. "I'll tell you what. I'll ask her, and if she says yes—"

"But that won't work," Bridie insisted. "He could disappear tonight. What if he does? How will we feel? How will poor Granny 'rene feel if she's decided she wants him?" She saw Peggy begin a protest, and she added quickly, "I saw some men pointing at him and shaking their heads before I went into the store. I really did. Please?"

Peggy supposed there was little harm in bringing the dog home with her. She could buy dog food to carry in the basket on the front of her bike. And with a little encouragement and a few dog treats, Banjax would probably lope along beside her. If Irene objected, as she surely would, Peggy could just bring him back the next time she came to town and hope someone else adopted him. Or she could send him back with Finn in the morning, if getting rid of him was important enough.

Bridie seemed to realize the odds were leaning Banjax's way. "I can help you get him home. I'll leave my father a note and tell him I bicycled out to Granny 'rene's. He won't mind. Really. And between us, we can get him there. I know we can."

"How old are you, Bridie?"

"Eleven."

"Once you're fifteen, we'll have a talk about the dangers of using those pretty green eyes to get everything you want."

Bridie smiled up at her, and Peggy thought her new young friend had already figured out everything she needed to know about green eyes and a charming smile.

"A dog? And a big, ugly odorous dog at that?" Irene stood on the stoop and stared down at Banjax, Peggy and Bridie. "Well, I declare, Peggy Donaghue. What were you thinking?"

"I've been bamboozled," Peggy said. "Tricked. My brain was turned inside out by a pair of lovely eyes, and not Banjax's."

Irene was trying to hide a smile. "Bridie, this was your idea, was it now?"

"He needs a place to hide, Granny 'rene. They were going to carry him out to the country!"

"So you did it before they could?" Irene couldn't hold back the smile any longer. "Well, he can't come inside, not ever. I put my foot down about that."

"I'll give him a bath," Bridie promised. She had bought a bar of flea soap with her own pocket money when Peggy bought dog food. "Tomorrow after school. I promise. But he needs you. He really does."

Irene looked at Peggy, and Peggy shrugged. "He'll make a good watchdog," Peggy said.

"And what will he watch for out here?"

"Crows? Butterflies?" Peggy couldn't even add snakes to the list. St. Patrick had taken care of that.

"We'll give him a try, poor old thing," Irene said. "He can sleep in my shed if he likes."

"I'll make him a bed," Bridie said.

Peggy heard a familiar wail from the direction of her bedroom. "Well, looks like my timing was good."

Nora came to the door and stared down at Banjax. "I know that dog. As useless as a chocolate teapot, he is. He'll eat and sleep and nothing more."

That seemed to strike a chord with Irene, whose days consisted of much the same. "He can stay. We'll see."

Peggy and Bridie followed her inside. Bridie peeked in the direction of Peggy's room. Peggy had told her about Kieran on the ride home. "May I play with him?"

Peggy tried to think of the best way of answering. Kieran didn't play, not the way Bridie surely expected.

"I'm good with children," Bridie said. "He'll like me."

She said it with such confidence that Peggy had to relent. "I bet you are. It's just that Kieran's not good with people he doesn't know." And even the people he did weren't sure how to approach him.

"Oh, that's okay. I'll just watch at first."

"Let me get him up. I'll be right out. Why don't you put some food out for Banjax?"

By the time she returned with a freshly changed Kieran, Nora had set a pot of tea on the table and a plate of freshly baked currant scones, and Bridie was digging in. She cooed over Kieran but was careful not to rush him. She continued to sit and watch him from the corner of her eye as she ate.

Kieran looked around the room with sleepy, suspicious eyes. As always, Peggy wondered what convoluted mixture of signals his tiny brain was sending. When he struggled to get down she set him on the floor, standing close by in case he wanted to be protected from yet another unfamiliar face. But Kieran was gazing at Bridie the way he gazed at light flickering on the wall. He toddled closer, peering at her, stopping, peering at her again. Peggy held her breath. Beside her, she knew Irene was doing the same.

"Hi, hi," he said at last. He moved closer. "Hi!"

Bridie took it in stride. "Well, hi to you, too, boyo." She went back to her scones, unaware of the small miracle that had just taken place right in front of her.

"Kieran was fascinated by Bridie," Peggy said that evening, as she and Irene sat studying a smoldering fire. "I think it's her hair. It's so bright, and light fascinates him."

"She's a beautiful girl." Irene leaned back in her comfortable armchair and rested her feet on a small padded stool. "Sheila was lovely, as well. Bridie resembles her, but her bones are finer. Sheila's beauty wouldn't have lasted past forty, but Bridie's will."

"She must miss her mother so much. A girl that age needs one." Peggy had lost her own mother at a much earlier age, but she'd had sisters and her aunt Deirdre to make up for it. Still, there was a yearning for Kathleen Donaghue that never quite went away.

"I suspect she'll be finding her way out to Tierney Cottage more often now that you're here. She's taken to you."

"And to Banjax," Peggy said. The dog had settled into the shed as if he'd lived there forever. Irene had made her way outside to supervise the placement of his bedding, even deigning to pat his bony head.

"A girl needs her father, too," Irene said.

"Bridie says Finn was working in Louisburgh today?"

"Construction. He wants nothing to do with medicine. He won't even work in a laboratory. He works so hard building houses, he sees little of his own daughter."

Bridie's plight was too familiar. Peggy had grown up without a father, too.

Irene pulled a knitted afghan over her lap, as if settling in for a very long time. "I needed my father and missed him every day I was growing up."

Since Peggy's arrival, they had hardly talked about Liam Tierney or his death in Cleveland. That had been the purpose of Irene's first contact with the Donaghue sisters, and Peggy had offered so little information.

"I wish I'd had time to dig deeper into city records," Peggy said. "Sometimes the amount of information that's out there is a curse in itself."

"I grew up wishing I knew more about him. The urge doesn't seem to go away. And I worry I'll die without that mystery being solved. It nags at me, although why it should, I don't know."

"Tell me what you do know," Peggy said. "Megan and Casey have promised to continue to search. You and I have the whole evening, if you're not too tired. Start from the beginning, and tell me everything. Maybe you'll remember something that will make their job simpler."

"I was very young."

"Then tell me what your mother told you."

Irene sighed contentedly. "A cup of tea would be nice, don't you think? If I'm going to tell the story."

Peggy rose. "I'll make it. You gather your thoughts."

"I'll do that." Irene closed her eyes. "It's a happy story, at least at first. The telling of it won't be so hard."

1923
Castlebar, County Mayo

My dearest Patrick,

As always, I think of you, my only brother, so far removed from Ireland, and I mourn your leaving for Ohio as if it only happened yesterday instead of nearly a lifetime ago. Cleveland is more your home now than Ireland ever was, and St. Brigid's still the center of your heart, even though you have now retired and serve as its priest only occasionally. But how sharp your mind has remained, and how astute your observations. We are lucky, you and I, that we still have our wits left, and that only an ocean separates us and not yet death.

How different our views on the plight of our people. Yours garnered at one end of our national tragedy and mine at the other. Yours when the immigrant steps off the ship or train and into a world of belching factories and hastily constructed shanty houses. Mine when the emigrant leaves his poor barren farm, prayers in his heart and hope glimmering in his eyes.

They say we live in a new Ireland. So far I've yet to see it. Last year assassins killed the Big Fellow at *Beal na mBlath,* a terrible loss to all men and women who believe our best fate lies in compromise. We Irish still fight among ourselves, as surely and naturally as we fought the British invaders. Men who survived the horror of Gallipoli fall in Dublin's streets, and sabotage, execution and other atrocities have become as symbolic of our ancient and honorable culture as rainbows and church spires.

You tell stories in your letters of new Irish blood for Cleveland, of men with surnames such as Durkan and Doyle, Heneghan and Lavelle, names as familiar to me as my own. I mourn for these men, although I never knew them, for their need to depart the country of their birth, and for unwelcome surprises on arrival. I remember too well your letters about the place called Whiskey Island, dear Patrick, and the horrors of life there for men who had only known Ireland's green splendors. Perhaps things are better now, but Cleveland will never be Ireland, will it?

There are still few enough opportunities here, particularly for those who allied themselves with the Republicans. Some wounds never heal. Perhaps it is better they leave for America's far-off shores, but perhaps it is not. For what will our beloved Ireland do without its strong, courageous sons?

Your grieving sister,
Maura McSweeney

chapter 9

At his father's knee, Liam Tierney had learned not to expect anything from life. At his mother's, he had learned he was not deserving of love. Fortunately for Liam, he met Brenna Duffy when he was still young enough to be skeptical.

Lorcan Tierney, Liam's father, was a hard man, and having a son late in life hadn't softened him. He provided the bare essentials without a smile and demanded nothing more of himself.

Walton Gaol, Liverpool's prison, had made Lorcan the man he was. As nothing more than a feckless boy, he had left the family home in Shanmullin to seek his fortune in England, but only a month later, overriding hunger, a slab of hastily stolen beef and an unlucky eyewitness to his robbery cured him of hope. Deeply ashamed, he told no one what he had done or where he was.

Upon his release years later, he returned to Ireland to find his family gone, likely all dead, and nothing left for him except the rocky soil and tumbling cottage he had abandoned with such expectations in his youth.

Liam's mother had been a spinster, sickly and morose, who accepted Lorcan's curt offer of marriage when a brother made it clear that she would have no place to live if she said no. She gave birth to Liam, her only child, with a maximum of pain and a minimum of joy. Had Lorcan not intervened, she would have left their infant son on the doorstep of the rectory that night.

Twelve years later, upon Lorcan's death, she made good on her threat and abandoned the adolescent Liam at the rectory doorstep, disappearing that same night, never to be seen or heard from again. Castlebar's conscientious parish priest sent Liam south to finish growing up under the strict tutelage of the Christian Brothers. Very little of what he learned in the orphanage served him well.

Lonely, angry boys find others like themselves as friends. Lonely, angry boys seek solace in action, in violence, in causes that fill the empty places inside them. Upon leaving the orphanage at sixteen, Liam Tierney found just such friends and just such a cause in the political upheaval of his time. Only the miraculous appearance of Brenna, an auburn-haired, blue-eyed angel and orphan from another institution, had saved him.

Now Liam and Brenna had come to Cleveland for a new life, a new start, a new home for their darling baby girl. Brenna had named their red-haired daughter Irene. It wasn't an Irish name, because at Irene's birth Brenna had hoped so desperately that someday the Tierneys would not be Irish anymore.

"Irishtown Bend?" Brenna looked at the tiny, lopsided house that perched on a hillside looking over the place the local people called Whiskey Island. "We've come all this way, Liam, gladly left everything behind, to live in a place called Irishtown Bend?"

It was so rare for Brenna to be critical that Liam felt her words in the pit of his stomach. "I'm aware of the irony," he said. "But we needn't live here forever. It's a place to start, and not such a bad place at that. Isn't it better to be with people we understand? People like us? So many of them came from Mayo. I might well run into people I knew there."

"Exactly what I hoped you wouldn't do."

Liam wanted the world for Brenna and Irene. He was going to give them the world, but unfortunately, not quite yet. And, of course, she wasn't asking for that. She only wanted freedom from worry, from a past that haunted her nights. *His* past.

"I think the house has charm." Liam cocked his head and stared up at it. The house was narrow as a young man's hips and tall as a young man's dreams. A rickety front porch ran across the front. His inspection had turned up boards so rotten that Irene's meager weight would crumble them to dust.

Brenna hiked their daughter higher on one hip. Most of the time Irene would not allow herself to be carried. She was a lively child, only content when she was moving. But the voyage, the nights in Boston, then the nights in a West Side hotel that housed as many rats as immigrants, had nipped at her good humor. She rubbed her eyes and angrily brushed red-gold locks of hair away from her face.

His daughter. His reason for coming here.

"Perhaps it has charm," Brenna said, "but I suspect it has mice and bugs, as well, and in winter, it will have icicles inside."

"By winter we'll live somewhere else, farther up the hill into the Angle, perhaps someday away from the Irish entirely." He hesitated. "Unless we find family."

Brenna looked as exhausted as their daughter, and that prospect didn't seem to please her. "There's little chance of it, Liam. You shouldn't raise your hopes so high."

Liam didn't need the warning. His hopes weren't high; in fact, he wasn't sure what to hope for. Once, in a rare moment of conversation, his father had told him of uncles who had come here during the last century, Lorcan's own brothers, Darrin and Terence, both of whom had died young and poor.

All the Tierney family had already died or abandoned Shanmullin when Lorcan arrived home from Liverpool, as had most of the villagers he had known as a boy. Even Shanmullin's priest had moved to America, but one neighbor recalled that Terence had married, and his wife might still be alive. The wife might even have given birth to Terence's child. In a place called Cleveland, where she and Terence had gone to live.

Liam knew so little of his family's past, and he cared only a little more. Family had failed him so miserably. What reason was there to think that anything might change? He had made his own family when he married Brenna Duffy and sired Irene. If Tierneys were here, he would observe them carefully before he told them who he was.

Now he tried to make the best of their bad situation, hoping to cheer his wife. "Be careful on the stairs," Liam said. "Best give me Irene. I know what to avoid."

He took the little girl, who was fussing, and jiggled her as he climbed. He skirted the worst of the holes and pushed open the door. The house was dismal inside but surprisingly clean. The former occupants had been too poor for repairs but too proud for dirt. Only the faintest dust filmed the rickety table in one corner and the ladder-back chair beside it. The windows were few but gleaming.

"Good people lived here." That was the most he could say, since the house had nothing else to recommend it. It was cramped and dark, and the moldering boards on the porch had close cousins here. He hadn't been inside before this. The house was all he could afford, and the state of its interior had hardly been at issue. It had a roof and a floor of sorts, a place to cook and sleep. Until he found work, there was little else he could ask for.

He didn't look at Brenna. He didn't want to see the horror on her face. He had brought her here, far from everything she knew. True, like him, she had no family in Ireland. The orphanage where she had been taken at birth was a cruel place, and her memories of Ireland were sad ones. But she had married him to improve her life. And this was no improvement.

"Oh, Liam, look at the way the sun shines in this window." She stepped carefully around the room and peered outside, down the gentle slope that led to the river and the smoke of Whiskey Island.

The sunlight wavered through the old glass, making patterns on the wall. He was pleased she'd chosen to notice them.

"And it's all ours," she said, turning to face him.

"It's not much—"

"All my life I lived in a room with twenty girls, sometimes more. I yearned for space like this, for a place where I could move without stumbling over someone."

He knew what she was doing, knew the effort this forced spate of optimism was costing her. He loved her more for it. "You'll need to be careful where you move here, as well. Or you'll end up on the ground below."

"But it will be our ground, won't it? Not charity. No one reminding us that we didn't earn it and we're lucky to have it. No sisters to beat us if we aren't thankful enough. Yes, it's meager, Liam. But I'm sorry about what I said before. If there are mice, they'll be our mice, won't they? And if the icicles form inside, then we'll know exactly where to patch, and we'll thank them for the insight."

"I'll get a job. I know there's work here, lots of it. I've been told so by every man I've encountered. We won't be in the house long. And I'll patch the floors. There's driftwood on the lakeshore. I've been told that, as well. I'll patch, and we'll make it a home until we can find better."

"I never expected to have this much. I have you, and our darling Irene, and I have this new land of ours, away from all our sad memories. We'll start again here. The three of us."

He set Irene down, and she ran to the window where her mother stood. Brenna lifted her daughter in her arms.

"Smoke," Irene said, pointing down the hillside.

"A sign of progress," Brenna said. "A sign of good things to come."

Liam followed his daughter. Brenna held out an arm, and he let her enfold him. The only moments of pleasure he'd ever experienced had been due to this woman. He felt the warmth of her breast pressing against his side, smelled the wind-tossed scent of her hair. He put his arms around the only two people in the world whom he had ever loved, and Liam Tierney counted his blessings.

chapter 10

Megan pulled into the parking lot of the Whiskey Island Saloon in Casey's red Mazda and turned the key in the ignition. She didn't move to open the door. Her hands gripped the steering wheel, and her foot continued to rest on the brake. She closed her eyes and reminded herself to breathe.

When she opened them again, nothing had changed. No fairy godmother had waved a wand in the intervening seconds to restore the rubble into a functioning Irish-American pub. The Whiskey Island Saloon would be a work in progress for weeks, maybe months, and Megan was going to have to accept the fact that life as she had known it was never going to be the same.

The driver's door opened. Startled, she looked up and saw her sister staring down at her. "You like my car so much you don't want to return it?"

"How did you know I'd be back today?" Megan stared up at Casey. "Is this sisterly ESP?"

"Nick called Jon and told him what happened. I brought Charity for you and came to get the Mazda."

Niccolo's phone call to Jon didn't surprise Megan. He was already acting like a husband, even though they'd only been married two weeks. He'd fallen into the role like Olivier into Hamlet.

"It's a long drive by yourself." Casey extended a hand. "He was sorry you had to make it alone. Not the way to end a honeymoon, huh?"

Megan hefted herself out of Casey's car. "Nobody's fault."

"Jon says Nick's mother had a heart attack? She's in Mercy Hospital in Pittsburgh?"

"Chest pains. They put her in yesterday morning for tests. I haven't heard any results yet, but Nick thought he ought to be there. He flew out last night. It was too late to make the drive home, so I stayed there alone until this morning."

"You had what, four nights together? Not much of a honeymoon."

At least they had been blissful nights. The lake lapping at the shore, Niccolo's lovingly chosen wines, gourmet meals prepared together, moonlight walks, the glowing eyes of nocturnal animals in the forest beyond their cabin. The big, soft king-size bed.

"It's a bad break, but it couldn't be helped," Megan said. "Marco told him not to make the trip home, but you know Nick. If he can't help, he doesn't exist. And she *is* his mother."

"You deserved longer. Between the tornado, the bids and estimates, the insurance adjustor, now this..."

"Hey, we were lucky to have any time at all. Between renovations here and Nick's work at Brick, it might be years before we can get away again."

"Don't even say that. You have to make time for each other."

Megan started toward the kitchen door. The old maple tree was gone now, and so was Niccolo's Honda Civic. The first brand-new car he had ever owned was a shiny silver cube in a Cleveland junkyard. Even the shifty-eyed insurance adjustor, who had clearly wanted to issue a modest check for repairs, had gasped when he saw it and declared it a total loss.

"I don't suppose the contractor's spent much time here," Megan said. She had come to terms on the renovations with a man from Westlake before she left. Casey had volunteered to supervise whatever visits the contractor wanted to make before Megan came back. "With all the rain you've had and everything else, I bet he's hardly been here."

They entered through the kitchen. It, like the rest of the saloon, had been picked clean. Before the brief Michigan honeymoon, Megan had hired a moving company to take everything that wasn't nailed down to a storage facility while the repairs commenced. The front facade of the building was shored up just enough for them to begin clearing the rubble, but security would be an issue until the walls were restored and doors could be installed again and locked.

"Megan, about the contractor." Casey followed her sister into the saloon proper, although there was nothing very proper about it now. "That's part of why I came looking for you."

Megan waved a hand as if she were wafting away the scent of boiling cabbage. "Look, I know he's no peach to deal with. He's got the manners of a bulldog, but his references are good. And his was the only estimate that even came close to the amount the insurance company is willing to reimburse us for. We're still going to have to come up with thousands of dollars ourselves. Expanding and improving went out the window fast."

"He never gave you the estimate in writing, did he?"

Megan frowned, turning to search Casey's face. "He said he'd send it to Nick's—*our* house. It's probably there. Why?"

"I don't think so."

"Casey, what are you trying to say?"

"He called me the day before yesterday. He reworked his figures before he put it all in writing. He was way off, Megan. Now he says he can't do it for what he promised. His new estimate's in line with the others. It's a lot more."

"He can't do that!" Megan felt a surge of anger starting at her toes. "He already gave me a figure!"

"Not one you can hold him to. He had the square footage wrong, and the price of lumber's gone up in the last week. He says the only way he could do it at what he originally thought was to do a really shoddy job of it. And you don't want that."

Megan felt as if she'd been punched. She should have known the estimate was too good to be true. "We should have had more insurance. I knew it. I just didn't get around to doing anything about it."

"Jon and I will help, Megan. You know we will. And the others are going to pitch in—"

"What others?"

"The family. The offers are pouring in. Everybody's going to help get the saloon up and running again. Maybe it's ours on paper, but it belongs to all the Donaghues. All the memories and the connections to the past."

Megan rarely cried. Now her throat felt tight. She didn't want to accept help. Sure, the Whiskey Island Saloon was a family icon, and the Donaghue clan were her family. But none of them profited from it. For years she had run it, and they had enjoyed it. The system had worked perfectly, with no grumbling. Relatives played at tending bar and helping in the kitchen; then they went home at night to their other lives. The saloon was a hobby, a welcome family link. She didn't want the system to change.

"Uncle Frank and Aunt Deirdre will foot the whole bill," Casey said. "He already gave me a check."

"Tear it up." Megan swallowed tears. She couldn't cry. There was too much to do.

"He did it gladly, you know he did."

"He's a gem. I love him. I love them all. But we can't make this a family enterprise, Casey. It's too dangerous. Too many hotheads and firm opinions, and rambling lectures on tradition vs. modernization."

Casey didn't argue. Megan knew she agreed.

"So the other options?" Casey said at last.

The kitchen door slammed, and the two women looked at each other.

"Megan?"

Megan couldn't believe it. "Nick?"

He came through the kitchen door into the saloon. "Surprise."

"Nick!" She was so thrilled to see him that she forgot her dignity. She ran to him, falling into his arms as if she hadn't seen him for weeks. "What happened? Why are you back so soon?"

"Anxiety attack," Nick said. "And not mine. Mama's. Mama wasn't dealing with our wedding quite as well as we all thought." He held her away and grinned. "We've had a little talk, Mama and me. She's on the road to recovery."

"You're kidding!"

"It was real. She's not given to hysterics. Just too much change in her orderly life. But she'll cope. She's humiliated. Next time she'll die of a heart attack before she tells anybody she has pains in her chest. And she's going to take up yoga. My mother in the lotus position. I've demanded photographs."

"Poor woman," Casey said. "I actually liked your mother, Nick, even if she spent most of our time together telling me about the day you were ordained."

"You're okay?" Niccolo asked Megan. "The drive back went okay?"

"It was lonely." She smiled up at him; then she sobered. "Nick, Casey has bad news."

"Jon already told him," Casey said. "He thought Nick should be warned."

"Why? So he'd be prepared to come home to a basket case?" She tempered the words with all the smile she could manage. "Listen, you two, I'll cope. Maybe I'll take up yoga, too. I'm going to find a way around this, even if I have to do the damned repairs myself. And I could, you know. If I had to."

"You don't," Niccolo said.

"You know, I should leave," Casey said. "You're invited for dinner tonight. I'll see you two then. You can fill me—"

"No, I want you to hear this, too," Niccolo said.

Casey waited.

"Megan, since Mama was fine, I used the trip to Pittsburgh to spend some time with Marco."

Clearly Niccolo was on his way to being accepted back into the heart of the family, and that pleased Megan very much. She wanted Niccolo to be happy.

"I'm delighted." She didn't know what else was called for.

"It was like old times. But that's not my whole point. We talked about the saloon."

She wondered if Marco disapproved of Niccolo's new wife working as a saloon keeper. He was a traditional male. His wife, Carrie, stayed home with their two children and cooked. And cooked. Megan wished she could hire her.

"Marco has the contracting skills that I don't," Niccolo continued. "I could never tackle the repairs here alone, particularly if we expand the project and make the changes we need to."

Megan felt her mind slowing. She was afraid to let it move forward, afraid she might be wrong.

"But Marco could do this job with his hands tied behind his back. Problem is, he has to pay a crew, and even if he could bring them here and house them for free, with union wages and building supplies, we'd be out of our range again."

"And he couldn't get his crew over here, anyway," Megan said. "Why would they want to come to Cleveland?"

"No, but with Marco and me doing the work with the Brick kids and occasionally a temporary crew, we can do it for the insurance settlement, Megan. We went over and over the figures last night. I had Jon fax me all the estimates we'd already gotten, the plans I drew up for the changes you want. It's doable."

"But why would Marco come and do this? He has a business to run. Can he be away that long?"

"He'll go home as often as he can. In the meantime—and get this—Carrie's going to run his business."

Megan stared at him. "Carrie? Of the fabulous parsley pesto sauce? Of the sun-dried tomato ravioli?"

"She's been answering his telephones, printing up his bills, making calls to the lumberyard and supply houses for years. She's even bossed the crew a time or two when he was sick.

Marco says she can do it. He'll go back and forth. It's not that long a drive. A couple of days here, several days there."

"Why?"

Niccolo smiled. "Because he's my brother."

Megan couldn't believe her good luck. Casey could, though. She came over to hug them both. "This is so great! Now you can get everything you want, Megan. Expanded kitchen, a redesigned space behind the bar. And if you have to take money from the family, it will only be a little."

"I might borrow," Megan said. "And pay them back with interest." With her current rush of goodwill, depleting their bank accounts seemed like the least she could do.

"Then it's a deal?" he said.

"Of course it's a deal!" She hugged him. She hugged Casey. "Thank you so much for coming up with this. I can't believe it!"

"We'll be slower than professionals," Niccolo warned her. "It won't get done overnight."

"I don't care. Just get it done. I'll help. I'm good at this stuff."

"You are." He touched her hair. "Good at everything you do."

Casey broke away. "That's too much sweetness and light for me. Ever since you saw the Virgin in the tunnel, folks, it's been like an episode of 'Touched By An Angel' around here. Gag me."

"A couple more people want to see the Virgin," Niccolo said. "Marco, for one. How would you feel if I took him through the tunnel, Megan?"

She was feeling much too fabulous to worry about anything so inconsequential. In fact, she was feeling so kindly toward Marco that she would scrape the image off the wall and give it to him for Christmas if he asked for it.

"The more the merrier." Her smile was so broad it threatened to permanently stretch her cheeks. "I'm becoming a believer in miracles myself. Light candles, burn incense, make novenas. I don't care."

"I'm heading home before you start the Gregorian chants,"

Casey said. "The invitation stands. You two come for dinner tonight."

Niccolo looked at Megan. Megan looked at Niccolo. Casey looked at both of them.

"Another time," Casey countered. "I know that look when I see it."

"Thanks. And you can look after Rooney another night?"

"Not a problem. And Josh will hold the fort at your house. What hotel are you going to?"

"That would be none of your business."

chapter 11

Bridie had an insatiable need to connect with people, and Kieran had as strong a need to keep them at bay. Yet the two children were fascinated by each other. She was an intelligent girl, with problem-solving abilities far advanced for her age. She saw Kieran's desires and needs as puzzles to assemble so that, in the end, the picture that emerged would please everyone. She didn't gush, and she didn't ask for more than he would give. She seemed to have no need for hugs or kisses. When he shouted "hi" in her direction, she took it as her due. When he threw himself on the floor in an exhausted temper tantrum, she raised her slight shoulders as if to say "I warned you he was reaching his limit."

Bridie was almost a daily visitor now, and Peggy had quickly grown dependent on the eleven-year-old's common sense and insight, as well as her help.

"Red." Bridie picked up a red sweater and dropped it on the small table where Kieran was sitting in the "classroom" Peggy had made for him. She picked up a red slipper she'd brought from home and put that on the table, too. "Red." A third item, a lovely polished apple, followed the other two. "Red."

Kieran showed as little interest as usual, standing, then wandering around the table. Peggy gently guided him back to his little chair, and when he sat at her instruction, she gave him a tiny fish-shaped cracker.

Bridie had cleared the table in the interim. This time she set out a giant red crayon. "Point to red," she said. "Where's red, Kieran?"

Peggy didn't correct her. Bridie should have used fewer and simpler words, and not repeated the command in different terms, but Kieran seemed to be paying attention anyway. And he was sitting, just as Peggy had instructed him to. This was the biggest success of a day in which there had been few others.

He frowned, but not as if he was going to throw himself to the floor. He squinted at the crayon, looked up at Bridie, then swept it off the table. Peggy watched Bridie pick it up and put it back. "Point to red." Bridie demonstrated. "Point to red."

He got up and toddled off to stare at the lampshade in the corner. Peggy put her hand on Bridie's arm when the girl got up to follow him. "He's been working hard. Let's give him a few minutes on his own."

Bridie settled back into her chair. "He knows red."

Peggy wondered how she'd come to that conclusion, but wisely didn't question her. Bridie felt a connection to her son, and Peggy wasn't going to do anything to lessen it.

"You didn't tell me about school," Peggy said. "How was it?"

"Boring." Except for the lilt in her voice, Bridie sounded like any Cleveland child answering the same question.

"Did you have to give your book report?"

"I did, and no one liked it. Sarah McElroy said I went on and on, and it was the silliest book she'd ever heard of."

Peggy was indignant. "*Anne of Green Gables* was one of my favorite books. Sarah's the one who's out of step."

"*She* reported on a book I read three years ago. It was silly then, and sillier now."

"You like to read, don't you?"

"Our flat is quiet at night."

She said it as if that was a good thing, but Peggy knew better. In her own ingenuous way, Bridie had dropped a number of hints about life with Finn. After the death of her mother and brothers, Finn had sold their home and moved his daughter to a narrow flat in the village over the one and only craft gallery. He worked long hours, and the proprietor kept track of Bridie after school for him, but the girl was alone too much. Peggy suspected that even when Finn was home, the girl was still alone.

"Are you going to the *Fleadh Ceoil* this weekend?" Bridie asked.

The *Fleadh Ceoil* was a traditional music festival held every year on this weekend on Shanmullin's green. Peggy had been looking forward to it since her arrival. The village had begun the event a decade ago as an attempt to attract tourists, but the music and dance were authentic, and supposedly the fun was infectious.

"Nora's coming to get us." Peggy knew Irene was looking forward to it, and Finn had given his permission. "Will you be there?"

"The school is singing." She hummed a few bars of something Peggy couldn't place. "My da sings, too."

That surprised Peggy, but everything she learned about Finn O'Malley surprised her. Nothing surprised her more than the deep respect and admiration that people in Shanmullin still seemed to feel for him, despite his decision not to practice medicine. He had left them with only one doctor, a haughty young man whose practice encompassed several small villages and nearby Westport. But despite long waits and care they didn't relish, people still seemed to wish Finn well.

When Peggy watched Finn with Irene, she thought she understood why. He was a different person with the old woman than he was with Peggy or even his own daughter. She thought, perhaps, that at those times she was witnessing the man he'd once been. Warm, thoughtful, a good listener and caring healer. At those moments he was everything a physician should be, everything she had hoped to be herself someday.

Kieran wandered back, and Peggy told him to sit. He did, and she gave him another fish cracker.

"Point to red," Bridie said.

His little face crumbled, but he didn't cry. He stuck out his lower lip and glared in her direction. For a moment it looked as if he would meet her eyes, but instead he looked down at the table. "No!"

Peggy sat up straighter. "What did you say?" she asked. "Kieran, what did you say?"

"No!" He got to his feet and toddled off again.

Peggy laughed.

"Why is that funny?" Bridie sounded genuinely puzzled.

Peggy reached out and gave her a brief, enthusiastic hug. "Because I'm the only mother in the whole wide world who's glad her son has reached the terrible twos!"

Bridie looked puzzled.

"He said 'no,'" Peggy said. "He's never said it before, Bridie. Not like that. He knows what he's saying."

"Well, I should think you'd be sorry he's learned it," Bridie said wisely. "You will be before long."

Peggy was elated. In her opinion, the weeks of work with her son were beginning to pay off. After his outburst, Kieran had settled himself in the corner, where a large pile of blocks awaited him. When Bridie finally joined him and piled them high, he knocked them over, again and again, waiting almost patiently each time for her to finish.

"Not everyone would see that as progress," Peggy told Irene at supper. "I realize that. But every time, he waited until Bridie was finished. They were playing together."

"Well now, it sounds as if they were," Irene agreed. "And who knows but that he'll be the one building the towers and she'll be the one knocking them over before long."

"I got him to turn a page," Bridie said.

Peggy was doubtful about that, not certain Kieran actually

had meant to. She was afraid turning the page had been more annoyance than anything else. The real miracle was that he was letting Bridie get close enough that these accidents could happen. He sat beside her when she read to him, and even though he never looked as if he was paying attention, Peggy couldn't be sure. They were interacting, though. And it wasn't just Bridie who was having good luck.

"He let me pick him up when he fell today," Peggy said.

"Don't you pick him up all the time?" Irene set her fork on the plate. She had eaten only a dollop of mashed potatoes and half a small lamb chop. Peggy hoped she was only resting.

"Well, usually when I pick him up, he's as stiff as a poker. Today he curved into my arms." She'd almost been ashamed at how much pleasure that had given her. She knew better than to harbor expectations of intimacy, because Kieran might never be capable of that. But oh, it had felt so good, so right, to be needed, even wanted, in that brief moment.

"Then I'd say a celebration's in order," Irene said.

Peggy peeked at her son. Kieran was about to fall asleep. He had always needed a great deal of rest. Now that she was working so hard with him, he seemed to need even more.

Bridie seemed to notice, as well. "The boyo's about to land in his supper."

"I'll put him to bed, then we can have dessert," Peggy said. Nora had baked a layer cake that afternoon, and there was fresh fruit to go with it. Bridie was staying the night, because Finn was occupied for the evening.

"I'm thinking you should put him to bed, then go into town," Irene said. "With him so tired and Bridie right here, I believe we can manage just fine without you, dear. You could have a night out, all to yourself. Now what do you say to that?"

Peggy didn't know what to say. For the most part, the peace of Tierney Cottage was a welcome substitute for the hectic pace of her life in Ohio. Life here offered little in the way of actual entertainment, though. Irene had television and a satellite dish, but aside from "ER" and two BBC medical dramas, Peggy had found few programs that interested her. She'd read all the books she'd brought with her, then ordered more and read those, too. She probably did need a night out.

Peggy glanced over at Bridie, who was working on her second chop. She couldn't imagine leaving her here with so little to do. "I thought we could play Charades," Peggy said. "Bridie would like it."

"Oh, I have homework," Bridie said. "I won't be much company."

Peggy sensed a plot. Bridie had the entire weekend for homework. "What would I find in town?"

Irene pushed her plate away. "Well, the pubs, of course. But tonight they'll be setting up for the *Fleadh Ceoil,* and there'll be music there. Tonight's really the beginning, you know, just for us, not for the tourists. Go and have a pint on the green and listen. Meet some of the townspeople. Take that ridiculous dog with you and leave him there while you're at it." She winked at Peggy.

Bridie looked up from her chop, indignant. "Banjax likes it here, and you like him. Can you say you don't?"

"Oh, I suppose he's all right where he is for now. Mind you, though, he won't be coming inside ever again. I only let him in this afternoon because I was afraid it might rain and the wind would slam the shed door shut."

Peggy focused on her son in an attempt not to smile. The afternoon sky had been as clear as Waterford crystal.

"You'll take a night out?" Irene demanded. "It's a perfect opportunity, you know."

"I will." Peggy stood, setting her napkin beside her plate. She reached for Kieran, whose eyelids were drooping lower. In a moment he really was going to slip quietly into his mashed potatoes. "I'll bike in for a little while, if you're sure...?"

"We're both sure. You go ahead. Bridie and I will have an evening, just the two of us. And have a pint for me, will you, dear? Since it's clear I won't be having one for myself any time soon."

Finn knew that he'd disappointed—no, that was too mild a word—*disheartened* Shanmullin's citizens when he closed

down his medical practice. Even those who preferred his colleague Joe Beck's arrogant manner, equating Beck's insensi-
tivity with superior knowledge, had been upset, even angry,
when Finn pulled his door closed for the last time. With only
one doctor to serve the local population, everyone's care was
compromised.

Finn had done what he could to repair the damage. He had
presented Shanmullin's case at every turn, attempting re-
cruitment of friends or colleagues from other counties,
pleaded with national and county authorities to fill the gap,
even offering his surgery and all its furnishings at a bargain
rate. But no one wanted to live in the small Western Ireland
village beyond the far edge of Clew Bay. Oh yes, it was perfect for a holiday, scenic and traditional and a return to long
withered Irish roots. Friends recounted warm memories of
family gatherings in villages just like this one. Then they
headed gratefully for cities like Galway or even Westport, with
their larger opportunities.

And Shanmullin was left with one doctor.

Finn had disappointed so many people that when asked
each year to participate in the village *Fleadh Ceoil,* he could
not say no to that, as well. He longed to. He was tortured each
time he attended by memories of Sheila, baby Brian in one
arm and little Mark hugging her skirts, standing at the edge
of the crowd, staring up at the musicians' platform as he performed with the others. Sheila had played the harp, lovely,
ethereal Sheila with the pale blond hair bequeathed her from
some ancient Norse invader. Some years the committee had
persuaded her to perform, as well, and she had silenced the
raucous crowd with her mournful tunes and clear, haunting
soprano.

Sheila, Brian and Mark, gone forever.

"Ye're not looking so good, Finn," Johnny Kerrigan said.
"Ye're not catching that flu that's been making the rounds,
are ye?"

Finn looked beyond the milling villagers, who were chatting and exclaiming over children and grandchildren. A row

of trees at the end of the green was as good a place to focus as any. He counted treetops, darkening as the sun slowly sank into the ocean. In a moment the memories and the squeezing pain in his chest that always went with them began to ease.

"I'm fine." Finn lifted his tin whistle from its case and made a show of cleaning it. "A long day, that's all."

"Ought to go back to pushing pills, ye know. Hours are just as bad, but at least ye did it right here in Shanmullin."

Finn was so used to remarks of that type that he ignored it. "There'll be a crowd tonight."

"Gets larger every year." Johnny removed his concertina from its case, giving it a couple of squeezes for good measure. It squawked in response. "We're wanting to remember our traditional ways."

Finn wasn't sure that for most people, at least, tradition was the real point of the festival. Shanmullin's residents were grateful for any excuse to convene. Then the talking could begin.

"And who would that be?"

Finn looked up at the reverence in Johnny's voice. Johnny was closer to seventy than sixty, his head as bald as Croagh Patrick's peak and as round as its base. He fancied himself a lady's man and had confided to Finn that he was finally on the lookout for a wife after a long life without one.

Finn expected to see an aging widow, most likely one who'd kept her figure and sense of humor, since Johnny was determined to have both. Instead he saw Peggy Donaghue chatting with a group of older women just ten yards or so from the edge of the platform.

Her long hair was drawn back in a braid, and her cheeks were flushed with natural color. She wore a rust-colored jumper over black jeans, and practical hiking boots. And still, with no attempt at artifice, she was stunningly beautiful.

"The Lord our God took His time putting that one together, didn't He now?" Johnny said. "Then He sent her straight to Ireland to torture us all."

"Not so straight. She's an American."

Johnny whistled softly. "I'll be putting my passport in order." He turned to Finn. "Ye know her?"

"Peggy Donaghue. She's staying at the Tierney Cottage. A long-lost relative of Irene's."

"They always come back, ye know, the lost Americans looking for home and family. Do they flock to Poland and Portugal the same way, do ye suppose?"

"I think Irene convinced her to visit. Peggy's been good for her." The latter surprised him. He hadn't even thought it, and out it had come. It was true, however. Irene took great delight in both Peggy and the little boy. Even his daughter thought the two of them were the genuine article and was spending as much time at Irene's as she was allowed.

"Ye have yer eye on her, do ye now?" Johnny asked.

The unspoken corollary, of course, was that if Finn didn't, Johnny wanted to step in. Finn's first foolish impulse was to remind his old friend that he *had* a wife, but of course, he didn't. Sheila had been gone for two long years, and last year the village matrons had begun parading their daughters and granddaughters, oblivious to the fact that this was the twenty-first century and marriage was no longer crucial to a man's economic survival.

Or perhaps he was making too much of their desire to see him happy again. No one understood the height and breadth of his demons.

"Well, perhaps the widow visiting Mary Sullivan is more my style," Johnny said when Finn didn't answer. "Mary says she fancies older men." He preened a little.

Peggy took that moment to look up and meet Finn's gaze. He supposed she had little enough reason to regard him as a friend. Her smile was slight, but genuine enough. He doubted she expected it to be returned. She broke away from the group that had nearly swallowed her and moved toward the platform.

"I didn't know you played an instrument, Finn. Bridie tells me you sing, too?"

Unaccountably, he was embarrassed, as if performing against his will this way had opened some secret door inside him. He didn't even question why he wanted to keep himself apart from her. He only knew that he did.

"There's little to do here," he said gruffly. "I learned to play as a boy."

"I love music. I can't carry a tune in a bucket, but I think that's my throat, not my ears."

The other musicians were drifting up to the platform. Two fiddlers whose names he couldn't recall, Matt with his accordion, Sean with his bodhran and Sarah with the uilleann pipes. The musicians of Shanmullin played together whenever they could, in the pubs, in the church hall, strangers taking seats to play with them, neighbors leaving to have a pint or a smoke. The music had been played this way for centuries, changing only slowly and relying on the oral tradition for instruction. Variations on old themes, respect for those who had come before, tentative, very tentative, forays into a new century. No need to reinvent what had stood them so well for so long.

He wondered if Peggy could understand that. She might be Irish in heritage, but what did she know of a culture that held on so fiercely to what it had nearly lost in centuries of occupation?

"Isn't it a beautiful evening?" She cocked her head. "You see, if I ask you a direct question, you have to answer."

He realized he had been staring at her. Not as a man stares at a lovely woman, but as a man stares at his enemy, expecting she who had come in peace to suddenly and fatally wield a butcher knife.

He managed a curt nod. "A perfect evening. Don't tell me you walked in. I could have come for you."

"I biked. I need the exercise, sitting all day with Kieran the way I do. I'll be glad when his legs grow longer and he learns to like the wind. Then at least we can go for walks."

"He's afraid of the wind?"

"He's not an adaptable child."

It was a classic use of understatement. He realized how much he admired her attitude. She had faced up to the truth about her son, and she was doing everything she could to help him. He wasn't certain about her methods—indeed, he hadn't wanted to know that much—but he did know, without having to ask, that she cared enormously. Like the experts and the researchers, he didn't understand what caused autism, but he did know that this child was luckier than some. He would not be abandoned or abused. Peggy would be certain he had every chance in the world to succeed.

"I didn't know you could smile." Her eyes were warm, even compassionate.

"I didn't know I was smiling," he said. "I'll have to be more careful."

The fiddlers began to tune. Johnny, who had gone down into the crowd before Peggy arrived, came back to meet her. Finn made quick introductions and watched Johnny flush and stammer, consequences he'd never witnessed. When Peggy left, he turned to the old man.

"Have you never been that close to a beautiful woman, Johnny?"

"Not in donkey's years. And she's nice, besides. It's a fatal combination, wouldn't ye agree?"

Finn was about to shrug, but he thought better of it. For two years he'd lost his hunger for a woman. Any stirrings of interest had been immediately extinguished by memories of his past. But now his past was before him, the vision still intact of his Sheila standing at the platform edge, and yet his body pulsed with longing.

And not for a woman long dead. For the one who actually stood at the platform's edge, for the one who had spoken to him tonight.

"Fatal," he agreed.

"Most women as lovely as that one would live in yer ear and grow potatoes in the other, but not that one. There's more to her, I'll wager." Johnny wiggled his brows and picked up his concertina. In a moment the music began, and Finn was able to leave the subject and thoughts of Peggy Donaghue behind.

Peggy couldn't believe how much she was enjoying herself. She had grown up in a large family, petted and fussed over by people not so different from these. Maybe by some people's estimation the Donaghues were "plastic paddies," Americans of Irish extraction who wore too much green and made too much of St. Patrick's Day, but the real core of her family wasn't plastic but truly, distinctively Irish. She felt at home here.

"Are you heading back home, Peggy?"

She smiled at a woman who had introduced herself earlier. Tippy—short for Tipperary, she'd confided dolefully—had a daughter Kieran's age, and they had talked babies with great relish. She was black-haired, black-eyed and cheerfully overweight. Peggy had liked her immediately.

"I suppose I should." Peggy glanced at her watch and saw it was nearly ten. The sky was dark now, and, inevitably, since this was the West of Ireland, clouds had blown in. The road home was a long one.

"If you stay just a bit longer, they might persuade Finn O'Malley to sing the last song."

Peggy raised a brow. "He hasn't sung a note." Finn had played the tin whistle and the flute most of the evening, though, and played both with finesse and enthusiasm. She had never heard anyone play better.

"He only sings when he's made to. Too bad, since it's God's gift, isn't it? To be used, not hoarded."

Peggy suspected the subject of Finn's gifts was one that was often discussed here. "Maybe I'll stay."

"I've been thinking we should get our little ones together soon." Tippy gestured for her husband, who was standing in a line of men drinking behind them. He grinned at her and ignored the summons. Tippy rolled her eyes in frustration.

Peggy hadn't told her new friend about Kieran's problems. The time had come. "I would like that very much, but you need to know up front that Kieran's not going to be a good playmate for your Maeve. He's autistic."

She hadn't been sure that Tippy would understand that diagnosis. Peggy had been through a year of medical school and hardly understood it herself. But Tippy frowned. "Is he? And you've already determined it? He's a lucky lad, isn't he, to have a mother who's so aware."

"You sound like you know something about it."

"I'm trained to teach special children. I've worked with children like your Kieran."

Peggy had a million questions, but she wasn't sure she wanted answers. She didn't want to know more than she already did about what awaited her son, the limitations, the roadblocks. Not now. Not until she needed to.

"I'll bring Maeve to play whenever you'd like," Tippy said. "Or you can come to our house. The sooner Kieran begins to play with other children, the better for him, don't you think?"

Peggy knew that at this age, the term *play* was relative, even for children who weren't autistic. For a moment she had to blink back tears. She'd come so far and found warmth and acceptance. "I'd be thrilled," she said. "Thank you."

Tippy hesitated. "Peggy, I have a sister in Senior Cycle. She wants to go to university, then teach, just the way I did at her age. If you need help, I know she'd be pleased to help you. And it will give her some experience, and help her decide if that's the right path."

Peggy nodded, grateful beyond speech. Tippy squeezed her arm. "That's 'The King of the Fairies' they're playing now. It's one of my favorites."

Peggy focused on the stage and saw that someone, a middle-aged woman with a bad perm, had taken Finn's place. She looked for him and saw him talking to Tippy's husband and the men beside him. She supposed he deserved a drink and a break after hours of performing.

As she watched, she saw one of the men take a flask from his pocket and hold it out to Finn. Finn seemed to freeze. He did nothing for a moment, just looked at the flask, then the man. The other men were still, as well.

Then Finn walked away. As she watched, a man cuffed the one who had made the offer and said something to him that was obviously not flattering. The man with the flask put it away, shrugging, as if to say, "More fool, he."

The whole scene had taken place in seconds. She wondered if she had imagined it.

"The King of the Fairies" was followed by "The Green Fields of Ardkiernan" and "Nine Points of Roguery." Tippy, who was an admirer of all things traditional, kept her informed, even though Peggy had trouble telling when one song ended and another began.

She glanced at her watch again, just as Finn climbed back on the platform. Someone began to applaud, and others took it up. He grimaced, but he went to the microphone.

"We have to save something for tomorrow," he said.

There was more applause, and feet began to stamp. He grimaced again. "All right, if I sing it, will you go home peacefully?"

Laughter greeted him, and with a sigh of resignation, he cleared his throat. The crowd quieted. He stepped closer to the microphone and began to sing. She had heard the song before, although she couldn't give it a name.

"'The Parting Glass,'" Tippy supplied, as if she had read Peggy's thoughts.

Peggy was mesmerized. Finn had a clear, resonant baritone. He sang unaccompanied, and the evening air was filled with his vibrant voice, the lyrics and the melody. The combination seemed simple enough, yet it was more powerful for its simplicity.

The words began to weave their own spell. It was about saying goodbye, she realized. The final glass at the pub, moving on, acknowledging friendship and mistakes made. The graceful and last farewell at life's end.

She was profoundly moved. She was always moved by Celtic music, but never more than this. The air was cool and the breeze had stopped. Finn's baritone seemed to echo off the mountain where St. Patrick had walked. His voice seemed to extend to the shore so close to the place where her ancestors had sailed for America.

"But since it falls unto my lot, that I should go and you should not, I'll gently rise and softly call, good night and joy be with you all."

Beside her, Tippy sighed, and Peggy realized Finn had finished. People began to applaud. She joined them, although it seemed too much like applauding in church.

"No one sings it quite the way Finn does," Tippy said.

Peggy watched the crowds disperse. The sky was even darker, but she thought it made sense not to rush away until what little traffic there was had lessened. Her bicycling skills had improved in the past weeks, but the lanes were narrow, and the crowd had drunk its share. Prudence was called for.

She said goodbye to Tippy and to some of the others she'd met, promising to visit when she could. The crowd was thinner by the time her new friends were gone, and she started for her bicycle. Finn intercepted her.

"It's about to rain."

She didn't doubt it. She was just sorry the rare clear skies hadn't held. "I'd better get moving, then."

"I'll drive you."

She wasn't sure why Finn felt she was his responsibility, but she wanted to disabuse him of that notion immediately. "That's very kind of you, but I won't melt." She said it with a smile.

"I've got to go out there anyway. Bridie forgot to bring clean clothes for tomorrow."

"She can wear what she had on today. We didn't do anything to get dirty. Or you can bring them in the morning."

"You're not going to let me help you, are you?"

"Finn, you did enough picking me up at Shannon. I don't want to be a bother."

"Your friendship means a lot to my daughter. And to Irene. It's my responsibility not to let you die of pneumonia." As if his words were a meteorological signal, raindrops began to fall.

"What about my bike?"

"There's a rack on my car. Come on."

Arguing seemed foolish. She got her bike and followed him

through the street to the place where his car was parked. He lifted the bicycle out of her hands and set it in place on the rack before she could even offer to help. "Get in," he said. "It's easier if I do this alone. I'm used to it."

She did, and he joined her just before the heavens opened and rain pelted the windshield. The car rocked as the wind picked up.

"Just in time," she said. "I should be used to swiftly moving storms. The day before I left, a tornado touched down and nearly destroyed the family saloon. And everyone in it, besides."

"You were there?"

"It was my sister's wedding reception. Everyone had moved to the back to see her cut the cake. If they hadn't—" She shook her head. She'd had little time to think about her narrow escape, or how lucky Kieran had been that afternoon. The rain and wind brought it all back.

"Do you have tornadoes here?" she asked.

"Not often. But we get storms."

She heard the tension in his voice. Had he been anyone else, she might have probed. But this being Finn, she knew better than to try.

He didn't turn the key. She supposed he was waiting to see if the storm lessened before he pulled out. "I enjoyed the music tonight." She turned a little to face him. "You're very accomplished."

He gave a short nod. She expected it to end at that, but perhaps sitting this way in silence seemed too intimate. "You're not finding your days here too boring?"

"Not at all. I'm busy with Kieran and Irene, and in between, the quiet's wonderful. I've had little quiet in my life. And if I ever go back to medical school, there won't be much in my future."

"You still plan on it?"

"Someday, when I'm sure my absence won't harm my son."

Finn began to drum his fingers on the steering wheel. She was sorry he'd made this offer. She knew he hadn't bargained for being locked up with her this way.

Minutes passed, and she tried to start another conversation. "The song you sang was lovely. I've heard it, but I've never really paid attention to the words."

"Some of our best songs are drinking songs."

"The pubs are an important part of daily life, aren't they? I suppose it makes sense."

"You'd understand that, with your background."

"I know a few drinks will do wonders for conversation. A few too many will do wonders for hospital emergency rooms. I notice you're not a drinking man."

"Do you?"

"It must be hard to drink too much and play so beautifully. I saw you refuse someone's whiskey," she explained.

He was silent so long she thought this conversation had died, too. The rain was still coming down in sheets, but the wind had lessened. He started the car and backed out of the parking place.

"I refused the flask," he said, once he was on the road, "but I wanted to take it. I wanted to drink it all and everything else I could put my hands on. I can't drink. Or rather, I can drink, but I can't stop."

She hadn't known, and it surprised her that Irene had kept this hidden. Finn was a recovering alcoholic. The man truly had more than his share of sorrows.

She wanted to know if this was the reason he had stopped practicing medicine. Had he lost his license or been about to? Was he simply taking a hiatus until he was certain his drinking was under control? She didn't ask. That was much too personal. But she wanted him to know she understood something of his struggle.

"My father is an alcoholic," she said. "Only in his case it's more than that, I'm afraid. The alcohol was an attempt to cope with psychosis, although we've never been completely sure which came first. It's been a terrible struggle for him and for everyone in our family. I can appreciate, all too well, what you must have gone through."

"Gone through? As if it's over?"

"That's not what I meant. I'm sorry. I was just trying to let you know I've seen this up close and personal from another angle, and I admire anybody who fights it. I know it's a daily struggle."

"There's nothing admirable about it." He bit off the words. "I'm a drunk, and you've seen what drunks can do to the people who care about them. I should think you'd know better than even to offer sympathy. You should run as far and fast as you're able. Unless you see knowing me as a challenge of some sort?"

She knew she hadn't handled the conversation well. But she had thought by sharing a little of her past, she could let him know she understood. Now any compassion she'd felt died away, replaced by a slowly burning anger. She supposed he was intentionally being rude to keep her at bay. But what had she offered besides understanding? Was trying to understand Finn O'Malley a crime of such magnitude?

"You know," she said at last, as he turned on to the boreen leading to Tierney Cottage, "I haven't known you long. Maybe the people of Shanmullin have such good memories of you that they're willing to accept your rudeness in hopes the Finn they once knew will come back to them. But that man's only a story to me. So don't worry that I'm going to try to knock down the barriers between us or reach into your miserly little heart. I'm not. You may have suffered, but all of us have or will. And not all of us feel it's our right to be so unkind in retaliation."

"You *do* have the temper to go with the hair."

"No, as a matter of fact I don't. I'm the easygoing Donaghue sister. By now Megan and Casey would have had a knife to your throat."

He pulled to a stop, and she opened her door into the pouring rain. "I'll get the bike. Don't get out."

He got out anyway, but she'd already unfastened the bicycle and was in the process of lifting it down when he arrived.

"Thanks for the ride, if not for the conversation." She rolled the bike away from him, then thought better of leaving him that way.

"I have problems of my own, Finn. Don't worry that I'm planning to borrow yours." She turned her back. Behind her, she heard the car engine start again. She didn't look as he pulled away.

chapter 12

Work at the saloon was progressing. Marco and Niccolo had hired a seasoned crew to clear away the debris and shore up the building until safety and security were no longer major issues. A new roof was underway, and soon work on the interior could begin in earnest.

Niccolo was using the opportunity to teach the Brick kids about blueprints and design. Each youth had been asked to submit a plan for the renovations, and some of them had been surprisingly creative. Megan liked Winston's idea for inexpensive kitchen shelving so much that she asked Niccolo to incorporate it. Winston's sister Elisha, whose flair for interior decoration had been in evidence at their first meeting, suggested a hand-painted mural of Ireland in one corner of the bar area, and smaller tables to create a quiet area. *Relatively* quiet, of course, but Megan liked that, as well.

She knew she should be happy. She knew how fortunate they'd been, and how inconsequential the renovations were in the scheme of things. But something just wasn't right, and she tried to explain her feelings to Casey, who was taking an early lunch hour from her job at the Albaugh Center.

"I don't feel like I have a purpose anymore." In the shell of what had once been a bustling kitchen, Megan heated a kettle of water to go with the sandwiches Casey had brought with her. She didn't have a stove anymore, which was the lowest possible blow for someone whose self-esteem had revolved around one. She heated the kettle on a hot plate, which sat on a sheet of plywood resting on two battered sawhorses. That, the old sink and two plastic patio chairs were the sum total of their kitchen furniture. Even the ancient linoleum floor was gone, exposing rough planks coated in tar.

Casey twisted in her chair as if trying, in vain, to make herself comfortable. "Isn't your purpose to see that things get done right?"

"At least you're not pretending I have some greater mission, like inspiring others to greatness or making the world a brighter place with my smile." Megan grimaced to show there was no chance of the latter.

"I know it has to be frustrating, but can't you just use the time to get some of the other things done you never had time for before?"

"Like?"

"Haunting the antique stores on Lorain. Planting a perennial garden in your new backyard. Having tea parties on your front porch. You used to dream of that, remember? And now you have one. I could come over on my day off. We could be ladies of leisure in Edwardian white. We could learn to play croquet."

Megan didn't feel even a twinge of longing. She figured that indulging her interests might be good for two days tops. Those were spare time activities, not a focus, a reason for being.

She wasn't comfortable analyzing herself, but unfortunately, she had all the time in the world to do it now. "I've been working since I was a kid. How did you stand it when you quit your job and came back from Chicago?"

"I tended bar for you." Casey inclined her head toward the saloon. "Remember?"

"I can't even do that. No bar to tend. No tables to wait on. No meals to cook." She realized her lower lip was nearly as low as her spirits. She forced a pleasant expression. "I sound ridiculous, don't I? After all, it's just a matter of weeks."

Casey licked her lips, something she did when she was about to launch into an offensive. "It's not just the saloon, is it?"

"What else could go wrong? Isn't that enough?"

"You're not seeing much of Nick, are you?"

There were days when Megan wished she'd had brothers instead of Casey and Peggy. Brothers who couldn't care less about what she was feeling and couldn't figure it out if they did.

"He's busy," Megan said, trying a shrug and realizing the result was more like a nervous tic. "Of course he's busy. He's doing everything he can to help here. And he and Marco are doing a great job."

"And you don't see much of him."

"Do you know how many people have called Nick and asked for a private tour of the tunnel?" Megan was surprised at the censure in her own voice. Was she that unhappy?

"I have no idea. A lot?"

"I'm trying not to keep track. I really am. But the phone's been ringing off the hook, Casey. Family. Friends. Friends of family. People who know friends of friends." Her shoulders spasmed again.

"And Nick's taking them all through?"

"Ask him. Here he comes."

Casey turned just as Niccolo walked through the door. "Not a very cheery place for a reunion." He bent down and kissed the top of Megan's head. "Maybe we ought to get a picnic table for the parking lot. We could all use a better place for breaks."

That kind of thoughtfulness was typical of Niccolo. Nuances never eluded him. The kitchen was gloomy, and Megan knew she looked gloomy, too. Niccolo wanted to move her outside and into the light. Hell, he'd been moving people toward the light most of his adult life. She was annoyed by his good will.

Casey lifted her cheek for a kiss. "Nick, Megan tells me people are bugging you for tours of the tunnel."

"Just a few."

"Few dozen!" Megan wondered if he was really that oblivious.

"It's not a big deal, is it? Are you worried?"

Megan couldn't very well say yes. It seemed to her that once she began itemizing all the peeves in her life, the list would grow like Josh's long legs. "You're going to wear yourself out. That's all. You're already busy enough with the renovation and Brick."

He leaned against the sink. "I guess I'm more worried about what could happen if I didn't show it to people."

"What could?" Casey said.

"I'm almost certain it's a water stain. From what I can tell, there was a small leak seeping into the wall behind it. Maybe there still is. When we redo the pipes in the saloon, it's probably going to dry up and go away. But in the meantime, people are talking about it. And the best way to stop the talk is to show people exactly what it is."

Casey looked interested now. "What kind of talk?"

"Casey, in your line of work you must see this, too. People are always hoping for miracles. Somebody digs a potato and sees the crucifixion etched on its surface. Somebody notices rust on an old abandoned car and sees the ascension. I woke up from the explosion and saw the Virgin in a water stain."

Megan liked Niccolo's shrug a lot better than the ones *she'd* managed so far. "It's no wonder people are looking for miracles. The church promotes miracles. You probably preached about them."

"The church is very careful now. We live in an age of scientific explanation. Nobody wants to sanction a miracle that turns out to be a perfectly natural phenomenon. The church has enough problems. It doesn't want to look foolish."

"So you're showing this to people and explaining the science of it," Casey said. "That makes sense to me."

He grinned. "Just as long as nobody else experiences what I did down there."

"You mean the explosion?" Megan said.

"No, I mean *surviving* the explosion. That's part of the mythology now. Word is getting out that the Virgin saved me."

Megan wondered why they hadn't had time for this conversation before. At home, Rooney and Josh were often around, but she and Niccolo could still make time for each other if they tried harder. Why hadn't they?

"When is it going to end?" The question was pointed, but she didn't care. "When are the rumors going to die down so you don't have to tramp through the tunnel at all hours?"

He seemed to misinterpret. "I don't mind doing it. I show and I explain, but people still seem to take something important away with them. It's been kind of nice. The best part of being a priest was sharing other people's spiritual journeys."

"Sounds like you're handling it well." Casey got to her feet. "And I'd better go run some errands."

Her words were punctuated by a pounding at the kitchen door. Megan looked up to see an unfamiliar woman with her nose pressed to the window beside it. "Anybody we know?" she asked Casey.

Casey squinted into the sunlight. "Isn't that Beatrice Stowell? You know, the old lady who lives next door to Uncle Den? She's a good ten years older than he is, but she's been trying to get him in the sack for years."

"And I'm supposed to answer the door with that sentence ringing in my ears?" Megan did, though. By the time she opened it, she recognized Beatrice, too. The woman was somewhere in her eighties and the victim of a sadistic hairdresser who had clipped her fuzzy white hair like a poodle's. There were longer tufts over the ears and forehead, but the rest was short enough to highlight her pink scalp. Megan thought the rhinestone spangled house slippers adorning her feet might be an attempt to divert attention until the hair could grow.

"Your uncle Den told me to come," Beatrice said without preamble. "He said I should see the tunnel."

Megan stepped back, and Beatrice marched inside. She nodded primly to Niccolo and Casey. "Which of you wants to take me down? I'm ready."

Megan imagined her next conversation with her uncle. She might even suggest that the two neighbors deserved each other. "We're a little busy," she began.

"I'll take you." Niccolo pushed away from the sink. "But just a short visit. It's not that pleasant." He gazed down at her feet. "We have to climb some stairs. Can you, ummm, climb in those?"

"I said I was ready." Beatrice was eager, if not particularly polite.

"I'll come, too," Megan said, catching and holding Niccolo's glance. "I'd better learn to do the tour, huh? Just in case you get too busy." She paused. "You know, with the...renovations."

He grinned at her, and her heart did its usual flutter. She hated that he could still do that to her. Marriage had not been the magic cure.

Casey elected to come, as well. They sandwiched Beatrice between them for protection, and, armed with flashlights they slowly made their way down and through the storeroom. Halfway there and too late to turn back, Beatrice announced that she had arthritis and every step was like a knife stabbing her.

"I've been meaning to tell you," Niccolo told Megan when they'd finished the stairs and moved slowly into the tunnel. He snapped on his light. "There are a couple of side passages. They're so narrow that at first I just thought they were experiments before somebody finished the main tunnel. One's a dead end, but one of them leads to another storeroom. You're going to want to explore. It's filled with memorabilia."

"What, bats? Mice? Spiders? That last would be my favorite, by the way."

"It needs cleaning," he admitted.

Beatrice cut through the small talk. "I think you should be

more reverent. If Our Lady is here, she won't want to hear all the blather."

Megan, who was behind Beatrice, began to plot retribution scenarios for good old Uncle Den.

They made the rest of the trip in coerced silence. Niccolo stopped where he'd landed after the explosion. He shined his flashlight on the wall and illuminated the water stain. Megan hadn't been sure what to expect, since she hadn't been down here since rescuing her husband, but the image had remained exactly the same, except that today no water seeped from the region of the Virgin's eyes.

Beatrice fell to her knees and crossed herself, confirming Megan's guess that she was a Catholic, if not a member of St. Brigid's.

"We're certain there's a leak somewhere above it," Niccolo said gently. "Probably has been for years. There's a perfectly natural explanation. But it's a nice reminder of more important things—"

"Shhh..." Beatrice opened her eyes and glared at him. "For heaven's sake, be quiet."

Megan saw her sister's eyes widen. Niccolo only smiled sympathetically and fell silent. Megan waited. Minutes passed, and she was anxious to see the second storeroom. Her patience wore out at last. "Look, Beatrice, we didn't mind bringing you down here, but Nick explained that we couldn't stay long, and we can't. We have to go now. Let me help you up." She extended her hand.

"I can't understand why Our Lady came to a place like this one!" Beatrice put her hand on Megan's, not so disillusioned that she wouldn't accept her help.

Megan had expected to need assistance getting the old woman to her feet, and Niccolo, who'd obviously expected he would need to give it, stepped up to offer his arm. But Beatrice ignored it and sprang up with the grace and energy of a much younger woman.

She looked astonished at her own prowess. Her eyes widened. "Did you see that?"

Nobody knew exactly what she meant or how to respond.

"The pain's gone." For the first time since arriving at their doorstep, Beatrice smiled. "It's gone. Hallclujah, it's gone."

Niccolo caught Megan's eye. She signaled him to say something, anything. He turned to the old woman and took her hand. "I'm glad you're feeling better, Beatrice. But we'd better get you upstairs now while you're feeling so well."

"Don't you see? I'm going to feel well from now on. I've been cured. My arthritis is gone."

"It's cool and moist and quiet here. It's a change from the June heat. It's easy to see why it might feel like a—"

"Miracle," she said, jerking her hand from his. She slapped him on the arm. "It's a miracle."

Megan could see the future, and the vision was anything but joyful and filled with light. "This is not a miracle," she said too sharply. "And please, don't go telling people you've been cured here, or we'll have to close the tunnel for good."

"You would keep people away?" Beatrice was astonished. "You would keep people from being healed?"

Casey tried to intervene, but Beatrice ran right over her. "I'm going to tell everybody. You have no right to keep them away. If I have to, I'll go to the Holy Father. I can get to the Vatican now, you know. I've been cured!"

"She thinks she's been cured," Megan told Peggy later on the telephone. The two sisters had scheduled weekly calls, and Thursday was their chosen time. It was night in Shanmullin, and with Irene and Kieran asleep, Peggy had the house to herself.

Peggy made herself comfortable. She suspected tonight might be a long catch-up call. "And you tried to talk her out of it?"

"Nick thinks she's just lonely. The Albaugh Center has a thriving senior citizen program, and Casey's going to get Beatrice involved in it. She and Nick are sure that will take care of the problem. Beatrice will forget all about the miracle and move on to bingo."

Peggy laughed. "Like they equate."

"She was limping by the time we got her back upstairs. But

she still insisted she wasn't in any pain." Megan paused, and when she spoke again, her voice had changed. "I don't know what it's like to be old and alone. Maybe there was a miracle of sorts there. Casey's going to help her find some new friends and something to do. That's miracle enough for me."

"You're not such a tough cookie, are you?"

Megan ignored that. "Tell me about Kieran."

"Well, it's the oddest thing. He's made a couple of major breakthroughs." She waited, and Megan didn't disappoint her. She heard the low whistle of congratulations.

"What?" Megan asked. "Tell all."

Peggy wasn't sure how to explain. The gains would seem so small to someone else, but to her they were powerful examples of the things Kieran might do if she continued working with him. "I—we've been trying to teach him to point to specific colors. On Monday he pointed to red when I asked him. When I put two blocks on the table, one red and one blue, and asked him, he pointed to the right one. Every time. And he sat beside me when I read to him and even turned a page when I asked."

As she listened to Megan ooh and ah, she missed her sister more than she ever had. "And last, but definitely not least, he used a spoon today. First time, Megan. He's not very good yet, but he sure has the right idea. And all this when he's cutting a tooth and not feeling very good and not eating. In fact, he fed himself the little bit he's eaten all day. I couldn't get anything into him at all."

"This is really great news," Megan said. "I miss the little guy."

Peggy was always touched when she heard that. Kieran couldn't give back the affection he received. Someday, perhaps, but not now. The fact that he was so unconditionally loved by her family meant everything to her.

"How's everything else?" Megan said. "How about the doctor?"

Peggy had needed to tell someone about her run-in with Finn. No surprise that Megan had been the first one she thought of. "He's been polite. I've been polite. Bridie still comes after school most days and helps out with Kieran."

"Sounds kind of uncomfortable."

It *was* uncomfortable. Peggy was sorry she'd lost her temper with Finn, but she didn't feel that she needed to apologize. He had been out of line. "I wouldn't think twice about it, but he's obviously in pain. And I never intended to make it worse."

"I know you didn't. But some people are offended by sympathy. They don't want to know they aren't hiding their feelings very well."

As always, Megan made sense. Peggy hadn't thought about Finn's reaction from that angle. "I guess I stuck my foot in it, huh?"

"So did he. Don't take all the blame. Leave him his share."

"How's Nick doing?" Peggy stared out at the moonlit landscape.

Megan was silent for so long that Peggy worried they had lost their connection. When she spoke, her voice was tense. "He had a dream last night that he was a priest again."

"We all dream about our pasts. Don't you? Sometimes I wake up and I'm surprised I'm not eight again, spending the night over the saloon with you and Casey." When Megan didn't respond, she added, "Megan, surely you don't think he wishes he'd never left?"

"No."

Peggy thought her sister didn't sound as sure as the word would indicate. "He's been absolutely clear about that from the first day you met him," Peggy said. "And he didn't leave the Church for you. He didn't even know you."

"It's just that we're starting our life together, but he's dreaming about the life he left. It's..."

"Disconcerting?"

"I have too much time on my hands." Megan sounded more like herself. "And that's not such a bad thing. Because guess what I found today?"

Peggy listened as her sister launched into the story of the second storeroom off the main tunnel corridor. Although her enthusiasm sounded a little forced, it was much more natural than the doubt that had crept into her voice earlier.

"It's a treasure trove," Megan finished. "Piles of old newspapers, liquor crates, records—probably outcasts from some precursor to our jukebox—ledgers. I'm guessing the newspapers were packing material in the days when liquor was brought in by way of the tunnel."

"Every Donaghue's middle name is 'resourceful,'" Peggy said. "And what was a little thing like a constitutional amendment if it interfered with business?"

"I never had any doubt the saloon sold more than soft drinks during Prohibition, did you? But I'm amazed at how complex an operation this must have been. The ledgers are amazing. I haven't had time to pore over them item by item, but let's just say there are two completely different sets of figures, and in one of them, business was booming."

"Aunt Deirdre might know something about that time. Have you asked her?"

"I called her and told what I'd found. She says the apartment upstairs was a speakeasy, an invitation-only lounge where real liquor was consumed. The bar downstairs was converted into a sedate little restaurant and soft drink parlor. Obviously somebody was looking the other way, huh? I wonder how much of the profit went into paying off the local cops?"

"And to think I lived right there in that little piece of Cleveland history."

"I haven't gotten to the good part yet." Megan paused for effect. "I have some information on Liam Tierney."

Peggy was standing now, closer to the window. Outside, something moved in the shadows. As she watched, Banjax skulked toward the house and deposited himself on the front doorstep. Peggy wondered how long it would take before the dog slept every night in front of the fire. "I hope whatever you found won't upset Irene."

"You've really grown fond of her, haven't you?" Megan said.

"She's wonderful. You're going to love her." Peggy meant it, but sadly, she wasn't sure Irene would live long enough to meet her sisters. She wished Megan and Casey could come soon.

"I brought a stack of the papers home with me this afternoon. You'll be amazed at how cheap food and clothing were in the 1920s."

"What's that got to do with Liam?"

"Not a darned thing. Just amazed me, that's all. But I was leafing through the headlines, and I saw an article about a man who was grazed by a speeding car when he was crossing a street near Whiskey Island."

Peggy could see how the Whiskey Island mention had caught her sister's eye. The history of their family in Cleveland had begun there, along with that of so many other Irish immigrants. "Liam had something to do with this?"

"The car was being chased by the police after a routine check turned up crates of liquor in the trunk. Before the dry agent—that's what they called them in those days—could arrest the driver, the driver attacked him with a tire iron, then took off with the liquor."

"Tell me Liam wasn't the attacker." Peggy paused. "I'll just bet he wasn't the dry agent."

Megan laughed. "Liam was the man who was injured when the car sped up a hill and into the city. Apparently he was just an innocent bystander."

"I'll be darned. And you just happened to find this?"

"It's not as much of a coincidence as it sounds. I'm guessing the story ran for weeks, because they kept alluding to things they'd already reported. Slow news month, I guess. Judging from the article, they hadn't caught the driver yet and didn't expect to. Liam's name was only mentioned once."

"He wasn't killed, was he?" Megan had said "injured," not "dead." Peggy dreaded telling Irene her father had been run over in a gangland getaway.

"Not from what I could tell. Unless he died of his injuries later. I skimmed through the other papers, but I didn't have any more for that month or the next. Tomorrow I'm going over to the Historical Society to see if they have any newspapers from that era on microfilm. Maybe I can get more on the story."

"You have time? You're still a bride."

"I have nothing but," Megan said. "In addition to giving tunnel tours, Niccolo is so involved in the renovations and trying to get new grants for Brick that we just nod when we pass in the hall. I think I saw him more before I married him."

Peggy knew she was supposed to laugh, but the joke fell flat. "If you miss him, you'd better tell him. This sounds like a fight brewing."

"I'm okay."

Peggy knew her sister. Megan was always "okay," even when she wasn't. "I wish you would come and visit. Can't you tear Nick away for a quick trip once the renovations are finished?"

"By then I'll have to get back to business. We'll lose all our patrons if we don't open the doors again as soon as we can."

"They'd wait another week. They're a loyal bunch. Think about it."

As if she wanted to cut short this particular topic, Megan cleared her throat. "I don't want to say goodbye, but this is costing a fortune."

Peggy was sorry the link to home was about to be severed. "Give Casey my love. And Nick, and Jon, and Rooney and everybody else."

"They'll be calling." The sisters exchanged goodbyes, and reluctantly, Peggy hung up.

Outside, the Irish landscape was peaceful and still. She wondered how Liam Tierney and his wife had felt as they left the tranquil cottage where she stood for the bustle of 1920s Cleveland. Then to be injured in a foreign country without family or friends? As always, she was amazed at the resilience and courage of family members she'd never known.

Kieran's heritage was a hardy one. She was glad, because he would need every drop of Tierney courage and resilience he had been bequeathed.

1923
Castlebar, County Mayo

My dearest Patrick,

Your letters continue to arrive, and I pore over them as if they were holy writ. Your Irish remains as strong and pure as if you spoke it every day. Do you ever speak it now? Are there people in your parish who come to you, who whisper their confessions in the old tongue?

Our true culture has been steadily, heartlessly squeezed from us like whey from curds. We Irish are a race with so much potential and so little opportunity. Just yesterday the lad who delivers my bread told me that he will manage his father's bakery when the old man passes on. Not surprising, of course, but sad nonetheless. He is a lad of many abilities. He borrows my books and reads them again and again. He understands them all, the poetry, the philosophy, the stories of great heroes and lovers. He is comfortable with ideas in a way he will never be with flour and yeast. Yet what choice does he have? How well he knows his good fortune in inheriting his father's business. He will be able to feed himself and his family at a time when such a thing is never a certainty.

Oh for the day when Ireland will come into her own again, when the myriad strengths and talents of Irish men and yes, women, will be husbanded and nurtured. I had a dream myself, dear Patrick. I wanted to teach and travel, to roam the world as my ancient ancestresses must have. Hundreds of years ago Celtic women, whose blood still pulses proudly in my veins, were warriors, physicians, lawmakers. Oh, that even one of those choices had been mine to savor.

We Irish residents of this twentieth century pride ourselves on how far we have come. We are Christians now, and soon, God willing, we will be completely free of tyranny. Yet what did we lose along this journey? What have our Irish men and women lost in the passing sorrows of our centuries? How many poets and philosophers are baking bread and tilling barren land? How many have gone to America and found the death of their vast potential in your factories and mills?

I grow weary, dear brother. In your next letter home tell me of happy Irish families, of hope for our next generations, of the poets and philosophers who will rise up from centuries of darkness to reestablish a world that slipped away.

Your sister,
Maura McSweeney

chapter 13

Liam was happy enough at the job he'd found. After a week of looking, he'd been offered several opportunities, an embarrassment of riches for a young man who'd had so few in his lifetime. He had agonized over which position to accept. Until then, choices had always been simple, because there were so few available, but now he was confused to the point of dizziness. Finally, in the neat handwriting she had mastered at the tip of a sister's cane, Brenna made a list of considerations on the back of a paper sack for them to study.

The box manufacturer lay closest to their house, one streetcar ride away. The pay wasn't quite as good as that of U.S. Steel's wire mill, but if he was employed making boxes, Liam would be home for more hours. There was no thought given to which job would be more enjoyable. The smell of glue at the box factory more than made up for the heat and noise of the mill. Fatalistically, Liam was prepared for either torment and chose the box factory and more hours with his wife and daughter.

At first he found himself growing woozy as the fumes collected around him. Gradually, though, he grew used to the smell, the noise, the splinters that made hedgehogs of his palms and fingers. He thought of misty, craggy Ireland and the friends he'd left behind, and he laughed to himself.

Six months later he was promoted up the line and away from the glue. He learned to operate the simple machinery that bound wooden boxes with wire and learned to keep his fingers away from moving parts. He was well-liked, a man who didn't share his troubles and wasn't averse to an occasional sip of the bootleg whiskey made in stifling attic stills. Liam wasn't a man who paid too much attention to laws he hadn't made himself, nor one who wilfully searched for trouble. His Irish neighbors appreciated him for the first, his Slovak employers for the second. Liam had come into his own.

A year after his arrival, Liam was promoted out of the factory and onto a delivery truck. The pay was no better, but he was so pleased to be outside in the fresh air and relative quiet that he snatched the opportunity like a hungry man snatches bread, terrified the miracle might disappear. That night he told Brenna what he was feeling.

"I'd put up with all of it, you know, for you and Irene. Anything to give us more ease. But to have that and a chance to be outside again..." He grinned and shook his head. "We'll be sound as a bell now."

Brenna looked worried. "I know you want this, and I can't blame you a bit, but you'll be staying on the West Side?"

"Most of the time, and coming back here every evening."

"And I suppose you'll be meeting a great many people?"

"But it's you I'll be coming back to."

"Liam, the change worries me. I won't pretend it doesn't."

He knew she was afraid that with this greater freedom, he might get into mischief as he had in Ireland. The confines of the factory had lulled her into a feeling of security. He worked hard there, and he had little time or energy at the day's end for anything but his little family.

"The only change you need to worry about is seeing me

happy again," he promised. "And if we have any luck, I'll be driving the truck before long and making a good deal more money. We can move to a better house, farther up the hill. You'd like that, wouldn't you?"

She didn't look convinced, but she let him gather her in his arms. "I want you to be happy," she said, "That's all."

It wasn't all, and he knew it. But his arms tightened around her, and he kissed away any lingering fears.

As he'd expected, he loved this new phase of his job. He was strong, despite a deceptively slight physique, and he wasn't afraid of hard work. At first the driver and the other two deliverymen gave him the hardest jobs, standing to one side smoking and cursing as he hauled the largest boxes on his own. But after one good fistfight in which Liam proved his mettle, the men accepted his place on their team. He breathed the fresh air, took in the new, expanded sights and congratulated himself on a job well done.

One month later, after back-to-back deliveries all day and muscles that refused to relax, he jumped down from the truck for one final delivery near his own house. Whiskey Island held no fascination for Liam, despite stories that so many Irish had lived and died here. Now for the most part the island was the meeting place of ore and freight train, a business that continued around the clock.

He had heard about the saloons here, Fat Jacks and Corrigans, that had done a thriving business before Prohibition. The saloon keepers had rarely closed their doors, and their establishments had been places where a man could find friends for the price of a drink. He'd heard stories about another called Mother Carey's, where bank robbers once gathered to count their blessings.

"Let's get this done quick," the driver said. Herman was a giant with a pencil-thin mustache and overalls that ended above the ribbed cuffs of his hand-knit socks. When he lent his considerable weight to the task, the crew could finish twice as fast.

Liam looked for a sign in front of the small warehouse but saw none. The building was long and low, and the watchman who let them inside used a shotgun to point to a dirt-floored corner where a space had been cleared. After the first flash of interest Liam hauled and stacked boxes mindlessly until Herman cocked his head toward the corner.

"Some of that whiskey you Paddies like so much starts out right here," he said in a low voice.

Liam raised a brow. If he'd given the matter any thought he would have known. The building lacked a sign or any evidence of real work being done. The Volstead Act had created an entirely new breed of businessman, not only those who operated small stills from their basements or attics, or even those who supplied them with corn sugar and markets for their product, but an entirely different type of bootlegger. Rumrunners, they were called. Canada was directly across the lake, and Canada had no intention of changing its own laws just because its foolish neighbor to the south was so self-righteous.

"I just stack boxes," Liam said. "What they do with them is their own concern."

Herman straightened and rested his hands against the small of his back. "We're done. I'll do the papers. Wait outside if you want."

Liam made his way outside, glad to be finished for the day. Brenna had promised fish for supper, a rare enough treat even though a lake as large as an ocean taunted them with its hidden splendors. Afterward he had promised Irene a stroll, just the two of them through the crowded streets of the Angle, the larger area surrounding Irishtown Bend, while Brenna cleaned the kitchen. He had no memories of such simple pleasures with his own father.

The other men were leaning against the truck smoking, and since he had used all the tobacco for his own pipe there was no point in joining them. He decided to walk along the dirt lane running away from the warehouse to stretch his legs. Herman would stop and pick him up on the way back to the factory, but in the meantime, he would get a little air. He shouted his intentions to the others and started up the hill. At the junction with another larger road he turned right. This section of

Whiskey Island wasn't well traveled, but two cars quickly passed him, whipping up a dust storm in their wake. He had just enough time to jump to the roadside, and he frowned and cursed. "Be Jaysus!"

He marched to the center of the road and shook his fist after them until there was nothing but the glint of a rear bumper in the dust cloud. He was so angry he almost missed the roar of another car coming up behind him. He jumped to the roadside again, still cursing, and whirled to see this car coming directly toward him. The driver had the entire road, but in one horrifying instant, Liam saw that the man's head was turned, as if he was watching for something or someone behind him.

Liam scrambled backward and shouted, but before he could leap far enough out of the way, the car had swerved farther toward him, and suddenly he was flying through the air.

He landed in a broken heap fifteen yards away. The driver didn't even slow down. Liam, unfortunately still conscious, watched him speed away.

The foreman at the box factory was truly sorry, but what could he offer Liam now? There were no jobs available in the office, even if Liam was fit enough to do them. Until it was entirely mended, Liam could not stand for hours manning machinery on his bad leg. He could not lift crates with an injured back that might never heal properly. The company was family owned and certainly not heartless. Out of respect they gave him two weeks' pay and their sincere condolences.

"What will do we do?" Brenna asked, staring at what little was left after she'd paid that month's rent and bought potatoes, flour and milk. "I'll do anything I can, Liam, but I don't know where to begin."

Liam knew that this was the moment when having family was important. Unfortunately, his subdued inquiries hadn't turned up any leads in that direction. He and Brenna were alone in Cleveland, and there was certainly no one in Ireland to turn to.

"One thing the sisters taught well was how to care for a house," Brenna said, when he didn't answer. "I'll find work of some sort, but will you be able to care for Irene while I'm away?"

Liam knew better than to sink into false pride, which wouldn't keep food on their table. "I'll mend quickly. You won't have to scrub a rich woman's floors forever, Brenna."

She kissed his hand; then she plumped the pillow behind him. "It was just like you, wasn't it, Liam, being right in the thick of things? Even when nobody seemed to be around?"

"Don't you think I've asked myself how this happened? Fate had a good laugh at our expense, didn't she?"

The police had questioned Liam about the accident repeatedly. Along the way he had learned what had transpired right before he was hit. The dry agent's routine search. The bootlegger's tire iron. The men's escape. The dry agent had suffered a nasty concussion, but he, at least, had the government's help as he recovered. Liam had only a raft of questions he couldn't answer.

"And you still remember nothing of what you saw?" Brenna asked. "Nothing about the car? Nothing you could tell the policemen?"

He grimaced as he tried to move his foot, elevated on a wooden crate topped with a pillow. "Not a bit of it's clear to me."

Brenna looked as if she wanted to say more. But what was there to say? She'd been married to Liam long enough to know that once he made up his mind, he wouldn't change it. If he said he remembered nothing, he would go to his grave claiming that very thing.

"Mrs. O'Reilly down the road will watch Irene tomorrow while I look for work," Brenna said, rising to her feet. "After that I'll be leaving her here with you, Liam, but Mrs. O'Reilly will get the midday meal."

"The moment I'm better, I'll find another job."

"I know you will." She smiled warmly. "We'll get through this time. We had a bit of luck already."

At the moment he was too discouraged to know what she meant.

"You're alive." She shook her finger at him. "And only by the grace of God."

During the next week, he wasn't sure that surviving had been a lucky thing. He had endured more than his share of pain since early childhood and had thought himself immune to it. But the agony in his back was nearly beyond bearing. Irene seemed to sense it, and she acted the part of an angel, playing quietly in the corner, taking naps when told to, waiting for the arrival of Mrs. O'Reilly if she needed anything.

The old woman was blunt but kind enough. She brought food at noon, helped Liam outside to take care of his needs, helped him back in once he'd finished. Brenna found a job keeping house for an old woman and her three spinster daughters, and even though they were impossibly demanding, they treated her well enough, sending food home each night and handing on clothes they no longer wore. She took some of the clothes apart and used the fabric to sew dresses for Irene and quilts for their bed, staying up late each night and working by the light of a kerosene lamp.

At the end of the month Liam could make the trip out to the privy by himself using a crutch Brenna had brought home for him. The pain in his back was still fierce, but easing a bit each day. He'd discovered that, despite doctor's orders, a little movement made things better, not worse. He began to believe he might recover.

"There aren't as many jobs as there were at first," he told Brenna the next morning. Last evening she had brought him a newspaper, and he had been up since dawn poring over it and circling the few possibilities.

"The times are good, aren't they? I always hear it's so."

"Aye, but apparently not here so much as other places."

"But won't you be hired back at the box factory once you're well?"

He had explored that avenue when Herman the truck driver came for a surprise visit. "Not likely," Liam told her now. "Orders have dropped. They've laid off men who went to work there before I did."

"There will be something, Liam." She laid her hand on his. "There's always something, isn't there?"

There wasn't. By the time he could walk without a crutch and stand nearly upright, the economy of Cleveland had hit a downturn. On Brenna's day off he walked slowly through the streets, waiting painfully in lines to make applications for menial jobs but never getting as far as an interview. He tried gardening for hire with Irene in tow, but found that constant stooping made the muscles in his back freeze up again. He tried washing windows and discovered that constant reaching did the same.

"I'm running out of ideas," he told Brenna that night. He felt useless, and angry at his own limitations. Brenna's job paid barely enough to survive on. Another crisis would destroy them.

Brenna was growing thin-faced and tight-lipped from her long hours at work, but she patted his hand without complaining. "Just keep trying, Liam. I know you can find something. I believe in you."

The next morning he saw her off to work, then settled himself on the old bench overlooking their street of miserable hovels. Today he couldn't see the pride, the industry of some of his neighbors, the garden two doors away with shoulder-high hollyhocks, the new paint and porch on the house across the street. He saw despair and poverty, as if a filter had been placed over his eyes, the emerald-green filter of his island home.

He had never missed Ireland as much as he did at that moment.

A car chugged up the street, not a common sight in the Angle. This particular car was far less common than most, a distinctive and elegant example, in a different class from the common Model T that Liam hopelessly coveted. The sedan was shining black, with polished gold trim and high seats that looked as soft as a featherbed. The huge headlights glowed like a tiger's eyes. Two men sat in the front, and one sat alone in the back. Even from a distance, Liam felt certain that the man in the back was the one to take seriously.

He rose when the car stopped in front of his house. He waited stoically but poised on the balls of his feet. Liam knew trouble when he saw it.

"You Liam Tierney?" the driver asked. He was short and muscular, and both his hair and his mustache were slick with pomade.

"Who's asking?"

"I'm asking," said the man in the back. He had waited to exit until the other man in the front raced around to open his door. Now he stepped onto the spotless white running board and finally down to the ground. His lackey took out a handkerchief and wiped the board clean in the seconds after his foot left it.

"Tim McNulty's my name." He stepped closer, but stopped just below the stairs. Liam looked down on him, noting the broad forehead, close set eyes, portly physique and, most of all, the hand-tailored suit with its gleaming brass buttons and folded linen handkerchief.

"What can I do for you?" Liam asked.

"I'm here to inquire about your accident."

Liam shoved his hands in his pockets, but his hands were fists by the time they entered. "And why is that?"

McNulty took his time responding. His gaze flicked up and down the front of the Tierneys' house. His eyebrows grew together in such a thicket that they appeared to be one. He raised half now. "You haven't done well for yourself here, have you, Paddy?"

Liam gave a snort. "Not as well as you have...Paddy."

A faint smile played at the corner of McNulty's lips. The man beside him, the oversized brute who had escorted him from the car, made a sound low in his throat and started toward Liam, but McNulty held him back with a gesture.

"Yes, my family started out here," McNulty conceded. "A little higher up the hill, perhaps. A good wind and you'll be floating down the river."

Liam waited.

"You've recovered? From the accident?" McNulty asked at last.

"I don't know what concern it is of yours."

"I've come to help you." McNulty snapped his fingers, and the man beside him grudgingly pulled an envelope from his suit and held it out to Liam.

Liam continued to wait.

"Take it up to him," McNulty told his henchman.

The man started up the stairs, stopping before he reached Liam. He outweighed Liam by a hundred pounds at least, but he stayed where he was and extended the envelope again.

Liam reached for it, expecting an attack, but there was none. He opened the envelope and flipped through a dazzling collection of bills, more than he had ever seen in one place. He looked down at McNulty. "And?"

"You don't think this is simple charity?" McNulty laughed. "That's the Irish for you, lad."

"What exactly do you want from me?"

"Just the description you gave the police. The description of the car that nearly killed you."

Any hope Liam had entertained died immediately. He held the envelope out to return it, but the henchman had abandoned the stairs. "I don't want your money," Liam said. "Not a penny. Thanks all the same."

"Just a description." McNulty fingered his watch chain, a fine shimmer of delicate gold. "So very, very simple. And who would know?"

"I didn't see a thing," Liam said. He knew better than to hope he could get inside again before the men tackled him. Even if he did, the lock was a flimsy affair, easily breached by a shoulder or punishing foot.

"That's not what you told the cops," the henchman said.

The man's voice was as robust as his physique. Liam was sure the sound had reached his neighbors, none of whom appeared to be outside. He glanced up and down the street. Apparently those with faraway jobs were already gone; those who worked nearby hadn't yet left. Or perhaps their sudden disappearance had occurred at the sight of McNulty's Cadillac.

"It's *exactly* what I told the cops," Liam said. "I don't know your interest in this and don't care to, but I have nothing to tell you."

"It's a lot of money. For very little."

Liam sighed, but it was time to end the charade. He took the money out of the envelope, and one by one he let the bills drift down to the steps below. But he wasn't so noble that between the first and the last he didn't think about all that the money could have bought.

No one moved. He looked up once he'd finished. "I saw nothing. I remember nothing." Because there was no other place to go, he turned and crossed the porch, as if to go inside.

As he'd expected, he didn't make it to the door. He heard the rush, felt the air stir, and whirled ready to defend himself. But there were two men after him, and he was not at his physical peak. Despite a sincere attempt to defend himself, he was knocked to the ground and pummeled repeatedly. Despite himself, he groaned when the driver kicked his recently mended leg. He writhed in silent agony when the henchman pounced on him and every muscle in his back spasmed in defense.

"Just the description," McNulty said, above him. "And they'll stop. It would be a shame to injure you permanently, lad."

Liam knew he might die there. He wondered if Irene was awake, listening to sounds of her father's murder. The thought made him furious, and he lashed out as best he could, but even fury was no match for two opponents.

"Stop," McNulty said calmly after a few more minutes of struggle and pain, and the men stopped. Liam could hardly see. His vision was blurred, both by blood dripping in his eyes and a nauseating dizziness.

McNulty stopped and frowned at him. "Just a word or two, lad, and we'll be gone, you'll be alive, and no real harm will be done. Just the color of the car? A number from the license plate?"

"The devil take you," Liam said. He saw a massive fist poised above his face and steeled himself to die silently.

"Enough," McNulty said. "Off him now. Good lads."

Liam sagged against the uneven boards as the henchman's punishing weight lifted. Every joint in his body felt as if it had been severed.

"Neither money nor death, Tierney? Nothing persuades you? We could ask your little lass what she knows, I suppose. Ask her if you've told her anything?"

"If you...touch her, I'll hunt you to...the ends of the earth!" The voice didn't sound like his own, even though he felt the words in his throat.

"Would you tell us in exchange for her life? Or your wife's, perhaps?" McNulty said.

"I have nothing to tell!"

"I have a daughter of my own." McNulty laughed without mirth. "Children are obstinate creatures, but I suppose they shouldn't be harmed for their fathers' failures."

He signaled the other two men, and they started down the steps. An astonished Liam managed to sit up, even though the world was whirling darkly around him and pain sizzled through every nerve.

At the car McNulty turned. "Keep the money," he said. "And report to me once your bruises heal. You want a job, lad? I have jobs for scrappers like you, men who know how to keep to themselves. You won't be making boxes again any time soon. Who knows, you might be able to buy the factory in a year or two."

He laughed at his own wit and climbed inside. The henchman closed the door and wiped the running board clean once more. Then he raised a massive hand to Liam before he went around the car and climbed inside.

Liam watched the men drive away. As if by magic, neighbors came out of their houses to go about their business, although all were careful not to look in his direction.

chapter 14

Father Ignatius Brady was a sparrow of a man who seemed to be composed of equal parts fasting and prayer. He looked like an ascetic, ate and drank with the enthusiasm of a dieting hedonist, and managed, through his many years of priestly service, to keep an authentic twinkle in his eye. He had been Niccolo's mentor since his ordination and had remained so when Niccolo withdrew from active priesthood. He had celebrated Niccolo's marriage and hoped to baptize his babies.

Now, however, Iggy was simply gazing at Niccolo's "miracle," the talk of St. Brigid's.

"I don't know, Niccolo. As fine an establishment as this one is, I never would have picked it as a shrine to the Blessed Virgin Mary."

"You see the resemblance?"

"I do now that I'm staring at it. But I wouldn't have noticed the stain at all if you hadn't pointed it out."

"It was hard to miss when I woke up under it that afternoon instead of at the pearly gates."

"You did have a close call."

"I looked up and she was crying."

Iggy faced him. "The Virgin or Megan?"

"Definitely the Virgin. Tears from the region of her eyes."

Iggy said nothing.

Niccolo turned back to the image, which sported no tears now. "I felt this sense of well-being and peace. It was indescribable."

"A natural reaction for a man who has just cheated death."

"I know. You don't have to worry about me. I'm a skeptic." He smiled a little at the memory. "But even Megan crossed herself when she looked up and saw the image."

"Now we *do* have something to worry about," Iggy said with a chuckle.

"What we really have to worry about is how to play this down."

Iggy knew exactly what Niccolo referred to. "Beatrice Lowell has been to see me."

Niccolo groaned.

Iggy patted his shoulder. "She's not a member of our parish, but I have spoken to her priest. He claims she's always had an active imagination and a consuming need for attention."

"Casey got Beatrice involved in the Albaugh Center's senior program. Meals, activities, field trips. I thought it would make enough of a difference in her life that she might not need to tell the story of her miracle cure over and over again."

"I'm afraid it backfired. Now she simply has a larger audience. She's still taking her arthritis medications, though. I wormed that much out of her. But she claims she's only doing it as insurance and doesn't need them at all."

"And does she still limp?"

"She doesn't look like a woman who's pain free."

"Apparently she has everyone at the center talking about this. I've had half a dozen—" Niccolo paused. "More like a dozen senior citizen calls, I guess. People want tours. As soon as they can get down here."

"These are difficult times, Niccolo. People everywhere are searching for proof that God exists and is working in their lives."

"There are a million genuine miracles every day. A fire-fighter goes into a burning building to rescue people he's never seen. A passerby takes off his coat on a cold winter day and gives it to a homeless man."

"But those are the hardest to see, Niccolo. Or the hardest to admit we've seen, because they make demands on the observer. Admit it's a miracle that one human being can sacrifice for another and you're suddenly called on to do the same. So it's easier to turn away. This image of Mary, on the other hand, doesn't ask anything of us, does it? Prayer, perhaps, but nothing more. She does the work. She performs the miracles and we accept. Nothing more is required."

"Should I close off the tunnel? Tell people there's nothing more to see? Or should I let this play itself out? People will notice Beatrice's limp and realize she hasn't been cured of anything. And there's a logical enough explanation for what happened to me."

"Can you close it? Or by doing so will you increase people's curiosity and their determination to see the image for themselves? Will you create a supernatural phenomenon through sheer mystery?"

Niccolo really didn't know. He did know one thing, though. "Megan wants me to close the doors. She's adamant."

"Does she?"

"This is a saloon, not a church. She has a point. All the fuss might scare away some of her loyal customers, good Catholics a number of them, who might think twice about drinking their pints of Guinness directly over an image of the weeping Virgin."

Iggy chuckled again, and Niccolo smiled in return. "She's not comfortable with miracles, my Megan. She's not comfortable with other people believing in them, either, particularly not in the family saloon."

"So she'd have you lock the door?"

"It will dry up eventually, Iggy. When the plumbing's all

ripped out and replaced. There's a pinhole leak somewhere above it, an improper fitting, or condensation where there shouldn't be. We'll find it and fix it, and the Virgin will simply go away."

"And in the meantime you'll lose weeks of opportunity to talk about this with the people who could have seen it, won't you?"

Iggy knew him too well. Niccolo reached out and traced one edge of the Virgin's cape. "Beatrice Stowell is only one person. There have been others. Skeptics, most of them. But this image makes people think. I don't know about what and wouldn't care to control it, anyway. But they leave thinking. Some of them feel they've witnessed something out of the ordinary, even if they don't believe it's what the most faithful say it is. And..."

"And how can that be bad?" Iggy finished for him.

"I like being here to show it to them. I like sharing those moments with them. I have no desire to return to active priesthood—"

"Besides, you have the small matter of a wife now."

Niccolo grinned. "Small in stature only. She's a giant."

"Your giant, though."

"But just because I no longer wear a dog collar doesn't mean that spiritual things aren't important to me. And sharing someone else's spiritual journey is a gift. I don't want to lose it until I have to."

Iggy was silent.

"A problem, huh?" Niccolo said.

"Not for me."

"No advice?"

"Just a question. Why are you talking to me? Why aren't you talking to Megan?"

Niccolo bought a picnic table for the end of the parking lot where the villainous maple tree once stood. With it he purchased twenty-four-inch terra cotta pots of marigolds and petunias to set along the perimeter, and two eight-foot sections of pine paling fencing to help screen off the Dumpster.

It wasn't exactly a Tuscan terrace, but it gave them all a secret hideaway where they could take a break and enjoy the sun while the renovations continued.

This afternoon Niccolo had promised Megan a romantic lunch. Marco, of whom she was growing very fond despite his inclination to call her Meg, had gone back to Pittsburgh for the weekend, and only a couple of the Brick kids were still around to help Niccolo install the kitchen tile later in the day. Right now the kids were inside, having their own picnic in the main floor storeroom, which had become an ersatz clubhouse.

"Greek olives," Niccolo said, taking a white paper carton out of a shopping bag. "Fresh bread from the West Side Market. Hungarian smoked sausage, strawberries—some of the prettiest I've seen— a really nice Gouda cheese. I bought pierogies for dinner. Josh loves them."

"So does Rooney." She felt vaguely guilty that Niccolo, who worked so hard, had been the one to provide this bounty. But only vaguely. It was so wonderful to be indulged, and even more wonderful just to have him to herself.

"And to drink?" she asked.

"Lemonade." He looked wistful. The man really did love a good red wine.

"That's better when you're working."

Niccolo had the hands of a working man, rough, callused, broad, but his fingers were long and tapering. For a moment she imagined them wrapped around a chalice or cradling a communion wafer.

"You look perplexed," he said, halting the parade of picnic fare. "Something wrong?"

She shook off the vision of her husband as a priest. "I'm starved, that's all. I can't seem to get enough to eat these days."

He went still. "There wouldn't be a reason for that, would there?"

The reason was anxiety, but she wasn't going to tell him so. And besides, he had something completely different on his mind. "Nick, don't get your hopes up. I'm still on the Pill."

Disappointment flicked across his face but disappeared quickly. "Well, I assumed you'd tell me if you weren't."

"I know you want a baby."

"Just me?" He kept his voice light, but she heard all the echoes of heavier issues.

"Someday it'll be both of us. But we've only been married a little while. Don't we need some time together first? Time to work things out before we add someone else to the mix?"

"What's to work out?"

He seemed truly oblivious. Anger flashed like lightning, then just as quickly disappeared. Wasn't she lucky that he was happy? That the tensions she felt were one-sided and therefore hers to resolve? How many women had a man who loved them so unconditionally?

And blindly.

"You don't look happy," he said.

"Nick, this isn't about whether I love you. You know that, don't you?"

"I don't know anything. I don't know where the worry is coming from."

"Worry isn't the right word. Not exactly, anyway. We just need to learn to live together, to figure out what's working for us and what's not."

"We lived together for almost two years."

"Not the same way. I kept my place in Lakewood and spent a lot of nights there. Either one of us had plenty of time to back out if things didn't go well."

"Backing out was the last thing on my mind. From the very first moment I met you."

His wonderful dark eyes were shining for her alone. Suddenly she was melting inside, and she was sorry. Because they were on the edge of something here that they needed to explore. And how could they, when all she wanted to do was find a quiet place to make love to him?

"I've never wanted to back out, either," she said softly. "But sometimes I was so afraid."

"Was?"

How could she answer that? She was afraid of different things now. Afraid that marriage had brought with it a complacency that swept away all unanswered questions. That her husband, having achieved the goal of marriage, saw no need to set new goals for their relationship. That Niccolo was going to move on without her and still expect her to be waiting by the fireside each night when he returned.

"Well, it's been an interesting start," she said. "You've got to admit it. We've been apart more than we've been together."

He looked genuinely perplexed. "I come home every night, Megan. I see you here every day."

She wondered why she needed more. And why he didn't.

"We don't have much of a chance to talk with saws buzzing and hammers pounding," she said carefully.

"This is about conversation?"

The lovely melting sensation was now as solid as stone. "Let's just keep it about conversation, shall we? How has your day gone so far? Tell me."

He finished taking the food out of his bag, as if he needed the time to settle down. "We're making progress in the kitchen. We'll be able to install the appliances next week, maybe even some of the new cabinets."

"Then I can cook lunch for everybody." She filled her plate, but the food that had looked so appetizing seemed to stick in her throat.

"Iggy came by this morning, while you were at the Historical Society," he said.

Megan had gone in early to see if she could discover more about Liam Tierney, but she'd been unsuccessful. Microfilm had no search function. She had looked through the papers for the two-week period before and after the date of the article that she had discovered in the tunnel, but she had learned nothing new. If there were more mentions of Liam later that year or beyond, she had no way of finding them except by going through the paper page by page.

She reached for the lemonade he had poured her. "What did Iggy say?"

"He found the image interesting."

"Not miraculous?"

"No, but it was good to talk to him. He always has something valuable to add to any question."

"He's been a good friend all these years, hasn't he?" She wanted to feel nothing but gratitude, and that *was* most of what she felt. But a part of her was worried. Niccolo had told her of the many long talks the two men had had during his priesthood, the retreats they'd attended together. She wanted them to remain friends, she wasn't that insecure, but she did fear the reminders of Niccolo's other life. Maybe she wouldn't if she and her husband had more to talk about themselves.

"He's a good friend," Niccolo said. "I told him you want to close the tunnel."

"And his response?"

"Questions. He wouldn't give an opinion. You know Iggy."

"I'm worried about the legal issues, too. Those tunnels have been closed off for years, and they were never exactly lawful. What if something happens while somebody's inside?"

"Marco and I did a cursory inspection. We can have them checked out by someone else if you'd like."

"By who, the city?"

He grimaced. "Probably not a good idea."

"It won't be that long before somebody reports us."

"And we can deal with it then."

They fell silent. Megan felt as if she'd gotten nowhere but didn't know a new direction to take.

Niccolo pushed food from one edge of his picnic plate to the other. At last he sighed. "I'm sorry, Megan. I know this is hard to understand. It's just that I really like showing people the image. Not because I believe it's divine, but because most people understand it for what it is, and in spite of that, something good seems to happen inside them when they look at it. I'm sharing something with them. I like the way that makes me feel."

"Did you just realize that? Because you never told me before."

"Didn't I?"

She was about to answer when she heard a noise from inside the saloon, or at least she thought that was where it had come from. A muffled thud that was oddly prolonged. She cocked her head. "Did you hear something?"

Niccolo was already on his feet. "Roy and Pete are probably up to something."

Roy and Pete were both high school dropouts, too old to go back to regular classes now, but struggling with their GEDs at Niccolo's insistence. Megan liked both of them but didn't find either of them as trustworthy as most of the other Brick kids. Pete, who was blond enough to be Scandinavian, claimed he was a direct descendant of Chief Crazy Horse, and he seemed determined to prove that connection by his behavior. All discussions of Crazy Horse's *real* contributions to the Oglala Sioux, the chief's outstanding courage and leadership, had so far gone unheeded.

"Want me to come?" Megan asked.

"No, I'll be right back."

She watched him disappear through the back door. She was sorry they had been interrupted. Again they had seemed on the verge of real communication.

She was just finishing her lemonade when Niccolo came to the door. "I don't see them."

She heard the worry. "The tunnel?"

"Could be."

She stood and followed him through the saloon. The new front door was still locked, so clearly they hadn't gone out that way.

"I've been trying to get Roy to stop smoking when he's here," Niccolo said. "But he sneaks behind my back."

"Tobacco or other things?"

"Tobacco. I hope." Drugs were absolutely forbidden, and each Brick kid had to sign an agreement that he or she would stay free of them while participating in the program. "Let's go down and see if they're there," Niccolo said. The unspoken corollary was to go quietly. If the kids were up to something, it was Niccolo's job to know about it.

Megan hoped they would simply find the boys having a smoke. But that didn't jibe with the noise she'd heard. Perhaps they'd slammed the door at the bottom of the stairs going into the storage area down below. Or they'd brushed something on a shelf and it had fallen.

She grabbed a flashlight on her way down and followed Niccolo. The door was ajar, and no one was in the furnace room, but the light was on. She flipped on the flashlight and followed Niccolo into the tunnel.

She was just behind him, and she nearly crashed into him when he stopped abruptly. "Good God," he said. "Are you boys all right?"

Megan peered around him and saw why he'd stopped. The two boys stood motionless in a sea of plaster and concrete rubble.

"The ceiling fell, Nick." Pete's voice was shaking. He didn't sound like a wild man now. He sounded like a little boy who had just seen the monsters in his closet.

"Are you all right?" Nick repeated.

"I think so."

Nick was picking his way forward by then. The boys were standing in front of the Virgin. The ceiling there was intact. Not so the area before and just after it. Megan was reminded of the tornado, a reminder she'd hoped to avoid for the rest of her life.

"How did this happen?" Nick said.

"We just wanted to see what was behind it. You know. A leak or something, like you said. There's like a gap between the wall and the ceiling. I got on Roy's shoulders, and we were doing fine, but then he started to sway and I got scared, and I grabbed one of the beams up there, and Roy crashed against the wall, and I was left swinging, and the board groaned—"

Nick held up his hand for silence. "I get the picture."

"It all came crashing down. Everything. All around us. But I wasn't touched." In the beam of her flashlight, Megan saw him turn to Roy. "You either, right?"

"I'm okay. Yeah, sure."

"I don't know what you loosened up. The beam looks fine. But we'd better all get out of here until we can make sure this isn't going to happen again," Niccolo said.

"We could have been killed," Pete said. "Like dead."

"If we'd been standing over there," Roy said.

Pete began to sound more like himself. "You think it was a miracle, Nick? Like people are saying? Another miracle? If we hadn't been standing right here—"

"I think we'd better get out of here," Niccolo said. "That's what I think. Stay there and let me clear some of the rubble so you can get through without falling. Megan, hold both the lights."

She grabbed his and watched him haul chunks of concrete out of the way. The boys picked their way through after a minute, and the four of them started down the tunnel.

She was already several yards away when she stopped, turned and trained her light on the image of the Virgin. Just as she feared, water was trickling from the Virgin's eyes.

chapter 15

Tippy's sister Shannon was more enthusiastic than knowledgeable, but she was a quick learner. She wanted to teach, and that was why she came out to Tierney Cottage three times a week, to learn what she could and earn a little money besides. Her love for children was real, and once she'd got used to Kieran, she had grown fond of him, too.

But not today.

"He won't do anything. Not one thing." Shannon was discouraged and growing more so. Peggy understood only too well how the girl was feeling.

"We all have days like that, I guess." Peggy watched her son throw himself to the floor and kick his little legs. It wasn't the first time that day, and she was afraid it wouldn't be the last.

"He's getting worse." Being blunt was part of Shannon's nature and usually not a problem.

Today Peggy felt a surge of anger. Not so much at Shannon, she supposed, as at life in general. She rarely indulged in anger or self-pity, but sometimes they indulged themselves.

She forced herself to model the patience she demanded of Shannon. "He's not worse. He's just not making any gains right now."

"Well, when I first came he'd sit quietly for a few moments, and he'd point. He'd even listen while I read to him."

Shannon was a pretty girl, with a broad freckled face and curly black hair. Peggy remembered when she'd been sixteen herself and believed that hard work and tolerance could change the world.

"I know you're disappointed," Peggy said. "I'm afraid that's part of the game."

"At least *I* can go home at the end of the afternoon."

Peggy thought that was a particularly mature observation. Shannon might be frustrated, but she recognized how much more frustrated Peggy must feel. In Shannon's blunt way, it was a stab at sympathy.

"Why don't you go home now?" Peggy said, standing up and purposely turning her back on her son. "You're right. You're not getting anywhere with him today, and it's not your fault. He's just having a bad time. Didn't you say you had a play to attend tonight?"

"It won't feel right, leaving you this way."

Peggy put a hand on the girl's square shoulder. "You're a good teacher's aid, Shannon. I don't know what I ever did without you. But there's no point in banging our heads against the wall."

"You ought to tell *him* that. Or the floor, for that matter."

Peggy smiled thinly. "A lot of good it would do, huh? Anyway, you go on. Full pay for the week anyway. You did your best."

Shannon looked longingly at the door.

"Go on," Peggy insisted. "I'll see you on Monday." She watched the girl stop in the living room to say goodbye to Irene before she bolted for the front door. Irene shuffled to the classroom doorway.

"She didn't stay long today." She looked at Peggy, not at the screaming toddler.

Once again Peggy was gratified that this woman, who had never had children of her own, could be so understanding about Kieran. She joined Irene and tried to make herself heard. "He's been a little monster today."

"Maybe he needs a rest, dear."

"I'd agree, but he's had more than usual. We've taken off early every day this week."

"He did have quite a siege with that tooth. Maybe he's still recovering."

Peggy didn't know what the problem was. She had been so sure the small gains Kieran had made were only the start of something bigger and better. Now, despite what she'd said to Shannon, she was afraid those were gone, as well.

"I'll find something quiet to do with him. I'm sorry."

"I'm only sorry he's not having a better day." Irene patted Peggy's shoulder before she left.

Kieran began to tire, and the tantrum ebbed. Peggy wanted nothing more than to pick him up and cuddle him, but she knew that was the last thing *he* would want. One of the saddest things about Kieran's autism was the way it worked against all her natural biological impulses. The comfort she yearned to give was like a match to dry tinder.

She searched the room for something that might interest him and saw a rag doll on the shelf in the corner. Bridie had appeared with it one afternoon, salvaged from some Shanmullin resident. Peggy had carefully washed and dried the doll, but she hadn't yet used it in play, afraid that with this, like his stuffed animals, Kieran would be more interested in picking apart loose threads.

Desperate, she decided to try it anyway.

"What a pretty girl," she said, taking the doll off the shelf. She pretended to ignore her son. "A pretty girl with pretty eyes." Peggy touched the eyes.

She knew she was using too many words if her point was to teach him the word *eyes,* but she was more interested in distracting him now. One goal at a time.

She sat in the armchair in the corner and put the doll on her lap facing her. She began to sing "An Irish Lullaby." Maybe it wasn't authentically Irish, but it had been good enough for Bing Crosby, and it was close enough for her purposes.

"Too-ra-loo-ra-loo-ral. Too-ra-loo-ra-li..." She thought she sounded pretty good, considering. Even though she wanted to scream her frustration, she kept her voice serene.

Kieran's legs flailed once, twice, then stopped. He didn't particularly like music, but something about her performance caught his attention.

"It's an I—I—rish Lull—aby," she finished. She remembered Megan singing the song to her when she was very young. Megan had certainly sung it better, but never with better effect. Kieran was silent now. Music therapy to the rescue.

Encouraged, she decided another song was in order. She settled for something all-American. "Hush little baby, don't say a word..." She stroked the doll's hair as she sang, paying no attention to her son. "If that mockingbird don't sing..." She always forgot the rest of the words, but it was more fun to make them up, anyway.

Out of the corner of her eye, she saw Kieran rising from the floor. She made a mental note to herself. This was working. Anything that worked was worth trying again. She might have stumbled on a combination here that appealed to the little boy, and hope nibbled the edges of the day's disappointment.

Kieran took one step in her direction. She didn't look at him, made no fast moves. She just let him come closer, a step at a time. She sang softer, nonsense words that didn't even rhyme. It didn't matter.

She loved this child, and she wanted so desperately to make things right for him. If she could just nudge him in the right direction. Gently. Slowly. Lovingly.

"If that billy goat bumps his head, Mama's going to buy a loaf of bread..."

He was standing right in front of her now, holding out his tiny little hand. She stopped singing. "Doll," she said softly. "Does Kieran want the doll?"

He didn't move away, though of course he didn't answer. Not even his favorite word, *no*. He just stood there, hand extended.

She thought she heard the door swing open, and she bet Irene had come to see if Kieran was doing better. She didn't hazard a glance. She didn't want anything to distract her son.

"Doll." She lifted the doll from her lap and held it out to him. "Kieran's doll."

For a moment she wasn't sure he would take it. Then he grabbed it, and, using the doll like a club he began to beat her with it.

Peggy sat in astonished silence for a moment. The doll was soft. There was no way he could hurt her, but his intention was clear. He wanted to. It was the supreme failure of her week. She was devastated, and her sharp gasp told the story.

"Kieran!"

He didn't seem to hear her. He beat her harder.

Peggy leaped to her feet. "Kieran, no!"

She picked him up, and he hit her again before she could wrench the doll from his determined grasp. "No!"

She dropped the doll on the chair, and he tried to dive for it. He began to scream and kick, managing to land one good thrust against her hip before she could prevent it.

She had never, in her entire life, wanted so badly to strike back.

She was prevented from considering it by a pair of strong arms. In a moment Kieran was out of hers and safely ensconced in Finn O'Malley's.

Peggy burst into tears.

"You stay here," Finn said. "Don't follow us."

He turned and left the classroom with the screaming child held away from his chest. Peggy gasped and ran after them, but Finn turned. His face was stern. "Do you need help or not?"

She wanted to say no, but she couldn't.

Her expression must have been answer enough. "Stay here, Peggy."

This time she didn't follow.

Somehow she ended up in the living room. Somehow she

ended up with Irene's bony arms around her and a cold cloth for her eyes.

"I shouldn't have come to Ireland," Peggy said. "You don't need this."

"On the contrary, it's exactly what I need, don't you see? I've had none of this in my life. I needed some before I died."

"Don't talk about dying!"

"I suppose the timing's not good, is it? There's a good girl. Have a good cry. Kieran's in the best of hands."

"Finn hates kids. He hates me. And I don't take it personally, you know. He hates everyone except you, and maybe Bridie."

"He hates no one except himself. Forgiveness is a long time coming for our Finn. But I'm hopeful."

"I'm a failure," Peggy said.

"You're a woman with a difficult task ahead of you and no guarantees. That's hardly the same thing."

"This isn't really me, you know. I'm the sister with her head on straight."

"Your head looks just fine to me, crooked or not."

Peggy stopped in the middle of another sob. A giggle bubbled out instead. "Aren't I supposed to be helping you? Isn't that why I came?"

"You help me more than you'll ever know." Irene patted her hand.

"Where did they go, do you suppose?" Peggy said.

"It doesn't matter, but they're together, and that's what counts. The two of them have so much in common, don't you know?"

Peggy looked up. She wasn't sure what Irene meant.

"Walled away from everything and everybody, both of them," Irene said. "Kieran can't connect to people, and Finn? Well, he simply refuses to. Perhaps they understand each other in a way that we can't. Perhaps after a time they can help each other move into the world."

Peggy felt fresh tears welling in her eyes.

Finn stayed for supper. He wasn't sure why, except that he didn't want to go home. After school, Bridie had gone to the country to spend the weekend with a classmate. He had wanted her to go away. Now he was almost sorry he'd said yes. Bridie was the sunshine peeking through the dark windows of his life, and even though he knew a child should never be burdened with an adult's happiness, he still missed her when she was gone.

He was careful, of course, never to tell her so.

"You're sure you didn't drug him?" Peggy asked as she passed a platter of baked parsnips. Beside her, Kieran was barely able to keep his eyes open. The spoon that had been his cherished companion for several weeks lay idly in front of him now. What little he'd eaten, some brown bread dipped in milk, he'd eaten with his fingers.

"He needed fresh air and silence." Finn took the platter and added the parsnips to a plate heaped with fresh salmon and boiled potatoes.

"He needed some time away from his mother." Peggy smiled, as if to say she knew the truth and was fine anyway.

There were few women who were still pretty after a storm of tears. Unfortunately, Peggy Donaghue was one of them. She had wiped her nose and dabbed her eyes, and even though her color was still high, she looked lovely. Sheila, whose complexion matched her pale hair, had looked splotchy and bloated for days after a good sob, and no one had remarked on it as much as she.

"He liked the view from my shoulders." Finn took a bite, then another. The food was delicious. He knew Nora had gone home at noon, which meant Peggy had cooked the salmon while he and Kieran were walking.

"I used to carry him in a backpack when he was smaller. Your shoulders felt like old times, I guess."

"Maybe his father carries him that way?" Finn knew that Peggy and Kieran's father weren't married, but Irene had told him their relationship was cordial.

"I don't think that's it. Phil's never been around much," Peggy said matter-of-factly.

Finn wondered about a man who could abandon both Peggy and his own child. Despite himself, he wanted to know more.

Peggy got to her feet, even though the meal had just begun. "I'm sorry, but I think you'd better excuse me. I'm going to put Kieran to bed. I'll be back."

"We'll be right here," Irene said.

"That was good of you," Irene continued, when Peggy and Kieran were gone. "Taking the boy that way for her. She's consumed by him, you know. The most conscientious mother I've had the pleasure to know, but it tires her more than she lets on."

He searched for something to say and found little. "It was the least I could do. Peggy's good to Bridie," he said at last. "And *for* her."

"I doubted you'd noticed."

"I'm not as oblivious to what's going on around me as you think."

"Resistant though, dear. Far too resistant."

"I don't know why you put up with me."

"Nor do I. I suppose it's your sainted grandmother guiding my steps from heaven."

He laughed, but he was afraid she wasn't joking. He was also afraid that before too long there would be two meddling old women in heaven trying to shape his life. He wondered if Peggy realized just how ill Irene was, and how small her chance of living long enough to see any real improvement in Kieran.

Peggy returned when he was halfway through his salmon. "I'm sorry, but I was afraid we'd have another scene if I didn't get him to sleep."

"I didn't hear a lullaby." He began to hum the one she'd been singing when he came into the classroom.

Peggy blushed. "That backfired, didn't it?"

"Autistic children often have hypersensitive auditory systems and no ability to screen out or make sense of sound. Combine that with your appalling voice, and it's good cause for a tantrum."

Peggy's head snapped up, but when she saw he was smiling, she burst into laughter. "So that was the problem." She held her napkin to her mouth, but the sputters continued around it. "Oh Lord, I was just trying to help him."

Irene was laughing now, and Finn found himself laughing, too.

"My father can sing. My oldest sister sings beautifully. Casey's passable, but I can hardly carry a tune. Why is that?"

"I'd say it's justice," Finn said. "I doubt they're as beautiful as you."

Peggy looked stunned. Finn was stunned that he'd said the words out loud.

"The Lord parcels out His gifts," Irene said. "And you've the Irish gift of blarney, Finn. Eat your supper now, before it grows icicles."

Finn washed the dishes, despite Peggy's repeated admonitions that he'd done enough.

"You've no concept, do you, of all the poor Irish mothers who longed their entire lives for their husbands and sons to help in the kitchen? The tide turns, and you swim against it?"

She laughed. Finn was someone different tonight, and she liked this new version enormously. He was allowing her to dry, so she stood beside him, carefully wiping each dish with a freshly laundered tea towel.

"Bridie's really been looking forward to this weekend," she said. "She talked about it all week."

"She's not happy in town. It's better for me, because I have people there who can look after her while I'm at work. But she likes to be outdoors. She had a pony, and I had to sell him when we moved."

"She said the friend she's visiting has ponies and they'll go riding."

"The parents are good people, and they invite her whenever they can."

"She's a wonderful little girl. Well, not so little, I guess. Before too long she'll be thinking about boys the way she's thinking about ponies."

"And I'll be out of my depth."

"Well, you were a boy once. That gives you a different kind of advantage. You can tell her what they're thinking."

"I can tell her that they *aren't* thinking, more likely."

She dried the final dish. Finn washed like a pro, not like most men, who felt that whatever spots or flecks of food they left were good seasoning for the next meal. She was surprised how homey working in the kitchen together felt. He was the most difficult man she'd ever met, at least the most difficult man who had interested her. When he dropped that pose, though—and more and more, she thought it was a pose to keep people at arm's length—he was warm and funny and intelligent. Those were the big three as far as she was concerned. Four—remarkably attractive—was the bonus that tied the other three together in an irresistible package.

"I owe you an apology." Finn faced her, leaning against the sink with his arms folded.

She didn't wave the offer away. Apology was good for the soul—that had been drummed into her by the other stubborn women in her family.

"I reacted badly the night I told you I was an alcoholic. I didn't want your understanding. I'm still not sure I do, but I do want your forgiveness."

This, too, was new to her. True, most of the men she'd known had little to apologize for. She had chosen them for the minimum of effort she'd had to put into knowing them. But when they had erred, most of them hadn't been willing to admit it. Phil, on learning of her pregnancy, had even blamed her for asking him to use a condom instead of taking care of birth control by herself.

"I appreciate the apology, Finn." She felt she needed to do more. He stood there, proud, alone, arms wrapped around his chest as if he expected her to come after him with her fists.

She took a step and touched his arm, just the lightest touch of her fingertips. It was rock-hard, as much from tension as a working man's well-developed muscles. "Would you like to go for a walk? I know you have already, you and Kieran. But I'd love to be outside for a little while, just to smell the ocean. I can't be gone long."

"It'll do you good."

"And how. Just let me get my windbreaker."

He was waiting outside, stooping and conversing with Banjax, when she joined him. The dog's head was cocked, as if he was following the topic with interest and just waiting his own turn to respond.

"I see Bridie's not the only animal lover in the family," Peggy said.

He got to his feet. "I'm glad Irene took him in. I don't think Bridie would have forgiven me if his life had ended badly."

"Irene's thrilled to have him here, though she'll never admit it."

"I'm sure she wonders what will happen to him when she dies."

It was the second time that day that Irene's death had been mentioned. From the beginning, Peggy had known that the old woman was dying. But she didn't want reminders. She wanted to enjoy this unexpected and very welcome link to her ancestors.

"Maybe Irene will outlast Banjax," Peggy said.

"You were a medical student." It wasn't a question.

They started down the lane. There was a well-worn path through the fields that led to a rocky shelf overlooking the ocean, and Peggy planned to take it.

"You're doing a great deal to make her final days good ones," Finn said, after they'd made the turn into the field.

She heard the subtext. *Despite what I suspected.* "I think that's another apology."

"Not at all. I had every reason to worry about Irene and want to protect her. How could I know you'd turn out to be a blessing, not a curse?"

"I doubt she felt I was much of a blessing this afternoon. Kieran's behavior was enough to give a healthy woman a heart attack."

"She relishes having you here. Irene has always been resourceful, and well able to keep herself busy and happy. I think when she was younger, living alone suited her well enough. But now she needs companionship. I've tried to tell her that for years."

"You just didn't expect the answer to be a young American woman with a difficult toddler."

"I didn't."

"I don't know what I expected, Finn. I'm normally rational to a fault. I think everything through and act on my conclusions. I believed if I could just get Kieran to myself, if I could just find a way to work with him for hours every single day, that his behavior would shape up, that he'd have a chance at something like a normal life. I didn't realize what a drain he'd be on me and, I'm afraid, on Irene, as well."

"You expected him to become normal in a month or two?"

She silently debated the question, but in the end she shook her head. "No. At first I was sure the doctors were wrong. It was his hearing, or attention deficit disorder, or something else we could fix with surgery or medication. But that only lasted a few days. Once I began in-depth reading, I realized the way everything fit together. And the long-range prognosis."

"There's a wide range of behaviors, as well as potential."

"I don't know what normal means anymore, but I don't expect his autism to disappear. I know it's going to be part of who he is for the rest of his life. But there's hope because we've caught it so early. Some autistic kids go on to college, to professions, to marriages. I want the best for him, the best he's capable of. That's all."

They walked in silence for a few minutes. Finn was the one to break it. "Perhaps I'm out of line here, but I don't think that's all you want." They had reached a group of boulders, Mother Nature's benches, overlooking the water. Finn put his foot on one and stared out at the ocean. "I think you want to make amends to him."

She sat on the boulder beside his, but she looked up at him, not at the water. The sun had gone down, and the rising moon was one sliver from being full. Already the countryside was bathed in an heirloom sterling glow. "There's autism in Phil's family. He has an autistic brother, who was born two years after he was. Phil's parents chose to put him in a residential treatment center after the diagnosis was made."

"Does Phil want the same for his son?"

"Phil can't articulate his feelings, so I'll probably never know what he wants. He married last year, and his wife got pregnant immediately. I do know he's worried that this new child might be autistic, too, even though researchers haven't completely proved there's a precise genetic link."

"He feels guilty about Kieran anyway. Is that what you're saying? Even if he can't say so?"

"I think he does."

"And what is it you feel guilty about, Peggy?"

She had hoped she was steering the conversation away from that. She was surprised he had followed up. "We have mental health issues in our family. I told you about my father. But I don't have any real reason to think my genes had much to do with it."

He was silent. She suspected he was waiting.

"I should have been there for him," she said at last.

"Kieran?"

"I thought I could have it all." She swivelled to look out over the ocean to Clare Island. "I was going to be Super-Single-Parent, a heroine worthy of her own Marvel Comics series. I finished college while I was pregnant, took a little time off after he was born, then plunged right into medical school. I'd planned to wait a full year, but Kieran was in such good hands. I had family clamoring to take care of him, and he didn't seem to need me, the way some children do. I thought that was because he'd always had so many people making a fuss over him. And they all adored him. What could be wrong with letting them help?"

"What could be?"

"You've been to medical school. I'm sure it's the same here as it is in the States. All-consuming."

"I still haven't caught up on my sleep."

He was encouraging her to talk. She knew it, and it made her uncomfortable, but still she couldn't stop. "I wanted to be a good doctor. I tried to spend as much time with Kieran as I could, but my time was limited. And when I was with him, my attention wasn't focused on him. He didn't seem to care, and I let that guide me. His needs were being met by people who cherished him, and I was preparing for a career that would support us well. I was even going to find a specialty with regular hours, so that I could be around for those weekend soccer games and Cub Scout campouts."

"And now you feel guilty about all that time away from him. Even though you know—since you say you've done all the research—that children like Kieran are born, not made."

She was silent, because of course she felt guilty. She had abandoned her son. Yes, to loving caretakers. Yes, in the name of a better future. But she had adored medical school and everything that went with it. As her own child deteriorated, her personal dreams had been fulfilled. And she had missed the signs.

"I should have known." Simple, forthright and true. "I'm his mother."

"But you don't want to be his mother, do you? At least not sometimes, like today. And that's what you feel the worst about."

"He's my son. I love him."

"I have no doubt of that."

The silence stretched. Moonlight sparkled on the water now, and stars had begun to appear.

"There are days when I wish things were different," she conceded. She didn't know why she was telling Finn this, when she'd never said the words before.

He countered. "Every parent would say the same. Even parents of the most relentlessly normal children."

"I think he deserves better." Her voice dropped. It was barely audible to her own ears. "He deserves endless patience, unlimited resources, a mother who wakes up every morning knowing exactly what to do and how to do it. A father who's involved in his life on every level."

"Unfortunately, children are born on earth, not in heaven."

"I try not to have unreasonable expectations of myself. I really do. But there are days..."

He joined her on the rock, which surprised her. They sat shoulder to shoulder, like two people comfortable together.

"Let me tell you what I see," Finn said. "Enthusiasm and intelligence. Someone who saw the signs while her son was still young enough for the best outcome from intensive treatment. A woman with a sense of humor about her own shortcomings. More patience than any two women I've known. Look at the way you supervise Kieran's diet, Peggy. Only the freshest, purest ingredients. No sugar or additives. The well-thought-out educational plans, the constant striving. Coming all the way to Ireland, with no guarantees, because it seemed like the best choice for helping him."

"I'm no saint. Some mornings I wake up and I'm not sure which foot to put on the floor. I feel at sea when I'm working with Kieran and nothing's going right. I never wanted to be a teacher. I miss being in school. I wonder if I'll ever be able to pursue a medical career."

"Would you send him back if you could?"

"What, trade him in for a more normal model?"

"Supposing you could?"

She considered. "Can I keep Kieran and just trade in his neurological system?"

Finn laughed. She liked the sound. It was robust and unfettered. She could feel it rumbling through him, the twitching of his arm, vibrations in the hip nestled against hers.

"On my best days, I think he was sent to me for a purpose," she said. "Lessons both of us need to learn. That's pretty New Age for a good Catholic, but there it is. I think he's taught me so much already. So no, I won't trade him for another model. He's mine for the long haul, and I love him."

"Strength through adversity?"

She was enjoying this intimacy, and she was fully aware that she might be about to destroy it. "Did you feel this way about your children sometimes? Or about the losses you suffered? Not that those could be good in any way, but that something will come from it, despite the horror?"

"Have you simply tired of talking about yourself?"

"No, I'd like to know you better. You make it hard, as you well know."

"I don't talk about my children."

"Yes, but that's the ultimate burial, isn't it? It's like they never existed. Even Bridie is afraid to mention them."

She felt him stiffen. She sighed. "Finn, I'm not your patient, so you didn't have to make me feel better tonight. I thought maybe we'd reached a new plateau here. Friends who could really talk about their lives."

"Talk about my life? I killed my children, and my wife." He got up and walked to the edge of the cliff. There was a narrow rock-strewn beach six feet below, then nothing but water until the horizon was broken by Clare Island, three and a half miles away.

He faced her. "Is that what you wanted to know? Is that the plateau you'd hoped to climb?"

She sat and waited.

"You've heard the story by now," he said.

"I know it was a boating accident."

"We went out to Clare. Sheila loved the water. Her father was a fisherman, and as a child, she went out with him frequently. She felt at home in a boat, and she wanted our children to feel the same way. We bought one, nothing expensive or exotic, but sturdy and comfortable enough for the trip. Bridie gets seasick, and she didn't want to go, so she begged to be allowed to spend the day with a friend."

"I'm so glad she did," Peggy said.

"At first Sheila insisted Bridie join us, but in the end she gave in. We left early, and the crossing was problem free. We spent the day swimming and hiking. The weather changed in the early afternoon, but I didn't pay it much of a mind. It was only cloudy, a relief of sorts after the morning's sun. Others were staying. We stayed. Little Brian fell asleep, and Sheila was reluctant to wake him to strap him into his life jacket again and carry him to the boat. So we waited for his nap to end."

Peggy didn't want to stop him. She nodded but didn't reply.

"By the time Brian woke, the skies were darkening quickly and the wind had picked up. Waves were slapping at the sides of the boat, and I had a moment or two of hesitation about whether to make the crossing. Sheila felt we'd be safe, and I was afraid if we didn't leave then, we might be marooned for the night. So we got the boys in the boat and started across."

He turned away and stared out at the ocean. "We would have been fine. The rain began to fall. Softly at first, then the heavens opened. Still, we were safe. Our boat was sound. I opened the throttle to get us home quickly. To this day, I don't know what we hit. The seas were rough, but nothing seemed to be in our way. One moment we were speeding home, the next we were all in the water, somewhere between the island and the mainland, and the boat was in pieces around us."

Peggy shuddered. He had not gone into great detail, but she could imagine the horror. "Finn, if you don't want to go on..."

"You asked. Here it is. Part of the hull was still floating. Sheila was a strong enough swimmer to help me get the boys to it, although she seemed sluggish and dazed. I had been thrown clear, and I wasn't injured. I managed to lift Brian to the top. He was too young to cling effectively. The water was cold, and now there was no beach to warm ourselves on, of course. The waves tossed us in every direction, and Mark went under, despite his jacket. I tried to hold him up, to hold Brian on the wreckage at the same time. That was when I realized Sheila had been injured and needed my help, as well. I shouted for her to hang on, that help would come. But we were the last boat to leave, and of course the ferries had stopped until the weather improved."

He cleared his throat. "I turned my head to try to get a better grip on Mark, and when I turned back to her, she was gone. I never saw her again."

"Finn..."

"I couldn't look for her. I couldn't help her. I had the boys. Both of them. Brian kept sliding off the hull, and it was breaking up. Mark was clinging to me, but he kept going under, and I realized..." He paused. "I realized I couldn't save them both."

Peggy's stomach clenched. She felt nauseous, but if she felt this way just hearing the story, how must Finn have felt these past two years?

"In the end, I saved neither of them," Finn said at last. "I knew that I had to choose, that I had to try to swim to shore with one of them. I knew this with every fiber of my being. But I could not choose between my own sons. So I waited, praying, fighting, until Brian was no more. And by the time I set out with Mark, it was too late for him, as well."

"I'm so sorry," Peggy said.

"I don't know why I survived. I knew Mark was dead, but I held on to him. I thought I heard waves slapping at the shore. I kept swimming, praying for a miracle, then I passed out. I woke up the next day in hospital. Someone had seen me. Someone had launched a rescue boat and fished me out in what should have been the last moments of my life. Mark's body was retrieved the next morning after it washed up on the strand. Brian and Sheila were never found."

"You must have felt like your life had ended."

"I only wished it had. I was trained to save lives, and I couldn't save the people I loved most. I'm a scientist. I knew what I had to do, I understood the facts even when I was gripped by terror, and I couldn't act."

Peggy got up and joined him at the cliff's edge, although she was careful not to touch him. She knew he would not appreciate it. "Is that why you stopped practicing medicine? To punish yourself for acting like a father instead of a physician?"

He was silent for a while, as if deciding whether to continue. When he spoke, he sounded exhausted.

"I closed my surgery temporarily until I'd recovered physically. I made arrangements for three funerals. I put our house up for sale and moved Bridie into town. And when six weeks had passed, I went back to work. My first patient was a young boy. He reminded me a little of Brian. The child had a growth on his back, just a mole, as it turned out, but I stared at it, unable to decide what to do. Was it malignant? Was it worth a trip out of the village for another look by a specialist? In the end I sent them off to Castlebar because I could no longer tell the difference between a simple mole and a tumor. Then the next patient arrived. An adolescent girl with a sore throat. I didn't know how to treat it. I thought of all the children who had died of bad throats, the drug-resistant bacteria, the complications. I made an excuse and sent her off to be looked after by someone else.

"The third patient was an emergency, a man I'd known for years who had tenderness in his abdomen, a low-grade fever. Bad mussels, as it turns out, but I was certain he was dying, and that if I didn't rush him straight to hospital, I might be *his* murderer, too."

"Finn—"

He shook his head. "I closed my doors that day, this time for good. Does a man need to be beaten over the head with the truth? In an emergency, when it counts most, I can't make decisions. I can't act, even when lives depend on it. And now I don't even want to try."

The last sentence was the most telling. From everything Peggy had heard, she knew that Finn was an excellent physician, a diagnostician who had rooted out the rarest disorders, often in the nick of time. He had never given up hope of finding the right treatment until it was clear that none existed. Patients from all over Western Ireland had come to Shanmullin to see him, driving many miles because he was the best doctor and the most compassionate.

"You know recovery takes time," she said. "As a doctor, you know that. Six weeks wasn't enough."

"No amount of time will ever be enough. I didn't trust myself that day, and I don't trust myself now. I started to drink. Six weeks later I woke up and realized I might lose Bridie, as well. Irene helped me see it, so I got sober for Bridie and Irene, and I stay sober. But I won't stay that way if I have to face the day-to-day decisions I used to make so effortlessly. When I'm needed the most, I can't act."

"You did act, Finn. You made a decision and tried to save both your children. Had you done anything else, could you have lived with yourself?"

He turned. In the moonlight she saw that his face was pale. "Am I living now? I'm not sure anymore."

She thought of Kieran, who would not let her comfort him. Finn would surely feel the same way. She touched his cheek despite that. He closed his eyes, but he did not step away.

It was a beginning.

chapter 16

Megan woke up from a nightmare in which she was chasing Niccolo through a railway tunnel. A train was gaining behind them. She could hear the wheels clickety-clacking, faster and faster, the horn shrieking a frantic warning. She shouted for Niccolo to get off the track, but he couldn't hear her, no matter how loudly she screamed.

She sat bolt upright, her heart pummeling her breastbone. She gasped for air and couldn't find enough.

"Are you all right?" Niccolo sat up and put his arm around her shoulders. "Take it easy. I'm right here."

"Damn it, you weren't. You were...just ahead of me. And you couldn't hear me."

"It was a dream. Just a dream."

She knew what a dream was. This wasn't a dream. It was the starkest of warnings, a no-holds-barred, no-dream-dictionary-needed plea that she recognize and deal with the problems in her marriage. Next time her subconscious would simply clobber her over the head.

"You wouldn't get off the track, and a train was coming. I kept shouting, but you wouldn't listen."

He kissed her cheek. "Sit there. I'll bring you some coffee. Caffeine will shake the clouds away."

He was gone before she could respond. Good old Nick, taking care of her the way he took care of everybody else. She had given him something to do, a problem to solve, and that was what he liked best.

She was furious at somebody, she just wasn't sure who, exactly. When had the problems between them crept into every hour of her life? While she was awake she could be rational—most of the time. Niccolo had a lot on his mind. Brick was badly in need of additional funding if it was ever going to be as comprehensive and useful as it could be. Renovations on the saloon took hours of every day, and Niccolo felt the pressure to finish so she could open the doors again and send Marco home for good. The accident in the tunnel had created a new groundswell of interest in the image on the wall, and people who had ignored or joked about it before were suddenly moved to ask for tours. Fortunately for her, city inspectors had closed the tunnel. Unfortunately it could be opened again as soon as some repair work on the ceiling was completed. Not for business, of course, but Niccolo had been told that no one was going to close down the saloon if people wanted a tour. After all, the tunnel was architecturally sound and a piece of local history.

And fast *making* history, unfortunately.

She propped herself against pillows, stealing Niccolo's in a fit of temper to make herself more comfortable. If she was going to stay one step in front of a fast-moving train for his sake, he owed her something.

He nudged the door open a few minutes later, coffee and *Plain Dealer* in hand. "Here you are."

He had one cup. The paper was folded under his arm so he had an extra—empty—hand. "Where's yours?" she asked.

"I told Iggy I'd stop by early this morning. He wants to talk to me about something. I'll have coffee with him."

She could feel her forehead puckering. "It's not even seven."

"It will be by the time I shower and dress. And he's up at the crack of dawn. Besides, I have a full day."

"That's not unusual." The words sounded as if she'd strained them through a sieve, but he didn't seem to notice.

He handed her the cup and the paper. He had taught her the ins and outs of good coffee and spoiled her for anything else. This was dark roast with cream and more sugar than he ate in a month. From the first cup, he hadn't forgotten how she liked it.

"What's the meeting about?" she asked. "Or is it just priestly discussion?"

Again he seemed oblivious to the undertone. "Iggy didn't go into detail. But I think it has something to do with the tunnel."

"So did my dream."

She watched him glance at the bedside clock. She very nearly knocked it to the floor.

Niccolo lowered himself to the bed. He was wearing pajama bottoms, but not tops. He had a wide chest, with soft dark hair tapering toward a still-flat belly. He took her breath away. Most of the time.

"Tell me more about it," he said.

She had gotten what she wished for, but now she thought of the saying that went with that. Because sometimes the worst thing *was* to get exactly what you wanted.

"A train was bearing down on us. In a tunnel, of course. You were just ahead of me. I couldn't reach you. I couldn't warn you it was coming."

"You're saving us a lot of money on psyhoanalysts, aren't you?"

"I've never been much for symbolism." She set her coffee on the table. "I like to get right down to basics."

"We're not communicating, and you can't reach me."

"That pretty well sums it up."

He ran his fingers through his hair, a typical morning gesture, just one of many she had come to love. This morning it annoyed her. It seemed like a barrier, a moment of private thought before he explained rationally, calmly, that she was off base.

"I know I've been too busy," he said when he'd run out of hair to ruffle. "I don't know what to do about it."

"I thought after the roof caved in, you'd be done with the tunnel for good. Instead, you've just added it to your repair schedule. And there seem to be endless numbers of people who want to discuss the way the boys weren't touched when the ceiling fell around them."

"I know, Megan."

"Nick, I'm feeling a little desperate here. We're supposed to be starting our life together, and you're always gone."

He stared at her as if she were speaking in tongues. "I'm busy. I'm not always gone. I come home every night."

"And lock yourself away to go over costs and figures and grant proposals."

He plowed a new trail through his hair. She wanted to slap his hands.

"I know all this is important to you," she said through clenched teeth. "I'm trying to understand."

"I have to get more funding for Brick. The only time I can work on it is when I'm home in the evenings. I'm working on the saloon during the day. And nothing has ever convinced me more that I need funding than that cave-in. I'm trying to do too much—"

"And how."

He ignored her. "And I'm trying to do it alone. But we run on a shoestring. Either I shut down the program, get some substantial funding to hire help, or I keep working like a maniac. I'm trying to make this successful in the only way I know how."

Guilt was a glimmer on the horizon, but anger subdued it. She struggled to be rational. "And you're doing the saloon for me. I know. It's just that—"

"What?" He got to his feet and glanced at the clock again. "What can I do? Just give me one good idea. I'll do it. Whatever it is."

"Forget the tunnel repairs. Close it down and forget it. Maybe later, when everything else is finished and life's settled down—"

"By then the image will be gone. It probably has a short life at this point. Once we replace the pipes—"

"I don't care about the image. Let it dry up. Real miracles don't disappear when leaks are plugged. You can tell people that. They'll go away. Things will get back to normal."

"Just for the record, there's no train coming up behind you. I can hear you just fine."

She hadn't realized her voice had risen, but she was angry at him for pointing it out instead of dealing with what she'd said. "You hear the words and the tone, Nick, but I don't think you hear my message at all."

"I hear you making demands. I'm up to here with demands. I don't think I can satisfy another one. Not this morning. Not with so much else I have to do. And now I have to get going."

She watched him head for the bathroom. She carefully removed the coffee cup before she swept her hand across the table.

The bedside clock was not so lucky.

Iggy set a cup of coffee in front of Niccolo. "The archbishop's not happy."

Niccolo watched in silence as Iggy poured a cup of coffee for himself. His old friend had already set out a plate of freshly baked brioche, delivered that morning by a grateful parishioner. The rectory kitchen was bright and cheerful, and best of all, the housekeeper, a dour woman who counted each crumb and calorie, was gone for the day.

He waited until Iggy was blissfully sipping before he answered. "I never understood the urge to move up in the Church hierarchy."

"Clearly you didn't. Hierarchy never appealed to you. That's one reason you're a married man now. Although I suppose that's a different kind of hierarchy, isn't it?"

Niccolo thought of Megan and her morning demands. He was ashamed of himself for the way he had reacted, but he wasn't sure what he would do differently if he had another chance.

"What's the problem this time?" Niccolo buttered a roll while Iggy considered.

"Well, it's this talk of miracles," Iggy said. "Although that's not all of it, of course. He claims it's the rumors. The Church has had too many public relations nightmares lately. He'd prefer we not look like a bunch of raving lunatics in the newspapers. That's understandable."

"I suppose if the image had appeared in a church or charitable organization, we might look saner," Niccolo said. "But Mary finding her way to an old bootleggers' tunnel is pretty far-fetched."

"The rumors are one thing. The test of faith is another. An occurrence like this is a Rorschach for believers. Look at the wall and what do you see? The Virgin stretching out her arms, asking you to come into the Kingdom of God? Or a simple unattractive water stain?"

"What did he say, exactly?"

"I'm to do my best to quiet the rumors."

Niccolo wasn't surprised. Had he been the archbishop, he probably would have said the same. "And what did he suggest?"

"That I use my good sense." Iggy reached for a roll, sighing with pleasure as he held it in his hand. "He's much too good a man to tell me how to use it. Or even to make suggestions."

"In other words, he doesn't have a clue."

Iggy smiled. "Not the way I would have said it, of course."

"Have you given this some thought?" Niccolo didn't know why he'd asked. Of course Iggy had thought about it. That was why Niccolo was having breakfast in the rectory.

"Have you ever tried to quiet a screaming infant?"

"I have nieces and nephews."

"So do I. Grandnieces and grandnephews by the dozens, too. Not a one of them pays me the slightest bit of attention."

"But from them you learned...?"

"Tell a baby not to scream, he screams harder. Put your hand over his mouth, he bites you."

"You've never put your hand over a baby's mouth. Not in your life."

"But if I had, that would have been the result. It's the same with people spreading rumors. Tell them not to, they'll scream louder."

"Censor or censure them, and they'll bite your hand."

"Exactly." Iggy rolled his eyes in pleasure at his first, glorious bite. From experience, Niccolo knew he wouldn't eat much more.

"Then what exactly do you propose to do?" Niccolo said.

"I think we need to discuss this openly and honestly. Bore them to death with the theological implications. If you discuss how many angels can dance on the head of a pin and discuss it long enough, you won't see the gyrations. They disappear. Poof."

"So who asked you to discuss this?" Niccolo had already started on his second roll, but he took a break to lean back and eye his friend. "Because that's what this is about, correct?"

"Of course."

"And?"

"Newschannel 5 at Noon. You're invited, too. I told them yes for me. You can accept or not for yourself."

Niccolo ticked off the positives and negatives in his head. If Iggy had accepted, then clearly the television channel wasn't going to do a hatchet job. It was probably a local interest piece, and a great chance to discount some of the wildest rumors. Yesterday he'd been asked if the tunnel really smelled like roses, and if it was true that light from unseen candles illuminated the image.

"You think I should do it, don't you?" he asked at last.

"Of course I do. We'll answer questions about the tunnel, then you'll turn the topic to Brick. This is your chance for good publicity. Maybe you'll even get some new funding from it."

"The accident clarified the need for more funding, that's for sure. I don't know how much longer we can go on the way we are. I don't mind the work, but Megan does." He wasn't sure where that had come from and was sorry the moment he'd said it.

"Selfish to the bone, our Megan." Iggy took another bite.

Niccolo felt properly rebuked. Megan was anything but selfish. She had given up most of her life for her family and had never mourned a bit of it. The fact that at last she might be asking for something for herself was a sign of good mental health.

And a sign that she loved him.

"I'll do it," Niccolo said. "I'll call the station and set it up."

Iggy reached in his pocket and handed Niccolo a slip of paper. "Number and name of my contact. They want us on Friday."

"While I'm here, I have a favor to ask you." Niccolo was still thinking of his wife. "For Megan."

"Anything."

Niccolo had told Iggy the story of Irene Tierney. Iggy knew Peggy was in Ireland living in Tierney Cottage, and that she had promised Irene to search out Liam Tierney's years in Cleveland. Now he told him what Megan had learned so far.

"But she's come to a halt," Niccolo finished. "She doesn't have the time to go through the microfiche spool by spool. That could take months. So I wondered if it was worth checking the church archives to see if there's any mention of Tierney here."

"You certainly had good luck last time you needed information."

Niccolo knew what Iggy was referring to. Two years ago, in order to discover the details of a murder in the Donaghues' past, Niccolo had read the journal of a former St. Brigid's priest, Father Patrick McSweeney, which had contained the answers they sought.

"I don't expect to be that lucky again," Niccolo said. "Although it's too bad McSweeney discontinued his journals. He might even have been at St. Brigid's when Liam Tierney and his family were here, at least in some capacity."

"There are no more journals, at least not that we've ever

discovered. But we do have the letters his sister wrote to him in the 1920s."

"*Her* letters?"

"Just hers, of course, because his went to Ireland." Iggy smiled. "Never write to a priest. We collect and keep everything."

"I'll bet they're interesting. Half a correspondence..."

"Is better than none? In this case, yes. Although there's one problem. They're in Irish."

"Gaelic?"

"That's right. Some English from time to time, so she was obviously bilingual. Apparently she wrote to him in Irish to help him stay fluent. She was quite a Nationalist. We've translated some of them, but not all. A pity, too. They're a chronicle of the times. But Irish speakers are few and far between in these parts."

"Megan knows a little Irish."

Iggy's eyes brightened. "You don't say."

"Not much, but enough that she might be able to help. She's been going to college for years, taking a class here, another there; enough to assemble for a degree if she wanted one. She didn't want to take French or German, but she took Irish for three summers under a special program, and she's continued studying on her own. She doesn't speak it well, that takes a lot of practice with native speakers, but she could probably translate the letters. At least well enough to give you the gist of them. And these days, she has more time than she knows what to do with."

"Why don't you copy the letters and take them home? See if she's interested."

"I will. And may I browse through the parish hall library and see if Liam Tierney turns up?"

"It's all yours, and the archive storeroom besides." Iggy got to his feet.

Niccolo was pleased right up until the moment Iggy left him inside the walls of the library, instructing him to lock the doors behind him when he left. St. Brigid's needed a professional to catalogue and care for the plethora of information on its shelves. Some documents had gone to the Historical Society, but most had not. Iggy was always on the lookout for volunteers who would help with the process, but history was less important to most people than the other workings of the parish.

Niccolo browsed the shelves and knew how impossible his task was. Most of the information wasn't even arranged by date, and he knew for a fact that more documents existed in trunks and boxes in the storeroom. He had hoped for proof that Liam and his wife had been members of St. Brigid's, perhaps even an address or notation about rites of passage that had been performed for the family. But tentative forays into fading volumes turned up nothing helpful, and he already knew that the church's computer system had not yet extended this far into the past. Volunteers were working on it, but they hadn't yet keyed in data from before the seventies. And gathering it to input would be difficult.

He spent an hour paging through ledgers and volumes until the cramped, faded handwriting made his sight blur. He closed the last volume he'd tried and slipped it back on the shelf.

Before he abandoned Niccolo to the library, Iggy, who had an unerring sense of where papers resided in the chaos, had gathered together the letters of Maura McSweeney to her brother and taken them into the church office to be copied. Niccolo had the copies in a manilla folder ready to take home to Megan. The letters were in chronological order, and the ones on the top had already been translated.

Niccolo leafed through them now. He hoped Megan would find the letters interesting. At least he could tell her he'd tried to find some information and brought her a consolation prize instead. He might earn some approval points. Nothing else he'd done lately had.

He was leafing past the fourth letter when a name sprang out at him from the translation.

"Liam." He could hardly believe he'd seen it. He took the copy closer to the nearest table lamp and squinted. The sum total he knew of the Irish had come from the Donaghue clan.

He didn't know a single Liam, but wasn't this a common enough name? Liam Neeson was an actor he admired. He tried to think of others.

He read the sentence out loud. "You can be certain I share your concern for your flock, dearest Patrick. Yet what can be expected? A man does what he must to feed his family, and should he be faulted for breaking a foolish law he did not make? Your Liam has found a way to care for his own. Now you must find a way to care for him, despite his decision."

Niccolo was intrigued, despite himself. He had looked into this for Megan, but the unfolding drama interested him. In the twenties, the laws most likely to be broken had to do with Prohibition. He certainly knew about bootlegging. The saloon tunnel attested to it.

He read the rest of the letter, but Maura had gone on to other topics, none of which seemed to relate to the mysterious Liam.

The next letter made no mention of him.

The first paragraph of the last one that had been translated didn't mention the name he was searching for, but another familiar word leaped out at him.

"Shanmullin." He knew this was the village where Peggy was living now, the ancestral home of the Donaghues—or rather, the Tierneys—in Ireland. And Lena Tierney Donaghue had come from there, as well. So must Liam have.

He backed up to the beginning of the letter to read with more care, reading aloud when he reached the important part. "A young man from Shanmullin would have little to hope for here in Ireland. Someday, perhaps, but your Liam would have found little to sustain his family."

"Liam..." There was the name again. And the connection made it nearly certain this was Liam Tierney. Perhaps Maura McSweeney was using only first names to protect the St. Brigid's parishioner if anyone else got hold of her letter. Perhaps her brother had done the same.

He skimmed and came to another paragraph that interested him. "I would agree that a law that makes life worse for so many is worse than no law at all. We Irish understand only too well about laws that benefit those who are already wealthy and powerful. The criminal class thrives on needs that can't be met by legal means."

Niccolo was certain now that Maura was talking about bootlegging and rumrunning. During Prohibition too many people had died from the trade in bootleg liquor and from the liquor itself. Too many shady characters had made millions while legitimate distillers went out of business. Had Liam Tierney gotten involved in the illegal trade?

He read on to the end. "Your life has always been a study in balances, brother. Balancing God's word with the needs of man, balancing your own needs with those of the Church. Now it seems the balancing must continue. You have members of your flock on every side of this sad business. Your Tim, carving out his own piece of luck and threatening all who interfere. Your Glen, struggling to uphold a poor law that is law nonetheless. And now your Liam, trying to take care of those he loves. Life is far too often this way, isn't it? And there are no easy answers."

Niccolo wondered who all these people were. Tim? Glen? He felt the deepest sympathy for Father McSweeney, who must have hoped his retirement years would be a time of rest and contemplation but had found struggle instead.

He closed the folder. At least he had something to show Megan now. He hoped she would realize he had been thinking of her this morning.

1925
Castlebar, County Mayo

My dearest Patrick,

You write of the number of policemen in your parish and the way our young Irishmen are drawn to enforcing the law. Odd indeed, for those who had little power in their country and whose rural life hardly seemed to lend itself to the back alleys and vacant lots of large cities.

And yet we are a sociable people. I read tales of your American farms, of their vast expanses and distance from neighbors, and I understand well why my countrymen find them so unappealing. We saw our land yield terror and heartache during the famine, and we trust the land no more. Instead we settle naturally in America's cities, where our strong backs and deft hands are wanted and our own people have come before us. Perhaps we are not appreciated for our courage and intelligence, but we are hailed for our willingness to do work no one else will abide, work that requires close allegiance to others, work that requires little education and pays poorly.

If we have learned nothing, dear brother, we have learned to stick together. We speak with one voice, organize and march together, and offer a helping hand to those who are like us. This is how we survived and will continue to do so.

It is no surprise to me that there are policemen and firemen to spare at St. Brigid's. We were bred through years of suffering to work together for justice. Is that not a description of the jobs so many Irish are called on to do?

Your loving sister,
Maura McSweeney

chapter 17

At first Brenna refused to quit her job. "I've no faith in this Timothy McNulty," she told Liam. "I've heard of him, you know. He gives money to the church and community with one hand, and snatches everything he can with the other. He's a thief and a liar, and the fact that he's Irish makes no difference at all. Look what his men did to you. Do you think they'll stop next time if they believe you've crossed them?"

Liam had considered lying to Brenna, telling her that McNulty had interrupted another man's beating of him and offered Liam a job because of his courage. But too many people had been nearby to witness the actual event. Most likely Brenna would discover the truth and be furious with him.

"He's a hard man," Liam admitted. "But he was testing me. Now he knows I'm a man who keeps things to myself, a man who can be trusted."

"And you trust Timothy McNulty? A bootlegger? A rum-runner?"

"Can you say those things are wrong? People want what they want, Brenna. A harmless drink or two, and they can't get it any other way. Somebody always makes money off bad laws. Who knows that better than an Irishman? For once I'll be the one making the money."

Nothing she said could change his mind. She continued going to work, leaving Irene with a neighbor each morning and loudly proclaiming that if she was going to be widowed young, she might as well have a position lined up to support herself and their daughter. After six months, though, she came home one evening and announced that she had given notice and planned to quit at week's end.

"Irene needs her mother," was all she would say. Liam knew better than to inquire further.

He had been surprised to discover how mundane his new job really was. He rode with several other men in a car that followed McNulty everywhere. He stood, arms folded, outside a variety of buildings when McNulty had meetings. When called on, he loaded crates of unknown origin into cars, trucks or boats, asking no questions and receiving no explanations. He swept floors at the hardware store downstairs from McNulty's business office, sometimes waiting on customers, sometimes carrying bags for shoppers.

He was paid regularly, and as well as he'd been at the factory. He was issued no weapon, asked to keep no secrets. He was alternately relieved and disturbed. He had no wish to put his life on the line, but he had hoped for a job with a future. His future, it seemed, was a life of manual labor.

Three months after taking McNulty's offer, he was downstairs in the hardware store doing inventory with the manager when Jerry, the oversized brute who had beaten Liam, came downstairs and crooked an index finger in his direction. "Boss wants to see ya."

Liam would never enjoy Jerry's company, but the two men had a silent truce. Liam knew better than to make enemies in McNulty's own operation. If he was ever called on to do anything important, he would need these men protecting his back. And Jerry seemed to take very little that he did for McNulty personally. Beating Liam had been part of a day's work.

Liam dusted off his hands and started up the stairs after Jerry. He'd rarely climbed them. This was McNulty's inner sanctum, and it was the job of every man on the ground floor to keep interlopers away.

At the top of the stairs, Jerry signaled a halt. Liam stood with his hat in his hands, waiting to be taken down the hall. He stood that way for a long time, not shifting his weight, not sighing or grumbling. He was paid to do anything McNulty asked, and if he asked him to stand there, he would.

Half an hour passed before he was shown into McNulty's office. It was surprisingly neat for a man with so many businesses to juggle. Liam wondered if there were other offices hidden in other places, perhaps even in the building.

McNulty sat at a mahogany desk, the surface shining and dust free. He didn't look up when Liam was shown in, and he didn't look up for minutes afterward. He gazed at the desk, as if he was hoping it would show him something new, once drawing his finger across the top as if bisecting it for future purposes. At last he looked up. "You like your job? Things going well enough to suit you?"

"Yes, sir. I like it fine."

"I hear good reports."

"I'm glad."

"Your wife's not unhappy? She's not complaining to the neighbors?"

"Brenna comes from the same sort of place I did. We learned to keep to ourselves. It's not a lesson you recover from."

McNulty smiled. "You like where you live?"

"Well enough, thank you."

"But you'd like something better?"

"When the time is right."

"From the beginning I thought you might be a man who's easily bored. Is that true, Tierney?"

"I don't let it stop me from doing what I need to."

McNulty seemed to think that was a good enough answer. "You had a bit of trouble with the law in Ireland, didn't you?"

Liam was certain McNulty knew all about it. The man was no fool. "I did."

"I like a lad who does what he thinks best, regardless. A lad who puts Ireland's future first. I've a new job for you. You won't find it boring."

"I go where you ask me to go, do what you ask me to do."

"We'll be watching you."

"I've no problem with that, sir."

McNulty looked up and signaled Jerry, who stepped inside the doorway. "He'll need supplies for the job. Take care of it." He dismissed Liam with a nod of his head.

"Thank you, sir," Liam said. Hat still in hand, he followed Jerry out into the hall before he clapped it back on his head.

"Ever fire a gun?" Jerry asked as they started downstairs.

"You'd be surprised at what I've done."

The process of making bootleg liquor differed widely, depending on materials at hand. But barrels of raw alcohol, which could be distilled, flavored and sold at exorbitant prices, went at a premium. Much of the work was done by the time raw alcohol was obtained from the fermentation of water, yeast and some form of sugar, making it a commodity in high demand and worth fighting for.

"Here's what you need to know," Jerry told Liam. They were third in a line of cars heading toward the East Side neighborhood of Woodland and 25th, known locally as Bootleggers' Rendezvous. "Squeaky Frank Donatone has a beef with McNulty. For some reason, he thinks McNulty's been stepping in on his operation. So he stepped in on McNulty's and lifted two dozen barrels from our warehouse on Monday. We're gonna return the favor. You understand?"

Liam figured that if he didn't, he was a half-wit and not worth trusting with the information.

A sawed-off shotgun resided double barrels-down beside him. After handing him the weapon, Jerry had given him a lesson he didn't need, but there hadn't been time to practice. Liam had no interest in shooting the gun—he had never been fond of violence. Still, if he was required to defend himself, he wouldn't hesitate. And if he was required to defend McNulty, who was paying his salary, he supposed he could do that, as well. Squeaky Frank, despite the ridiculous nickname, had a reputation for ruthlessness.

"Why's he called Squeaky?" Liam asked.

Jerry snorted. "Got a fake leg that squeaks when he walks."

Liam figured that if he came across old Squeaky, that was the leg he would aim for if he was lucky enough to have a choice.

It was midafternoon by the time they got to Donatone's warehouse, and a cold wind blew off the lake, rattling signs and siding, and sending trash skittering across the street. When he stepped out of the car, Liam looked down to see the front page of *La Voce Del Popolo Italiano* wrapping itself over his shoe. "Voice of the Italian People." He didn't need an education for the translation.

"They ain't gonna have much of a voice, time we're done with 'em today," Jerry said.

Liam didn't have anything against Italians, or the Jews, for that matter, who also had their hands deeply in Cleveland's bootlegging till. He figured everybody was out to get their share, and the more downtrodden they'd been, the more they figured their share was worth.

He thought about that now as he followed Jerry through the undergrowth on the warehouse's east side. The alley where the warehouse resided was tucked away, but even at that, the neighborhood was strangely quiet. He was reminded of the morning that Jerry and McNulty's driver had beaten him nearly senseless on his front porch. The working people of Cleveland knew how to mind their own business.

The main door was on the other end of the building, but McNulty's men were now stationed in the back and at the sides. They flanked their door and waited. Nobody had told Liam the signal, but when a whistle blew, he knew what was required. Together he and Jerry lent their weight to the door, and it crashed open. Liam snapped his gun waist-high and cradled the trigger with his finger.

The warehouse was nearly empty. Two frightened watchmen stood in the middle with trembling hands held high. Jerry laughed. "They better be scared, and not of us. Squeaky's gonna be one unhappy fella, and that's no baloney. Tie 'em up."

Liam saw some wire that was similar to the kind he'd used in the box factory. He grabbed it and sat the men in a corner, back to back, using smaller pieces to secure their hands, then stretching the remainder around and around them, finally bending it back and forth until it snapped and he could fasten it off.

As he worked, the other men loaded barrel after barrel in the truck that had followed Liam and Jerry. It was a city truck, or one painted to look that way. When they had finished, they pulled a sheet of brown canvas across the top, fastening it on all sides so it wouldn't blow away.

"Done," Jerry said. "They're secure?"

Liam hoped he hadn't wired the men together to make them a better target. "You're going to leave them like this?"

"No reason not to. Squeaky will know who did this whether these guys squeal or not. Stuff something in their mouths."

Liam settled for some rags in the corner, folding them to make gags, which he tied securely behind their heads.

Things had gone too well. He'd developed a sixth sense in early childhood, a survival tool that had gotten him to this point in his life. He had learned to feel the winds of change, and he felt them now.

"Hear that?" He got to his feet. "Listen..."

Jerry scowled over his shoulder, striding to the back door where the cars and the truck were parked. "Don't get all balled up on me, Tierney. Just get going. We're gonna be the last to leave."

Liam was halfway toward the exit when he heard the screech of tires and slam of car doors. He grabbed Jerry's shirt and hauled him backward. "This way."

Jerry didn't need a second invitation. They backed toward the door through which they'd entered, shotguns raised for business.

"Treasury agents," Jerry said, just loud enough for Liam to hear him.

Liam had been prepared for trouble with Squeaky and his gang. He wondered if the dry agents had guessed McNulty's men would steal back what belonged to them, or if this was just an unfortunate coincidence. In the greater scheme of things, it didn't really matter.

"Not that way. This." Liam jerked his head toward a storeroom, where some of the barrels of alcohol had been kept. He'd seen a window large enough to slide through, offering them a better chance to get out without being seen. The window looked out over a vacant lot filled with rusted machinery and factory debris. If they got out fast, they had at least a chance of hiding there.

A blast from somebody's shotgun sizzled the air, and the rat-a-tat of a machine gun followed. Tires squealed; a bevy of single shots were fired. McNulty's men were making a getaway. Liam and Jerry dove for the storeroom. The window was high, but two crates under it made a perfect ladder. Liam unlocked and lifted the window and put his head outside. The action was all in the front, and if they were lucky, all the agents would follow the getaway truck. He motioned for Jerry to follow and launched himself out the window to the ground below.

Jerry joined him, although squeezing through the window wasn't as simple for him as it had been for Liam. For a moment Liam thought they'd made it unseen; then a man came around the corner, pistol pointed directly at Liam's chest.

"Prohibition Agent Glen Donaghue. Guns down. Hands in the air."

Liam dropped his shotgun at this formal announcement and raised his hands. Beside him, Liam could see Jerry begin to comply. He had observed the man and been on the wrong end of his fists. He knew giving up was a sham, and he was ready.

Jerry's shotgun whipped up just as Liam careened into

him, knocking the big man off balance in a surprise attack. Pellets sprayed the air but did no damage. Jerry didn't even stumble to catch his balance. He fell hard, knocking his head against a concrete post as he hit the ground. He went limp.

"You trying to save my life?" Glen Donaghue had gone pale. He was a young man about Liam's age, with the healthy physique of a generation that had survived both the Great War and Spanish flu. The clean line of his jaw, broad, clear brow and gray eyes were an ancestor's contribution. The aura of character was his own.

"Not much chance of that, lad," Liam said. "I just thought you were about to shoot him, that's all."

Glen stared at Liam. More shots came from in front of the warehouse, another squeal of tires. "You're part of this?"

"I came along for the ride." Liam had heard stories of Treasury Department agents. The job was thankless; the men were poorly paid, and graft was as common as fancy badges. Men quit the department every year to join forces with the criminals they'd once pursued. This man seemed different.

"Bad idea." Glen's eyes flicked to the man at Liam's feet. "You're better than he is, Mick."

Liam doubted that, but he was in no mood to argue.

"Put your hands out in front of you." Glen pulled out handcuffs.

Liam did as he was told. He wasn't sure what to do next. Even if he *had* saved Glen Donaghue's life, he was still going to jail or back to Ireland in chains unless McNulty paid for a very good lawyer. He thought of Brenna and Irene and what could happen to them.

Donaghue took a step forward, and his toe caught on a root. The moment he stumbled, Liam took advantage of the situation and leaped forward, using his clasped hands like a club on the back of Donaghue's neck. In a moment the agent was on the ground, head to head with the unconscious bootlegger.

Of the two men, Donaghue was the one Liam would have preferred to save, but Liam knew Donaghue would be all right without him. In a moment someone else would come around the building, find him and call for assistance.

With a curse, he turned Jerry onto his back, and, grabbing the big man under his arms, he heaved him into the lot and down into a ravine to safety.

chapter 18

Peggy spent every evening making notes on Kieran's progress that day, or lack of it, and drawing up lesson plans for the next. There were so many goals to balance that she couldn't be casual about any of them. Her son needed time to play and be a child, to work on social skills, behavior management, language and general knowledge, and that was just for starters.

On Friday nights she wrote a report to the therapist who was working long distance with her. If Mrs. Blackpool saw anything extraordinary on which to comment or make suggestions, she telephoned Peggy as soon as the report arrived. Otherwise, she made notes and mailed them back. The system wasn't perfect, but the guidance and feedback were helpful, and the mail between Ireland and the United States was surprisingly fast.

On this Friday night Peggy worked on the report while Kieran played by himself in the corner. She had made large blocks out of cardboard boxes and covered them with colorful paper. He liked stacking them, as well as crawling into one that she hadn't sealed and lying there, the box squeezing against him. She wondered if her son had been particularly sorry to leave the womb.

"He seems remarkably happy in there."

Peggy looked up from her notebook to see Irene in the doorway. "He's like a little turtle withdrawing into his shell."

"A box turtle," Irene said, with a smile. "He's had a good day?"

Peggy wasn't sure how to answer that. In the past week there had been no more extravagant tantrums, and that was welcome progress. But his verbal skills had taken a giant leap backward. "He's had a happy day," Peggy said. "No tears." No words, either, and little interest in any of the activities she had planned. "He *is* using the spoon again. Only he's using it to beat on his little toy drum."

"When he's angry?"

Peggy considered that. "Maybe. I hadn't really made the connection, but could be."

"That's an improvement, I'd say. Finding some way to make himself heard."

Peggy stood and stretched. "He prefers the noise the drum makes to my singing. And who could blame him?"

"I've had a thought about tonight, dear."

Peggy hadn't had a one. Her days and nights were a seamless continuum of working with her son, thinking about her son, and talking to her sisters and Mrs. Blackpool and anyone else who would listen about her son. Her last conversation of depth had been two weeks before, when Finn told her about the loss of his family. He had hardly spoken to her since, peeking in to see Irene every morning and most afternoons, but sparing Peggy any need to figure out how to treat him now that he had bared his soul to her.

"We could watch a video. I could make popcorn." Peggy had learned that Irene had an insatiable appetite for both. She enjoyed good old-fashioned love stories or mysteries, just one more way that she and Peggy were alike. She also enjoyed salt and half a cup of butter on her popcorn, but she let imagination suffice, and Peggy had learned to, as well.

"I have company on the way," Irene said.

"Oh." Peggy was glad to hear it. Irene had frequent visitors but rarely any at night. "I can make myself scarce, if you'd like."

"I would, as a matter of fact."

"I'll just hole up in the bedroom with a good book. I—"

"Scarcer than that. I'm thinking a trip into town for you. A night at the pubs is just what you need."

Peggy was immediately suspicious. "Who's on the way?"

"Shannon, the dear girl. She has a houseful of relatives from Sligo and no place to go to get away from them. And she has papers to fill out for university, so I offered her a quiet place to do both, and sole use of my computer."

Irene looked angelic, with her soft white hair forming a near halo around her aged face, but Peggy knew that under the halo dwelt a woman quite determined to get her own way. "In other words, you asked her to baby-sit."

"In a manner of speaking. But don't make it sound so harsh. It suits us both admirably. And you, as well."

Peggy started to protest, but as usual, Irene had seen her needs clearly. Peggy was restless and in need of more than a video to help her unwind. She needed music or conversation or both, which were standards at Irish pubs. She felt a stab of nostalgia for the Whiskey Island Saloon.

"Then it's all settled?" Irene said. "After supper you'll let us put Kieran to bed and go along your way?"

Peggy knew that Shannon would manage just fine without her. "It's a very welcome gift."

Tully's Tavern was one of four pubs in Shanmullin, a small enough number to make some residents grumble. Peggy had stopped by two of the other three but found little to interest her. The crowd at one was mostly old men, and the billows of cigarette smoke had sent her on her way. Another had been unacceptably dingy and nearly empty of patrons, a sure sign of a local feud or the final stage of a terminal illness.

Tully's had none of those problems. She could hardly get in the door, and before she even tried, she heard music from inside—and not U2 from a Galway radio station. The pub was paneled in dark wood, with a stone floor oddly paired with wooden planks in the niches that sat away from the bar and beyond them in the lounge. Shelves lined every wall, filled with odds and ends of pottery, ceramic horses, small outdated appliances and framed photographs. The mirror hanging over the vast mahogany bar looked to be older than the ancient building itself.

A young man smiled at her, and she measured the smile she sent back, just wide enough to be polite but not a watt warmer. She was looking for conversation and fun, not someone to take back to Irene's for the night.

Before he could wend his way through the crowd, Peggy felt someone grab her arm and looked up to see Tippy.

"Well, hi." They pumped hands like old friends. "Shannon's baby-sitting for me," she shouted through the din.

"Would you like a pint?"

Peggy nodded, and Tippy disappeared into the crowd. Only then did Peggy see an opening in the throng blocking the door way into the next room, where the music was coming from. She peered around the people still in her path and saw six musicians. Finn was in the front with his tin whistle. Their eyes locked and held.

The music halted and the crowd applauded raucously. Clearly this was going to be a good night at Tully's.

"'Peggy Bawn,'" Finn said, and the musicians began a cheerful ditty that wasn't familiar to her. Finn began to sing, and as before, she was more than impressed with his voice.

"Oh Peggy Bawn, thou art my own, thy heart lies in my breast..."

She couldn't hear the rest of the words, but Finn's eyes never left hers. She was mesmerized.

"He doesn't usually sing in here, and I've never heard him sing that one," Tippy said, coming up to hand Peggy a mug of Guinness. She refused Peggy's Euros with a shake of her head. "It's older than the leprechauns."

"Finn could make 'Beowulf' sound like a love song," Peggy said.

"Not so's you'd notice, Pretty Peggy-o. At least not most of the time."

Peggy realized that indeed Finn had chosen another "Peggy" song and was singing it right to her.

"Our captain fell in love with a lady like a dove, and the name she was called was pretty Peggy-o," Finn sang.

"Are there an endless supply of Peggy songs, do you suppose?" Tippy asked, when that song had nearly finished. "If so, he'll know them all."

"I'm sure it's inadvertent," Peggy said, not at all sure. Finn was still singing directly to her, and her heart seemed to be forging connections with every note.

"When first I saw sweet Peggy, t'was on a market day..." he began, as if to answer the question.

"I haven't seen him like this in such a long time." Tippy took her arm companionably as they listened. "I was half in love with him as a girl, but then, so was most of the town," she said as the song ended. "He was a rogue, our Finn, and he left a trail of broken hearts when he married Sheila. We didn't expect him to come back after his training. That was too much to hope for. Everyone knew he'd be wanted for better things, but he came back anyway. And we loved him more for it."

"And that's why he's been forgiven for all the rough spots in the past years." It wasn't a question. Peggy had noted the way people all through the village talked about Finn, the affection and concern, with only a hint of dismay.

"He's had more than his share of troubles. Perhaps that time is ending?"

"Peggy O'Neil is a girl who must steal any heart anywhere anytime..." Finn smiled this time, and Peggy smiled back.

Tippy saw the smile, too. "If you don't want to stay in Ireland, if you don't want a man in your life, Peggy, you might want to walk away now, before someone is hurt."

Peggy had been so caught up in Finn's singing that at first

she didn't hear Tippy. She broke eye contact with Finn and turned to her new friend. "What?"

"He doesn't need more trouble." Tippy wasn't smiling. "I don't mean to preach, truly I don't, but if he's moving out of the shadows now, he doesn't need anything that might push him back."

"If she walks like a sly little rogue, if she talks with a cute little brogue... Sweet personality, full of rascality, that's Peggy O'Neil," Finn finished the song.

Peggy knew flirtation and all its guises. This seemed remarkably innocent to her.

She glanced back at Finn. He nodded, lifted a brow and began one more song. "O Peggy Gordon, you are my darling. Come sit you down upon my knee and tell to me the very reason why I am slighted so by thee?"

She couldn't see the future, but if she'd had that ability, she would not have accepted an outcome that included Finn O'Malley. Still, at the moment, she was powerless to walk away from him.

She was mesmerized by a man who was still down for the count. She had never been one to adopt wounded birds unless she wanted to practice her medical skills. She had her hands full with a child who would need everything she could give him, possibly for the remainder of her life. And still she could not walk away.

Finn didn't know what had possessed him. Had someone questioned him about the number of "Peggy" songs he knew, he would merely have shrugged. He had even ended the evening with the instrumental reel "Over the Moor to Peggy." He supposed the tunes had been going around in his head for weeks now. He certainly thought enough about Peggy Donaghue.

"Well, ye have taste, lad," Johnny Kerrigan told him as Johnny put away his concertina. "Yer not the only man here tonight who fancied her, ye know, but yer the only one she paid any mind to."

Finn didn't pretend confusion. "She's been kind to my daughter."

"Ye made a holy show of yerself for something as simple as gratitude?" Johnny winked.

Finn had already lost track of their conversation. He searched the room beyond for Peggy, who seemed to have disappeared. The pub was clearing for the night, and he supposed she had already started back to Irene's. He stooped to get his whistle and push his chair back against the wall, and when he turned to leave, she was standing there.

"You forgot 'Peg O' My Heart,'" she said.

He was surprised by how glad he was that she hadn't gone. "An early product of your Tin Pan Alley."

"Maybe so, but my father sang it to me when I was a little girl. It's one of the only memories I had of him when I was growing up. I'm partial to it."

He smiled at her. "Next time."

"Thank you. You made my night."

"Make mine."

She didn't look surprised. She raised a brow in question.

"There's a view I want to show you. Before the village closes down completely for the night."

"I don't know, Finn. It's a ride back to Irene's, and it's late."

"I'll take you home again."

"That's a Kathleen song, not a Peggy." She hummed a few bars. Badly.

He winced. "Will it do for the moment?"

"I'd like to see the view."

She stayed at his side as he said his cursory goodbyes and introduced her to the people she hadn't yet met. He saw looks exchanged among locals who had known him since his christening. He knew what kind of rumors would be flying by morning.

"Everyone's so nice," she said as they went to retrieve her bike for the walk to his car. "And such fans of yours, Finn. They all made sure to tell me."

He could only imagine those conversations. What little

privacy the village had given him after the accident would disappear now. Mourning had officially ended, and the village had its duties.

"What a gorgeous night." She stopped and lifted her hands. "I've never seen so many stars, not even in astronomy class."

The moon was a waning crescent, and he was reminded of a fuller moon and their last conversation. Peggy liked simple things, not something he'd expected from an American woman who had grown up amid so many more attractions.

They found her bike, and Peggy walked it to the street where his car was parked. "What's Bridie doing tonight? Would she like to come with us?"

He wondered how many other women would think to invite his daughter. "Another weekend away. She's gone camping just east of here."

"What fun. I was a Girl Scout. My aunt insisted, and I'm glad she did. I can roast a mean marshmallow."

"Worth a badge by itself."

They had secured the bike and were in the car pulling away from the curb before he spoke again. "Sisters, aunt and father. You've never mentioned your mother, Peggy."

"She died not long after I was born. I had an eclectic upbringing. My father disappeared soon after—I told you about his problems. My oldest sister fought to keep us together, but she was too young to be in charge. So I went to live with my aunt and uncle, and Megan and Casey remained in our apartment over the saloon. I went to stay with them whenever I was allowed."

"No mother, but a lion's share of mothering."

"Exactly. They're all wonderful women. I'm luckier than I can say."

"Not everyone would look at it that way."

"They would if they knew my sisters and aunt." She paused. "They're a large part of the reason I thought I could manage being a single parent."

"Are you?"

"Managing? What's your take on it?"

"I don't know anyone who would do a better job with Kieran." He paused, knowing the next part was none of his business, but forging ahead anyway. "But you shouldn't be so alone. I'm sure your sisters and the rest of your family help enormously, but this ought to be a partnership."

"Phil, you mean?"

"I suppose that's what I'm saying."

"He's not as irresponsible as you think. He offered to marry me when I told him I was pregnant. And he's generous with child support, even though I suspect his wife isn't happy about that."

"You didn't want to marry him." It wasn't a question.

"Scarlet woman and all that?"

"I'm not judging you. Not at all. It's just that it would have been an easy choice for someone who wasn't as strong as you are. Marry the man and share the burden."

He had driven steadily uphill. Now he pulled off on a side road that climbed higher into one of the area's rare forests. At the top he parked on the roadside and came around to open her door. She let him, which pleased him for no discernible reason. He knew she was used to taking care of herself.

He held out his hand, and when she was standing beside him, he didn't let go. Her hand was warm and soft and seemed to fit with his. He linked fingers. "Come on."

She didn't resist. "My aunt told me not to follow men into the forest."

"Those were American forests."

"I've heard my share of Irish fairy stories. The grogochs, the banshees, the dullahan. Your forests are more dangerous than ours."

"Not when I'm with you."

"That was the part my aunt had in mind. Internationally."

He knew they were flirting. So many years had passed since he'd tried that he doubted he was very successful. And even now, part of him was screaming no, that the pleasure of her touch was a blasphemy. He did not deserve to feel this youthful giddiness. Never again.

"Oh, will you look at that."

He had led her to a clearing looking over Shanmullin. Now he dropped her hand regretfully. Beyond them was the ocean, sparkling faintly under the sliver of moon. Lights shone from dozens of windows below them, but they were already being extinguished for the evening. The view was enchanting, and the clearing well known to local lovers. Tonight, luckily, they were alone.

"Do you come up here often?" she asked.

"Not in many years. It's one of those things you take for granted if you've lived somewhere forever."

"I feel that way about Lake Erie. I forget to appreciate it. Then one day I'm passing by, and I realize all over again what a treasure the Great Lakes are."

"This isn't a place anyone passes by. There's nothing here but this view."

"Reason enough."

He was wearing a light jacket, because even though it was July, the evenings could still be chilly. He took it off now and spread it on the ground. "I know you have to get back, but let's stay a few minutes and admire it."

She smiled and lowered herself gracefully. "Room for two." She patted what little was left.

He chose the ground beside it. For a change they'd had little rain that week, and it was dry enough.

"In the car you seemed to want to know why I didn't marry Phil."

"I shouldn't have brought it up."

"I wanted more. Silly and romantic, I know. I've always taken relationships slowly and carefully. I had too many plans to let myself fall in love. Unfortunately, Phil and I had one of those instant attractions that disappears almost as instantly, but since it was a first of its kind for me I thought it was the real thing. Fortunately I figured out right away that it was a flame that had burned out, and we went our separate ways. *Un*fortunately, good intentions didn't prevent pregnancy. I considered Phil's offer of marriage, but I thought Kieran deserved better."

She sighed audibly. "It's funny, I guess. I don't know if Kieran will care if his parents aren't married to each other. I don't know if he'll ever be capable of that kind of feeling."

"You wanted more. Did you find it?"

She laughed, a light, quicksilver sound. "When have I had the time to look?"

"Kieran doesn't leave you much time or energy."

"And I was in school, remember."

"All those young men."

"I had enough complications in my life, thanks, without having a fling with a fellow student. And now that Kieran's part of the bargain, it will take a very special man."

There was no one on the horizon. He heard that clearly but wasn't comforted. He wondered if he had been looking for an escape from his growing feelings, a way of cutting them off so he could withdraw from her and, to a lesser extent, from the world again.

"Do you disapprove of me?" she asked.

"Does it matter?"

"I don't know."

"For the record, I'm not that traditional. I think you did what was right for yourself, and what you believed was right for everybody else, as well. It probably was. No one should be locked into a loveless marriage."

"You married young, didn't you?"

She always led him back to his past. Tonight he felt no rush of resistance—he had already told her the worst. "Sheila was pregnant."

"Please tell me it wasn't one too many visits up here."

He found himself laughing. "One visit on my part to her parents' house when they weren't at home. We got carried away just once, but that was enough."

"Infertility doesn't seem to run in our families, Finn."

He took her hand and squeezed it, laughing again. "We were parents nine months later, and Bridie was a handful. By the time she wasn't, Mark arrived, then Brian. Sheila and I never had a chance to really know each other, the way some men and women seem to. I knew her as a wife, but even more so as my children's mother."

"And from all accounts she was a wonderful one. Bridie talks about her frequently. She adored her."

He was surprised to hear that his daughter, who never mentioned Sheila at home, talked freely about her with Peggy. He knew how necessary that was, and how therapeutic. Like the coward he was, he was glad she hadn't chosen to talk about Sheila with him.

"She *was* a wonderful mother." He stared out at the village lights, dimming softly, one by one. "She died to save her sons."

"What do you mean?"

"I think in her final moments Sheila realized no one was coming to save us. I was struggling to hold on to the boys and to get to her, and even though she'd been injured, I think she realized what I was doing. She pushed away from the boat. She knew if she didn't, I would try to help her, and she knew I couldn't manage. At first I didn't understand. Now, of course, I do. She died to save Mark and Brian."

She brought his hand to her cheek. "Do you believe in heaven?"

"No. Do you?"

"I reserve judgment, I guess. No one's convinced me otherwise."

"If it's true and I'm wrong, then Sheila's where she wants to be. With our boys."

"And if it's true, she knows you're here, watching over her daughter. Maybe that afternoon she realized you were too far from shore to save anybody but yourself, and she wanted you to live on for Bridie's sake."

It seemed strange to Finn that Peggy, who had never met his wife, would think of that possibility. Because he'd thought of it, as well, and even though he always tried to discard the idea, the thought of it stayed with him.

"I didn't want to tell you about that day," he said. "I haven't talked about it unless I had to. For two weeks I've been asking myself why I let you convince me to."

"Do you have an answer?"

He couldn't put the answer into words. So he showed her. He kissed the back of her hand, and when she leaned toward him, he kissed *her*. She smelled of citrus and jasmine and some earthy fragrance that was unique, he was certain, to her skin. Her lips were warm, and softer than Irish rain. She wasn't hesitant or shy, not a virgin startled by this turn of events. She wasn't bold, like a woman so experienced that performance eclipses pleasure. She was Peggy, mature, intelligent, independent, and more desirable than anyone he had ever known.

He dropped her hand and put his arms around her, holding her so that her breasts pressed against his shirt. She ruffled his hair with her fingertips as she kissed him back, and he felt that lightest of touches radiate through his body in waves of feeling.

He felt poised on the brink of something, the world he'd made for himself, the only world he could bear to live in, crumbling under his feet.

She was the one who moved away. She smiled at him and touched his lips with her finger. In the darkness, he thought her eyes were moist.

"Answer enough," she whispered. "We'll take this slowly, Finn. No quick moves for either of us. You can walk away any time you want."

"And you?"

"Me, too."

No false promises. No regrets. No warnings. He heard caution and concern, and a decision to live, for now, with both.

He stood and held out his hand, scooping his jacket off the ground when she'd joined him. But she was in no hurry to leave. She kissed him again, leaning against him and reaching up to claim his lips with hers. "Irish magic," she said at last.

"Fairies in the forest after all?"
"There must be."
He suspected stronger forces at work.

chapter 19

Casey's house was a tasteful blend of simple contemporary pieces and antique reproductions—neither her salary nor Jon's went as far as the real thing. She liked color and used it lavishly on walls sporting inexpensive framed posters. The living room sofa was covered with faux leopard skin pillows, and a faux polar bear rug adorned the floor in front of the fireplace.

Megan liked earth tones and collectibles, anything handmade or nostalgic, but even though Casey's taste was completely different from hers, she still felt at home in her sister's house.

On Saturday afternoon, Megan handed Casey a glass of iced tea she'd brought into Casey's cozy den. Casey had preceded her with a plate of homemade cookies provided by a grateful client. "I like the color of these walls," Megan said.

"Aubergine. Just another word for purple."

A massive gilded mirror hung on the wall opposite the sofa, reflecting colors from the garden behind them. Casey had surprised them all with a talent for growing flowers. The side yard was ablaze with the results of her remarkable green thumb.

The sofa was burgundy suede cloth, and Megan sank into downy softness as she made herself comfortable. "I'm glad you thought of this. I was at loose ends today. There's really nothing else I can do at the saloon until some more of the big work gets completed. Then I can help with the finishing."

"You surprise me. I thought you'd be framing walls and installing pipes and insulation with the Brick kids."

Megan had expected to. She had always been handy, and her years with Niccolo had honed her skills. But she had quickly seen that helping with the saloon renovations was not going to work. Niccolo was distracted and harried, and her irritation with him mounted every time she tried to help.

"I'm trying to save my marriage," Megan said. "I get so annoyed with everything that if we work together, Jon will have to recommend an attorney."

"That bad, huh?"

Megan didn't want to talk about her marital problems. Casey adored Niccolo, and, for that matter, so did Megan. Besides, she had managed most of her life not to ask for advice, and she was determined not to change.

"So, how are things?" she asked instead. "You still like the job?"

"It's running me ragged, but I do. And the board has agreed to hire another staff member, so that will ease some of the burden."

"That doesn't sound like you."

"No?"

"No, ever since you took over the Albaugh Center, you've been one hundred percent hands-on."

"There was a lot that needed to be reorganized. But the worst of that's over, and I don't need to work that hard anymore. Other people can do the day-to-day administration."

"Leaving you time to do the bigger stuff?"

"That, and other things." Casey lifted her glass, smoothing the sides against first one cheek then another. "What a hot afternoon."

Megan was enjoying the weather. Clevelanders liked to complain about summer heat, but most years there were only a couple of weeks when an air conditioner felt like a necessity. This wasn't one of them.

The scent of newly mowed grass drifted in through the open windows, along with the laughter of children playing in a sprinkler next door. Megan sipped her tea and felt herself relaxing. In a moment she would be asking for a soft bed and a window fan.

Casey set down the glass without a swallow. "Have some cookies. Jon says they're great."

"I'm surprised you left the man any. I know you and cookies." Megan helped herself to a respectable handful. "Which are better, the pecan or the chocolate chip?"

"I don't know. I haven't tried either of them."

Megan stopped mid-bite. She began examining the evidence. Casey had lost her taste for cookies. The tea was herbal. Casey's color was high, and probably not from the heat. And to top it off, she was looking forward to more help at work.

"You're pregnant," Megan said without preamble. "When were you going to tell me?"

Casey looked sheepish. "I hadn't decided."

Megan dove for her, pulling her forward for a quick embrace. "It's fantastic, Case. I'm so thrilled for you. Why on earth didn't you just tell me right away?"

Casey was silent.

"Because things aren't going well with Nick?"

"I just hate to parade how well things are going for us. I know you and Nick are still in that adjustment phase we all go through."

"You didn't go through it."

"Okay, so Jon and I adjusted to each other in high school."

"How could you let our little problems spoil telling me your news? Who cares if Nick and I are going through a rough spot

or two? We'll get past it. And that shouldn't take away from
your excitement."

"Jon's beside himself with joy." Casey smiled wanly. "I'm
basically just beside myself. I've been sick as a dog all week.
How can you eat in this weather?"

"With great gusto. I'll eat for you, too. How far along
are you?"

"Not very. Two months or so."

"Peggy didn't have much morning sickness."

"I hate her for that."

The news was really starting to sink in now. Megan knew
Casey and Jon had planned to have a baby and that it hadn't
happened as fast as they'd expected. Casey, who was thirty-
two, had worried that she had waited too long to try. So
Megan really was delighted for her sister, but she wondered
exactly what the news would do to Niccolo.

She decided to contemplate that later. "Have you thought
about fixing up a nursery? Do you want a boy or a girl?"

"It's such a cliché, but I just want a healthy baby. I don't
care about anything else."

Megan knew where that thought came from. "Phil has an
autistic brother. If heredity had anything to do with Kieran's
problems, then it probably came from Phil's side."

"And our side is so extraordinarily healthy, huh? Exactly
which Donaghue would you like this kid to take after?"

Megan burst into laughter, and Casey joined her. "Let's
hope Jon's Hungarian genes are strong," Megan sputtered.
"This baby will need all the help it can get.

Megan didn't tell Niccolo about Casey's pregnancy. The
perfect opportunity never seemed to arise. He was gone more
than he was home, and when he *was* home, he was distracted
by paperwork and telephone calls. His television appearance
had generated real interest in Brick and new hopes of increased funding. He worked on grant proposals and fielded re-
quests from locals who still demanded to be shown through
the tunnel. A reporter from the *Plain Dealer* had stopped by

the saloon for photographs and an interview, and even though Niccolo and Iggy had carefully explained the so-called miracles as natural good fortune, the article had stirred up more interest in the image.

Both Rooney and Josh had been around the house more than usual, too. Rooney was wandering less and growing more content with his life on Hunter Street, and Josh, who was attending summer school to earn extra credit, was home every night studying. Megan wouldn't have had it any other way. After years of wondering where her father was, she was thrilled to have him under her watchful care. And Josh was too old to be her son, but she thought of him as one and loved watching him set his life on track.

A week after her talk with Casey, Niccolo came home from the saloon bedraggled and remote.

"I'd like to talk to you." He flopped down on the couch to remove his work boots.

She was surprised, because talking was one of the things they didn't do anymore. "Here? Now?"

"Have you made dinner?"

"No, I didn't know what time—"

"We'll go out."

This didn't feel like a date, or even an invitation. It felt like a command performance.

"What about Josh and Rooney?" She folded her arms, preparing for a fight. As much as she yearned to be alone with Niccolo, this was not the way she wanted to begin the evening.

"Josh can cook macaroni and cheese and slice some tomatoes."

She knew Josh wouldn't mind that, would, in fact, probably enjoy having the house mostly to himself so that he could turn up his stereo or call his friends without worrying about tying up the phone.

She decided not to argue. "Should I change?"

"We're just going to Great Lakes."

He was acting like the stereotypical Italian male and nothing like himself. She almost called him on it but decided not to. She would know soon enough what was bothering him.

She fluffed her hair and changed her shirt while he showered and dressed. They didn't talk in the car. The Great Lakes Brewery was within easy walking distance, but he didn't seem inclined to consider a stroll in the evening breeze. Under more cheerful circumstances she would have been delighted to go. The brew pub was about fifteen years old, but the building itself was more than a hundred, and a local legend claimed that the bullet holes in the wall had been put there by no less a man than Eliot Ness himself.

They were seated outside on the patio before he spoke. "We'll order, then we can talk."

She nearly rebelled, but she decided to give him this one last concession and not one thing more. The next time he told her what they were going to do, she would tell him where to put his orders.

She studied the menu and settled on the tortellini salad and a cold glass of the brewery's Edmund Fitzgerald Porter. They were seated next to each other so that they could hear their own conversation. It was a perfect night to eat outside, and the attractive patio was crowded and noisy.

"I've heard tell that John D. Rockefeller had law offices just above the pub," she said, after their server had come and gone.

"What else have you heard tell, Megan? Recently, that is."

Now she understood what was wrong with him. "If I had my drink, I'd toast my sister." She lifted an imaginary glass. "To Casey and Jon and the baby to come."

"Why didn't you tell me? Or didn't you think I'd want to know?"

"I wasn't trying to keep it a secret. There just wasn't an opportunity, and I didn't want to blurt it out."

"Come on, Megan."

She started to protest, but there was nothing more she could say. Maybe if a perfect opportunity had presented itself she would have told Niccolo. But she hadn't even attempted to find one. The truth was that she hadn't wanted to face him with news of the baby. Because she had known what would come afterward.

"I guess I was trying to forestall another argument." She waited until their mugs had been delivered and she'd had a few sips before she went on. "I know how you feel about having a baby, and I just didn't want to see your disappointment that they were first."

"I don't care who's first. Don't you know me better than that?"

"How'd you find out?"

"Jon stopped by the saloon. I think he was hurt when I didn't congratulate him."

She rested her fingertips on the back of his hand. "I'm sorry. Let's buy some champagne and stop by their house on the way home. Casey can't drink it, but she can watch."

"Jon's over the moon."

"Casey is, too. Only *she* got sick on the trip."

"The night before I was ordained, I had a dream about three little dark-haired boys. Stair steps, each one half a head taller than the other. They were waving goodbye to me from across a river. I very nearly called off my ordination."

She swallowed a lump in her throat and more of her beer. It was such a lonely vision, a man being parted from a future he would never be allowed to experience. "You have obvious dreams, too, Nick. And that's not the only one."

"Meaning?"

"You're still dreaming about being a priest, aren't you?"

He didn't deny it. "How do you know?"

"I sleep beside you, remember?"

"What, am I chanting the Gloria? Reciting the Eucharistic prayer in Latin?"

"Even I know that's not done anymore." She tried to soothe him. "I'm not angry, and I'm not worried. But we're both in transition here. This isn't the right moment to add a baby to the mix."

"At least this is a different argument than the one that says

I'm too busy and preoccupied to be a good father. That I'm more worried about ersatz miracles than about my own wife."

Her empathy was eroding. "It's part of the same argument. You're not ready. I'm not ready."

"If I thought you might be ready while we're both still fertile, I wouldn't even bring it up."

The comment was so unlike him that she just stared. He had never before used their advancing ages as a reason to hurry into pregnancy. Now she wondered how long he had been worried.

"Forget I said that." He reached for his beer, as yet untouched.

"That would be pretty tough. You did say it. And you meant it."

"I could have said it better."

"Let me make sure I understand. You think we're ready, right this very minute? In fact, if we rush home without eating, we might catch the next ovulation and just in the nick of time?"

"That's not what I said."

"You need me to prove that I will be ready soon. That's what you said."

He put his head in his hands for a moment, like a man who was too weary to hold it up. After a few seconds he straightened. "I want what Casey and Jon have."

"If you were looking for a brood mare, there were better choices."

"None of them were you, and I was looking for Megan Donaghue."

"You want me to tell you that I'm one hundred percent certain I'll be ready to have a baby next week or next month, but I'm not. Every day we seem to drift further and further apart, Nick. This is the first time we've been alone in ages. We haven't even..."

"Made love?" He looked increasingly exhausted. "I know."

"You want a baby *and* an immaculate conception?"

"I thought this was going to be easy. How can two people

who love each other as much as we do suddenly be so far apart?"

She was glad he realized that it wasn't a question of not loving each other. "Let's enjoy tonight," she said. "Let's talk about something, anything, besides Brick and funding and the renovations. I won't tell you about the kitchen sink I've picked out if you won't tell me about your latest grant proposal."

"Deal."

"Then we'll buy champagne and visit the Kovats family. You can watch Casey turn green. Maybe it will convince you that waiting a while for a baby's not such a bad idea."

"A stellar evening to come."

"Then we'll go home and act like a newly married couple. You won't ask Josh about messages, and I won't ask Rooney if he remembered to take his bedtime medication. At least not more than once."

"And I won't fall asleep as soon as I hit the bed."

"You'd better not, or I'll hit *you*."

She hadn't told Niccolo she was hurt by his lack of attention. It was a reality that had only slowly occurred to her. She had thought herself beyond such a thing. She had never been emotionally needy, and she was a practical soul who was tolerant of the imperfections of others. Logically, she understood that Niccolo's exhaustion and preoccupation, even his demands, were a result of needs that had little to do with her.

She was surprised that even though she understood all this, she was still hurt. And she was too bewildered at her own reaction and too ashamed of it to tell him so.

The remainder of the weekend was a truce. Niccolo pulled himself away from his work on Sunday morning to make coffee and homemade ciambella to celebrate A's on two of Josh's summer school exams. In the evening they convinced Rooney to take a stroll through the neighborhood and wandered toward Casey and Jon's with the leftover cake in hand. But on Monday morning Niccolo was ready to go by six, and before he left the bedroom, he warned her he might be late for dinner, too.

"I have a breakfast meeting with someone from Catholic Charities," he said on his way out the door. "They want me on their board."

She turned over to glare at him. "And you're going to say no, right?"

"Most likely."

She didn't like the sound of that, and her reaction must have been obvious. "The contacts would be great," he added. "That's the only reason I'm hesitating."

"You could open a new branch of the United Way while you're at it. Those contacts would be great, too."

"You're going to be at the saloon?"

She had told him she would be. Now that the necessary repairs had been done to the tunnel, she wanted to finish clearing the second storeroom. She didn't know whether she would ever use it or not. She was inclined to permanently seal off the tunnels as soon as she and Niccolo could come to an agreement, but in the meantime, cleaning out the stacks of trash was something to do. She had asked Niccolo to build a small display case at the front of the saloon for memorabilia. She knew others would find some of the correspondence and newspapers and lists of supplies as interesting as she did.

She turned away from him and pulled the sheet higher. "You can find me in the bowels of the earth if you need me."

"I'll see you there."

She doubted it very much.

She did see him for a few minutes at lunchtime. He stopped by the picnic table on his way out to buy more supplies. "Good meeting this morning?" she asked.

"Productive."

"You told them no?"

"Almost. I said I'd think about it."

"There are probably a few free minutes between midnight and 12:05 to give it some thought."

"Megan, I'm sorry, but don't hold dinner for me. You go ahead and eat, and I'll grab something when I get there."

She didn't even ask where he would be. Somebody needed him, and he felt compelled to go. "Let me write down our address, in case you forget where we live."

He had already turned to go. Now he turned back. She'd expected irritation, but he looked contrite. "Let's plan a weekend away. Soon. Just you and me. Where nobody can get to us. Okay?"

She managed a smile, although she suspected this was an invitation that would never materialize. "Okay."

"I'll see you later."

She shook her head as he walked away.

The afternoon was hot and muggy, and she wasn't sorry to go back down into the tunnel, which was cooler, even if not the most pleasant of atmospheres. She hurried past the image without a glance, then turned back to study it, training her high-powered flashlight directly on it. Niccolo and the Brick kids had redone some of the plumbing that week. There had been no indication of a leak, but he'd asked her to check and see if the image had changed. It looked the same to her, eerily like the beckoning Virgin Mary. No tears today, but the image was as clear as the first day she'd seen it.

She remembered her own reaction, and it bothered her. After her mother's death and her father's desertion, she had abandoned God as a time-consuming hobby. She had spent the hours she should have been in church trying to keep her sisters together. When compelled by family members to go to a First Communion, she always arrived at the last minute and departed before the sign of peace. She hadn't so much been angry at God as dismayed by his indifference. She had returned the favor.

After the tornado, then the explosion, she had run back through this tunnel praying silently that Niccolo had survived. She hadn't even realized she was praying. The words had been wrung from deep inside her, snippets of long-buried prayers that her mother and the St. Brigid's nuns had taught her. And she had found Niccolo alive, when by all rights he should have been dead or seriously injured.

The spot still felt holy to her. Not because of the image. And perhaps not because she had found her husband alive after all. But because she had turned back to God in this place. Not demanding a miracle, not bargaining with something she would later forget to deliver, but simply asking for the strength to face what was ahead of her.

And strength was only a piece of what she'd been given.

She stared at the image and wondered if Niccolo felt something of the same here and if that was at least part of the reason why he didn't want to close the tunnel. His life had been spared on this spot. Perhaps his willingness to show others this place was his way of expressing his gratitude.

She passed on to the storeroom. She had made a good start here, but she hadn't been back for a while. Niccolo had rigged a long extension cord from the furnace room and a high wattage portable light for illumination. She switched it on gratefully and debated where to begin.

An hour later she had gotten through two cartons. Anyone else would simply have heaved the contents into the nearest Dumpster, but she was too entranced. Life in the twenties had been so different, and some forefather or mother had hoarded every record of it. She found candy tins filled with receipts, moth-eaten leather albums with sample menus, hardcover ledgers with painfully neat writing and more painfully detailed expenditures. The menus were a find, and she set them aside to display. She was gratified to see that some of the signature dishes she served had been favorites then, as well.

The receipts went into trash bags, since most of them weren't labeled or even decipherable. Then she took a closer look at the ledgers. She was still going over them item by item when she heard a noise in the tunnel. She looked up to see her aunt Deirdre in the doorway.

"Well, hello." Megan closed the ledger and stood up to greet her. She and her aunt "Dee" had survived a somewhat rocky start to become friends. As a girl, Megan had resented her aunt for taking Peggy to live with her, but now, as an adult, she realized the necessity and was grateful for the care as well as the sensitivity that her aunt had displayed. Megan hadn't been the easiest teenager to love, but her aunt had never stopped trying.

"Welcome to the mess." Megan gestured to the still unopened boxes.

"You weren't kidding, were you?"

Aunt Dee made up excuses to check on her at least once a week, and Megan had told her about the second storeroom during their last telephone call. Megan knew she was worried that Megan wasn't handling the enforced time off very well.

"Look at these." Megan handed her the album. "Same food, different prices."

Deirdre scanned the pages. "I hate to say it, but I remember back nearly this far."

"You weren't even born."

"Not that long afterwards. This is fun. What else have you uncovered?"

Megan showed her the stack of treasures. "I was just going over the ledgers. Considering Prohibition, we were doing awfully well in the twenties. I'm sure the tunnel helped, huh? All that bootleg booze?"

"We sold our share, there's no doubt."

"There's a lot more to look through."

"Want some help?"

"I'd be thrilled. Although once this is done, I'm not sure what I'll do next."

"Relax and read? Take up sewing?" Deirdre laughed at Megan's grimace. "You're not having fun, are you?"

"I miss seeing everybody. I miss all the regulars and the family dropping in, and the noise and even the work. And I miss cooking."

"Nick says it won't be that much longer before the kitchen's done."

The kitchen was going to be beautiful. Megan practically drooled every time she walked through. She could hardly stand not being able to whip up her famous Irishman's stew or Lenten Cod Cobbler.

"Give me a box," Deirdre said. "We'll have fun."

Megan explained what she was keeping and what she was tossing. "Anything interesting that we don't want should go the Historical Society for a look," Megan said. "Otherwise, toss."

They worked in companionable silence for fifteen minutes. Deirdre never pried or made demands, and Megan was grateful.

"Aunt Dee, look at this." Megan held up a cigar box stuffed with newspaper clippings.

"What is it?" Deirdre stood, putting her hands against the small of her back as she straightened. Cartons weren't the most comfortable of seats.

"Articles and pictures about Glen Donaghue," Megan said.

"My father Glen?"

"Looks like it." Megan had seen photographs of the older Glen Donaghue, who had died when she was only four. Glen, her grandfather, had adorned the walls of the saloon along with other long dead ancestors. He had married in his thirties, and she hadn't seen many photographs of him from before that. "What a good looking guy. A heartbreaker. I'm surprised he made it as long as he did without some woman snagging him." Megan set the cigar box where her aunt could go through it, too. "He worked with Eliot Ness, didn't he?"

"After Ness became safety director. In the mid-thirties sometime. Boy, the stories we heard when I was growing up."

"These look like they come from an earlier era."

"He was a Prohibition agent in those days." Deirdre scanned the article. "A good one, at that. Some profession for the son of a saloon owner, huh?"

Megan perched on the edge of a box with her clippings. "I've been looking for information on Liam Tierney, and Nick brought home some letters from St. Brigid's." She explained about Maura McSweeney. "Some of the letters that were already translated mention a Liam who seems to be from Shanmullin, so it looks like that could be Liam Tierney, and one of the letters mentions a Glen, who was trying to uphold the law. Did they cross paths, do you suppose? Wouldn't that be a hoot?"

"I don't know much about Dad's years with the Treasury Department. He didn't talk about them."

"A Tim is mentioned, too." She tried to remember the wording. "Something about him carving out his own piece of the world...no, carving his own luck and threatening anybody who interfered."

"Well, that one's easy. She's probably referring to Tim McNulty. Quite a celebrity in these parts. I know for a fact he was a member of St. Brigid's. And Dad definitely knew him. There's quite a story there, though I never heard it from Dad. I heard bits of it from Dad's sister, Maryedith, just before she died."

Megan remembered her great-aunt well. Maryedith had been sharp-tongued and intolerant, which was too bad, because she had also been the family historian, the one to remember all the family stories in Technicolor and Dolby Stereo. They'd all been forced to put up with her complaints and marching orders if they wanted to learn anything.

"She used to pinch my fanny every time she thought I was getting out of line, which was most of the time," Megan said. "Not too easy to love, our Maryedith."

"Apparently men thought so, too. She lived alone all her life."

"What did she tell you about Tim McNulty and your father?"

"Well, you'll see why he never told me himself once you've heard the story."

Megan's curiosity was royally piqued. This was almost enough to make her forget her problems. "There's iced tea in a cooler upstairs. We could sit on the picnic table. We can take the cigar box and ledgers up with us."

"I like the sound of that. You're on."

"Switch on your flashlight and prepare to depart." Megan closed up the larger box and stowed her new treasures under one arm.

"I waited a long time for this, you know."

"What? To find these clippings?"

"No. To be your friend."

"I'm sorry I was so awful all those years, Aunt Dee. I know you did what was best for everybody. We owe you a lot. All of us."

Deirdre switched on her flashlight as Megan flicked off the portable. "You don't owe me a thing. I did it because I knew someday we'd sit upstairs in the sunshine and have iced tea together. It was worth the wait."

1925
Castlebar, County Mayo

My dearest Patrick,

You ask why I never married, an odd question in these closing years of my life. The answer has to do with choices, of course.

I had mine. In my youth there were two men who asked me to share their homes and bed. The first, a farmer, had a sizeable brood of children that needed raising and a wife newly in her grave. I had no interest in the man or the children, and particularly not in the farm, which had neither beauty nor tillable earth. I was careful, of course, not to tell him this, only that I was a woman not inclined toward marriage nor with any of the gifts such a woman needs. He gladly searched elsewhere.

The second man was not so easy to refuse. He was a good man, a handsome man, and life with him would not have been difficult. Perhaps we might even have traveled, read the books I love so well and talked about them, watched our children grow older and laughed about them in our twilight years.

But marriage is never a certain prospect for a woman. We are born to serve. Duties to church, duties to parents, duties to those superior to us. We are inferiors, overworked, poorly paid, if paid at all, often undernourished, if there are men who must be fed first. I watched our own mother suffer at the hands of our father, dear Patrick. You saw less of this, leaving home when you did. But I watched her carefully as her spirit was extinguished, heartbeat by heartbeat, shout by shout. I did not learn to hate men, only what our society allows them to become.

I said no to my beloved. I told him I would live with him outside the bonds of marriage so that my choices remained my own. Being the godfearing man that he was and wanting children, he refused.

And now I have shocked you. Perhaps you pray for my soul? Or perhaps you pray for Ireland's, where decisions such as this are forced upon women. I no longer know you well enough to guess which.

Your sister,
Maura McSweeney

chapter 20

The first time Glen Donaghue approached Clare McNulty, a cloche hat covered most of her shining brown hair, but the ends curled enticingly at her nape and forehead, and the hat mirrored the blue of her eyes. He knew who she was, and he knew she was the last woman he should be seen with. That didn't stop him from picking up the rosary she dropped as she started out of St. Brigid's after the earliest morning service. It was warm in his hand, and smooth, and even without lifting it to his face, he smelled the soft fragrance of roses.

"Oh, thank you." Clare stopped and smiled. "It was my mother's. I would be so sorry to lose it. She made it herself, of rose petals she shaped and dried."

"A garden of roses to crown the Virgin's head." Glen smiled and held it out to her. "It's lovely and fitting."

"Really? My friends think I'm hopelessly old-fashioned. Their rosaries are sterling and jet." She gave him a side glance before she added, "I've seen you in church before."

Clare walked through the doorway and extended her hand to the usher who was collecting money for candles that morning, speaking a few words before she started down the stairs.

Glen knew he could delay following her by engaging the old man in a conversation himself. By the time it ended, Clare would be gone, and he could not be accused of rudeness.

Good sense did not prevail. He caught up with her easily, because she was walking so slowly. "I've seen you, too. But usually not alone."

"Oh, I'm my father's greatest treasure. He makes certain I'm under guard." She sounded as if this was not something she appreciated.

"Aren't fathers supposed to love their daughters?"

"You sound like a traditional man, Mr....?"

"Donaghue. Glen Donaghue."

"And I'm Clare McNulty. I said treasure, not love."

"There's a difference?"

"We don't have to love what we treasure. We only have to value it for whatever it's worth to us."

"And you're worth something to your father?" He wondered what exactly.

"Women have been property to bargain with for centuries. If there was ever a time when we weren't, I've yet to hear about it."

"This is the twentieth century, and we have laws against slavery. How can you be forced to do something you don't want to?"

She changed the subject. "I left home before anyone even knew I was up. That's why I'm alone. I come to this service whenever I can."

"I know who your father is." He debated the next sentence, but in the end, he knew he had to tell her the rest. "I'm the last person he'd want you to talk to. Me and my kind are the ones he's probably trying to protect you from."

She stopped, and for a moment she looked concerned. "You're one of Squeaky Frank's men?"

He laughed. "Do I look like one of his men? And with a name like Dona*ghue?*"

"You look young enough to be in knee pants when you do that."

"Do what?"

"Smile. Laugh. The corners of your eyes crinkle like a little boy's."

"I'm afraid I'm old enough to be a booze agent."

Her eyes widened; then she laughed, too. "So that's what you meant. Tell me, did you station yourself at the door hoping I'd drop something?"

"Not a bit. In fact I told myself to stay as far from you as possible."

She started back down the sidewalk. "Then why didn't you?"

"I don't know what to tell you."

"The truth would be nice."

"I guess there's just something about you, that's all."

"There's something about me, all right. I'm a dangerous woman. Especially for a man like you."

"Why, are *you* making gin in your bathtub? Cruising back from Canada once a week with a hold filled with whiskey and rum?"

"I run my father's household, and I go to school. There's not much time left for bootlegging."

She had the most beautiful skin he'd ever seen, as pale, fine-grained and smooth as his mother's wedding gown. He knew himself to be a serious man. He had grown up on stories about his grandfather Rowan Donaghue's long career as a policeman. Glen knew his own father was only a Donaghue by adoption and that he had none of Rowan's blood in his veins. But Rowan was Glen's hero, and he had decided long ago to pattern his life after him. Now that he had achieved the first steps up the ladder, he knew better than to throw everything away for alabaster skin and forget-me-not eyes.

"You sound too busy to be dangerous," Glen said.

"I imagine that you're busy, too. Too busy to tangle with Tim McNulty."

"I tangle with him more often than you think."

"But never directly."

He smiled a little to let her know she was right.

She sighed softly. "He has a dozen men to keep men like you away from him, but if we have any more of these conversations, you'll get to know him personally."

She looked sad at the thought, but resigned, as if she understood that her life would always be lived at her father's mercy. She was slight, almost fragile in build, and he had the absurd urge to pull her into his arms and vow to protect her.

"He has plans for you?" Glen asked.

"He has plans for everybody he's ever met."

Glen had never had a conversation this personal on such short acquaintance. Part of him was shocked; part of him thought fate was at work. He wasn't one hundred percent Irish for nothing.

"Do you come to this Mass often? Are you able to get away?" he asked.

"Every day if I can."

He was a devout Catholic, and traditional enough to attend Mass whenever he could. In his line of work, the more religion the better. "Then I'll be seeing you," he said.

She smiled, small white teeth and rosy pink lips that owed nothing to a flapper's artifice. Her navy-blue dress was stylish but conservative. He liked everything about her.

"Then that will be another reason to get up early." She turned away and started down the sidewalk. He didn't follow, although he was sorely tempted. He knew they would find time together in the coming weeks, and he knew they shouldn't.

Somehow, that last part didn't seem to matter as much as it should have.

When she wasn't with Glen Donaghue, Clare dreamed about him. She only saw him at early Mass, and then only when she was able to get away by herself. They talked each time, and once they went across the street for coffee, a daring and probably foolish adventure that had given her that much more to dream about.

Glen was quiet but strong, blond but not too blond, tall but not too tall, handsome but not one bit a pretty boy. His family was Irish, too, "harps" like hers, but loving and happy—which wasn't like hers at all. He had only one sister, Maryedith, but dozens of cousins.

His family ran the Whiskey Island Saloon, which Clare, of course, had never visited. His job was an odd one, considering his family's occupation. He confessed that he'd chosen to be a Prohibition agent instead of a policeman because of them. As a policeman, he might well have been called on to raid his own family's place of business. His job with the Prohibition Bureau required him to keep liquor from getting to places like the saloon, cutting it off at the source.

His job required him to thwart *her* father, not his own—at least not quite as directly. His family tolerated his decision and his absence from all events at the saloon, and his superiors didn't ask him to spy on his relatives. Glen walked a fine line, but so far he had walked it with success.

Clare walked a fine line, too. Her father would be furious if he knew she had fallen in love with anyone, much less a Prohibition agent. Tim McNulty had already chosen a man for his daughter. His choice, Niall Cassidy, was part of the North Side Irish gang in Chicago, and Tim wanted nothing more in life than to affiliate himself with Bugs Moran and his pals through her marriage.

Cassidy was a junior associate of Moran's, a senior-thug-in-training, and Cassidy had kept Clare in his sights since their first meeting at a "conference" of bootleggers Tim had hosted. Cassidy had managed to find his way back to Cleveland once or twice a month ever since. He was brash and uneducated, and his effusive Irish charm barely concealed the soul of a boa constrictor.

Clare's father, a big fish in the relatively small pond of Cleveland, Ohio, had aspirations to become something more. Clare had observed him her entire life. The word *enough* was not in her father's vocabulary. The words *small time* were enough to send him into a lather. Marry Clare to Niall, and he was sure his influence and earnings would automatically increase. Doors would open for him that were closed now. Her own needs or desires weren't worth consideration.

So far, she had thwarted Cassidy. She pleaded headaches or prior engagements when he arrived unannounced, and managed to disappear when she knew ahead of time that he was coming to town. Her father was growing wise to her tactics, however, and her day of reckoning had arrived. Cassidy was coming in that afternoon to consult with her father on some minor business matter. Tim had informed her that she would be present for dinner that night, arranging something impressively festive for all to enjoy, and that afterward, if Niall Cassidy wanted a quiet moonlight stroll, she would by God accompany him through their lakeside neighborhood.

Clare had no desire to parade her household management skills for the likes of Niall Cassidy. She set the maids to dusting the countless pieces of Victorian bric-a-brac that her father equated with wealth and good taste, the Staffordshire shepherdesses, the framed coats of arms, the Majolica vases. She made sure the silver was polished—and carefully inventoried, since Cassidy was a man who would cheerfully pocket anything that pleased him. She didn't arrange fresh flowers or choose the menu with his tastes in mind. He seemed like a man who might relish a roast and potatoes; she chose chicken a la king on toast. He probably enjoyed rich pies or cakes; she chose baked fruit. The rolls were a day old, and she used the everyday china.

Cassidy arrived with her father promptly at seven. She greeted them in a mousy brown chemise that didn't suit her coloring.

"Mr. Cassidy," she said, taking his Chesterfield and handing it to the downstairs maid. She was careful not to touch him or smile.

"Niall," he corrected. "And you look lovely, as always, Clare."

She had pulled her hair back severely from her too-high forehead and donned none of the jewelry her father had given her to parade his wealth. "Elmira has set out canapes in the parlor." The canapes were made with hard-boiled eggs and sardines, the least engaging combination she could find. She had made certain that gin, vermouth and olives had been set out for fashionable martinis, since her father despised anything that stood between his glass and straight whiskey.

"You'll be joining us, Clare?" There was no question in her father's voice.

"I'm afraid I can't," she said sweetly, "although, of course, I'd love to. But if I don't supervise, I'm sure the dinner will be ruined. And we can't spoil Mr. Cassidy's evening."

"We'll take that chance." Tim took her arm.

Clare stood her ground, even though she knew her arm would be black and blue in the morning. "Then goodness, at least let me check on things in the kitchen, Daddy. Elmira is expecting me."

His fingers tightened in punishment. She didn't wince. Finally he released her. "We'll expect you shortly."

She nodded graciously and fled to the kitchen.

Elmira wasn't good with cream sauces. A scorched smell greeted Clare as soon as she opened the kitchen door. Clare smiled for the first time that evening. "Things aren't going well in here?"

"Oh, miss, I'm so sorry. It burned so quickly. I just turned away and—"

"Don't you worry. Just leave the burned part in the pan and scrape out the rest."

"Oh, I don't know, miss. It tastes bad. There's plenty of chicken. I could make more—"

"Oh, no. This will be fine. Don't forget the peas and carrots, and make sure they're very, very crisp."

She wasted as much time as she dared, but finally she joined the men. Both were gamely sipping martinis and working on a pack of Camels. She observed Niall for a moment before she entered the room. By the standards of most young women, he was the cat's meow, with smooth Rudolph Valentino hair and heavy-lidded green eyes. He dressed impeccably and smiled easily. She still found everything about him offensive, from the tobacco stains on his teeth and fingers to the cloying bay rum odor of his skin.

"Dinner will be ready soon." She entered the room and took the lone seat beside the fireplace, noting with satisfaction that the canapes had not been a roaring success.

"Niall was just telling me that he's coming up in the world." Tim looked pleased to hear it, but when he turned his gaze on Clare, she saw the glint of steel.

"Congratulations," she said primly. She knew better than to ask in what ways Niall was becoming a success. In her father's world, questions were never appreciated.

"And he was telling me that he would like to settle down and raise a family."

She considered telling the truth, that she would rather give birth to Lucifer's children than Niall Cassidy's. Instead she nodded. "I'm sure the young women of Chicago are pleased and excited."

Both men stared at her. Her voice had been modulated and her tone sincere. Clearly they weren't sure if she was being flippant. She stood before they could dig their way to the truth. "Shall I reheat the canapes?" She took the plate and held it aloft.

"Nothing short of hellfire will help them," Tim said. "Sit down, Clare."

She obeyed, rotating the plate in her hands for something to do.

"How is school?" Niall asked. "Are you learning anything useful?" Both men laughed, as if that were so impossible as to be humorous.

"The plays of Shakespeare, the philosophy of Kant." She looked wistful. "I might like to teach someday. The Ursulines do such important work. I pray for a vocation every night." She smiled—nunlike, she hoped.

"A colored girl will be Pope before I allow that," Tim said darkly.

"They do say one of the earliest popes was a woman."

"Blasphemy!" Tim mixed himself another martini. "Maybe you've had enough education, girly."

"Do you think a woman can have too much education?" Clare asked Niall. "What do they think in the Windy City?"

"My mother couldn't write her own name, but she raised ten kids and not a one of us passed away."

She nodded in mock admiration. "Happy years and high standards for everyone, I'm sure. She must be proud of you."

"Ah, she kicked the bucket a couple of years ago."

Clare spared a second of pity for the departed Mrs. Cassidy. If the other nine were like Niall, the poor woman hadn't died a moment too soon.

Elmira saved the day by announcing dinner. Niall escorted Clare into the dining room, and she was forced to take his arm. He seated her at the head of the table, and her father took the opposite side, gesturing for Niall to sit beside her.

Elmira served, and Clare watched the men from under her lashes. She was not a petty woman, and most of the time she prided herself on making others happy and comfortable. It was a thankless task in her father's home, but she labored without grudge or expectation. Tonight she only wanted her father to be as unhappy as she was at this charade of civility.

"What is this stuff?" Tim demanded.

"Chicken a la king. It's all the rage. Don't you like it?"

"If I wanted toast, I'd ask for eggs to go with it."

"Mr. Cassidy, you like it, don't you?"

He managed a nod, crunching uneasily on a mouth filled with carrots.

"Good." She smiled sweetly and set about cleaning her plate.

"There'd better be something good for dessert." Tim pushed away his portion and nursed the whiskey he'd poured before leaving the parlor.

"Fruit. It's so healthy, don't you think?"

He pushed that away, as well, after it arrived, glowering at Clare for the remainder of the meal.

She excused herself when it was clear no one was going to eat another bite, standing to signal that they could leave, too. "I'm sure you gentlemen need to smoke. I'll just help Elmira get organized for tomorrow's breakfast."

"Let's go for a walk, Clare," Niall said. "Your father's given me permission to take you out for a little while."

"I'm afraid I can't. I must study for a test."

"You'll go," Tim said pointedly. "Or there won't be anything to study for in the future."

She knew the more she argued, the worse her chances of getting away from Cassidy. "I'll get a sweater. But only if Mr. Cassidy promises to return me early."

She rejoined them a few minutes later to find the men's heads together in the midst of a discussion. She stopped in the doorway. "Should I come back later?"

"No, I'm ready." Niall took his coat and slipped it over his shoulders; then he escorted her out the front door.

"You and my father seemed to be having a chat about something important," she said, when they'd cleared the expansive McNulty yard. The house loomed behind them, a monstrous brown-shingled mansion that was suited to the gloom of a Cleveland winter and little else.

"Nah, we was just talking about you."

That was one conversation she was grateful she hadn't heard.

She had half expected one of her father's goons to discreetly follow them, but for once she was alone with a man. That did not bode well. Her father was set on her marrying Niall Cassidy. Apparently Niall had Tim's unspoken permission to use any means possible to make it happen.

"You like Cleveland?" Niall asked.

"I've never lived anywhere else." She lifted a hand to wave to a neighbor, but the woman turned away quickly, as if she hadn't seen Clare. When Clare was alone the neighbors were friendly, but they knew better than to draw attention to themselves when any of McNulty's men were with her.

"You'd like Chicago. It's bigger and better. Lots of speaks. Lots of fun. I could show you a good time." He winked.

"I don't think our idea of a good time is the same."

"Yeah? What d'ya like to do?"

"Reading. Opera. Attending Mass." She wasn't as stuffy as she made herself sound, but she didn't elaborate on the finer points.

"I like a classy sheba."

She stopped on the sidewalk. The lake was just ahead of them, a small strip of beach, then choppy water as far as any one could see. They might as well have been standing at the edge of the Atlantic. Overhead, a seagull cawed to complete the illusion.

"Mr. Cassidy, you have the wrong idea about me. I don't know what you and my father have discussed, but I'm not looking for a boyfriend or a husband." She tried flattery. "There have to be a dozen or more girls in Chicago who would be thrilled to take a walk like this with you."

"I like a sheba who plays hard to get."

"I'm not playing anything."

"What, I'm not good enough for you?"

There was a dangerous edge to his voice, and he was a dangerous man. She knew better than to be blunt or even honest if she wanted to survive the evening unscathed. "Of course that's not it. I'm not good enough for *you*," she said. "We're not the same kind of people, you and me. I'm dull. You need a girl who likes the things you do. Somebody who can help you get ahead."

"I can find other girls to have my fun with. I want a wife who does what she's told, a natural born mother."

"I'm neither of those things. I'm just trouble for you. For both our sakes, let's part as friends. You can find someone so much better."

He grabbed her arm and spun her around. His eyes were dark with anger. "You think I don't know what you're doing? You think you're something special, and I'm nothing? A nobody?"

She was afraid, but she was also angry. "I do have some say in this, you know. It's 1925. Women have the vote. And if I ever marry, it won't be to a man who doesn't listen to me. Now let go."

Instead he jerked her closer. "You know what your problem is? You never been kissed by a real man. Maybe some pansy's been kissing you."

"Let go!" She tried to wrench her arm free, but his grip tightened. One moment she was in his arms, trying desperately to avoid his lips and the grinding of his hips against hers, then suddenly she was free.

"The lady said to leave her alone."

Through a blur, Clare saw Glen Donaghue knock Niall to the ground. He was up in a moment, rushing toward Glen headfirst, but Glen stepped aside as a matador might with a raging bull. She jumped back just in time. Niall turned and rushed him again, and this time Glen moved just slightly, bringing up a knee.

The air left Niall's lungs in an audible whoosh, and he doubled over, moaning. For a man with a dangerous reputation, he wasn't much of a street fighter.

She didn't know where Glen had come from or why. She wanted to warn him that Niall was probably armed. Only rarely did her father's men go out on the streets without a gun. A man like Cassidy would consider himself undressed.

A car pulled up beside them, and two men got out. One flashed his badge. "You Niall Cassidy?" he asked.

Niall moaned in answer.

"We got questions for you. Like where you were last night, and why there's a false bottom in the floor of your car."

"Come on, Miss McNulty," Glen said, gently taking her arm. "I'll escort you home."

She watched in horror as the two other men searched and disarmed Cassidy, then unceremoniously dumped him in the back seat of the car and drove off.

"He'll kill you," she said. "He's not a man you can humiliate like that, Glen." She drew back, and he dropped his arm. "You were following me?"

"I wish I could follow you, but no, we were looking for Cassidy. Your house was the logical place to start, and we've been parked down the street all evening. We saw the two of you come outside."

And none of her father's men had been watching, because Tim McNulty had wanted to give Cassidy time to woo his daughter. The irony wasn't lost on her. "He's an ape. I hate him. My father wants me to marry him."

"And you're going to go along with it?"

"No!"

He stepped into the shadows, and she went willingly after him. He took her in his arms. "He's your father," Glen reminded her. "Honor thy father and mother."

"You can honor somebody, but that doesn't mean you should do what's not right just to please them."

"This is crazy," Glen said, right before he kissed her.

She kissed him back, her arms threading naturally around his neck, her hands into his hair.

She stepped back at last, and the world seemed like a different place. Not filled with menace, with deceit and arrogance, but filled with possibilities.

"I can walk home alone," she said. "I *have* to walk home alone. My father can't know about you."

"What will you tell him?"

"I'll tell him the truth. That three men stopped us and took Niall away."

"Will you tell him Cassidy roughed you up?"

She smiled sadly. "He probably expected it."

"Will I see you at church?"

"And anywhere else you name."

He lifted her hand and kissed it. Then he stood on the sidewalk and watched her walk home alone.

chapter21

Peggy and Bridie wore shorts, both with legs as pale as the whitecaps of Clew Bay. Wind blew in gusts, but the August sun was hot enough to make up for it. Bridie turned her face up to the sky and closed her eyes in pleasure.

"I love sunshine. I want to pour it in a bottle and keep it for rainy days."

"Me, too. When you live in a place where sunshine isn't guaranteed, you learn to treasure it."

"Kieran likes it."

Peggy looked over at her shorts-clad son, who was sitting in a sandpile with a bucket and toy shovel. He was surrounded by wooden blocks, but so far he had only showed interest in the patches of light filtering through tree limbs. Banjax lay in the shadows, guarding him and enjoying the summer heat.

"At least he's not afraid of the wind, the way he was when we first arrived."

"He learns things." Bridie paused. "Just not very fast."

And that, thought Peggy, was the reason she awoke every morning with a heavy heart. Because Bridie was right. Kieran's progress was so slow that she had run out of improvements to report to her sisters. She almost dreaded their phone calls and the inevitable questions about her son.

"I'm glad you could spend the day with me." Peggy motioned for Bridie to move closer, and when she did, Peggy unplaited an unsuccessful braid, combed it with her fingers and plaited it again. The gesture was nearly automatic. She and Bridie had grown even closer over the summer, and now small affectionate intimacies were commonplace.

"My mom used to do that," Bridie said. "Daddy tries, but he's not very good. And I don't think he likes it."

Finn's stiffness with his daughter concerned Peggy, but it was a subject they had never discussed. She knew he loved Bridie and that Bridie loved him, but the two were like strangers walking through the same forest on parallel paths.

"No one teaches boys to braid hair." Peggy wrapped the elastic band around the end and patted Bridie's shoulder. Bridie didn't leave, she just snuggled against Peggy, and Peggy put her arm around her for a companionable hug. Bridie needed an adult who could show her love, and Peggy needed a child who could return it. The relationship was mutually fulfilling.

After a moment Bridie flopped down on her stomach. "When I grow up, I want to live far, far away."

"Do you? Away from Ireland?"

"Why should I stay? This is where bad things happen."

For a moment Peggy didn't understand; then she realized Bridie wasn't talking about politics or the country's history of repression and famine. She was talking about herself and her family.

"Your daddy's here," Peggy said. "And he would miss you."

"I don't think so." Bridie rolled to her back. "He doesn't notice me very much."

Peggy would rather have heard anger in the little girl's voice than resignation. Clearly Bridie saw little chance of affecting the way her father felt.

"It may seem like it." Peggy felt her way. "When sad things happen, the way they did to your family, everyone's affected. Sometimes people don't know how to go on, what steps to take, how to act or even how to think."

"Is that how you felt when Kieran was born? Because it doesn't seem that way. I think you love him more just because things didn't go quite right with him."

"Your daddy loves you, Bridie. Maybe he's just forgotten to show it as often."

"What are we going to do with Kieran today?"

Peggy had a lesson plan. She'd brought her son outside to work on nonverbal imitation skills. Having a schoolroom was important, but Kieran needed to be taught how to block out distractions and learn in other places, as well. So she'd chosen the sandpile, and she'd made a list of behaviors for him to copy. If he learned to imitate nonverbal behaviors, then other behaviors might follow more naturally.

Of course, in one way or another they had been doing imitation exercises for months with little success. On his best days he paid attention and cooperated, almost seeming to enjoy the activity. More often he became annoyed or frustrated and refused to follow along.

"Why don't you see if he'll follow you today? He's tired of me." Peggy's morning alone with her son hadn't gone well.

"What should I do?"

"Let's start by putting toys in the bucket. You put one in yours and see if he'll put one in his."

"And I'll praise him if he does it."

"You're very good at this."

Bridie went over to sit across from him. Kieran objected, because she disturbed the shadows that had so fascinated him. Bridie sat her ground, guessing, Peggy thought, that if she didn't, Kieran would be so engrossed in watching the shifting light that nothing she did would get his attention.

"No," he said.

"Yes," Bridie answered. She picked up her bucket and put a block inside it. Then gently she lifted his hand and closed it over a block. When he grasped it at last she moved his hand over the bucket and waited for him to drop it in.

Kieran snatched his hand back and threw the block at her. Then he grabbed handfuls of sand and began to hurl them at Bridie's face.

Peggy was up like a shot, but before she could get to the children, Bridie picked up a handful of sand and tossed it back at him. The sand landed in his lap. Kieran looked down, then up at her. He picked up another handful, but this time instead of hurling it at her face, he dropped it in her lap, exactly the way she'd done to him. He followed that with a giggle, the giggle of any child engrossed in a new game.

This time Bridie tossed a block in his lap. Kieran fished for another and tossed it to her.

Peggy was so fascinated by this turn of events that she didn't hear footsteps until Finn was nearly on top of her.

"What next? Firebombs and grenades? The activity of the day is exploring the troubles in Northern Ireland?" He lowered himself to the ground beside her.

Peggy's breath caught in her chest. She and the children weren't the only ones wearing shorts today. Finn's long, muscular legs were bare and, unlike her own, tanned. The hours he spent outside showed on his sun-kissed face, too. Her gaze fell to his lips, and she smiled. "Hello."

"Hello to you." His gaze was warm, but he didn't touch her. As far as Peggy knew, she and Finn were the only people in the world who knew their relationship had blossomed into something more than tolerance. In the month since he had kissed her at the overlook, their intimacy had increased steadily. They found excuses to see each other whenever they could. The sexual attraction that had simmered between them almost immediately was rising to a slow boil.

"Don't tell me you came to take Bridie home." She raised her gaze to his. "You can't. Who'll throw things at Kieran?"

"She's going to Dublin with Sheila's cousin's family for a week. Didn't she tell you?"

"I forgot she was leaving today."

"We're meeting them in town later. They're stopping by Shanmullin on the way from Westport."

"I'll miss her."

Finn didn't respond in kind. She remembered Bridie's earlier comments about her father and wondered how he could be so oblivious to the little girl's needs.

The children were still happily tossing blocks in each other's laps. It was unorthodox, but it was definitely imitation. Eight out of ten times was the standard, and Kieran had already exceeded the maximum. It was time to go on to something else, but Peggy had no energy for a change.

"Did you come to see Irene?" she asked.

"I stopped in to let her know I was here, but she waved me away. She's watching something on the telly. I really came to spend some time with Bridie before she goes off for the week."

That pleased her. He wasn't oblivious to his daughter after all. "I guess I can lose my helper for a good excuse like that."

"Not at all. I thought we'd stay here and work with Kieran, and you could go inside and spend some time with Irene. I know how she loves to have you to herself occasionally."

She wasn't certain she understood. "You're going to work with Kieran?"

"Work may well be inaccurate, since I doubt I can accomplish the lofty goals you have for him. But tell me what you planned to do with him today, and I'll give it a try. Bridie can help."

She understood so much. That Finn wanted to relieve her of some of the burden of Kieran's therapy. That Finn wanted to spend time with his daughter. That Finn needed a project he and Bridie could do together. Without one, he wouldn't know what to say or how to treat her.

"This is such a luxury."

"You deserve it, Peggy-o."

She smiled at him. "Then I'll take you up on it. I know he'll be in good hands."

Kieran was tiring now. Bridie took the cue and picked up a block to drop in her bucket again. This time he followed suit. On that positive note, Peggy fled the scene.

Irene was thrilled to see her. They sat companionably and watched "Crossroads," Irene's favorite soap opera. The show took place in a busy hotel, a revival of a much earlier version that had taken place in a motel—a creative update for Irish sociologists to ponder. Irene attempted to acquaint Peggy with the confusing lives of all the characters. Someone's dog had been used in illegal dog fights. Someone else had hidden out in a rock quarry. By the time the episode had ended, the only thing Peggy was sure of was that she didn't want to vacation at the Crossroads Hotel any more than she wanted to take up residence on Melrose Place.

They turned off the television, and Peggy brought Irene the snack that Nora had left for her. Half an apple, a low-fat oatmeal cookie and a glass of skim milk.

Irene took it gratefully, but Peggy noted her lack of interest.

"What I want," Irene confirmed, "is a wedge of good cheddar and a slice of rich fruitcake. Don't grow old, Peggy dear."

"They say it beats the alternative."

"That it does. Particularly when you have reasons to keep living. Since you arrived, I wake up every morning excited to see what the day brings. The bits of information you've turned up about my da have done my poor heart good."

Peggy was touched. She hadn't been sure Irene would be glad to hear the details of her father's shady past that were coming to light. "I wish I could take you back to Cleveland, Irene. There are so many people there who want to meet you."

"I'm satisfied just to know they're there, although I would like to meet your sisters."

They talked until Irene grew droopy-eyed. Peggy made sure she got to bed and that the head of her bed—hospital issue—was cranked up enough to facilitate easier breathing. No sooner had she closed the bedroom door than Finn and

Bridie arrived with Kieran. Peggy said goodbye to Bridie, who was practically dancing with excitement at the thought of her upcoming holiday. Bridie went out to wait for her father in the car as he handed Kieran over to Peggy for his nap.

"A good hour, I think," Finn said. "He used his shovel to dig in the sand and even piled it up the way Bridie showed him."

"Thanks so much, Finn. It was a welcome break."

"Irene's gone to sleep?"

"I'm afraid you missed her."

"Then I missed my chance for her check-up, too. I'll need to come back later."

"I can check her blood pressure and heart for you, if you prefer?"

"I prefer to come back and have supper with you both."

She touched his cheek. "Just give Irene time for a good nap. She seems tired today. Maybe my company wore her out."

"That I doubt." He kissed her cheek and left.

Peggy quickly bathed Kieran and offered him a snack, but sleep claimed him halfway through a cookie. She carried him to bed and decided to join him. When she awoke an hour later, the house was silent, and she tiptoed into the living room to see if Irene was up. When she discovered she was alone she looked over Nora's preparations for the evening meal and added a carrot and raisin salad to go with them.

The afternoon wore on. Kieran awoke fussy and inconsolable. She was surprised he didn't wake Irene with his whining and one lulu of a tantrum that nearly brought down the thatch. At last she settled him on the front porch with a bowl of ice cubes and a pitcher of water. When every last cube had melted she gave him a box of toy cars to play with on the flagstones. After she'd demonstrated how to roll them along the stones he stopped fussing and shoved her away. Then, one by one, he turned the cars on their backs and kicked them into submission.

She was so absorbed in her son's rebellion that she didn't

hear Finn's car. She was surprised when she saw him coming up the walkway.

"I suspect that's not what you had in mind for him," Finn said.

She shook her head; then she bent and gathered up all the cars and put them back in the box. She spoke calmly. "Kieran, you can play with the cars when you don't kick them."

"Want some input here?" Finn asked.

"You bet."

Finn stooped in front of the little boy who was gearing up for another tantrum. "Kieran, would you like to choose one car to play with?"

Kieran stared suspiciously at him, but the tantrum, at least, seemed to be on hold.

Peggy knew that giving children choices was an important part of their growth and learning, and autism didn't change that. But normally, when she tried offering choices, it provoked angry outbursts.

Finn reached in the box and chose two cars, holding them out to the little boy. "Which one would you like?"

Kieran's little eyes narrowed, and his rosebud mouth puckered in a frown.

"You may have this one." Finn held it out. "Or this one." He held out the other.

Kieran seemed to struggle. Peggy could almost read his little mind. Throw himself to the ground, which felt familiar and to some degree comforting, or participate in this new and suspicious game. Finally, when her own patience was beginning to fray, he stepped forward and took the car in Finn's left hand. Then, as if he'd known all along what to do with it, he put it on the ground and began to run it along the flagstones.

Finn stood and dropped the other car in the box.

"Too many cars?" She knew her son better than anyone else did, but she was not always privy to the way his tiny mind worked.

"Maybe, but I think he staged that scene because he saw me coming down the road."

"I don't get it. He didn't want you here?"

"On the contrary. Remember the day I took him for the walk during his tantrum?"

She remembered well. It was the day Kieran had used the rag doll as a weapon. "You think he was angling for another?"

"Tantrum plus Finn equals a ride on my shoulders. Add it up yourself."

"He really is a stinker, isn't he?"

"I think we can assume he's quite bright, just locked away from ways to display his intelligence."

She was warmed by his words. Intelligence was difficult to measure with autistic children, particularly those of such a young age. But even though IQ was no guarantee of a successful life, a high one was a factor in Kieran's favor.

"Now let's wait until he's been a good little lad for a few minutes, then we can take him for a walk together."

"Some days I feel like I'm in a brand-new version of 'The Miracle Worker.' He can see and hear, but he's just as shut away from the rest of us as Helen Keller was."

"And look what she accomplished," Finn said.

"Yeah, but where's Ann Bancroft when you need her?"

He smoothed a piece of hair back from her forehead. "Right here."

Before they left, she went to see if Irene was up, but there was still no sound from her bedroom. By the time they returned with a calm and happy Kieran and Irene still hadn't emerged, Peggy was growing concerned.

"I think I'll peek in on her," Peggy said.

Finn didn't argue. She knocked softly, and when there was no answer, she opened the door and went to Irene's bedside. Irene opened her eyes, but for a moment there was no recognition in them.

"I'm sorry I woke you," Peggy said, "but you were asleep so long I was worried."

A long moment passed. Irene's breathing quickened. "I'm not feeling so well," she said at last.

"Finn!" Peggy motioned for him to join her. "She says she's not feeling well."

"Hello, dear." Irene spoke softly when Finn joined them. "It's nothing to worry about."

"I'll check that out, if you don't mind." Finn sat on the bed beside her and lifted her wrist to take her pulse.

Without being asked, Peggy went for his medical bag. He accepted it with a nod. "Call me if you need me," she told him. "I can put Kieran in his crib."

When he didn't call for her, she settled Kieran at the kitchen table with cheese cubes and grapes, but her mind wasn't on her son. It was on Irene, whose pallor had been noticeable and breathing labored. Peggy was no fool. She knew the extent of Irene's illness and the prognosis. Every day was a gift. Peggy just wasn't ready to let go.

Finn appeared a few minutes later. "She needs to be in hospital."

"Let me guess. She won't go."

"So right. She's terrified she'll die there."

"She wants to die in her own bed." Peggy knew that was Irene's wish and, in theory, an admirable one. But Peggy wasn't ready for Irene to die at all.

Finn shoved his hands in his pockets. "There's a fairly new drug on the market, an injection I can give her that has a good success rate. If I do it here, I'll need to stay and monitor her blood pressure. I know you could do that, but I should be here if it goes down too low."

"You can stay?"

"I can."

She realized he was asking for permission to treat Irene here at home. Peggy was Irene's closest relative. If she objected,

Irene could still override her decision, but giving permission would make his task easier. "Is there anything I can do?"

"We can take turns staying with her, if you'd like."

She nodded. "You have the medication with you?"

"I knew this day was coming." He left the kitchen. She waited until Kieran seemed to be done, then she set him on the floor and cleaned up.

In the living room, she turned on the television and put in a tape of "Sesame Street," a treat he was rarely given. Kieran had too much to do and learn to spend his time watching images flicker across a screen, even creative, educational programs. But this unexpected bonus would keep him occupied for a little while, at least.

When he was settled and murmuring excitedly to himself, she went to stand in Irene's doorway. "How are you doing, Irene?"

"I don't want to go to hospital."

"I know you don't. But I don't want to lose you, either."

"I...I want to find out what happened—"

"To your father, I know. We're closing in on it. You've got to stick around, even if that means a short trip to a place where they can take care of you."

"I'm not going...anywhere."

"Well, if I had any doubts you were related to me and my sisters, they're all gone now." Peggy went to her bedside. "Look, promise me you'll let Finn and me decide if you get worse? Please? You know we'll do what's best for you, don't you?"

Strains of "One of These Things is Not Like the Other" drifted in from the living room while Irene considered.

"Let's...just see," Irene said.

Peggy frowned at Finn, but he nodded. "I think the injection I gave her will work. If it doesn't, I'll thump her on the head, throw her over my shoulder and dump her in the back seat of my car."

Irene smiled and drifted off to sleep.

"Tell me about the drug," Peggy said softly.

"It's a synthetic version of a natural human hormone. Essentially, it dilates arteries and veins. It's manufactured using recombinant DNA technology, and it's reported to be more effective than nitroglycerin for shortness of breath in circumstances like this one. It needs to be given in low dosages, though, or hypotension can occur. That's what I'll be checking for."

Even under the circumstances, she was thrilled to be discussing medicine with him. Some women wanted roses and soft music. Peggy found chemistry and physiology a turn-on. Quietly but avidly, they discussed treatment alternatives as Irene dozed. Peggy thought the old woman's breathing had eased by the time Finn stood.

"She's not out of the woods, but we might have turned the tide." He grinned ruefully. "Pardon the mixture of metaphors. I was a doctor, not a language professor."

"You *are* a doctor." Peggy considered her next words carefully, but if she and Finn were to have any kind of relationship, she needed to say the things that were on her mind. "You didn't have any trouble making a decision about this, Finn. You acted decisively and quickly."

"She gave me no choice."

"And if she had, would you have done anything differently?"

"I would have done it in hospital, where she could be carefully monitored."

"But the treatment would have been the same."

"What is it you Americans say? I'm a sucker for technology?"

"One of the most important things I learned in med school was not to overtreat. A doctor has to know when she's accomplished her goals. Sometimes it's easy to assume illness when health is present."

"I don't think you're talking about Irene."

"No, I'm talking about you."

"One decision does not a doctor make."

"One after another does."

"Not here, Peggy, and not now. This isn't the time for this discussion."

"No, but it was the time to begin it." She rose on tiptoe and kissed him. She almost expected to be rebuffed, but he put his arm around her waist and pulled her closer.

When Peggy stepped away, she glanced at Irene. The old woman's eyes were open, and she was smiling.

chapter 22

By the time Irene drifted into a more natural sleep, Peggy had fed Kieran supper and given him another bath. All the outdoor play had taken its toll, and he went down earlier than usual for the night.

She was dishing up two plates when Finn came into the kitchen.

"How's she doing?" Peggy put an extra helping of roast potatoes on his plate. Nora's were always superb, even reheated.

"I think she's turned the corner."

"She didn't eat any supper."

"Did she have a good lunch?"

Peggy tried to remember. "Just soup, but she finished a whole bowl, and Nora makes it with lots of lean meat and fresh vegetables. And she had a snack in the afternoon."

"She's been sipping water every time she wakes up. I think she'll be fine. I'd rather let her sleep than force her to eat. She's exhausted."

"Our dinner's all ready." Peggy took the plates over to the table and motioned for him to sit.

"Would you like to take it outside?"

Peggy wished she'd thought of that. With the windows open they could easily hear Irene or Kieran if they awoke, and the sun went down so late that there was still plenty of light. "I'll get a tray."

"I'll spread a blanket."

She met him outside a few minutes later. Poached salmon wasn't exactly picnic fare, but it tasted even better in the evening air. They ate and listened to the sounds of sheep in nearby paddocks and the persistent call of a cuckoo, which never failed to delight Peggy. The temperature was dropping, and clouds were moving in. Peggy had changed into sweatpants as evening approached, and now she was glad. Before he returned, Finn had changed out of his shorts—which she silently mourned—but the man did justice to a pair of jeans, too.

"I think it's going to rain," she told him, looking up at the sky. Wispy clouds were gathering force, and she knew from experience what that meant in the west of Ireland.

"Then it'll be a good night for a fire. Would you like one?"

She was fond of the smell of burning turf, which had seemed familiar almost from the beginning of her stay here. She supposed the acrid fragrance had wormed its way into and attached itself permanently to the Tierney genes. The centuries of plant life compressed into those slabs had seen Ireland's triumphs and sorrows, and many of her family's, as well.

"You're sure you want to stay?" she asked. "Because I can monitor her through the night, and you're just a phone call away."

"I'll feel better if I'm close by. Move your plate."

She looked down at her lap. "Why?"

"Because my head's going there."

She was glad he wasn't monitoring *her* heart rate. "And if I say no?"

"How can I tell you stories if I'm not looking up at the heavens?"

"Stories?"

"Well, most of our stories take years to tell. We're a talk-ative people."

"We took that with us to the New World. You should hear my family."

"I could tell you a bit about Fionn Mac Cumhain, for whom I'm named, but we'd still be here next week."

"That's Finn McCool the giant?"

"One and the same. More or less."

She smiled. "I know some of the stories. I grew up on them. What was your mother thinking?"

"She let my grandmother do the honors. I was to be a giant of a man, in whatever way I chose. Do you want to hear about our stars or don't you?"

She moved her empty plate with no reluctance. He lay down, knees up, head nestled in her lap. "We'll start with the sun, since it's sneaking over the horizon. Did you know that if a woman sleeps outside in the sunshine, pregnancy is nearly guaranteed?"

"Does sunscreen prevent it?" She smoothed his hair back from his forehead. She liked the broad expanse of his fore-head and the way his hairline dipped into something just short of a widow's peak. The intimacy of this position certainly didn't escape her. It felt absolutely right.

"There's no research on that," he said. "Maybe we could apply for a grant."

"What else?"

"The moon has her stories, too."

Peggy had her own. "We had moon stories in the emer-gency room where I worked. When it was full, we had to triage our patients. The place was always a zoo."

"Must be universal and timeless. The ancients believed the moon caused insanity."

"It's that old devil moon...." She hummed a few bars until he winced. "You know, you're going to have to get used to my singing."

"I'm terrified I might."

She laughed and gently tugged a lock of his hair. "What about the stars?"

"The luck, or lack of it, you have in your life depends on what star you're born under."

"Astrology, huh? Irish style?"

"When a soul moves from purgatory to heaven, a meteor streaks across the sky." He paused. "I may just have run out of sky lore."

"Where did you learn all that?"

"My grandmother—the one who named me—lived on *Inis Mór*, in the Aran Islands. Stars are the nightly entertainment. I spent summers with her and learned all the constellations. I'd point them out if it were darker."

"Always a scientist, huh?"

"I preferred the myth to the science. The romantic Irish soul. I was born a storyteller."

"Do you tell Bridie stories?"

"Not anymore."

She waited, giving him time to elaborate. Talking about himself was Finn's greatest trial.

"I used to tell stories to the three of them," he said at last. "Every night. Mark loved them the most, even before the words made sense to him, I think. He loved the rhythm, the rise and fall of my voice. He would sit there, wide-eyed, nodding as if I was one of the heroes I spoke of."

The picture tore at her heart. "Tell me more about him."

"Why?"

"Because that's the only way I'll ever know him, the only way anyone will now. You have to tell Mark's story, and Brian's, too. So they'll be remembered. It's the Irish way."

"And if remembering them is like walking on hot coals?"

"It won't always be."

"You would know that? From personal experience?"

She stroked his hair. "Finn…"

He was silent so long she didn't think he would speak again. When he did speak, his voice was rough. "His hair was darker than Bridie's. More golden brown, and his eyes were dark like mine. He had a child's turned-up nose and freckles. He had colic as a baby, and Sheila was desperate to trade him in. I promised we would if he still had it when he was three."

Peggy laughed softly.

"He loved Bridie's pony. I'd promised him one of his own on his next birthday."

"The anticipation must have been delicious."

"He was marking off days on the calendar. It was the first thing I saw when I came home after the accident. Mark's calendar, one childish X after another."

"Each one put there with great joy, Finn."

"If only I'd bought him the pony for Christmas."

She smoothed his forehead. "Tell me about Brian."

"Smaller than Mark at the same age. The darkest hair of the three. It probably would have been nearly as dark as mine. More precocious, but more the baby, too. He liked the way everyone hovered over him. Mark tolerated him, and only a little at that. But as Brian got older, they showed signs of becoming friends."

"How did Bridie get along with them?"

"Bridie was in charge, and nobody disputed it. For a fragile-looking child, she's surprisingly strong."

"I think she's the most delightful little girl I've ever met."

"She talks about nothing but you and Kieran."

"She's so patient with him." Peggy hesitated, then went on. "I think Bridie can sympathize with the way it feels to live in a world you don't understand. Kieran's days are a mixture of confusing signals, and in some ways, hers are, as well. I'm not sure life feels very safe for either of them."

"Because she lost so much?"

"Yes, and because she's not sure what she still has."

"I suppose you're referring to me."

"I'm not judging you. It would be foolish to believe you could simply adjust and move on after such a terrible thing. The world changed for both of you. You have to feel your way."

"She needs more than I can give her. I know that."

"Were you close before the accident?"

"I fell in love with Bridie the moment I saw her. I was too young when she was born. I was married to a woman I really didn't know, and the pregnancy was difficult, so between that and my education, we didn't get to know each other very well in those months, either. Sheila spent more time at the home of her parents than she did with me. By the time Sheila delivered, I was fairly certain I didn't want an infant cluttering our lives. Then I saw Bridie, and that was that."

"I was glad you came to help out with Kieran today. It was a good way to spend time with her."

"I don't think I could be around your son so much if he wanted more from me."

Clearly Finn was a man of hidden depths, she just hadn't realized he was so well acquainted with them.

"I don't think Kieran knows what he wants," Peggy said. "And I'm not sure there are any books to help me teach him. But if we can teach him to respond outwardly the way most children do, maybe he'll be able to understand and express his feelings someday."

"We?"

"Don't worry, I know today was an anomaly. I'm not expecting an hour of your help every day."

"Help for you, or for Kieran?"

"Both."

"I'm impressed with the way you're handling your life and his. You take chances not many women would take, like coming here, quitting what you really love to devote yourself to helping him."

"I loved medicine. I love him more."

"Does it really have to be an either-or?"

"It does on my budget. He needs intervention now, not after I've finished my residency and I can afford the best programs for him."

"How is it going?"

"Not well."

"Then what's the next step?"

"It's too early to think about that. Three months isn't long enough to see a marked improvement. If nothing's changed by next spring, I'm going to have to reevaluate."

"You'll leave Ireland either way?"

"Are you trying to get rid of me?"

He moved from her lap and propped his head on one hand. "Did I tell you my favorite piece of sky lore? I don't think I did."

"Try me and we'll see."

"Come down here first."

The idea of lying beside him on the blanket sent warning signals jangling along Peggy's nerve endings. She peered at him through lowered lashes. "What happens to a woman who lies outside in the light of a rising moon?"

"She gets cold unless she has a warm man lying beside her."

She wondered if warning signals were the right explanation for what she was feeling. Anticipation might be a better term. She lowered herself to the ground beside him, and their thighs caressed companionably through denim and fleece.

He pointed above them. "Look up at the sky."

The sun was finally gone, and the streaks of glorious color it had left behind were gone, too. The light was quickly fading, and the sky seemed to turn darker as she watched, spurred on by gathering clouds.

"What am I looking for?" she asked.

"The first star."

"It's too cloudy."

"Not if you're observant."

She took up the challenge. They lay side by side, quietly gazing up, until she thought a thousand stars could come out and she would be too blind to see any of them.

She closed her eyes for a moment. When she opened them, a glimmer of light appeared in the sky directly above them. "Look." She pointed. "First star."

"Very good."

"Now, what's the story?"

"Well, if a woman sees the first star in the company of a man who kisses her, she'll get her fondest wish."

Her breath left her lungs in a whoosh. "That part about

being in the company of a man who kisses her? That's entirely new to me."

"You still have things to learn."

"How long can my wish be?"

"Don't waste a good opportunity. One long run-on sentence is the norm."

She made her wish as he leaned over her, a wish that began with Irene's improvement and ended with Kieran's. And in the middle were wishes for Finn and Bridie, and one for herself. They flowed together into one fervent "please" as she wound her arms around his neck.

Finn was satisfied with Irene's progress. Her color was better, her breathing much easier. She woke up when he took her vital signs, seemed oriented and coherent, then drifted back to sleep without a fuss once he'd finished.

He joined Peggy in the kitchen, where she was washing dishes. She was a modern, no-nonsense woman who still seemed to take pleasure in the simplest of things. Her hair swung as she swayed from side to side in rhythm with the washing and rinsing. Her sleeves were pushed up over her elbows, exposing delicate wrists. There was nothing about Peggy that didn't physically please him.

She turned when she realized he was standing in the doorway. "How is she?"

"I think she's out of the woods. For now."

"But these acute episodes will become more common, won't they?"

"It's an old heart, and a weak one. You might go in to wake her next time and find she's gone."

She halted in the midst of rinsing a plate. "She needs monitored long-term care, doesn't she? Did I delay that by coming to stay with her?"

"She needs to be *here*. Adding months to a life she despises is no gift. I just want you to understand your own risk. You'll feel guilty. You'll be certain you could have done more, that if you'd only checked on her earlier, or left her door open so you could hear her call you, or decided not to take Kieran for a walk, she would still be alive."

"Thank you." She took a deep breath, almost as if she was inhaling and absorbing what he'd said. "It's a good warning. And you? Will you be able to let go of Irene without feeling you failed her?"

He had thought about it enough to know he could. "I'd fail Irene if I insisted she move away. If I hadn't agreed to look after her, she might already be dead. Of course, insisting I care for her here is her way of proving to me that I'm still competent. Two birds with one stone. She was never a woman to mince words or waste time."

"Or maybe it's her way of helping you learn to let go. More gradually and naturally than you were forced to before."

"This is the way people should die. After a long life lived, for the most part, the way they wanted. Surrounded by people who love them. Happy with what they had time to accomplish." He hadn't meant to sound bitter, but the undertone was there.

"Oh Lord, I want that fire." Peggy shivered. The wind had picked up as the sun went down, and Finn felt the chill coming through the old walls, despite being used to it. They didn't need heat, but it was a perfect night for a small fire on the hearth.

"How soundly does Kieran sleep?" he asked.

"Why?"

"Because I have an idea how to entertain you tonight."

She raised a brow, and he laughed, because he knew she was thinking of their kiss on the blanket. "How soundly?" he repeated.

"If I drop him on his head, he might wake up. If I set off firecrackers under his bed..."

"Good. And Irene's room is far enough from the fireplace that I doubt we'll disturb her, either."

"My curiosity knows no bounds."

"I'll finish up in here if you'd like to check on Kieran."

"Let me finish here so you can start the fire. And I checked on Kieran a little while ago. Sleep is the only time when no one is making demands on him. He indulges with gusto."

"Then I'll see you in a few minutes."

Blocks of turf were smoldering nicely by the time she finished. Finn was stretched out on the soft rug in front of the fireplace, and he motioned for Peggy to join him.

She settled beside him, although not as close as he would have liked. "More stories? Twenty questions? Accounts of your childhood? You haven't told me a thing about your family, you know, and I've told you so much about mine."

"I was an only child raised on a small farm. I played with wounded birds and bugs and made animal hospitals for them. After all those years my parents decided they despised the country, so they moved to Cork four years ago and set up a small florist business. They aren't good with children, and Bridie won't visit them unless I stay with her. They only come back to Shanmullin if they're forced to. They're good people, just a trifle odd."

"That explains why they aren't around to help you with Bridie."

"They would have no idea what to do with her. Sheila's parents moved to Belmullet after the accident to get away from the scene of the crime. They wanted to take Bridie with them. If I hadn't stopped drinking, they would have."

"Does she see them?"

"They blame me for what happened, so they don't want to see me if they can help it. They won't come here to see Bridie, and I'm afraid to send her there alone. I'm never sure they'll return her, and the law can move slowly."

"She deserves better, and so do you."

He heard the undercurrent of anger in her voice. "We cope in whatever ways we can. They were close to Sheila and the children. I think the fact that Bridie looks so much like her mother makes it hard for them to be with her, and harder to let her go afterwards."

"This is not entertaining. It's sad. We need entertainment. What's next?"

He was glad to change the subject. Despite what he'd said, he had felt the absence of both sets of parents keenly, and he knew Bridie had, as well.

"Close your eyes."

"Do I know you well enough for this?"

"Don't you trust me?"

"Enough, I guess." She squeezed them shut.

He'd seen that face before, on her son. "Stay right there, and don't move."

"I can probably only bear the suspense for a minute at most. I was a youngest child and not good at delaying gratification." She paused. "Which, I suppose, is the reason I have a child myself."

"I was an only child. It seems to have little enough to do with self-control, witness Bridie's existence."

"Thirty seconds longer and my eyes pop open. I'm sorry, but you're forcing me to play against type here."

He retrieved what she hadn't noticed when she entered the room. Then he sat behind her, leaning on an armchair for support, and put his arms around her, pulling her back against him. "Okay, you can peek now."

"It looks like a tin whistle." She stroked a finger up and down the expanse of it. "It feels like a tin whistle."

"Your powers of observation are extraordinary."

"I scare myself."

He relinquished it as she grasped it. "You love music, and you claim it's not your ear that's at fault. I'm correct?"

She snuggled deeper against him. "Did Mozart sing? Did Beethoven? Can we judge their musicality by voices we'll never hear?"

"You're not claiming to be Mozart. Please tell me you aren't."

"Well, maybe Elton John?" She laughed at his grunt. "My aunt made me take piano lessons, but I wasn't very good at it. I'm slightly dyslexic. It took me an extra year to learn to read, and trying to remember which hand was my right or left was a trial."

"I'd rule out surgery as your speciality. Brain surgery in particular."

"That was a long time ago. I spent two years with 'R' printed on one hand and 'L' on the other. I'm going to be very good at this."

He didn't really care how good she was. She *felt* good in his arms, much better than good, in fact. She felt elemental and essential. He had been celibate for two years, despite offers of comfort from an older widow and a young mother who had scandalized the village by seeking a divorce the moment Irish law allowed it. He had considered both, since neither offer came with any desire for commitment. In the end he'd refused, afraid recreational sex would drive him deeper into depression. He hadn't been ready to feel good or to lose himself in sensation.

He seemed to be ready now.

"All right, here's what you need to know." He circled her with his arms. "There are two types of whistles. This one's in the key of D, which is what's called for when you're playing with others."

"As a child, I got high marks for playing with others."

"Then clearly this is the right whistle for you."

He wiggled the mouthpiece. "This moves so the whistle can be tuned to play with other instruments."

"I also believe in being in tune. I told you I'd be a natural at this."

"Peggy, you've yet to put it in your mouth."

"Technicalities. I've got all the right stuff."

"Okay, here's the test. Put it between your lips, and whatever you do, don't chew. Just hold it there gently, then blow. And try not to wake the household."

"Don't I need to know how to hold it and change notes? That sort of thing?"

"Are you teaching me, or am I teaching you?"

"A stern taskmaster, huh?" She did as he asked, blowing softly. The tone was steady and clear.

"I'm impressed." He actually was.

"I'm sure you are. You thought I'd squawk, didn't you?"

"Now I'm going to show you how to hold it." He demonstrated. There were six holes, three to cover with fingers from each hand. "Rest your thumbs behind the index fingers. Like this." He tipped it so she could see, then he handed it to her.

Her fingers fell over the holes and her thumbs moved naturally into place. "Like this?"

"Perfect. Now keep all the holes covered and blow softly. That will be a D."

"I beg to differ. It will be an A+."

"The note will be a D. The quality remains to be seen. Are you going to give me trouble every step of the way?"

"I'm hoping to." She put the whistle between her lips and blew a well-rounded D. "This is fun."

His arms tightened around her as she settled back against his chest. Her hair brushed against his jaw; her hips settled against the insides of his thighs. His body reacted noticeably.

He swallowed, moistening a throat that had suddenly gone dry. "Take the fourth finger of your right hand off the bottom hole and you'll have an E."

She did and blew. Another pure, sweet note. She uncovered more holes at his instruction and played more notes.

"Now try them all, starting again with all holes covered, and go up the scale."

She did, with very little wavering in tone.

He demonstrated tonguing, using the tongue to end notes cleanly. She wasn't bad, although she needed practice. "Now, here's the hardest part for most people. You'll need more notes than you've learned in order to play most songs, and higher ones at that. And the only way to get them is to blow harder. It's not something you learn right away, and the first attempts aren't fit for human ears."

"In other words, you don't want me to try the higher notes here and now."

"You've got a lot to practice already, don't you think? I'm going to leave this with you so you can practice on your own. I have more than one."

"You don't trust me, do you?"

"Trust has nothing to do with it. I just think—"

She squirmed in his arms, turning so that her breast pressed against his chest. "You think I'll make a racket and wake Irene and Kieran and every Tierney in the parish graveyard."

"You're determined to show me differently, aren't you?"

She eyed him for a moment, then raised the whistle to her lips. Then, with her gaze locked with his, she played God's sweetest version of "The Foggy Dew" from beginning to end.

"You never asked me if I knew how to play," she said once she'd lowered it.

He tried not to smile. "Don't blame me. You were letting on that you didn't, allowing me to make a holy show of myself."

"Hubris, Finn. Pure and simple."

"Mind yourself, Peggy-o."

"Why? And by the way, that's the only song I know how to play. So the lesson wasn't strictly for nothing."

"Where'd you learn?"

"A cousin. She plays in an Irish band. She hoped I'd pick it up quickly so I could join in, but right after she taught me 'Foggy Dew,' she moved to Milwaukee. Nowadays she's into something she calls Celtic rap. Scary stuff, that." She set down the whistle. "You know, Finn, this wasn't a bad way to get close to me."

"You think that's what it was about?"

She touched his cheek. "I'm wondering how long we're going to go on like this."

He knew what she was asking, but he didn't have an answer. These days, he walked around in a state of arousal. He wanted her, thought about her night and day, always followed closely by thoughts of Sheila and his sons. He had no right to feel anything.

"Would Sheila have wanted you to die with her if she'd known you couldn't save your boys?" Peggy asked softly. She touched his lips before he could answer. "Not if she loved you, Finn. Did she?"

After that first burst of passion and fertility, love had come slowly. He had grown to love Sheila, too, perhaps not the way he would have loved a woman with whom he'd had more in common, but as the mother of his children, the presence who both ordered and softened his life, the sweet ethereal fairy princess who charmed him with her harp and high, mournful voice.

She saw the answer in his eyes. "She wouldn't want you to be half dead, either," Peggy said. "She wouldn't begrudge you this. Lie down." She put her hands on his chest and nudged him toward the rug.

He knew better than to let this happen. He wasn't ready, not for Peggy, who was more to him than a pretty face and pleasing body. Yes, his body screamed for release, but he also yearned for her in ways that had little to do with sex. Peggy made him feel young and alive, and he knew that was part of the reason why he had fought so hard to stay away from her.

He was on his back now, and she was over him, unbuttoning his shirt. She smoothed the fabric apart and touched his chest, then she laid her cheek against it. His hands came up to tangle in her luxuriant hair. When she began to kiss him, all his doubts assailed him at once, as if they had gathered and planned this final assault.

"Shhh..." she whispered. "You can't bring them back with your unhappiness. You're alive, and this is right."

He turned her to her back in one frantic movement. "Is this sex or grief therapy?"

"It's two people who need each other here and now. It's just you and me, Finn. But don't make love to me if there's anyone else in this room."

He waited for guilt to make its fatal thrust, for memories to wrap their fingers around his throat. He realized that all he felt was the wild beating of Peggy's heart against his chest and the soft warmth of her breath on his cheek. Then he kissed her, and there was nothing between them except their clothes. And soon, not even that.

He didn't tell her that he loved her, but when he sank into her at last, for one fleeting moment of awareness he knew that what he felt was more than lust or even gratitude. And fear followed quickly when they had both found their release, and he lay with her head cradled on his shoulder.

chapter 23

The kitchen at the Whiskey Island Saloon was finished. Megan had never expected to have such a beautiful, organized space to work in. Everything was at her fingertips, and for the first time in memory there was enough built-in storage that she and the staff wouldn't have to juggle pots and pans with supplies.

"The only problem is that there's nobody to cook for," Megan told Casey after giving her the tour. "Except the work crew. And they're more a peanut butter sandwiches and pizza crowd. No one's breaking down the kitchen door for my soups and stews."

Casey perched on the edge of a counter, careful not to mar the cabinet below with her muddy shoes. The west side of Cleveland was in the midst of a heavy downpour. Fall and cooler temperatures weren't too far in their future. "When are we due to reopen?" she said.

"Nick thinks another month, max."

"Are you going to start off with a bang?"

"Free food and one dollar Guinness for all our regular customers and family. That ought to wipe out whatever's left over from our insurance money."

"It's really going to be beautiful. Nick and the boys are doing great work." Casey accepted the herbal tea Megan had brewed for her. "The place is nice enough for yuppie businessmen now. Maybe we ought to add tapas to the menu, or sponsor Saturday afternoon wine tastings."

"Just so you're the first one through the pearly gates to deflect the unfriendly fire. I don't want to explain tapas to the Donaghues who ran the place before I did."

"You think we've lost customers?"

That was a very real concern, and it preyed on Megan's confidence. What if Nick, Marco and the kids had done all this work and the place folded because people forgot to come back?

She tried to be positive. "I hear complaints every single day about the other places people have to go instead. I get another five or six phone calls a week from people who want to know when we're going to reopen."

Casey was reassuring. "Then as long as we do it soon, we should be all right. For a lot of our patrons Whiskey Island's like Grandma's house. Maybe Great-Aunt Fifi's condo has a better view and a fancy elevator, but it doesn't feel like home."

"If I had a great-aunt Fifi, I'd move somewhere far away and forget to leave a forwarding address."

Casey sipped her tea, and Megan puttered, wiping down spotless counters and disinfecting the sink. Niccolo and Marco had gone out for materials and promised to return an hour ago. She wondered if Niccolo had been so busy lately that basic skills like dialing a telephone had been lost.

"Are things going any better, Megan?"

Megan looked up from her extraordinarily clean sink. "What things?"

"You and Nick."

"He's still too busy."

"Will things ease up when he's finished here?"

Megan seriously doubted it. Last night, on the way home, Niccolo had driven by a house for sale in their neighborhood.

It was exactly the kind of house he liked to renovate. Structurally sound, a poor job of remodeling that he could dispense with quickly, enough room that an addition wasn't necessary. He'd called the Realtor that evening and signed a contract this morning. It would be Brick's next project.

"Things are never going to ease up for Nick," Megan said. "The busier he is, the happier."

"He has a high energy level."

"He has no desire for intimacy." Megan stopped scrubbing and turned to lean against the sink. "He's absolutely driven, and I'm beginning to think he just wants me hanging around the edges of his life for those rare moments when he has time to do something that's not connected to Brick."

"You don't think that will change when funding's secured?"

"Truthfully? I think once he gets the money, he'll work even harder. He'll be determined to show the funding organization that their money was well spent. He'll come up with new projects he'll need funding for." She shrugged. "Sometimes I wonder if he doesn't keep himself this busy just so he won't have to think about his life."

"What doesn't he want to think about?"

"His decision to leave the priesthood. His decision to marry."

"Oh, come on, he's crazy about you."

"Casey, I could leave him and it might take days for him to notice."

"That's insane."

"He was supposed to be back here an hour ago. We were going to run out and get some lunch together. I finally ate some soup just before you arrived."

"Maybe something happened."

"I'm sure something happened. He and Marco thought of something else they needed clear across town. He'll walk in here in a little while with McDonald's wrappers to toss in the garbage. He'll see me, and he'll remember, and then he'll feel bad and ask me to forgive him, and like a dope I'll do it."

As if she had the gift of prophecy, the front door slammed and Niccolo came striding in, followed closely by his brother.

The two men were similar in appearance, although Niccolo's features were a shade more refined, and he was thinner than the overweight Marco. Marco looked like a linebacker going to seed. Niccolo was a quarterback in prime condition.

"Megan, I'm sorry. The time got away from me. Did you eat?"

"Uh-huh." She caught the wadded up white bag as he tossed it in the kitchen garbage. She held it up for Casey's inspection. "Burger King, but I was close."

"That's Marco's. I thought I'd better make sure you weren't waiting for me," Niccolo said.

She knew a better woman would have offered him some of the soup she'd eaten herself. She just shrugged, then turned to her brother-in-law. "What kind of wild-goose chase did he lead you on?"

"Some call from Catholic Charities." Marco's eyes twinkled. "This guy of yours is sure popular. Good thing he has a cell phone."

"Catholic Charities?" Megan turned to Niccolo. "Are they still after you?"

He held up his hands as if warding off a horde of bees. "I told them I couldn't be on their board."

She felt a moment of sheer unadulterated pleasure. He had listened to her, and he had refused the position, even though it would have meant valuable contacts.

"It's a conflict of interest," Niccolo continued. "I'm applying for funding from them, and it looks like I've got a good chance of getting it."

The pleasure died. He hadn't done it to please her or even as an admission of how overextended he was. He must have realized what she was thinking, because he put his hand on her shoulder.

"I would have said no anyway."

"Sure you would have. It's just a difficult word to pronounce."

"Near as I can tell, every organization in the Midwest wants a piece of Brick." Marco went into the refrigerator and came out with two soft drinks, tossing one to his brother. "Anybody else?"

"I'm fine," Megan said. "What do you mean?"

"The way that phone rings. All that publicity stuff didn't hurt."

"I've been through this funding thing." Casey got up to wash out her cup. "When I was trying to put Albaugh back on its feet. Our problem was that every bit of money I applied for came with a million strings attached. We had to make so many changes in staff and services that every time a check came in it was almost as bad as starting over."

"That's a problem for us, too." Niccolo flipped the tab on his can and took a big swallow, as if he hadn't had anything to drink all day.

Megan sighed and went to the fridge, nudging Marco out of the way so she could take out the soup. "Do you want some of this?" She held it aloft so that Niccolo could see it.

"For sure." He turned back to Casey. "I've already turned down offers that looked good on the surface. My favorite was the one that insisted that none of the kids use power tools. Another one insisted that each participant be born again."

"You'll find the right money and the right source." Casey glanced at her watch. "I have a doctor's appointment. I'll see you later." She saw the look on Megan's face and smiled. "Just a routine check."

Marco tossed his can in the garbage. "I've got to get going if I'm going to make it back to Pittsburgh in time for dinner. Carrie's promised pasta fazul. I'll see you next Wednesday, Nick." He grabbed Megan for a goodbye kiss. "See you then."

Megan heated up the soup in the new microwave while Niccolo walked them to the door. It was ready when he returned, and she set it on the counter. He pulled up a stool. "Looks great."

"Good day for it."

"I'm sorry about lunch. I used my phone so much that the battery went dead and I couldn't call you to let you know we weren't going to make it. I looked for a telephone booth, but no luck."

"It's not the first time I've been stood up, and it won't be the last, I'm sure."

"The rest of the week's a bear. I don't have a single afternoon free."

There were a hundred clichés coined for moments like this. *So what else is new? I've heard that song before. Tell me another one.* The possibilities were an embarrassment of riches and too hard to narrow down. She simply nodded, tight-lipped and resigned.

"But I don't have a single thing planned for the weekend," Niccolo said when she didn't answer. "I'm free Friday and Saturday night. Let's plan something fun for one of them. Just you and me. Somewhere nice."

A warning seemed prudent. "But cheap."

He rested his hands on her shoulders. "Nice and not too cheap. Just us, a bottle of wine and fresh seafood. How about it?"

She rotated her head as he began to massage her shoulders. "You're sure you can find the time?"

"I'll make the time, Megan. We need an evening out. We'll get dressed up for once, maybe go dancing afterwards."

She liked the sound of that, although she could do without the dressing up. "It's a done deal, then."

"Great." He pulled her close and nuzzled her ear with his lips. "Do you want to make the arrangements? Or do you want me to act like an old-fashioned man and try to figure out what would please you the most?"

"I'll make them." She turned so she could look up at him. "Maybe you should miss lunch with me more often."

"I never want to make you unhappy. You know that, don't you? I want to give you everything you ever wished for."

"Right now I'll just settle for you, Nick."

When he kissed her, she thought maybe she'd asked for something he really could give her, after all.

Niccolo had suggested dinner and dancing. Megan decided on something a little more romantic. There was a resort about an hour and half south of Cleveland in the heart of Ohio's Amish country. She had heard that rooms at the Inn at Honey Run were lovely, that there were woods to walk in and nearby shops to explore. Better yet, it was far enough away that Niccolo couldn't easily return to Cleveland if somebody needed him. The resort wasn't expensive, and there probably wasn't a place to go dancing or buy a bottle of wine for fifty miles or more. But she would willingly settle for two nights of glorious sex.

She called, discovered they'd had a last-minute cancellation and booked a suite with her own credit card.

Her good mood lasted until four, when Niccolo called home to tell her he had a dinner meeting. Just came up, couldn't refuse, and he'd be home just in time to turn off all the lights and lock up for the night.

Josh had gone to Niagara Falls for one final summer fling with his Explorer Post, and Rooney, who was supposed to be at Deirdre and Frank's house for dinner, hadn't yet returned. Megan ate leftover salad and a microwaved potato at the kitchen table with *Newsweek* for company, then labored over the letters of Maura McSweeney with an Irish dictionary on the table in front of her and her Irish textbooks open beside it. So far the letters she'd managed to translate hadn't mentioned Liam again, but she found them interesting anyway. She was sorry she'd never met Maura McSweeney.

One frustrating hour later, she was trying to drum up enough interest to watch Humphrey Bogart seduce Lauren Bacall when Rooney came in the front door.

She heaved the usual sigh of relief that once again her father had come home. His hair was windblown and his cheeks red from too much sun, because once again he'd left the cap she'd bought him at home, but he looked as if his day had been a good one. He came into the living room and settled himself in the old armchair he'd claimed as his own.

She was never quite sure what kind of answer she would get if she asked her father a question, but lately Rooney had been on target more often than not. Better medications, a healthy diet and no worries about where to sleep at night seemed to be doing their part to improve his life. Love that assisted but didn't smother seemed to be helping, as well.

She gave conversation a try. "Still raining?"

"Not so bad."

"I hope you had a good dinner."

"Steak."

"I had wilted lettuce and a potato with more eyes than Mississippi."

He chuckled, and she was encouraged. The Rooney of her childhood had been a man with a wonderful sense of humor and the ability to share it.

"Dee says hello," Rooney said. "Frank, too."

Rooney was having a good day. Not only was he oriented to reality, but he seemed happy to be with her. She was always grateful for these moments that other people simply took for granted.

She took advantage of his good mood. "I had a nice talk with Aunt Dee a couple of weeks ago about your father."

"What'd she tell you?"

"Well, we were talking about the days when he was a Prohibition agent. Did you know he fell in love with the daughter of Tim McNulty the bootlegger?"

"Course I do."

"We didn't get to finish our conversation. That's about all I know." Deirdre and Frank had gone off on a cruise two days later, and Megan hadn't had a chance to corner her aunt again to see what else Deirdre could tell her.

"I know a lot more than that. More than Dee."

Megan was intrigued. "Do you?"

"He talked to me." Rooney smiled. "Thought I was falling in love with the wrong woman."

"Not Mama!"

"Not Kathleen. Shame on you."

She put a hand over her heart. "Well, you had me worried."

"She moved away." Rooney frowned. "Don't remember her name. Just as well."

"I'll say. You wouldn't have *me*. Or Casey and Peggy."

Rooney shot her a fatherly smile, and Megan smiled back at him. "Do you remember the stories your father told you about Clare McNulty?"

He was silent so long that she wondered if he was drifting off into the world that no one else could enter with him. Then he nodded. "You're old enough to know. Sad, though."

She was touched, because the last part was an obvious warning. He was worried about her feelings.

"That's okay," she promised. "Life can be like that."

"Good woman, wrong one to love," Rooney said. "I'll tell you what I remember."

She wasn't sure which to be more grateful for. That her father remembered the story or that he could articulate it now.

1925
Castlebar, County Mayo

My dearest Patrick,

I've had quite a fright here, and I hesitate to write you about it. Yet what news do I ever have to make you sit up and take notice? So tell it, I shall. Be assured before I begin that I am fine now and wiser than I was a week ago.

Perhaps you remember the Fitzgerald family far down the Ballinrobe road? Sean Fitzgerald and his wife, Rose, had twelve children, each of whom settled in the area, some on the family land itself. The land has never produced well, and each child has gone out to work from time to time. They are an admirable bunch. They will do anything, these Fitzgeralds, to feed their families, even the lowliest jobs. The eldest son, Hugh, had two sons of his own. On the youngest, Jack, hangs this tale.

I listen, as old women are apt to do, to news of my neighbors. It's a harmless enough pastime most days. It was not harmless the day I heard that Jack was determined to marry Fiona O'Shea. You could not know the O'Sheas. They are Church of Ireland and newly come to Castlebar. I've yet to determine how Jack met Fiona or spent the necessary time in her company to fall in love. But suffice it to say both things happened. And the two decided to be married.

Jack does work for me at times. He is a charming lad, determined to make his way in the world. He has some education and a desire for more. He has read every book that I own and absorbed every tidbit of knowledge I possess. I know less of Fiona, only that she seems both kind and spirited. When Jack confessed that they were going to run away to be married, I tried to dissuade him. Perhaps someday in the future our people will remember that we worship the same God and have more in common than centuries of disagreement. But that time has not arrived, and I feared for them both.

I was, of course, correct to be afraid. Jack presumed on my friendship, and on the night he eloped with Fiona, he brought her here to wait while her family searched for them, thinking they would not come this far and once it was completely dark they could avoid apprehension on the roads.

They were wrong, of course. They escaped only minutes before her father and brothers arrived, followed closely by Jack's. Someone had seen them nearby and felt duty-bound to report it.

I was alone when the families arrived, one after the other, and can only say that the good Lord prevailed and they did not set the house on fire. I can not report what happened to Jack and Fiona. For if they were caught, would anyone be told? Are they sharing a grave somewhere in the Irish countryside instead of a marriage bed?

I am ashamed sometimes to be a Christian, dear Patrick. We are far too frequently a most unchristian people.

                                        Your loving sister,
                                        Maura McSweeney

chapter 24

Glen had fallen in love with Clare McNulty at first sight, and even though he denied the strength of his feelings, he found countless ways to see her. After Niall Cassidy was hauled to the police station for questioning, Clare's father was even more careful about letting her out of his sight. But Clare was bright and resourceful, and Tim was a busy man. Glen and Clare met when and where they could, and each time Glen was a little more certain that he had found the woman he wanted to marry, despite the obstacles between them.

Today they were going on a picnic, and Glen had asked his grandmother to pack a lunch. Lena Donaghue was beloved by her grandchildren, and she doted on them one and all. His own mother would have questioned him relentlessly until she squeezed out every thought he'd ever entertained about a woman. But Lena was more discreet and more inclined to cook up a true feast to impress Clare.

He stopped by his grandmother's house on the morning he

was to meet Clare at Edgewater Park. As always, he was forced to wind a path through a cadre of great-grandchildren who were playing jacks and dominoes on the front porch. In the parlor he stepped over two teenage cousins who were listening to John McCormack warble a sentimental ballad on Lena's brand-new radio.

He found her in the kitchen, as he knew he would. Her hair was white, with just a few strands of red, and she had it pinned on top of her head in a knot. No fashionable bob for his grandmother, but she was still slender, despite giving birth to six children, and the lines in her cheeks did little to detract from a face that remained lovely in its way.

His grandfather Rowan, who had passed away nearly ten years before, had insisted that his wife teach her children to cook so that she would have help both at the saloon and at home. With one exception, Lena had taught her offspring the basics and little else. Only to Terence, Glen's father and her oldest son, had she passed on the sacred family recipes. By not giving them to everyone, Glen suspected that Lena was making certain that her family continued to congregate at the saloon after she died. They would be forced to if they wanted a real taste of home.

"Something smells wonderful, *Mamó*." She had always been *Mamó* Lena to him and to the other grandchildren, a word she'd brought over from the old country. It was just one of the ways she remained Irish, along with a musical brogue when she spoke.

"And what else but it should, darling?" She leaned over and kissed his cheek when he came to stand beside the stove. "I'm making enough for every Donaghue ever born."

Glen suspected his grandmother missed cooking for her customers at the saloon, even though a fierce battle with pneumonia had weakened her lungs and forced her into retirement. But she had grandchildren enough to keep her happy, and a son and Irish daughter-in-law who kept the saloon running to her strict standards. And there was always someone in the family, like Glen, who needed her to cook something special.

He spied a straw hamper on the counter and peeked inside. It was already filled with food. If he and Clare began to eat the moment he found her at the park and continued to eat until they parted, they might be able to dispense with half of it.

"Now don't you go saying it's too much," Lena told him. "Take whatever you can't finish back to that tiny room in a stranger's house you call home."

Glen had moved out of his parents' home when he became a Prohibition agent. He suspected his family understood, although it was something of a scandal, but he knew better than to live where he might hear tales that would test his morals. He visited frequently, but the move was a reminder to his family that they needed to exercise care in his company or risk a raid.

"I'm sure we'll eat every bite," he said. "It looks wonderful."

"This girl of yours, she enjoys good cooking?"

"I don't know. We've never eaten together."

"And why hasn't she had you to her house for Sunday dinner? Have you met her family?"

He wasn't sure how much to tell her. Lena could be discreet if she chose. But if she was too worried about him, she would probably share her fears with his parents. "Her father wouldn't approve of me," he said, trying for the most minimal of explanations.

Lena faced him. "Just tell me she's a good Catholic girl."

"That she is. We met at church."

"Then I might well know her."

"*Mamó*, there are complications. She's all the things you'd want for me. Her father is a different story."

"Perhaps it's only that you haven't given him a chance to know you. Can you be sure he's so bad? Or perhaps he doesn't like the Irish?"

"He is Irish."

Lena looked as if he'd given her the moon and the stars.

"He's a bootlegger, *Mamó*."

"Tim McNulty!" Her smile became a grimace. "Glen, are you daft, child? I've seen the daughter. She's a lovely girl, but surely there are lovely girls all over the West Side whose fathers don't walk the streets with bodyguards?"

"You're the only one who knows. Please don't tell anyone else. I don't know what we're going to do. Her father wants her to marry a man from Chicago, another bootlegger. And she despises him."

"Is she using you as a way to get out of a bad situation?"

"She's not like that. I don't know how she turned out the way she did, but she's kind and gentle and well bred. You'll love her once you know her."

"I *will* love her? Does this mean you've made up your mind already, Glen? You're going to fight for her?"

He *had* made up his mind, although facing it hadn't been easy. He was an old-fashioned man in a changing world. He didn't like the fact that he was going behind McNulty's back to court his daughter. He didn't like the fact that if Clare married him, her father would disown her.

Most important, he didn't like the fact that their relationship put Clare in danger. He knew McNulty's reputation, and he knew the man wouldn't allow his daughter to foil his plans for her, not easily, anyway. McNulty was dangerous, and he held his daughter in low regard. It was a frightening combination.

"I'll fight for her," Glen said. "But I'm not a fool. I may not win."

"And that would be a shame, wouldn't it? Because it sounds as if she needs you."

"You'll keep this between us?"

"For now." Lena turned back to the pot bubbling on the stove.

Tim McNulty was in Chicago, and Clare had been expected to go, as well. She had agreed cheerfully and packed her suitcases, but at the last moment she had pleaded female problems, the one excuse that Tim wouldn't probe or discuss. He railed at her for allowing such a thing to happen, but in the end he left her behind.

Jerry was supposed to look after her, but Jerry was a goof,

easy to fool and scared of women to boot. When she told him she was going to spend the day in her room sleeping—and after she issued a few discreet moans when he walked by— he quickly deserted the upstairs. From experience, she knew he would make himself at home in the parlor with a deck of cards and a hip flask of hooch. If she came and went through the servants' stairway at the back of the house, he would never even discover she was gone. And if he did, she would simply tell him that she'd desperately needed fresh air because she was feeling so faint.

It wasn't the sort of thing he would report to Tim.

An hour before noon, Clare made it as far as the kitchen without being detected. She had her hand on the doorknob, ready to exit the house, when she saw a new man watching the rear yard. He was tall and lithe, younger than Jerry and clearly a great deal fleeter of foot.

She hadn't counted on that. With her father in Chicago, she had assumed that bodyguards would be minimal. While gangsters might kill each other without qualm, they rarely turned their rage on family members. She was in no real danger. She suspected Tim was more afraid she might get out.

She was debating what to do when the man turned and walked toward the front of the house. She heard a car pull up and the faint tones of conversation. Her chance had arrived.

Clare closed the door softly behind her and scurried behind the river birches clumped along the walkway to the alley. The boxers Tim kept as guard dogs ignored her as she passed their pen, and she was out the back gate and halfway down the alley before she ventured a glance behind her. No one was about. She cut through yards, taking care to stay as far away from the street as possible, until she reached the corner where she would catch the streetcar. She waited until it had nearly reached her before she dashed from behind a neatly clipped boxwood hedge and boarded for the trip to Edgewater Park.

Glen was afraid Clare wouldn't come, but when he saw her waiting beside the pavilion, he was so pleased that his own reaction dismayed him. From the beginning, he had tried to take their romance slowly, to be cautious and sensible. But one glance at her rosy lips and gleaming hair, and he knew that he had stepped over an important line. From the look on Clare's face, she had, too.

He kissed her with no regard for the people milling around. He felt like a man who had fasted for weeks and was finally sitting down to a banquet.

"I almost didn't get away." She rose on tiptoes and kissed him again; then she took his arm. "My father was having the back door watched, too. Someone new to me."

Glen knew that McNulty had an entire stable of goons working for him. He doubted that McNulty would entrust Clare to just any of them. The new guy must be an up-and-comer in the ranks.

"Let's find a place to sit." Glen led her toward the lakeshore. The day was sunny, and they were surrounded by people enjoying the lake and the August weather. A cool breeze blew off the water, making the temperature nearly perfect. Off the main path they found a tree for shade and spread the blanket Glen had brought with him.

He unpacked the hamper and told her about his conversation with his grandmother. "You will love her," he promised. "And she'll love you. Everyone will."

"Glen..." She set down her plate. "Once my father finds out about us, there'll be no going back for me. You understand that, don't you? If I defy my father and survive, he will never acknowledge me again. I'll be dead to him, and he'll try to exact revenge. You'll always be in danger as long as he's alive or free. This should be the last time we see each other. It would be better."

"For who? For you? For me? For him?"

"For you."

He lifted her chin so he was staring into her eyes. "And what about you, Clare? What would be better for you?"

She tried to look away. "Don't ask."

"I have to know."

"You know how I feel."

"Just say it."

"I love you. Can't you tell?"

"I hoped you did. I love you."

"We never should have begun this."

He dropped his hand. Of course she was right, but they *had* begun it, and the rest was behind them.

"Maybe you're right, but what would you have done if you hadn't met me? Married Cassidy? At least now we have a chance for real happiness, Clare. What if we'd never found each other?"

"What are we going to do?"

"We're going to get married. I don't make much money, and I can't support you in the style your father does, but we can live with my family until we find a place of our own. My grandmother has room in her house, and once she meets you, she'll want us to move in with her. She'll insist."

"And my father will try to get even."

"Maybe not. Once we're married, our children will be his grandchildren. He won't want to lose them. And maybe he cares more about you than you think."

She shook her head. "You don't know."

"Then we'll move away. If it gets bad here, I'll ask to be transferred to another city. Marry me, Clare. As soon as we can make the arrangements."

"You would leave Cleveland and your family?"

"You'll be my family."

Tears shimmered in her eyes, but she nodded. And when he leaned over to kiss her, her response was passionate.

They ate Lena's lunch and made plans. He told her that Father Patrick McSweeney, who had retired from St. Brigid's, had married his grandparents and his parents, and Glen wanted him to perform their ceremony, too.

"His health isn't good, and he only does the occasional wedding and funeral now, but he'll do a private ceremony for us. I know he will. He's been a good friend to our family. And maybe he'll have some influence with your father, as well."

"Or my father will have influence with him," Clare said sadly.

"Not with Father McSweeney. It doesn't matter how much your father's given St. Brigid's, or who intercedes for him. He'll do what's right."

"Will your family come?"

"Yes, of course. Is there anyone from your family who might?"

"No one. But my mother will be watching from heaven, I know she will. And I'll wear her dress. She put it away for me."

He took her hand. "We'll have to be careful, Clare. It was probably foolish to meet in such a public place. Until we're married, we'll need to be more cautious than ever. I don't want your father to hurt you or send you away where I can't find you."

"How will we make plans?"

"If I have to, I'll find someone to bring messages to you. And if you can slip away to early Mass in the mornings without arousing your father's curiosity—"

"I will. You know I will."

"You said there was a new man watching you?"

"I got away from him today. I'll get away from him again."

"Do you think you ought to go back now?"

She looked torn, but at last she nodded. "I'd better."

"I'll walk you to the streetcar." He started to stand, but she put her hand on his arm.

"Don't. Stay here. I'll disappear into the crowd. You were right. It's better if we're not seen together."

He took her hand. "It'll only be for a little while. Then we'll be married for the rest of our lives. We'll make this work. You'll see."

She lifted his hand to her lips; then she stood, and in a moment she had blended into the crowd and disappeared.

Glen sat watching the space where he'd seen her last. At first he didn't see the shadow falling on the blanket. By the time he realized he had company, the man was towering over him.

The man was familiar. Glen realized that immediately. But the rest, where and when he'd seen him, danced at the edges of his memory.

"Donatone's warehouse," the man supplied.

Glen started to get to his feet, but the man motioned for him to sit. He joined him, pulling his legs up and hugging them against his body as if he was enjoying the sun with a close friend. "Last time I saw you," the man said, "I had to knock you out."

Thinking about it made Glen's neck hurt. Once he'd come to, he'd had trouble living down that fiasco. He hadn't dared tell anyone that the same man who had rendered him unconscious had also saved him from another bootlegger's bullet. Despite past glories, he doubted the department would ever have sent him on another raid.

"What are you doing here?" Glen demanded. "I could haul you off to jail."

"I'm here keeping an eye on Miss McNulty."

Glen heard Ireland in the man's words; he also heard a warning. He didn't bother to lie. "She's not here."

"I know. I saw her leave."

"*You* were the goon in her backyard. She didn't give you the slip after all. You followed her."

The man grinned. "That's me."

"Do you have a name?"

"Who doesn't?"

"I guess I'm the last guy you'd want to give it to, huh?"

"Liam will do."

"Pleased to meet you, Liam Willdo."

Liam's grin broadened. "And you? Pardon me if I've forgotten."

"Glen Donaghue."

"Well, Glen Donaghue, I'm here to give you a warning."

"That's all? Too many people around to deliver a beating to go with it?"

"You could hold your own, I'm thinking."

"I could."

"Mr. McNulty has plans for his daughter. They don't include the likes of you."

"And hers don't include him. It's the twentieth century. Women like Clare vote. They turn their stockings down and

bob their hair and smoke cigarettes. They go to school and decide who they're going to marry. They don't let their fathers
pawn them off on men they despise."

"That so?" Liam tugged at a piece of rye grass and put it
between his lips. "She despises this Cassidy fellow?"

Glen realized how strange this meeting was. Liam was a
thug, and all thugs were hazardous. But from the first moment
he'd seen him, he'd felt drawn to the man. Of course, Liam
had saved his life immediately, which went a long way toward
creating a bond.

"She hates him," Glen said.

"And she loves you." Liam chewed on the grass.

"I didn't say that."

"Didn't need to. She's not the kind of girl who would sneak
around for anything else."

"How do you know? She said she'd never seen you before."

"I listen. I pay attention."

"Well, you've delivered your advice. You can go now.
Make sure she gets home safely."

"That was no advice. That was a warning, Donaghue. I told
you, I pay attention. And here's what I know. Tim McNulty
isn't a man to trifle with. Don't be fooled by the wink and the
charm. He's as ruthless as a Prussian soldier. He won't think
hard before he'll have you killed. He'll kill her, as well, if he's
forced into it, or, worse, he'll make her wish he had. You're
putting yourselves at risk."

Glen's conversations with Cleveland's criminal element
had never gone quite like this one. Liam Whoeverhewas
seemed genuinely concerned about him.

"Why are you telling me this?" Glen said. "Are you trying
to save yourself some work? Or don't you have any stomach
for murdering innocent young women?"

"I have no stomach for murdering anybody."

"Then you're in the wrong business."

"Not so far. And I'd like to keep it that way." Liam threw
the gnawed blade of grass to the ground and stood, stretch-

ing as he did. "I saved your life once. Maybe I feel responsible for making sure you don't throw it away."

"You don't owe me anything and never did." Glen stared up at him; then he grimaced. "But thanks for the last time, and for the warning."

Liam was staring down at him with an odd expression on his face. "You say your name's Donaghue?"

"That's right. Why?"

"Nothing. You look a little bit like somebody I used to know, that's all." Liam doffed his hat in farewell.

"If you keep Clare away from me, you're guaranteeing her a life of misery. I'm the only hope she has for a real life, Liam."

"No, by keeping you away from her, I'm guaranteeing my wife and daughter a real life. I do what I'm told. And I, at least, have better sense than to cross Tim McNulty."

chapter 25

Rooney's story ended abruptly. He stood and stretched.

"Rooney, what happened to Clare?" Megan said. "Did she decide to obey her father and marry Niall Cassidy?" She was thinking fast. "Since she wasn't my grandmother, I can assume she didn't marry Granddad. Unless she was his first wife and nobody told me he'd been married twice?"

"Going to bed." Rooney started up the stairs, unaware, she was afraid, that he was leaving without answering her questions. The storytelling had been convoluted, but the basics had been clear. Unfortunately, his mind was wandering now, as it still too often did.

She knew better than to put pressure on him. She was just lucky she had learned as much as she had. "Good night, Rooney. Sleep tight." She watched him go.

She was still staring at the steps when the front door opened and Niccolo came in. He looked so tired that, despite herself, she felt a stirring of sympathy. Besides, staying angry at him was counterproductive when they had a long, romantic weekend ahead.

She got up and kissed his cheek. If he'd had a briefcase, she would have taken it. If he wore slippers, she would have gone to get them. "How'd your meeting go?"

"Long and exhausting. How was your evening?"

She wanted to tell him about Rooney, but she decided it could wait. She was afraid she would get a nod and an "uh-huh," and then tomorrow, if she quizzed him about anything she'd said, he wouldn't have a clue.

"Why don't I make us a toddy?" she said. "You'll sleep better."

"I feel like I could sleep right here standing up."

"Toddy?"

"Uh-huh. Great."

She was standing at the stove stirring the milk and honey when he came into the room. He was barefooted, and he'd shed his tie and sportscoat. His shirt was open at the throat and hung over his hips.

"Making yourself comfortable, I see." She reached for mugs above the stove. "This will cure what ails you."

"What ails me are too many long nights away."

"It ails me, too."

"Would it bother you so much if the saloon were open?"

"Probably not as much. I'd be over there doing inventory or checking on things. But I'd always rather be with you."

"I like the sound of that." Niccolo flopped down at the table. "The good news is that the worst of this might be coming to an end."

"Really? How so?" She turned off the burner but left the milk to warm a little more before the burner cooled.

"I think I may have found the funding source I need."

"Really?"

"An organization that's run out of Indiana. They fund youth projects all over the country, and they're interested in Brick. They concentrate on crime prevention. Their motto is keep kids busy, give them skills and attention, and they grow up to be productive citizens."

"That's great. Sounds like they're right up your alley. And there aren't any strings attached that you don't like?"

"There are lots of strings attached. I won't know if I can live with them until this weekend."

A warning alarm buzzed in her head. "This weekend?"

"I know. I know." He ran his hands through his hair. "I told you I was free."

"Actually, you *promised* you were free." She kept her voice calm, but the effort was great.

"And I was when I promised. Look, Megan, please understand. I wouldn't do this to you if it wasn't absolutely necessary. But I have to fly to Indianapolis on Friday afternoon, and I won't be back until Monday. Their board meets this weekend, and if I'm not there, I'll have to wait for their next regular board meeting, which isn't for three more months. They have a host of questions for me and me for them. And this will expedite things."

"You can't ask questions on the telephone?"

"Sure, I could, but this makes more sense."

"How much do you know about them?"

"Not nearly as much as I need to. What I do know sounds promising. I—"

"So you're flying to Indiana without having the facts in place? Leaving on the only free weekend you've had in months, on something that sounds dangerously like a whim?"

"Look, you can come with me if you'd like. Do some shopping. Relax poolside while I attend meetings."

"Gee, doesn't that sound like fun. It's always so nice to be alone in a strange city."

"You know, I thought you'd be a little more understanding in light of what this could do for Brick. It was just one night out. There'll be others."

"Nick, I made reservations at the Inn at Honey Run for the whole weekend."

"I never said I could spare the whole weekend. I said we'd go out one night."

She thought of a hundred things to say to that. She restrained herself to the most practical. "At this late date, I won't get my deposit back if I cancel."

"Then let it go. I'm really sorry, but this is just one getaway. We have the rest of our lives."

"Don't count on it."

"What does that mean?"

"It means don't count on it, Nick." For a moment she'd thought she was going to explode, but now an icy calm filled her. She looked at the clock above the table. "I'll be spending the night at Casey's. Don't worry about me. Don't take even a moment away from the rest of your life."

"This is unbelievably childish."

She didn't answer. She went upstairs and packed a change of clothes and her toothbrush. He was nowhere in sight when she closed the front door and started toward her sister's house.

Casey made up the guest bed and sent Megan down the hall for clean towels.

"You're sure you want to do this?" she asked when Megan returned from the guest bath.

"I'm sure." Megan sat on the freshly made bed. The quilt beneath her was an eye-popping tomato red, and the guest room walls were a deep curry gold. A large batik of Hindu deities in compromising positions hung over the bed. She hoped she would be able to sleep.

"This is no way to work things out."

"Look, no lectures, okay? I've just got to have some time away from Nick to think things over."

"How long are you going to stay?"

"It depends."

"You know you're welcome to move in permanently, but I don't want Nick to blame me for this."

"Casey, I'm going to Ireland."

Casey looked puzzled, as if Megan's words had been spoken in an unfamiliar language.

Megan tried again. "Ireland. The Emerald Isle? I'm going to

stay with Peggy and Irene. I can't do it once the saloon is ready for business. I'll be swamped, so the timing's perfect now. Peggy's been after us both to visit. I gather Irene's health is worse than she'd guessed, and she's afraid we'll never get the chance to meet her. So I'm going to take her up on her invitation."

"Did you tell Nick?"

"No, but I'm going as soon as I can get a reservation. Tomorrow, if I can."

"Doing it at the last minute is going to cost a fortune."

"You know what? I don't care. I'll put it on my credit card. I'll pay it off a little at a time. Hell, I won't hire a night cook when the saloon opens again. I'll do it myself for a few months until I've made up the difference. Nick won't even notice I'm not home."

Casey sat beside Megan and took her sister's hand. "Don't you think it's dangerous to go off half-cocked like this? Shouldn't you work this out, then go to Ireland if you still feel like it? But please, don't go angry. Remember when I left Cleveland and what it did to *our* relationship?"

As a teenager, Casey, angry at Megan for not selling the saloon and giving each sister her share of the profits, had left Cleveland, vowing never to return. It had taken the sisters years and maturity to patch up their differences.

"*We* were kids," Megan said. "Nick and I aren't. And I'm so close to the trees right now that I can't see my way through the forest. I need some time and distance to work things out in my head. I need to get away so it doesn't feel so personal."

"You need to work this out together."

"Right now I'm too angry to try."

Casey squeezed her hand before she released it. "Then what can I do?"

"Take care of Rooney. Will you do that for me?"

"Of course I will."

"As long as Josh and Nick are there keeping an eye on things, he'll be okay. But if you could visit, particularly this weekend when Nick's gone, and make sure they have everything they need? Make sure Rooney's taking his meds, that they don't need groceries."

"Easy enough. I'll stop over every day, and I'll cook for them while Nick's away. Rooney really likes Jon's chicken paprikash. I'll bring him here to stay if I need to."

"Thank you." Megan fished around for something else to say. "It will be great to see Peggy." Her eyes filled with tears.

"Of course it will."

"And I can check on this Finn O'Malley."

"Don't do too much checking. She won't like it. Be her friend, not her big sister."

"I hate all this, Casey."

Casey put her arm around Megan's shoulder and squeezed. "I know you do."

"Leave me alone, okay?"

"I'm on my way out the door." Casey stood and left.

Megan changed into a long T-shirt, her eyes brimming. She made it into the bathroom to brush her teeth and wash her face. But back in the guest room, when she was staring at the ceiling, the tears arrived, as she'd known they would.

"Damn you, Niccolo Andreani," she whispered fiercely. "Why did you want to get married in the first place?"

chapter 26

Peggy wasn't sure how to feel about Megan's surprise arrival. She was thrilled to see her, and thrilled that her sister had the chance to get to know Irene, but obviously the decision to come had been a sudden one. She was alone, and Niccolo was in Cleveland. That did not bode well for the honeymooners.

Between the long flight and hours of driving on the left side of the road in an unfamiliar country, Megan was exhausted but still too wound up to rest. Irene had greeted her warmly, then gone in for her own nap to leave the sisters to catch up on their lives. Peggy had made them a pot of tea and set out a plate of Nora's scones. Kieran was conveniently asleep, as well.

"This is just too picturesque." Megan was wandering nervously, examining every nook and cranny of the cottage. "I know people who search their whole lives to find their Irish roots, and here ours are presented to us on a silver platter. Not some pile of moss-covered rocks in an empty field, but this." She swept her hand through the air in emphasis.

"You must be starving. Settle down and have some tea."

"I'm afraid if I sit I'll fall asleep and miss the rest of the trip."

"How long can you stay?"

"I haven't decided. I have an open ticket."

"Megan, that must have cost the moon."

"I don't care. I've always wanted to see Ireland. Now I will."

"I know you wanted to come for your honeymoon—"

"But we're much too practical, Nick and I. We carved out a few days together in Michigan and thought it would be enough."

Peggy waited, hoping that was the beginning of something, but Megan just wandered silently, lifting each knick-knack and examining it.

"How is Nick?" Peggy asked when Megan came to the end of the line, a ceramic Eiffel Tower that Irene had bought as a girl on a trip to Paris. "You haven't said much."

"Busy. You should see the saloon. Of course you will when you come back home. He and the Brick kids have done a fantastic job. The kitchen's all done, and there's actually enough room to put all the pots and pans. And the new oven heats up so fast I'm afraid I'll burn everything until I get used to it."

There was a frantic quality to Megan's story, as if she was afraid if she stopped talking about how wonderful things were, she might lapse into the truth. Peggy understood part of her sister's operating code. Peggy was the "little" sister, the one who was to be protected and coddled. Never mind that Peggy had maturely faced her own problems and was coping with them. Never mind that at a mature twenty-three she was well able to lend support herself. To Megan, she was still little Peggy, as close to a child of her own as Megan had yet to come.

"And how is Brick?" Peggy probed.

"Nick's working hard to get more funding. He's going to Indianapolis this weekend to meet with an organization who might provide it."

"So you thought you'd come to Ireland while he was away? A good excuse?"

"I knew I wouldn't be able to do it once the saloon opens again. The timing seemed right."

"I can't help but think there's more—"

"Did I tell you about Rooney? He just seems to get better and better. The other night he told me a story about Granddad, and he claims he's the only one who knows it all. He didn't finish, but he got a good start. He's on new medication, and it's helping him focus. He seems happy, too, and even less prone to wander."

Peggy was delighted her father was happy. She was afraid he might be the only one in the house on Hunter Street who was. "You'll tell me the story?"

"What I know so far. And Casey's doing well. She's not showing yet. She has that long, thin body, and I'll bet she won't show for a long time. If I ever got pregnant, the baby would probably be visible the second day."

Peggy heard the "if" louder than the rest of the sentence. "When are you going to stop chattering?"

Megan turned, inspired, most likely, by the edge in Peggy's voice. "Chattering? I was just telling you about the family."

"And not a thing about yourself."

"There's nothing to tell."

"Not to me, I guess."

"What does that mean?"

"It means that we've reached a crossroads, Megan. I can go through the rest of my life as a little girl for you to protect and take care of, or I can finally be an equal partner in this relationship. You tell me your problems, I tell you mine. You offer comfort, I accept it. I offer comfort—"

"I accept it." Megan took her chair and looked down at the teacup steaming in front of her.

"That's right," Peggy said. "You know I love you, and I'd do anything for you. But the one thing I won't do is play this game anymore. I'm a grown-up, you're a grown-up. I was never your daughter. I'm your sister. Treat me like one."

Megan's hand trembled slightly when she reached for the

tea. Peggy knew that exhaustion could do that to a person. So could sorrow.

"I don't know what to say." Megan lifted the cup to her lips, then set it down. "We're not happy. I'm not sure why. Nick works too hard, and I think it's because he doesn't want to spend time with me. I think he's sorry we ever got married."

Peggy knew better than to tell her sister that was ridiculous. She knew how much Niccolo loved Megan, but clearly Megan was no longer sure.

Megan looked up. "The moment I can talk about it, I'll talk to you. Is that a deal? Right now, I just don't know what to say. That's why I'm here."

"It's a deal." Peggy held up the plate of scones. "Eat something, then I'm putting you down for a nap with Kieran."

"I can use both." Megan managed a smile. "Peggy, old habits die hard. If I try to grab your hand when we cross the road, just slap it, okay?"

"I'll be grabbing your hand while you're in Ireland. You'll look in the wrong direction for the first week and be liable to get run over."

Irene was as friendly and natural as Peggy had reported, and Megan liked her immediately. The cottage was charming, the landscape breathtaking.

And she was deeply depressed to be there.

"You got a little sleep, then?" Irene asked when Megan came out of the bedroom.

"Enough to make me realize how much I missed." Megan stretched. "But I do feel better. How about you?"

"I spend far too much time in bed as it is. Sleep is not the way to spend whatever time is left to me."

Peggy came in from the kitchen. "It's the best way to make sure you *have* time left to you."

Megan had tiptoed out of the bedroom, careful not to wake her sleeping nephew. But despite her best effort, something had done the deed. The new sounds coming from behind the closed door were unmistakable. "Shall I get him? Will he remember me?"

Peggy looked troubled. "I'm not always sure he remembers *me,* Megan."

Megan forgot her own problems for the moment. "Things aren't going as well as you hoped?"

"Maybe you'll be able to tell me. You might notice some changes that we're too close to see. Go get him if you like."

Megan did like. She went back into the bedroom, and this time Kieran was standing in his crib rattling the bars.

"Hey, buddy, it's Aunt Megan." She moved slowly, since she knew he needed time to adjust. "Still sleepy?"

Kieran's little mouth puckered, as if he was going to cry.

"Shhh..." She picked up the stuffed Pro Bear she'd bought on her way out of town, a Cleveland Browns collectible in an orange-and-black jersey. She wiggled it in front of him. "Look what I brought you, Kieran. Just for you."

He stared at her as if she'd arrived from another galaxy. Then he began to wail.

She threw Pro Bear on the bed and crossed to the crib, lifting him into her arms. "It's okay, sweetie, I know just how you feel."

She was unsuccessfully rocking him in her arms when Peggy came in and relieved her. Kieran continued to scream as Peggy changed his diaper.

He calmed a little when Peggy took him into the kitchen and poured him some juice. But he refused to look at either of them, and stared at the sunlight flickering through the window even when she added a cookie and a bunch of grapes.

"I know you'll want to work with him this afternoon," Megan said. "I won't get in your way."

Peggy was trying not to look discouraged, but Megan knew her too well to believe it. "I think we'll take the day off. Bridie's coming for a cooking lesson. And Finn's coming for dinner, though he doesn't know it yet. Nora taught Bridie a few things, and I've taught her what little I know, but she seems to have a natural talent. And she wants to impress her father. We're having fresh trout a friend brought Irene and garlic mashed potatoes."

"Maybe I can pick up a few tricks from Nora while I'm here and write off the airfare. New authentic specialties for the saloon."

"She's great, but you could teach her a thing or two, I suspect. Don't worry about Kieran. He can use a break, and so can I."

"So I'll get to meet Finn?"

"Uh-huh."

"And you two are still seeing each other?"

"I wouldn't put it quite that way." Peggy joined her sister at the window but moved to the right when Kieran began to fuss. She had disturbed the light on the wall.

"How *would* you put it?"

"We're friends. Close friends. We're taking it slowly. He's just beginning to come back after a very difficult time."

Megan thought Peggy had already experienced enough difficult men. Megan had never liked Phil, and despite the excuses Peggy made for him and the modest support he provided, Megan thought he was irresponsible and selfish. Her sister had always been too understanding and too patient, and now Megan was afraid she'd adopted another deadbeat, only this time a deadbeat with a brogue.

"You've had a difficult time, too," Megan pointed out. "Is anyone taking care of you?"

"It's not like that, I promise. You'll see when you meet him. And this wasn't exactly an existential crisis he went through. He's not trying to figure out the meaning of life. He lost his family."

"Tell me about Bridie."

"I adore her." Peggy's eyes brightened. "She's wonderful, and so good with Kieran."

"Are you falling in love with the father because you've already fallen in love with the daughter?"

Peggy's cheeks bloomed with color. "What makes you think I've fallen in love with him?"

"I don't know for sure. But I will by the time I get ready to go home."

"You can't know what I don't know myself."

They heard the front door slam, then a child's voice. Irene and one of the prettiest girls Megan had ever seen came into the room. "Look who's come to cook for us," Irene said.

"I brought a cookbook from home, Granny 'rene." A beaming Bridie held high a thick volume that looked as if it had seen many a meal. "You must be Megan. Peggy talks about you all the time. I never thought I'd get to meet you. Hi, Kieran." Without waiting for an answer, Bridie went to stand right in front of the little boy, disturbing his concentration. "Look at me, not at the wall, boyo."

Kieran looked up at her, his brow furrowed. Then he pitched forward and began to pummel her. As if this was the most common of greetings Bridie set him on her hip and, blocking his punches with one hand, mopped his face with a paper napkin with the other.

Megan looked at Peggy and found her sister was watching her. Megan shrugged. "Sometimes love's like a smart bomb, isn't it? Aims right for you, and there's not a blessed thing you can do about it."

Finn hadn't had a good day. Twice now he had refused a supervisory position with the construction company for which he worked, but lately he'd begun to suspect they had awarded him the job anyway, without the raise in pay.

He liked physical labor and found it was a good way to put everything else out of his mind. He did not like telling other men what to do or how to do it, and he did not like making decisions about what they should do next. Today he had been forced to do all three.

He had never intended to keep the job, not for any length of time. He'd needed time to reconsider his life and his options. A year had slipped by, then two, and he was still installing pipe and water lines and ducking responsibility whenever he could.

The job was only part of today's discontent. He had worked hard, doing his job and the foreman's, but he hadn't been able to put Peggy out of his mind. He had not intended to become involved with her. He had fallen into the relationship despite every struggle not to. Perhaps if they hadn't been thrown together each time he checked on Irene... Perhaps if his own daughter hadn't preferred Peggy's company to any of her friends...

Perhaps if he hadn't found Peggy so overwhelmingly alive and appealing...

Finn was aware of the slippery ground under his feet. Until the death of his wife and sons, he had been strong and confident, the student most likely to make a success of himself, the graduate courted by hospitals as far away as Edinburgh and London. As a young father he had effortlessly solved problems and doled out rewards, and as a husband he had supported and encouraged Sheila to find her own place in the world.

That self-assured young man had died off the coast of Ireland, and the hollow shell who remained broke into a cold sweat each morning when contemplating which shoelace to tie. That young man, who only shared the occasional leisurely drink at the pub with friends, had been replaced by a desperate, broken alcoholic, striving each day to remain sober.

And into this life—or what passed for one—he had invited a woman. Not just any woman, of course, but one with a child who, even under the best of circumstances, would require constant supervision and extra doses of love and initiative. Peggy needed a man with both to spare, as well as a proven ability to stay the course.

Peggy did not need him.

He, of course, did not need the complications of any relationship or the added burden of an autistic child. He made it through each day, put food on the table and made certain his daughter had clothes to wear. He avoided the pubs, and when he couldn't, he found the strength somewhere to refuse all drinks. He cared for Irene, but no one knew how badly he doubted his ability to do so.

What did a man like Finn O'Malley have to offer a woman like Peggy Donaghue?

The question had haunted him all day. The answer was deceptively simple. He needed to tell her goodbye. They had made no promises, exchanged no vows. Peggy knew how limited was his potential as a long-term lover. He had made no secret of his battles or his losses. She might be sad, but she would not be surprised.

The problem was that he didn't want to end what had barely begun. Since the start of their affair, he'd had moments of painfully intense pleasure. Making love with Peggy was like blood pouring back into a sleeping limb. He was afraid he could not go back to existing as he had without her. By withdrawing from the world he had cushioned himself, but now that he had been drawn into it again, he was afraid that cushion was gone forever.

He drove to Irene's, no closer to a decision than he had been all day. The closer he got to her house, the more his problems seemed to melt away. He wondered what they would find to talk about, if she would tell him the small details of her day, if they would find a moment or two alone. Before he could stop himself, he wondered what it would be like to go home to her each night.

He'd half expected Bridie to be waiting for him outside, but no one except Banjax was about. The foolish old dog lay in the meager shade of a wind-sculpted ash, and when Finn approached he wagged his tail briefly but didn't even lift his head.

Finn stooped to rub his ears. "If you look a wee bit more pitiful, she'll bring you inside."

Banjax thumped his tail again, perhaps in appreciation of the advice.

Finn rapped on the door, then let himself in. He heard

laughter from the kitchen, and, despite everything, his spirits lifted. He remembered a party for Bridie's fourth birthday and a cluster of helium-filled balloons presented by Sheila's mother. They had nearly swept the little girl away. Now his feelings were like balloons soaring above him, and all the weight he could muster would not bring them back to earth.

"Finn, hello." Peggy poked her head into the kitchen doorway. "Have we got a surprise for you. Two actually."

His heart sped up at the sight of her. She wore green shorts that exposed slender, shapely legs and a paler green top that exposed a band of skin at her midriff. Her hair was pulled back in a knot, and he longed to loosen it and send it tumbling around her shoulders. She would like that. Peggy might look like a fresh-faced country girl just now, but she was a sophisticated and surprisingly sensual young woman. He had a terrible suspicion that he had only just begun to discover the depths of her sexuality.

"Is Bridie part of it?" He didn't dare to get closer. He wasn't sure who was around or what they might see if he did.

"Part of one surprise. I'll give you a hint. You're staying for dinner."

It wasn't a question. He frowned. He had intended to check Irene, then take his daughter home. She had already been here most of the day, and although Peggy claimed Bridie was a help with Kieran, as her father, he knew that, like any child, she could be wearing, too.

"Don't look like that," Peggy warned. "You'll be glad you did." She turned around and motioned for someone to join her in the doorway.

Another woman, shorter and more compact than Peggy, joined her. Her hair was a mass of short red curls and her face a practical square. On the surface there seemed to be little of Peggy in her, but he knew somehow that this was one of Peggy's sisters.

"Meet Megan," she said. "My wonderful sister Megan."

There was nothing for him to do except move forward as Megan extended her hand.

"I'm happy to meet you at last, Finn."

For one crazy moment he wondered if Megan had come all the way from America to persuade her little sister not to take up with an Irishman. He grasped her hand and murmured greetings. Her eyes never left his face. He was certain he had been judged and pronounced, although the verdict was a mystery.

"I didn't know you were coming," Finn said.

"Neither did I," Megan said. "Whimsy overtook me."

"I know Peggy must be thrilled. Have you ever been to Ireland before?"

"I've hardly been outside Cleveland."

"Then you'll have lots to see." He had run out of things to say. Once he'd had an endless supply of conversation guaranteed to make anyone feel comfortable. Now he thought in monosyllables and only muttered them when absolutely necessary.

"I'll be content just to stay here in Shanmullin and get to know the village and Peggy's friends."

He understood that with no trouble. He didn't know the whole story of why Megan had come, but at least part of the reason was to check on her sister.

"Daddy." Bridie squeezed in between the sisters, and Peggy rested a hand on her shoulder. "Will you stay for dinner?"

He looked down at his daughter's bright little face and knew he had no choice. "Is dinner the surprise?"

"I made it!" She covered her mouth with her hand. "Uh-oh."

Peggy laughed. "It's okay, Bridie. He had to find out sooner or later. Now he can sit in the living room and think about what a lucky man he is."

Finn knew something was expected of him. "You cooked it yourself?"

"Uh-huh. Trout and potatoes and all kinds of stuff."

She was beginning to sound like an American. Too much television or too much Peggy, he wasn't sure which, but her enthusiasm was universal.

"I'm looking forward to it," he said.

"I used Mommy's recipe for dessert."

In the seconds while she waited for an answer, he thought of a hundred things. How proud Sheila would be of Bridie. How pleased she would be that Bridie wanted to cook her favorites. How unfair it was that Sheila would never know how the daughter who looked so much like her was growing up to be a beautiful, generous girl.

Words stuck in his throat. Peggy saw his dilemma and spoke for him. "Your mother would be thrilled her recipes are being used so well," Peggy said. "Let's go make sure everything's cooked to perfection." They left for the inner sanctum.

Megan stayed in the doorway. "She's a great little girl."

"I know."

"Peggy's very fond of her."

He waited for the punch line, but she didn't deliver it. "Make yourself at home," she said. "I'll send Kieran out if you get bored. Irene's entertaining him with wooden spoons and an upside down kettle. Our very own percussion section."

He wanted to reassure Megan that he hadn't set out to hurt her sister. But what could he say? Of all people, he knew that good intentions could backfire dramatically.

"I'll be glad to take Kieran for a walk if there's enough time," he said instead.

"He's happy. You look like you've had a hard day. Why don't you rest?" Megan disappeared into the kitchen.

He knew he was not invited to follow. He took the most comfortable armchair in the living room and immediately fell sound asleep.

He awoke when Peggy came in and put one of Irene's old '78s on a gramophone that, until that moment, he had thought was purely for show. The scratchy sound of a '40s dance band filled the air. "I found a stack of records in the closet last week. Isn't this neat?"

He expected to see young ladies with pageboys and flowered rayon dresses fox trot their way into the living room. "Brilliant."

"We're ready for you."

He followed her to the tiny kitchen and the sight of a table set with china, flowers and candles in silver candle holders. Bridie had folded the napkins into swans, and she could hardly stand still for the excitement of it. The pots and pans she had used—a considerable number, from what he could tell—were hidden under another tablecloth draped over the counter.

"Isn't it beautiful?" Bridie asked.

"Beautiful," he confirmed. He remembered other evenings like this one, when Bridie had been nearly beside herself with joy, but he hadn't seen her this way since Sheila's death. He hadn't realized how subdued she had grown. Now he wondered how much of that had been for his benefit.

"Will you sit at the head of the table?" Peggy asked. "Irene will be at the other end."

He did not want the prime seat. Night after night, he had sat at the head of his own family table, watching his children squabble and laugh. He and Sheila had exchanged looks that only parents understand. Meals had been among their happiest times.

He took the seat because what he wanted tonight wasn't important. He reminded himself that he was doing this for his daughter, and to some degree for Peggy.

Bridie arrived at his side and held his napkin high, flipping it open. The swan became a parachute straight into his lap.

Even Kieran looked interested in the proceedings.

Everyone was seated, and Bridie brought the food from the counter by herself. She set each platter and bowl as close to her father as she could. Steaming trout, creamy potatoes, roasted vegetables sprinkled with herbs and what might be almonds. The aroma was mouth-watering. His fingers itched to pick up his fork.

"Bridie, you've outdone yourself." He smiled at her. "This looks delicious."

Bridie beamed proudly.

"She's a natural cook," Megan said. "That's not something

you can teach. You can teach someone technique and how to follow a recipe, and they'll be pretty good, but Bridie understands food and flavor and texture."

Finn took a fillet and passed the platter of trout. The next moments were taken up with the happy silence of diners filling their plates. When everyone had finished, Irene looked up at him. "Finn, will you please say the blessing?"

He had not said the blessing before a meal since the accident. Bridie said it sometimes, and he sat there as she did, pretending to pray. But Irene had never before asked this of him. He wondered what had possessed her to do so now.

"I'd say we have particular reason to give thanks this evening," she elaborated, as if she was answering his unspoken question.

Like sitting at the head of the table, this was not an option. He waited as everyone bowed their heads; then he made the sign of the cross, and the rest of the table followed suit. He remembered two graces. He began, without giving himself time to think, on the one he had least often used.

"We give Thee thanks, Almighty God, for all Thy benefits. Who livest and reignest, world without end, Amen. May the souls of the faithful departed through the mercy of God rest in peace. Amen."

The words seemed to ring long after he had said them. He had as much as brought his wife and sons into the room with the words, then laid them to rest. He wondered if anyone else had noticed. He glanced at Peggy, who was seated on his left, and saw that she certainly had. She gave a slight nod. He felt as if she'd squeezed his hand in comfort, even though she hadn't touched him.

He noticed the others were eating and beginning to chat. Peggy turned to put bits of fish and vegetables on Kieran's plate. Bridie and Megan were discussing the pros and cons of rosemary, and Irene, in her favorite blue housedress, was listening intently, putting in a good word for parsley whenever she could.

The fragrance arising from his plate was mouth-watering; the friendly buzz of conversation was like that in millions of homes throughout the world as families sat down together to review their days and engage in this most basic of communions.

He lifted his fork, and hunger turned to bile. He was physically ill, and for a moment he doubted he could leave the table in time.

He shoved his chair back and strode out of the room, his head spinning, then throbbing, and his stomach twisting in a terrible knot. Outside, in the cooling air of evening, he rested his cheek against a porch pillar and took deep breaths. The nausea dissipated a shade, but his knees grew weaker. He circled the pillar with an arm and sagged against it.

"Da?"

He closed his eyes. "Go back inside, Bridie."

"Are you all right?"

"Go on."

"No." She came up beside him. "Are you ill?"

"I said go back inside."

"And I said no!"

His eyes flew open, and he stared at her. She had never in his memory addressed him in that tone.

"My dinner made you sick." Bridie crossed her arms. "I worked all day on it, and you didn't eat it. So I want to know why. Is it because *I'm* the one who cooked it?"

He realized he was breathing too fast. He understood hyperventilation and its effects. He wondered how long he had been gulping air to quell his panic. His skin was cold, and his hands tingled in warning.

There was a bench under the same tree where he'd last seen Banjax. He made his way there and fell onto it, putting his head in his hands and cupping them over his mouth and nose. He breathed in his own exhalations, and in a minute the worst of the sensation abated.

Bridie came to stand in front of him. "It's my fault they're dead. I know it is, and that's why you hate me."

As the roaring in his head eased, her words replaced it. For a moment he was confused. "Your fault?"

"Don't you think I'm old enough to understand? You blame Mommy's death on me, and Mark's and Brian's. If I'd been with you that day, I could have helped save them. I'm a strong swimmer. I could have taken one of the boys, and you could have taken the other. And Mommy could have hung on to the side until she was rescued! But I wasn't there. I was selfish. I wanted to play with my friends. I wanted to ride Sally's pony. So I stayed here, and everybody died but you! And that's why you hate me and have ever since."

She began to sob.

He could not get to her. His arms felt like lead weights, the way they had the afternoon he had tried so desperately to haul his older son to shore. He had tried and failed to save Mark, and he knew he was failing Bridie the same way now. But he was paralyzed.

"Bridie..." The name sounded as if it had been torn from him. "No. No. You're wrong."

"I'm not wrong! I know what happened. I know it wouldn't have happened if I had been there, but I wasn't!"

He found the strength to reach for her, and he hauled her into his arms, forcing her to his lap. He began to rock her, but for whose comfort he wasn't certain.

"You're wrong, so wrong." He kissed her hair and held her tighter. "I thank God every day, every single day, that you weren't with us. Because what would I do without you, Bridie? And make no mistake about it, you would have died, too. You couldn't have helped the others. As good a swimmer as you are, the waves were too high, the water too rough and cold. You would have perished just the way they did. Don't you know that *you* saved *me,* dearest? You saved my life because I knew I had to get home to you. I would have given up if you hadn't been waiting. So you did save a life just by staying home that day. You saved mine."

She turned her face into his shoulder. She was sobbing so hard she could hardly speak. "But...but you...hate me!"

He held her harder. "How can you say that?"

"You act...like you do!"

"Bridie...Bridie." He smoothed her hair and kissed it, and he wondered when he had last held her this way. After the accident he had been too ill. After his recovery, he had felt too guilty.

"I can't explain this very well," he said. "I blame myself, Bridie. The way you do. I...I couldn't save them. And every time I look at you, I remember that *I'm* the reason they're gone and you have them with you no longer."

She put her arms around his neck. "But I still have you."

He kissed her cheek. "Oh yes, of course you do." He repeated it fiercely. "Of course you do!"

"And it wasn't your fault. Everyone says it wasn't. That you're the only one in the world who thinks so. Even Gram says so. She says she can't live with your pain and hers, as well. That's why she and Granda moved to Belmullet."

He could not believe that Sheila's mother had said such a thing to a child. Yet was this worse in its way than not saying anything? To allow Bridie to believe for so long that he held her responsible for the deaths?

By not talking honestly and openly about his own pain and guilt, hadn't he foisted it on her?

"None of us have shared our suffering as we should have." Finn continued to rock her. "We've let it eat at us separately. I'm sorry, so sorry, that you ever believed, for even one moment, that I didn't love you. I love you so much it hurts me sometimes, Bridie. But it also gives me the greatest joy."

"Why couldn't you eat my dinner, then?"

She was still a child, and this was the question of the day. He tried to think of an excuse, but there had been far too many of them. He settled for the truth.

"I was reminded of other times. It pressed in on me, and for a moment I felt ill, and I couldn't breathe or swallow. Can you understand that?"

"In the night, sometimes, I feel like someone is sitting on my chest. Is that how it feels?"

He smoothed back her hair and kissed her forehead. "Oh, yes."

"Will it always be this way?"

He shook his head, but not in denial. He really didn't know. "Bridie, in the night? When that happens to you? Come in and wake me up. I'll get up, too, and we'll make cocoa. I'll tell you stories of Fionn Mac Cumhail to make it go away."

She leaned against him, and he held her there for a very long time. Dinner was cold by the time they returned to the house, but neither they nor those inside, who had waited for their return, seemed to care.

chapter 27

"I feel on top of the world this evening," Irene said. "And Nora and I have mittens to knit for the annual parish bazaar. She'll be keeping me company and listening out for Kieran."

Megan glanced at her sister to see if Irene's argument was having any effect. It was her second day in Ireland, and she had already learned just how stubborn the deceptively sweet old woman could be. Irene wanted the sisters to have an evening of pub hopping in the village, but Peggy was concerned about leaving for the night.

"When will she be coming?" Peggy asked. "She didn't say anything to me this morning."

"Any moment. And we firmed up our plans this afternoon by telephone."

"Peggy, you've been bested," Megan said. "And Irene would probably like a quiet evening without us. Last night was excitement enough."

"Last night was a turning point," Irene said. "And I'm glad

I lived to see it. For two years now I've watched Bridie and Finn moving like shadows in each other's company, and I had begun to worry they would never find their way back to each other." She hesitated. "But it nearly stopped my poor old heart. So yes, a quiet night is just the thing."

"What do you think?" Megan asked her sister. "Want to show me the sights?"

"I'd love it. I only wish Finn was playing at Tully's tonight so you could hear him. But he and Bridie went north to see her grandparents for the weekend."

"And not a moment too soon." Irene hobbled toward her room to ready herself for company.

"She'll be all right without Finn on call?" Megan asked once Irene was out of earshot.

"I'll monitor her and call him in Belmullet if need be. There's another doctor I can call in a real emergency."

They settled on a time to leave. Megan put Kieran to bed, tucking him into the crib with his new stuffed bear and his favorite blanket. He seemed oblivious to her presence, but as she left the room he said "hi," not once but twice. She was thrilled; then she realized how low her expectations had become. Peggy had left for Ireland certain she could work a miracle with her son. But in the months she had been away, Megan was afraid very little had been accomplished.

Megan tried to put that out of her mind as she drove her sister to Shanmullin. They wandered the village, feeding the swans in the brook on the green and chatting with the strangers who stopped to put in a good word. Everyone seemed to know Peggy. Megan wasn't surprised her sister had already made an impression. Her warmth was bone deep, and Peggy was a born healer. Two minutes into a conversation she had solicited life stories, without even seeming to try. She knew what to say and what not to when silence was required. People felt better just for having spoken to her.

Or at least that was the way her proud sister viewed the matter.

"You like it here, don't you?" Megan squatted to pet a cat

preening on the sidewalk in the last rays of a setting sun. A window opened above their heads, and someone called for Blackie. The cat looked around, as if to be sure no other feline had noticed, then rose majestically and started through an open shop door.

"I do, and I wasn't sure if I would. I thought of myself as a city girl, but I like the slower pace and the chance to concentrate on limited numbers of people."

Megan got to her feet. "Would you like to practice in a small town, do you think? Somewhere outside of Cleveland instead of the heart of the city?"

"So much depends on Kieran. I don't know if I'll ever really be able to leave him long enough to finish med school."

They walked slowly, and Megan knew it was time to tell her sister the truth. "I've been looking for signs of improvement."

"And haven't found many. I know." Peggy shook her head. "Sometimes I think I'm getting through to him. When he was teething, he took a sharp turn for the better. I don't know why. But it's weeks later, and little else has improved now that he's feeling better. Even his therapist doesn't seem to have any long-distance answers."

"Maybe you should come home where you can get him into a good program. You know everyone will help out with the bills."

"No, I have to give this more of a try. It's too soon to accept defeat."

Megan debated her next remark. All day she had pondered ways to introduce Peggy's relationship with Finn O'Malley into their conversation. Megan had hoped for someone very different for Peggy, a romance hero with shoulders broad enough to carry the weight of the world, a knight who would sweep her off her feet to an easier life. As much as Megan loved Kieran, she was not blind to the lifetime of problems ahead for both the son and his mother. Peggy would need a great deal of support in the years to come.

And what could Finn offer?

Megan decided the opportunity had arrived. "And you don't want to leave Irene. Or Bridie." She paused. "Or *Finn*."

"Here's Tully's." Peggy stopped at a bright yellow door. "It's my favorite." She listened. "No music tonight. Maybe it will start later. It might be ten o'clock, but it's only just turned dark."

Megan knew better than to push the subject of Finn here and now when her opening gambit had been so soundly rejected. "The Guinness is on me."

"Did you hit the lottery, Megan?"

"You only live once."

"Not according to the New Agers. Who knows, we might have been in this very spot a hundred times before."

They debated that possibility as they found seats at the bar. Tonight was not as crowded as Peggy had expected, but as he readied himself to leave, the man beside her explained. There was a wake at the church, and the departed was known to all. They were invited to come and pay their respects, but Peggy graciously declined.

The bartender arrived and introduced himself as Jimmy. He was a large man, with a bulbous red nose and a wreath of peach-colored hair. Megan would have hired him for the Whiskey Island Saloon on nothing more than his smile. A few minutes later he came back with two brimming pints.

Peggy excused herself to go to the ladies' room, and Jimmy came back to talk to Megan when he saw that Peggy was gone.

"So what brings you to Ireland?"

She saw her chance to get information. She knew from personal experience how vast were the resources of a bartender.

"Well, I'm in Ireland to visit my sister and meet her friends. She lives with Irene Tierney and spends quite a bit of time with Finn O'Malley and his daughter. I met them both yesterday."

"Ah yes, the American woman who was just here with you."

"That's the one."

"Yes, she seems to have caught old Finn's eye." Jimmy winked.

"He's a stranger, and that worries me."

"Worried about Finn? He's had a bad time of it, but there's no reason to worry now."

"Then you like him?"

"Best doctor we ever had in the village. Everyone liked him, from the babies to the dying."

Megan was less concerned with Finn's skills as a physician than with his emotional health. "It's just that she's still young, and I feel responsible for her." She hoped that would prompt him to say more, and that if Peggy ever heard about this conversation, she would forgive her.

"So you're staying at Tierney Cottage?" he asked instead.

"Uh-huh."

"Now, you want to know secrets about Shanmullin, that would be the place to start. Ask old Irene about her father. You could learn an earful."

Megan had been poised on the brink of asking more about Finn, but she paused. "Earful?"

"Aye, there's quite a story there. Old Liam Tierney was either the devil himself or a Republican hero, depending on who tells the tale."

"I don't know much about Liam's years in Ireland." Megan realized she had just become the champion of understatement. "I've hoped to learn more. Irene doesn't seem to know a lot."

He frowned, as if to say that was impossible. "Well, it's no secret, that's for certain. He left here when he was a lad, and the cottage sat empty for years, just a place for mice and bats, you know."

"It looks like he might have moved to Cleveland at some point during that time and died there. That's where I'm from."

Someone hailed Jimmy to take another order. Megan sipped her Guinness and waited for Peggy to return. Clearly the only story she would get out of Jimmy tonight was about Liam, not Finn.

"I'm back." Peggy slid onto the seat beside her.

"Listen, Jimmy was just telling me about Liam. Sounds like there might be a real story there. And it sounds like Irene might know more of it than she's told us."

Peggy looked surprised. "I don't see how, Megan. She says she knows very little."

Jimmy returned. "Can I get you ladies another pint?"

Megan declined, since her glass wasn't empty. "We'd like to hear about Liam, though, if you know anything more."

"Oh, there's lots more. After his mother left the village without so much as a word to anyone, he was sent away by the village priest to an orphanage in the south. He came back here some years later as a married man with a baby and set about trying to fix up Tierney Cottage for Brenna, his wife, and baby Irene. But he couldn't escape his destiny."

When Jimmy paused to savor what he knew and they didn't, Peggy asked the obvious. "What destiny?"

"He was an IRA man, don't you know, and not afraid to do anything for the cause of a free Ireland. That's the way I've heard it told. In '23 he killed a man during an ambush and left Mayo and all of Ireland one step in front of the law."

Megan was trying to remember her Irish history, never a central point of American education. "But didn't Ireland become independent in 1921 or '22, when the treaty with Britain was signed?"

"Not so's you'd know it. We were still forced to have ties with England. Some thought things were fine that way, that we'd move a bit slower but reach a state of total independence in the long run—which we did in '49, except for the north, of course. But some, like Irene's da, were convinced things had to happen all at once. And they tried to make sure they did. We had our very own Civil War, you remember."

"So he killed somebody who didn't agree with him?"

"A policeman, not just somebody. The Republicans smuggled Liam and his family out of the country and into America."

"That seems awfully charitable of them." Megan wished that she'd taken Jimmy up on his offer. Her glass was empty now, but Jimmy's story was still in full spin. "And forgive me if I'm wrong, but I've never heard that the IRA was a philanthropic organization."

"Oh, it was a different organization then, I can tell you. But helping him leave Ireland was more than charity." Jimmy turned for a rag and wiped the counter as he talked. "They sent him to America to raise money for the cause of the Republic."

"In Cleveland?"

"I don't recall I ever heard where the lad went. I just know that years later Brenna came home without him, and Irene was a little girl by then. They moved back into Tierney Cottage, such as it was at that time. Brenna was a lovely young woman, I'm told, although I'm too young to know firsthand. But a local man fell in love with her, and they were married right here at the village church. He was a man of some means, and together they bought the land outright and made the cottage what it is today." With a friendly salute, Jimmy left to chat up another customer.

Megan turned to her sister. "Peggy, that's a *whole* lot of background Irene's never bothered to mention."

"You don't suppose she was ashamed of what Liam did and kept it from us?"

"Two reasons why not. One, even though Liam killed somebody, it was probably considered an act of war. I'm sure some people, maybe most people in Shanmullin, think of him as a hero, or at least as a man who was trying to do what was right. Two, she must have known you would discover the truth from someone once you came to live with her. It's only surprising you didn't learn it before this."

Peggy set her glass on the counter. "I didn't ask anybody about *Liam*. I believed Irene when she said she didn't know anything more than what she'd told me. I guess I just assumed nobody else in the village knew anything, either."

Megan was trying to find a charitable explanation. "Maybe she really *doesn't* know the way he died. From the beginning, that's what she asked us to discover."

"If she wasn't straight with us about Liam's reasons for fleeing Ireland, then maybe she hasn't been straight about that, either."

Megan acknowledged that possibility with a nod.

"Nothing of great interest here tonight," Peggy said. "But there might be something of interest waiting for us at the cottage. Let's go home and see if Irene and Nora have finished with their knitting."

Between them, Nora and Irene had completed a pair of creamy white mittens. As girls in school they had been taught to knit by the nuns, who had viewed a perfect stitch as a rung on the ladder to heaven. Even though the two women's education had been years apart, the mittens still matched perfectly.

"You've no idea how many rows we were forced to pull out only because our gauge was off by the tiniest fraction of an inch." Irene put away her knitting. "I could pick up and finish any jumper Nora began, and no one would be the wiser."

Nora had already gathered her things and was on her way out the door. Megan offered to take her home, but Nora insisted that she preferred to bike.

"She owns a car, you know," Irene told Megan once Nora had gone. "She just prefers her bicycle. Claims she sees more along the way."

Peggy motioned for Irene to stay where she was. "It seems there's a lot the Donaghue sisters don't know about a lot of things. Why don't I make you a snack before you go off to bed?"

"Oh, thank you, dear, but Nora and I had toast and milk just a while ago. Did you girls have fun in town?"

"It was a lovely night. Not many people were about, since they were all at the wake."

"Ah yes, for Thomas Harrigan, poor man. I'll be going to the funeral tomorrow. Nora will take me. Dropped dead milking his cow, and no one knew it until he didn't come in for dinner."

"We did hear some interesting gossip," Megan said.

Irene's eyes sparkled. For a moment Peggy glimpsed the younger woman she had not been privileged to know. "You're sure you don't want some tea or another glass of milk?" Peggy asked.

"No, but a report would be nice. Pity an old woman who has to depend on others to keep her informed."

"Well, I know how you must feel." Peggy settled herself on the sofa. "Depending on others can be tricky, because they don't necessarily tell you everything."

"That's God's own truth."

"For instance, when I heard this evening that your father had left Ireland one step ahead of the law, I was so surprised. Because in all our conversations, you've never mentioned it."

Irene didn't look shocked or even guilty. "Did I somehow omit that?"

"Irene!"

Irene smiled. "Well, I suppose I didn't see much point at first in telling you that your very own cousin was a wanted man."

"And I'm sure he wasn't the first and only relative who was." Megan dropped down beside her sister. "I could tell you some things about the Donaghue clan that would curl your hair, but the question is what else haven't you told us? We know Liam was involved with the IRA, that he was sent to America to raise funds after he killed a man here—"

"He never meant to kill anyone. My mother told me he was defending another IRA man, and that even then, he only meant to injure the man he shot. He never liked guns."

"I'm sure that's all true," Peggy said. "And even if it weren't, it happened so long ago it hardly seems to affect us. So why didn't you tell us?" She paused for effect. "And what *else* haven't you told us?"

Irene didn't look offended, even though Peggy's gently voiced question was, in its own way, a challenge. "I've been less than honest about my da's activities in Cleveland. I knew, for instance, about the bootlegging and his job with Timothy McNulty."

Peggy took a moment to digest that. "But I don't understand. Why didn't you tell us? Right at the beginning, when we didn't have a thing to go on? That would have put us so much further ahead."

Irene didn't answer directly. "As a matter of fact, I know

more about those years with Mr. McNulty than you do. Tonight you learned about my father's connection with the Republican Army. And how they helped him make his escape. You haven't yet put the rest of it together, but I can help. My father took the job with Tim McNulty because Mr. McNulty was an Irish patriot, or so Da believed. And he hoped that once he was deep in Mr. McNulty's trust, that he would give some of his considerable money to the cause."

"The IRA cause?" Megan said.

"The very one. Da was convinced the only real hope for Ireland was to toss the Brits out fairly lively. Remember now, he'd grown up with a father who was a bit away in his head after all those years in an English gaol. My father was no great admirer of Great Britain."

"And?" Megan waited, and when Irene didn't respond, she added, "Did McNulty give the IRA money? And did that have something to do with your father's death?"

"Mr. McNulty was a poor example of the human race. After a while it became clear enough to my da that he was, excuse the expression, like the barber's cat, full of wind and piss."

Peggy curled her legs under her rump and pulled a pillow to her chest, hugging it close. She had a feeling this was going to be a long story. "I guess we don't need a translation for that one."

Irene nodded. "And like many a political man of his generation, Da decided not to get angry. He decided to get whatever else he could."

Unlike Peggy, Megan didn't make herself comfortable. She leaned forward. "Irene, you sidestepped when Peggy asked you why you didn't tell us this before. I think we need to know. I think there are two stories here, yours and Liam's. I'd like to hear both of them."

"Both in due time." Irene held up a finger to stop Megan's retort. "I *will* tell you this. I did hold back, and I'll admit it. And I misled you. I'll admit that, as well. But there's nothing devious about why I did it. It was my way, you see, of getting to know you. We might be related by blood, but that was no reason to be certain I could trust you. So I asked you for help, then I waited. And you stepped forward to help an old woman you'd never even met. What further proof did I need?"

"You had to trust us? For what reason? You were afraid we would think less of you if we knew Liam's real motives for coming to Cleveland? That was eighty years ago. Why would we care about the past of a man we never knew? *You* hardly knew him."

"T'will all come clear. For now, though, will you settle for a bit more of Liam's story?"

"It's pretty late." Peggy had just noticed the clock and realized they had already gone an hour past Irene's bedtime. As much as she wanted to learn the whole story, she still felt responsible for Irene's health.

"I had a long nap this afternoon, and I'll sleep better for having told you more."

"More?" Megan asked. "Not *all?*"

"Do you want to hear what I have the energy to tell tonight, dear?"

Megan looked as if she wanted to say more, but she settled herself much as Peggy had done. "Okay, shoot." She winced. "Whoops. Maybe that's not the best expression under the circumstances."

"It's good to see your sense of humor hasn't bolted, dear." Irene closed her eyes and leaned her head against the back of her chair. "I've known for a very long time that I was related to the Donaghues who ran the Whiskey Island Saloon in Cleveland. Let me tell you how I knew."

1925
Castlebar, County Mayo

My dearest Patrick,

In your last letter you asked me to make inquiries about the Tierney family of Shanmullin. You have forgotten, I fear, how rambling our distances and how primitive our communications. But you have remem-

bered well the way we Irish love to know the comings
and goings of all within our reach. Ireland may yet be
a poor country, (no thanks to the landlords, who are only
just being dispensed with, and not a moment too soon)
but we are rich in what we know of each other and what
we share with a willing ear. So this much I can tell you
already, from conversations with my neighbors.

Years ago there was a family named Tierney who
lived near the village of Shanmullin. Good people, by
all accounts, even in the days when goodness often
meant starvation. After the famine they dispersed as our
poor families were so often forced to do. For years the
cottage was deserted and the landlord raised sheep on
their acres. Then a son returned, and the landlord took
pity and let him farm the land. He married and had one
son, who was later orphaned and sent south to Cork. That
son returned as an adult, although as to why he might, I
have no insight. Views of the ocean will not feed a starving sparrow. The young man, however, seemed oblivious to that fine point and returned with a wife and child.

There was trouble, Patrick dear. Of what nature I've
yet to uncover, although of course I have my suspicions. Some things are not talked about freely in Ireland
even yet. I only know the young man, Liam Tierney, disappeared with his wife and child one night after a policeman was murdered. And the Tierney Cottage once
again lies empty and neglected on a windswept hill.
How odd, is it not, that your young man's name would
be Tierney? Was not this the name of the young woman
living on Whiskey Island of whom you wrote me so
many years ago?

Yes, my Patrick. My memory is as long as my life. I
find this both a curse and a blessing.

chapter 28

Liam made discreet inquiries about Glen Donaghue's family but discovered nothing of interest. No one remembered exactly when the Donaghues had come to Cleveland. Years ago, for certain. The Donaghues had built the Whiskey Island Saloon themselves and made it a success by working hard and making friends of thirsty men. Someone thought that Rowan Donaghue was the first to come from the old country. Even those old enough to know seemed to think the saloon and those who had founded it were simply a part of Cleveland history. Always there. Always accessible. Standing, perhaps, before the first still was built on Whiskey Island to give the land its name.

"You'd do well to speak to Father McSweeney," counseled an old woman who lived in the corner house on the Tierneys' street.

Liam had stopped to chat as he strolled with Irene through their quiet new neighborhood. The houses were just recently built and spacious; in fact, several at the opposite end of the block were still under construction. There were established oaks and maples to lend shade, and wide porches for enjoying the fragrance of a neighbor's roses or the song of a cardinal on a summer evening. After six months of living there, Brenna still marveled at her very own sweep of green yard and her gleaming oak floors. Liam could only rarely coax her from the kitchen, where she baked and scrubbed and hummed hymns that the sisters had taught her.

Liam tried to place Father McSweeney in his mind. "The old priest they trot out on holy days?"

"That would be the one."

Liam only went to church because Brenna said they must for Irene's sake. He found little there of interest, having released his tenuous grasp on religion the day he was sentenced to grow up under the squinty-eyed gaze of the Christian Brothers. Now he tried to remember what Father McSweeney looked like. He only recalled that the priest was frail and bent, and his voice quavered when he chanted.

"I've only rarely seen him," Liam said, hoping for some information.

"Oh, he was a magnificent priest, he was," the old woman said. "Put the fear of God in you, he could, and at the same time help you know God loved you, too. He married my Colleen to her Arthur, he did. They used to say that to be married by Father McSweeney was God's own blessing, that all his marriages were happy ones."

"And he knows something of the history of the area, does he?"

"Oh, much more than something. He knows it all." She leaned forward in confidence. "But I'd be quick about it, were I you. His health isn't the best. And he won't go south, although they want him to retire where the weather is kinder. He says his life is here."

Liam wondered if a priest had a life. He doubted it, but perhaps the old man had friends, even people he had come to love. Surely he hadn't stayed because he found the climate pleasing.

"Perhaps I'll ask him, although it's of little importance," he told her.

"You'd be interested for a reason," she said, her eyes narrowing in question.

"Oh, it's only that young Glen Donaghue resembles a man I once knew." Liam lifted Irene onto his shoulders, said his goodbyes and started back home. But the old woman's suggestion intrigued him. Why had he not thought of the priest? Priests meddled in the lives of everyone they met. Christened and married, absolved and buried. He resolved to visit Father McSweeney to find out what the old man knew about Glen Donaghue.

He found the opportunity later that week. McNulty and his bodyguards had gone to New York for a meeting, and Clare, who had become Liam's personal charge, was visiting her mother's sister in Buffalo. McNulty himself was depositing her there on his way to the big city, and Liam's watchful eye was not needed. His list of responsibilities while they were gone was short and uncomplicated.

He called the rectory and spoke to the housekeeper, who relayed his message. Surprisingly, Father McSweeney agreed to see him that very afternoon at four.

Liam was waiting, hat in hand, when the priest made his way into the rectory parlor. Each step was measured and shuffling, but when Liam offered an arm to help the old man seat himself, the priest waved him away. More than age afflicted McSweeney. Some form of palsy held him in his grip, and disease withered his body. But the man's blue eyes were still clear, and once he began to speak, it was obvious that the mind behind them remained sharp.

"You're welcome here, but you've come for more than a chance to see the rectory, I suppose?"

"Yes, Father." Liam perched on the edge of an overstuffed horsehair chair. Both arms of the chair were covered with crocheted doilies, and he was afraid he would knock them to the ground. He wasn't yet over his discomfort with priests and the punishment they could mete out.

"You have questions for me?" Father McSweeney seemed

to be trying to ease Liam into revealing himself. There was no hint of impatience in his voice.

"The conversation will go no further than this parlor?"

"Well, it's not the confessional, but it's nearly as good." Father McSweeney searched Liam's face. "But you haven't been in a confessional for some time now, have you?"

"How would you know that?"

Father McSweeney smiled. "I can't read your mind, son, nor the stains on your soul. It's only that I've never seen you there."

"Oh." Liam realized he was twisting his hat in his hands. "I met a man. Glen Donaghue is his name. And I'm trying to find out something about his family. Someone told me that you would be the one to ask."

"I know something about *you.*"

Liam was surprised. He had not expected this. "Do you, now?"

"I made inquiries some weeks back. In Ireland."

Liam was more surprised, and growing alarmed, as well. "Now why would you do such a thing?"

"Perhaps for the very reason you're here to ask about the Donaghues."

As the priest struggled to make himself more comfortable, Liam pondered that possibility.

Finally Father McSweeney sighed in resignation and stopped fidgeting. Clearly comfort was not to be had. "I saw you at Mass on Easter Day, and you reminded me of someone. I asked your name of another priest. You're from a village called Shanmullin?"

"That's right, Father." Liam placed the hat at his feet and leaned forward. "*Who* did I remind you of?"

"Someone long dead. Also named Tierney."

Liam waited, breath held.

"A man named Terence Tierney," the priest said. "Your uncle, if my information serves us both correctly."

"Long...dead." Liam had known as much, but the news was still something of a blow, although why, he couldn't say.

Father McSweeney continued. "Terence had a son, how-ever, who is alive today. And that son has two children."

Liam thought he knew the name of one of them. "Glen Donaghue?"

"Yes."

"The wife married again?" It was the only explanation Liam could see.

"Yes. Lena Tierney gave birth to Terence's child after his death. She called the son Terence, as well, but she married a man named Rowan Donaghue soon after, and he adopted lit-tle Terry. Terry was always called Donaghue."

"When I arrived, I asked about for Tierneys, but there were none to be found. So that's the reason. Why did you ask about *me?* Before you even knew my name?"

"I saw something of Terence in you. A flash, a gesture. For a moment you took me straight back to another time. I thought it was only an old man's whim, but I asked, just in case. When I discovered your name, I asked with more interest."

"And *I* saw something of my father in Glen Donaghue. Glen is very much like Da must have been at his age, but I see no resemblance between the two of *us.*"

"Perhaps not, but each of you resembles, in some small way, the other's ancestor."

Liam thought how odd it all was. He had saved Glen's life, never knowing they were cousins. Now Liam worked for Tim McNulty, and Glen struggled to find ways to put Tim out of business.

"I wasn't certain what to do with what I had learned," Fa-ther McSweeney said. "I'm glad you came to me. Will you tell Glen?"

"What else do you know about me?" Liam asked.

"Enough, I'm afraid."

"Then you'll understand why I *can't* tell him. Will he want to know that his long lost Irish cousin is a bootlegger?"

"His parents keep a saloon, you know. His grandmother began it."

"His parents don't work for Tim McNulty."

"You don't have to, either."

Liam considered that. If he quit, he could tell Glen who he was and how they were related. Ironically, Liam's job was to keep Glen and Clare McNulty apart, a mission he had found distasteful even without knowing that he and Glen were cousins. Now it seemed worse, and he could end it by leaving Tim McNulty's employment.

Yet could he quit? Even if he wanted to? Would McNulty allow him to simply walk away, knowing all he did? And there were other considerations. Brenna, Irene and the lovely house they could now afford. And men at home in Ireland who expected him to show proper gratitude for helping him bypass America's traditional immigration procedures.

Then, of course, there was the IRA cause. Something bigger than himself, the *only* thing bigger that he really believed in.

"Perhaps breaking with Tim McNulty isn't as easy as it sounds?" Father McSweeney said. "Would you like to pray about it with me?"

"Thank you, but no. I'm not a believer, Father, and if there's a God, He stopped listening to me long ago."

"Impossible."

Liam picked up his hat and rose. "I'm grateful to you for speaking with me. You won't tell Glen or the other Donaghues?"

"They would help you make a new start, you know. It's a good family. And Lena, Terence's wife, would be happy to know that some of the Tierney family survived. We're old friends, and I see her often. She grew up in your village. I suspect she knew your father when he was a lad."

"Perhaps, but she never knew the man he became. That's a story she's better off not knowing."

Father McSweeney struggled to his feet. "If you won't pray with me, I'll pray *for* you." He held up a trembling hand when Liam began to protest. "It can't hurt, can it? And it will fill an old man's final days with something more than letters and endless contemplation."

"Then pray for Glen, and for Tim McNulty's daughter, too, will you, Father? She and Glen believe they've fallen in love.

And if they really have, they'll need more than prayers. They'll need all the heavenly hosts to avoid McNulty's retribution."

"And you would allow such a thing? For your very own cousin?"

Liam set his hat on his head. "I do what I'm told."

"And it got you in trouble once before, didn't it, son? In Ireland, just before you came to America. *That's* why you believe God has turned away from you."

Liam could think of nothing to say about that. He turned and left before he could.

Tim McNulty was a rich man who wanted to be richer. It was not an uncommon ailment. Liam had seen the disease frequently in his homeland. Ireland had come to a sorry state because of greed, as pervasive and destructive as the blight that had attacked the potato crops.

McNulty's greed was matched by a fierce need for power. It wasn't enough that his own little bootlegging empire thrived, and that he was the undisputed crime king of Cleveland's West Side. He wanted more, needed it the way most men needed whiskey and a willing woman. And the only way to guarantee more of everything was to take chances.

McNulty, born to be a gambler, was about to take a big one.

"I won't pretend this is any ordinary haul, lads," McNulty told the men assembled inside one of his warehouses. "If I do, then you won't know that you *have* to give this one your all. So I'm telling you now, this is the real thing tonight, the thing you lay your life on the line for if you have to. Because if all goes well," his eyes narrowed, "and it had better, then every man here's going to leave for home a lot richer. There will be large bonuses for every one of you if we come through this with no problems."

Liam was more interested in McNulty's appearance and tone than his words. McNulty was sweating like a washerwoman bent over a laundry press. And the smile that characterized all his dealings, even the most grisly ones, had disappeared, melting away in his personal deluge.

McNulty fished a handkerchief from his pocket and mopped his forehead. "So if anybody has any questions, now's the time to ask them. Otherwise, you lads are on your own."

Nobody said a word.

"Okay, then." McNulty waved them away. "Come back with all the goods, or I'll find you, and you'll be returning in a pine box." This time he did smile, a sickening imitation of his usual. Then he turned his back on them, and stepped out of the warehouse and into his Cadillac.

The men waited until the car had been driven away before anybody moved.

"Exactly what's going on?" Liam asked Jerry. "What's he so flustered about?"

"You criticizing the boss?"

"No, but if I'm about to risk my life, I'd like to know the stakes."

Jerry motioned him farther away from the others, three of McNulty's favored "assistants," who were talking among themselves. "I can tell you what all I heard."

"Good enough."

"This panther sweat they're bringing over from Canada tonight? Well, it's better stuff than usual, see? A lot better, and there's a lot more of it. The boss has everything tied up in this haul." He looked around before he spoke to be sure no one else was listening. "He borrowed money to make this deal. That's why he went to New York, but his regular source in the Bronx turned him down flat. So he took big simoleans from Bugs Moran and his gang, and they don't give nothing unless they get a whole lot more something back, you know what I mean?"

Liam knew. Obviously McNulty had gone into heavy debt to get the money for this shipment. If it all went well, he would make it back and a whole lot more, plus gain some muscle with the North Side Chicago gang. But if things didn't go well...

Jerry pulled out his watch. "We gotta get going. One at a time." He signaled to one of the other men, who nodded. Jerry turned back to Liam and winked. "You're the end of the line. Put the cat out, and lock up nice and tight for the night. I'll see you there."

Liam forced a smile. "That you will."

The others left, one by one in four separate vehicles with five-minute intervals between. Liam waited another ten before he slipped out the door of the darkened warehouse. He had been told to walk down to Whiskey Island, where the shipment was supposed to arrive. The walk took him twenty minutes more, along rugged paths lit only by a cloud-dusted moon and the occasional flickering glow from some resident's shanty.

The clouds congealed and gathered forces as he walked, and he hoped that the storm that was brewing held off until the night's business was complete. He skirted what industry there was, and the railyards, too, kicking twice at packs of stray dogs who were searching for rats or garbage. The bars that had once dotted the landscape were gone now, casualties of Prohibition. He was just as glad, since that meant fewer people to mark his presence.

The others had hidden themselves well on the peninsula's most deserted shore, assisted by skies that were growing steadily more menacing. Lightning flashed on the distant horizon, but it was the only light he saw now.

This spot was a favored destination for rumrunners, and it wasn't Liam's first visit. Had he been in command of the booze agents, he would have assigned a man to live right here and reap the frequent harvests of Canadian hooch. But he wasn't in charge, and he supposed the Lake Erie coast had plenty of other places as ripe for business as this one. He stood behind a line of scrub and waited for the others to show themselves.

They did, one by one, materializing like stories he'd heard of the half-fairy *grogoch*, which only appeared when it had grown comfortable with its surroundings.

"Anybody see anybody he shouldn't have?" Jerry asked when they had gathered into a tight little bundle of nerves and flesh.

No one had. Men shuffled uncomfortably, afraid to smoke

and draw unwanted attention. When they spoke, they did so in low voices, chopping off words as if final syllables might get them arrested.

Liam couldn't see his watch, a gift from Brenna on his last birthday, but he figured another half hour passed before Jerry shook his arm. "Look."

Liam followed Jerry's pointing finger. Something was moving in the water just off the shore. Two somethings, if he was right. "Two boats?"

"Three. Look farther that way."

Liam turned his gaze to the left and saw the outline of another cruiser in the wake of the second. Liam whistled softly. McNulty had been right. This was going to be some haul.

"First boat lands, you take it with Slim. Unload everything you can into the first truck. You do the last boat, too. Then you ride shotgun."

Liam knew the plan was not to drive the first truck to the warehouse, which might be watched, but to a restaurant in Lakewood owned by somebody who owed McNulty a favor. The first truck had Finegan's Fruit Company painted on the sides. The crates of "fruit" would reside in the restaurant's defunct wine cellar overnight until they could be delivered to a variety of speakeasies. Two other businesses would get truckloads two and three, and finally a funeral parlor would be similarly blessed with a crop of brand-new and surprisingly heavy caskets from the fourth truck.

"Where are *you* going to be?" Liam asked.

"Delivering the money." Jerry patted the inside of his coat. "Making sure we got everything we was paid for. I'll be counting what you bring back, but they'll have to come ashore to get their money. I'm not taking any chances on getting shanghaied."

Jerry might not be the brightest of McNulty's men, but Liam figured he was the most loyal. "Just watch your back," Liam said.

"Yeah, I know." Jerry peered into the darkness. "Okay, get going. Slim will take you out."

The plan was to use a small motorized skiff to get out to the larger boats. Two others of McNulty's men had brought them here just after dark. The moment Liam boarded the larger of the two, both were pushed out, and in a moment they were on their way. The crew of the Canadian boat started handing over the crates before they'd even finished tying the skiff to the cruiser. The men on board were silent and grim, and from the swift and efficient way they worked, Liam would have known they were pros, even if McNulty hadn't dealt with them half a dozen times before. He was speeding back to shore before his back could begin to ache.

Jerry helped pull them in. He counted crates, using a crowbar to pry off lids on random samples to make sure they contained what they were supposed to. A couple of bottles were opened and sampled. By the time he'd finished with their load and okayed it for the truck, the second skiff was back.

Most of the next hour was spent going back and forth to the boats, loading and unloading, packing the crates of whiskey and scotch into containers appropriate for the businesses inscribed on each truck. The first truck was ready to leave for its destination, as was the second, but the men lingered to make sure there were no problems until the deal was complete. The first two boats had already left for their return voyage.

When it was time for the skiff's final run out to the third boat, Liam went with Slim and silently unloaded the crates that were handed down to him. Then he motioned to a crew member. "You the fellow who's collecting the money?"

"No." The man turned, and in a moment the captain, silver-haired and stocky, came to the side.

"I'm the one you're looking for."

Liam figured a good percentage of the money must have been paid up front when McNulty made the deal. Now it was time to fork over the rest.

"My man's on shore," Liam said. "We'll take you there and bring you right back."

"Better not be any funny stuff. These guys'll have guns

pointed on you. Besides, McNulty ever wants another drop from Canada, you'll pay up just the way you said."

"I think the guy with the money is afraid of the water," Liam said. "He's a big fella, he'd float, but he's not too sure of himself."

"Let's make it quick, before the rain starts."

Liam couldn't have agreed more. So far, things had gone without a hitch, but the longer this took, the more chance of trouble.

The captain climbed over the side into the skiff, and Slim set out for shore. Jerry was waiting where the ground was firm, and the captain jumped out and headed toward him the moment the boat made shallow water.

He addressed Jerry from several yards away. "You did your check?"

"I did." Jerry reached into the inside of his jacket and pulled out a wad of bills. "Count it. S'all there."

The captain grabbed the money and riffled through the bills. Liam had never seen so many in one place. His mouth was suddenly dry. He could think of a hundred things to do with all that money that didn't include giving it to the Canadians.

"Looks okay." The captain nodded in affirmation just as the heavens opened and the storm erupted overhead.

Jerry cursed, pulling his jacket over his head for protection. Around him, the other men were doing the same. "Slim'll take you back out. Make it quick."

The captain carefully pocketed the money, and the two men shook hands. The captain turned back toward the skiff.

Lights flashed from the road above them, and a voice bleated into the storm, "We got you surrounded. Hands up, and don't move!"

"Shit!" Jerry spoke for them all.

Liam's gaze jerked through the curtain of falling rain toward the lake. Out on the water he saw lights that hadn't been there before. Two boats were closing in on the remaining Canadian vessel and the skiffs. The raid was coordinated. No one had simply happened upon them.

"Scatter!" Liam knew better than to stay and face the coast guard or the booze agents. Captured, he faced deportation or jail. If he was sent back to Ireland, he faced the gallows. Better to die here.

He dove headfirst into the scrub behind him, hoping that even though that put him temporarily closer to the men who wanted to arrest him, it also made him less of a target. The storm would provide some protection. Around him, he heard the others racing for parts unknown, the scuffling of feet, the muttering of oaths.

Shots were fired, and one bullet sprayed sand just in front of him. He crawled farther into the brush, finding his way one hand and knee at a time. He was moving as fast as he could, slipping and sliding, away from the gunshots and the agents who were brandishing lights, but he was sure he wasn't moving fast enough. At some point he would have to crouch and run, hoping he wasn't spotted until he could reach firmer ground and sprint to freedom.

Someone crashed through brush close to him, and for a moment he thought the chase was over and he was going to be forced to fight. Then he caught a glimpse of silver hair and broad shoulders and realized the Canadian captain was making his escape in the same direction. The man was so intent on finding his way through the brush and the pounding rain that he didn't see Liam. Liam kept him in sight, letting the captain blaze the trail and brave a first hail of bullets if one came, but the man's instincts were unerring. He zigged and zagged through the thickest cover. Yards and seconds to his rear, Liam followed in his footsteps.

Behind him, Liam heard shouts and scuffling. Overhead, lightning split the sky, followed immediately by a lion's roar of thunder. More gunfire erupted, and he winced. He was armed, as were all McNulty's gang, but he had no intention of turning fire on faceless men. He told himself that was simple humanity and nothing to do with the fact that one of those men might be his cousin. He pushed forward, keeping the captain in his sight and leaving the gunfire farther behind.

He didn't know how far they'd gone when the captain slowed, then stopped. The shouts and the lights were well behind them now, but the rain was heavier, a solid black sheet. Through no particular plan or instinct, it seemed they had made a good stab at escape, although they weren't yet out of danger.

The captain seemed to realize this, too. As Liam watched, the man paused a moment, then reached inside his jacket and stooped, both simultaneously. Then, as he watched, the captain straightened and started off through the thicket again. Intrigued, Liam planned to follow when the man had gained twenty yards, but shouts deterred him.

"We got you, mister. Don't move, don't even flinch."

Liam took one step into deeper cover. He realized he was trembling, although from exertion, chill or reaction he couldn't have said. He drew his gun and waited, but nobody appeared.

"Hands over your head. Look, Jake, we got a real rumrunner here."

The captain was in custody, and Liam knew the chance that the men would come this way was excellent. He looked for a better place to hide. There was a depression just below the knob where he stood. A large tree had been uprooted and lay on its side across a shallow pit. He edged his way back to it and crawled silently and cautiously underneath, lying parallel to and beneath the trunk. Rain sluiced over him, and he knew the water surrounding him was probably rising. The hole was shallow enough that eventually it would fill completely. Before it did, of course, he would drown.

He wondered which would be worse, hanging or drowning? The rain drummed against the trunk of the tree and echoed all around him. From this hiding place, nothing else was audible, just the drumming and sloshing of Heaven's floodgates draining into the sanctuary where he lay.

He wondered if Glen had been in on this raid, and how the Treasury agents had got their information. Somebody in McNulty's confidence had talked, but whom? McNulty would never rest until he found out. And what if somehow McNulty discovered that Liam was a relative of Glen Donaghue's? At that point Liam would be the prime suspect, even though he hadn't even known about the haul until McNulty's pep talk at the warehouse. But McNulty might think that Liam had wormed it out of someone, Jerry, perhaps, or someone else higher up than he was. Liam was doomed if McNulty ever discovered his connection to Glen.

Liam told himself not to throw stones at a dead dog. There was no use worrying about something that was never going to happen. Only he and Father McSweeney knew the truth, and why would the Father tell anybody?

The water was rising. The night had been warm enough, but it had cooled as the storm moved in. Now the rain felt like melted snow sliding under his collar and seeping up his arms. He wondered how long he had lain here already and how much longer he should stay?

He closed his eyes and thought about the rumrunner captain who was now a guest of the United States government. What exactly had the man left in the woods below? As the water rose around him and the storm raged, Liam wondered if he would be able to find this place again. If he remained a free man, he planned to take a walk by the lake someday soon when the skies and the woods were clear.

chapter 29

Niccolo was standing at an altar, staring up at the wooden beams crisscrossing a towering ceiling. One glorious stained glass window of Jesus blessing three small children illuminated the space where he stood. His voice boomed, and his hands were rock steady.

"And looking up to heaven, to you his almighty father, He gave you thanks and praise. He broke the bread, gave it to His disciples and said—"

A piercing shriek cut short the speech. He paused, attempting to turn around to find the source, but his limbs had grown heavy and his head refused to move. His heart began to pound faster, and his chest constricted. The downward pull of his alb and green chasuble seemed to drag him toward the floor, while the snakelike twining of his stole bound him in place. He could not catch his breath. He could not fight his way clear. Fear enveloped him as closely as his garments.

As he struggled to break free, he awoke to the sound of his alarm clock and the twisted length of a top sheet around his hips.

The moment he realized where he was, *who* he was, he ceased struggling.

Blindly he reached over the telephone, nearly knocking it from its cradle, and turned off the alarm. He had forgotten to reset it last night, and now he'd paid the price. He was breathing rapidly, and his heart was skittering. He forced open his eyes and stared at a very different ceiling. He had plastered this one himself, and not with any great expertise. He was better with plaster now, better at so many things, but he was a failure at the things at which he wanted most to succeed.

He was in no hurry to rise. There was little to get up for today. Meetings later in the morning. Tedious telephone calls. More people anxious to see the water stain that gave them faith in something beyond themselves. He had no Mass to celebrate, no confessions to hear, no pastoral calls, no meetings with church officials. He had been laicized; he was not a practicing priest. He was his own boss, lying in his own bed.

Without his wife beside him.

His eyes closed involuntarily. Megan was gone, and suddenly the hurly-burly rush of his life had slowed to nothing. Not that much had changed since her departure. The nonprofit organization in Indiana in which he'd put so much hope had agreed to help fund Brick, then their board had listed all its requirements, and he had walked away. Not just because they were petty and absurd, but because he would become an instant bureaucrat. And Niccolo knew that his real calling was to change lives, not to document the changes made by others.

So his own life had not been transformed since Megan left for Ireland. Brick continued to limp toward some imaginary finish line. The bootleggers' tunnel continued to attract visitors. And Niccolo Andreani, who missed the active priesthood but had no regrets about leaving it, continued to dream he was celebrating Mass.

He felt a rush of loneliness as profound as any he'd felt while living in a Pittsburgh rectory. He wanted his wife beside him. He wanted children of his own. He wanted to know that the kids he worked with had every chance to grow and hone their talents. He wanted time to interact with them, to listen, to advise. He wanted to watch them graduate from high school and college and know that he'd done what he could to set them on the right road.

And now, every single dream was in danger.

The telephone rang, and for a moment he debated whether to answer. He did on the third ring, knowing that it might wake Rooney or Josh, or, more important, that it might be Megan. She had called home upon her arrival in Ireland so that he wouldn't worry, but she hadn't called since. Clearly Megan had no desire to talk long distance when they hadn't been able to talk in the very same room.

Iggy was on the other end, and when they'd finished their conversation, Niccolò had a reason to get up and get dressed.

"Croissants," Niccolo said, placing the white bag filled with pastries on the kitchen table of St. Brigid's rectory. "From the bakery around the corner from my house."

Iggy looked rapturous. "I've got coffee and eggs to go with them."

The housekeeper made passable coffee and excellent scrambled eggs. The morning was looking up.

They served themselves from a pan on the stove and poured their coffee, taking it back to the table. Iggy took a croissant and broke it open, holding it up for Niccolo to see.

Niccolo looked at Iggy's uplifted hands and was reminded of his dream, of the fact that the dream recurred and recurred and each time alarmed him more.

"You always know exactly what to buy," Iggy said. "You have an unerring instinct about food. Only the best, the freshest. The Italians and the French. What would the world do without them?" He popped a bite of croissant in his mouth and smiled blissfully. "What would I do without you, Niccolo?"

Niccolo had planned on small talk. Discussions of next week's fund-raiser to upgrade the parish hall, whether to cut down a tree menacing the St. Brigid's parking lot, if Brick should move forward with renovations on the new house even though they would have to make them on a wing and a prayer. Now he couldn't utter a syllable.

"Niccolo?"

Niccolo looked up and knew he could only talk about one thing. "I dreamed I was celebrating Mass. It's a dream I have frequently." He paused, then exhaled audibly. "Nightly."

"Since you moved on from active priesthood?"

Niccolo appreciated the way Iggy had phrased that. "No."

"When did it start?"

Niccolo didn't answer.

"With your marriage." Iggy did not phrase it as a question.

"Yes." Niccolo lifted his fork and slid eggs on to it. They tasted like rubber.

"Let me guess further," Iggy said, popping another piece of croissant into his mouth. "Not right away. After the honeymoon?"

"Yes."

"I see."

"I don't!" Niccolo looked up, ashamed at his own sharp tone. "I'm sorry. Where did that come from?"

"I believe you're angry, Niccolo. That's where it came from. But don't worry, I know the anger isn't directed at me."

"I am angry. I feel like I'm being punished. I don't need these reminders of what I left behind. I don't need to walk around with a guilty conscience."

"You think God is punishing you?"

"No, God and I are fine. I'm punishing myself. And I don't understand why."

"Of course you don't, because that's not what's happening."

Niccolo didn't know what to say to that. He had pondered his dreams over and over and gotten nowhere. Now Iggy, who had just heard the story, seemed to understand what Niccolo himself could not.

"What *is* happening?" Niccolo said.

"I think we have to back up." Iggy started on his eggs.

"Back up to what?"

"To those moments not so long ago when you stood at the altar."

"In the dream?"

Iggy looked up. "No, in real life. Back to the days when you did celebrate Mass."

Niccolo smiled ruefully. "I'll back up to my days in utero if you think it will help."

"I think that's a bit premature. Start with Mass."

"What do you want me to say?"

"Do you remember how you felt at those moments?"

"United with God. As if He were working through me. Humbled. Reverent." Niccolo shrugged.

"Always?"

"Truthfully?"

"I think that would be most helpful, don't you?"

"No. Sometimes I was thinking about everything else I had to do that day. And at the end of my tenure at St. Rose of Lima, when I knew I would be leaving soon, I was thinking about how sad it would be not to stand at that altar anymore."

"Just sad?"

"Relieved, as well," Niccolo admitted.

"And?"

Niccolo tried to dig deeper, without success. He shrugged.

"Put yourself there, Niccolo. Put yourself back in the robes for a moment. What are you doing in the dream?"

"Holding up the host."

"Imagine it, then."

Niccolo put down his fork. He was not comfortable with this, but comfort had little to do with getting past the problem. He had counseled too many people himself not to know this.

"I'm standing at the altar. I feel sad that I won't be doing this much longer, but glad that my decision's been made." He could almost feel the cool, humid air of St. Rose surrounding him, hear the slide of clothing against wooden pews, the occasional wail of an infant.

"It's easy to say the words. I know them so well. I've repeated them so many times. I could do this every day until I died without stumbling over a word."

"And what are the people in the church thinking about you?"

"That I know exactly what I'm doing. That I'm their leader and they can trust me to do what's right."

"You know that you'll be leaving soon. You say you're glad the decision has been made...."

"I am." Niccolo remembered the relief well. The decision had been anything but easy, but with it had finally come peace.

"What else?" Iggy prompted.

"Fear." Niccolo looked up. "No, terror."

"Ah..."

"Not terror that I'd chosen wrong, but terror about what I would do next. I knew I was supposed to be a priest from the moment I was old enough to think about a vocation. My parents wanted it for me, my grandparents did. I thought I wanted it for myself."

"And when you discovered it wasn't right for you, Niccolo, how much time did you have to think about what *was* right?"

"I gave myself time afterwards, remember? That's why I came here to Cleveland. I wanted time to think about what to do next. I bought my house and started working on it as a stop-gap measure. I was going to sell it for some extra cash when I'd finished."

"And little by little the neighborhood kids came to see what you were doing, and before long Brick was born."

"Brick feels right, Iggy. Brick is the right thing for me to be doing."

"I have no doubt about that."

"And I fell in love with Megan. And I knew that was right, too."

"Again, I have no doubts."

"Then what?"

"Niccolo, you're standing at the altar. And you're feeling great confidence about what you're doing. You could do it every day for the rest of your life without making one mistake. The people in the pews have confidence in you." Iggy quirked a brow in question. "Was this, perhaps, the very last time you knew exactly what to do?"

Niccolo couldn't believe he hadn't seen this himself. The truth of it washed over him. Doors swung open, and for a moment he was engulfed in fear. He couldn't speak.

Iggy spoke for him. "You knew how to be a priest. You were slated to become one, nudged into it, trained, supervised, nurtured along the way. But who ever taught you to become a husband?"

Niccolo closed his eyes.

"On the contrary," Iggy said. "You were taught the best ways *not* to become one. How to avoid intimacy. How to be celibate. How to avoid loving a woman."

So in his dreams, Niccolo, feeling his way into marriage, trying and yes, failing badly, returned to the moments when he *had* known exactly what to do, and when the people surrounding him believed in his powers and competence.

The fear was fading a little, and relief was seeping into the hollows fear abandoned. Relief that the dream had been not self-flagellation but enlightenment.

"I *don't* know how to be a husband." He opened his eyes. "I'm doing a really lousy job of it."

"Tell me how you went about being a priest?"

"I don't know what you mean."

"What did you try to do for your parish?"

This seemed so obvious that Niccolo didn't understand the need to recite it. "I struggled to make it the best parish I could, the way any priest does. I worked all day, every day, counseled, prayed, visited, administered——"

"Does that sound familiar?"

Now Niccolo understood. This truth, too, had been so easy to see, yet he had missed it. "I've been going about being a husband the way I went about being a priest."

"Exactly." Iggy went back to his eggs, which had certainly grown cold, as had Niccolo's own.

"Because it was the only thing I knew to do," Niccolo continued. "It *is* the only thing I know to do."

"Of course it is. You were trained for the priesthood practically from the cradle. So you took what you knew how to do so well and transferred everything you'd learned into your marriage."

"I don't know how to be a good husband." The truth was hard to swallow. Niccolo believed himself to be a good person. Surely a good man with good intentions should know how to give the woman he loved what she needed.

"Tell me. What does Megan want from you?"

The truth was so simple that Niccolo winced. "Intimacy."

"And what have you been giving her?"

"I've been trying to make things perfect again. Renovate the saloon, make Brick something to be proud of. I wanted us to start a family right away. I wanted everything to be perfect."

"You want what a marriage *looks* like, not what a marriage *feels* like."

"Megan wants *me*. She doesn't care about the trappings. They come with time. But I'm good at trappings. I'm right at home when I'm working hard."

"And where does the image in the tunnel fit into all this?"

"I was giving the image and the people who were flocking to see it more time and attention and love than I was giving her." Niccolo didn't need Iggy to point out why. "Because the image was something I understood. People's need for faith and hope was something I understood."

"And marriage was not."

"Intimacy." Niccolo shook his head. "It wasn't a big enough project. It wasn't something I could throw myself into and see results."

"So?" Iggy looked up.

"I feel like a fool. The harder I worked to make things right, the worse they got. All I ever had to do was stop working and start listening."

"She'll be coming home, you know."

"Yeah, I know. She's got a saloon to run."

"And in the meantime, you'll have some time to ponder this."

Niccolo thought about all he had nearly lost. He just hoped it wasn't too late to reclaim it.

He hoped it wasn't too late to learn how.

Casey was just going up the front walkway when Niccolo drove up to his house. He was surprised to see her, but he supposed she had come to look in on her father.

He hadn't talked to her for a few days, because he had been too busy. No surprise there.

Niccolo pulled into the space in front and got out. "He's doing great," Niccolo said from behind her. "I should have called to let you know. I'm sorry."

Casey turned. She wasn't in maternity clothes yet, but she was wearing an oversized T-shirt over leggings, probably for comfort. She looked rested and content. He hoped the worst of the morning sickness was over.

"Rooney? Don't give it a thought. I've seen him every day. I pop by late in the afternoon, before you get home. I bring him something for his dinner or invite him to our house, but he's told me in no uncertain terms that Megan's cooking is better. He misses her."

"So do I." He paused. "Enormously."

"Good." She waited on the porch until he unlocked the door; then she preceded him inside.

"Can I fix you something?" Niccolo asked. "I have decaf coffee if you're not drinking regular these days. Juice—"

"Nothing. I just came to tell you I'm going to Ireland."

"I don't believe it. You, too?"

"Why should they have all the fun?"

He ushered her into the living room, and Casey flopped down on the sofa, automatically hugging one of Megan's quilted pillows as if it were the baby to be. "Megan called last night. Irene's health is pretty precarious, and I got to thinking. What if she dies before I make the trip to meet her? Once my pregnancy is further along, I won't be able to travel long distances. Then once the baby's here, I won't want to travel until he or she is ready. I have some comp time. Between that and vacation days, I can spare a few days there, then a few days here to recover from jet lag before I go back to work."

"And you don't want to miss anything. Them there, you here."

"You know me well." Her eyes lit up. "Want to come with me? Just drop everything and come?"

He considered, but in the end he shook his head. "No. I have too much to do."

"Nick, I—"

He held up his hand. "I know, Casey. I know what you're thinking. I've really been an idiot. But I have loose ends here that need to be tied up before my wife comes home. I think I understand a lot more than I did before she left. And I want our reunion to be here, in Cleveland. Just the two of us." He smiled a little. "Not surrounded by avenging Irish-American redheads."

"Aren't you funny." But she smiled, too. "She adores you, you know."

"I adore her."

"Good." Casey got to her feet. "Is Rooney up? Will he be okay with you guys for a week? Jon says he'll look in on him every day."

"We'll all bach it. We'll take good care of him. Why don't you find him and explain, but see me before you go, okay?"

"Sure." She looked curious.

"I just got back from St. Brigid's. Father Brady found more letters from Maura McSweeney, and these have been translated. The copies are in my car. When I saw you going up the walk, I forgot to bring them in, but you can take them to Ireland with you. There's quite a stack. I hope they provide some insights." He paused. "And if you dawdle with your dad a little, I'll have time to add a letter of my own. To Megan."

She nodded, understanding. "I'll read them on the plane—except the one to my sister."

"Thank you."

She crossed the room and kissed his cheek.

1925
Castlebar, County Mayo

My dearest Patrick,

Your letters are my greatest indulgence, both those I read and those I write to you. So it was with much joy that I opened your last. I fixed a pot of tea and took it to the parlor where the light is best. Oh, how I wish I hadn't seen that letter with my others, that it had slipped unnoticed to the ground, never to be found again.

I feel as if I know the young people you've so often written about, each of them as individual and promising as the first wild roses of the summer. Winds may batter and rains may lash, but the roses, fragrant and robust, are somehow better for the experience.

Not so, my dear brother, with the gentle souls of lovers.

For the moment, I can find nothing else to say.

Your loving sister,
Maura McSweeney

chapter 30

Although he hadn't been in attendance, Glen knew all about the Whiskey Island raid. The agents who had been there were peacock proud and not afraid to brag. In that one evening's work they had waylaid enough premium liquor to dry up more than a dozen high-class speakeasies. The papers were full of it, and even though no one had proof that Tim McNulty was behind the shipment, it was widely speculated that the raid would put him out of business.

Two local men believed to be in McNulty's employment had been captured, but both of them were bailed out before uttering even one useful syllable. A Canadian crew and their captain were in jail awaiting interpretations of international justice, and they weren't talking, either. Still, the liquor was useless to McNulty now, and most likely so was some large portion of the money McNulty had agreed to pay the Canadians.

On hearing of his colleagues' great adventure, Glen's first thought was of Clare. McNulty was a bad father under any circumstances, but, distraught and anxious, he was bound to be even worse. Now Clare would be kept under lock and key, and meeting her would be impossible.

As it turned out, his worries were for nothing. He came home from work one evening just three days after the raid and found Clare waiting in the hallway of his apartment building.

"Clare." He looked around, then unlocked his apartment door and pulled her inside. "What are you doing here?"

"Don't worry, nobody followed me."

"Are you sure? That guy who watches you is pretty thorough."

"There's a meeting tonight. Everybody's there except a flunky who's half-blind and lazy, too. He was sleeping when I left. Besides, I don't think my father even remembers I'm supposed to be watched."

Glen suspected he knew the agenda for McNulty's meeting. "Are you all right?" He cupped her face in his hand and examined it. She looked tired, but she smiled.

"Oh, I am now. But things have been tense at home. I'm sure you know why."

He didn't want to talk about her father's business. No matter what Clare was to Glen, she was also McNulty's daughter. "I've been worried about you."

"For the most part my father's ignored me. He's had more important things to think about. But I don't know how much longer that will go on. I —" She sighed. "I have to be honest. I've been snooping, Glen." She placed a finger over his lips when he started to speak. "No, don't. I don't like it any more than you do, but the truth is that if I don't know what my father is up to, I can't protect myself. I can't protect *us*."

Unfortunately, she was right. He couldn't protest.

"He's had a large financial setback," Clare continued. "And the money wasn't his. It belongs to men in Chicago, the same men Niall Cassidy works for."

Until that moment, Glen, idealist to the core, had believed he could keep his job, his family's saloon, and his love for Clare separate. Now he knew that was a fantasy. Because he couldn't refuse to hear the rest of what she had to say. And once heard, he could not pretend ignorance. He was sworn to uphold the law.

He stepped away from her and reached in his pocket, removing the badge that he had foolishly believed he could balance with the other complications of his life. He set it on the table. "From this moment, I'm no longer a Treasury agent."

"Glen, no."

"Clare, it's okay. I can't be your husband and a booze agent, too. It's been hard enough with my own family's occupation. Impossible with yours."

"Then I'll go." She turned as if to leave for the door.

"Stop." He put his hands on her shoulders. "Don't you know I'd rather have you than the job? Besides, we aren't going to be able to stay in Cleveland. We need to go where we can't be found. And once settled, out west or down south, I'll apply for another job in law enforcement."

She was shaking her head before he finished. "I'm asking you to give up too much. Your home, job, family."

"I'll give up everything for you—without a backward glance. I have no choice. I love you. That's the one thing I can't walk away from."

She faced him, but reluctantly. "It's so much, too much."

"Not nearly enough. I'll do anything to keep you."

She still looked torn. "Whatever we do, darling, we have to do it soon. The men I spoke of, the ones from Chicago, are coming the day after tomorrow to collect their money. That's what the meeting is about. My father is trying desperately to come up with what he owes them. But he isn't going to be able to. Not right away. He has to sell everything, including our house, and that takes time. Even then, he might come up short."

"And they aren't patient men." Glen knew that.

"I'm afraid I'm the bargaining chip."

Glen felt as if he'd been punched. "With Cassidy?"

"Niall has enough clout with his bosses to keep them at bay for a while. *If* he's a happy man. And I'm the only thing that will make him happy."

"You know this for sure?"

"I heard enough to put it together. My father's frantic enough to sacrifice me on any altar. Cassidy's is the most appealing at the moment."

"The bastard."

She didn't ask to which man he referred.

Glen wondered at the greed of a man like McNulty, who would put his life and the happiness of his only daughter at stake this way. The loss of the Canadian hooch had been more than he could absorb, but from the beginning, he must have known the risks. He was a gambler of the worst kind.

"Tomorrow," Glen said. "I'll go to Father McSweeney tonight, and I'll tell him everything. I'll ask him to marry us without the usual announcements. If he refuses, I'll find a justice of the peace, but we'll be married tomorrow night. Then we'll disappear."

"I have some money. My mother always hid money away for a rainy day, and after she died, I added to it whenever I could. It's a small nest egg, but it will help."

He was a traditional man who believed he should be able to support and care for his wife, but he was not a fool. "Someday I'll be sure you get back every penny."

"I consider my life with you a worthwhile investment."

He kissed her, hard. She pressed herself against him. When they parted, each was breathing faster.

"Tomorrow?" she whispered.

He wanted her now. Not tomorrow after the ceremony, but now, here in his apartment. He had never been so tempted to go against everything he believed in.

With great effort he turned his back on her. "Yes, tomorrow."

"Where shall I meet you?"

"I want my family there, Clare. I want them to meet you before we disappear. Are you willing?"

"Of course!"

"Then we'll be married at the saloon."

"You can make the arrangements so quickly?"

"With their help. And they will help. Can you be there tomorrow about dark? Will you be able to get away?"

She nodded. "Glen, once this is settled, once my father cools off, maybe we can come back."

He knew the only way they would ever be able to come back to Cleveland was if her father was killed or imprisoned. And even then, Niall Cassidy would still be looking for her. He wasn't a man who would ever take rejection in stride.

"Stranger things have happened." He took a deep breath and faced her, but he was careful not to touch her again. "Wherever we live, we'll have each other and children and a life we can be proud of."

"It will be enough?"

He touched her hair. One quick touch. "Please believe me. More than enough."

Clare spent the next morning preparing to go away with Glen. She had so little she wanted to bring with her that one suitcase was all she needed. She packed her mother's wedding dress to wear that evening, photos of her mother and one of her father as a young man holding his baby daughter. She hoped he'd been a different person in those early days of his marriage, a man not yet corrupted. It was small comfort, but a thought to hold on to.

She packed a few clothes, the money she'd told Glen about, her mother's rosary and missal, and the personal items she would need. She was coming into the marriage with so little, but in a way she wished she had less. She was sorry she had to bring anything of her life with her father along. She planned to replace every piece of clothing the moment she could.

She was preparing to dress for the day when someone knocked on her bedroom door. Before she could ask whoever it was to come in, the door opened and her father entered.

She was glad she'd hidden the suitcase. As a child, she had learned that anything personal, anything important, had to be kept secret. That had served her well today.

"Why aren't you dressed?" he demanded.

This was one instance when the truth would serve no one but the man in front of her, and she lied without qualm. "I had a headache. I decided to take my time and see if it might go away."

"Your health seems precarious these days, daughter. Or have you just become adept at making excuses?"

"It was only a headache. I don't think it's contagious or fatal." She smiled so he would know she was treating it lightly.

"You feel better now?"

She was feeling worse by the moment. She wondered why she had remained in this man's house for so long. Why hadn't she taken her life in her own hands?

"I'm okay," she said. "I think I just need some breakfast. I'll dress and come downstairs. You must have eaten hours ago."

"Do you have any idea what's going on around here?" He pounded a fist on the closest piece of furniture, which happened to be her vanity table. Cut-glass bottles leaped and slid in protest.

She was not afraid. She lifted her chin. "And how would I know? Have you ever included me in anything important?"

His eyes narrowed. "You like living here, don't you? You like having anything you want. You like the way people look at you and know you're somebody!"

She knew he was spoiling for a fight. She also knew that if she gave him one, her whole future could change for the worse. And yet she wanted to tell him what she thought of the life he had given her. She wanted, just once, to tell Tim McNulty how she despised the man he had become, despised her own father and everything he stood for.

She opened her mouth to tell him so, then realized that if she did, she would never be allowed to leave the house tonight.

"I've never complained, have I?" She was only sorry it was true.

"Well, it's about time you gave something back for everything I've given you, daughter."

She knew exactly what he wanted her to give, but she feigned ignorance. "I thought caring for the house, making sure all your personal needs were attended to, was a way of giving something back."

He stared, and a muscle jumped in his cheek. Clearly he was torn. He wanted to continue lashing out at her, because at heart her father was a bully. But he was also a clever man who knew that this encounter needed a little finesse.

"Your mother taught you well in that regard," he said with obvious effort. "You'll make a good wife."

Yes, she thought, and sooner than he knew.

"Niall Cassidy has his eye on you," he said at last. His voice was softer, more a plea than a demand.

"I know."

"It would help me if you would encourage him."

"Encourage him?"

"His intentions are honorable, Clare. He wants a wife. I'm not asking you to do anything your beloved church would disapprove of. Tell him you'll marry him."

"He hasn't asked."

"He's coming this afternoon!" Tim threaded fingers through his oiled hair. "And I need you to play up to him a little, let him know you're willing...to marry him."

"This afternoon?"

"What do you think I just said!"

"I'm just surprised, that's all. It's terribly short notice, isn't it?"

"It doesn't matter what kind of notice you have! Give the man what he wants."

"Why don't you just put an apple in my mouth and serve me on a silver platter?"

He lifted his hand to strike her but seemed to think better of it. "I will not have you talk to me that way in my own house!"

"It's a fair enough question. Are you even a little bit interested in my feelings about this?"

He frowned, as if the idea had never crossed his mind. "He's an up-and-comer, in with people who can make him a rich man, and your marriage will benefit me. Besides, he'll make sure you have everything you've ever wanted, just the way I have."

There was so much she could have said to that, but she knew better. She had said enough already.

It took everything she had inside her to smile gently. "I just want to know that the way I feel about this is important to you." She placed her fingers lightly on his arm. "I want to know I'm important."

He made a noise low in his throat, as if to clear it of any latent sentimentality. "Just tell me what you're planning to do. Because if you don't do what I'm asking—"

She cut off his threat. "I'll encourage Niall. This must be very important to you."

He took her response as his due. "Yes, well. Wear something pretty, and tell him yes when he asks you to marry him."

The absurdity of this struck her. She, who had seriously considered entering the convent before she met Glen Donaghue, was now about to be engaged to two men simultaneously. At least for a matter of hours.

It seemed so absurd that the dishonesty and even the danger of such a move seemed inconsequential, even funny. She was living a bad joke. Once she disappeared, Cassidy deserved whatever disappointment he experienced. And her father? She waited for a pang of filial affection. Guilt was the only possible antidote to the lies she was preparing to tell.

Instead she looked at Tim McNulty and felt nothing except pity. He was a man empty of everything that mattered. Perhaps he had not been this way from the beginning, but at some point on his life journey he had managed to quench all human instinct. She was nothing to him except a pawn in his power game.

She managed one final smile. "I'll wear my prettiest dress. When is Niall expected?"

"I don't know. Just be ready." He turned and left the room.

She would not look back tonight when she escaped from this house, this man and this life. She would never look back.

Glen expected resistance from his family. As always, he decided to go to his grandmother first. Lena would understand why the marriage had to be performed tonight and why they had to leave town immediately afterward. He hoped she would intercede with his parents and put in a good word with Father McSweeney, who had seemed reluctant last night, even when Glen had explained the situation.

Lena was close friends with the priest. He knew the two old people often spent afternoons together, talking of times they had known, of world politics and scandals. Their relationship had always seemed odd to him, the revered, learned priest and the poorly educated Irish saloon keeper. Yet clearly the priest admired the same things that Glen saw in his grandmother: virtue, raw intelligence, the strength to do whatever was required.

He hoped her strength was up to this particular task.

He went to her house the next morning, rising early to reach her before the rest of the family descended. He found her in the kitchen, which was no surprise. But she wasn't cooking. She was reading the newspaper.

"Anything of interest?" he asked.

She looked up and smiled. "My favorite grandson."

"You say that to all of us."

"And it's always true." She patted the seat beside her and started to rise to get him tea.

"No, I've had my breakfast. Please, sit."

"Bad news or a request?"

She knew him too well. He shrugged. "Some of both, I guess."

"The day will be filling up quickly," she prompted. "Spit it out."

"*Mamó,* I'm getting married tonight."

She looked up from folding the paper. "Did I hear you right?"

"I've no choice." When her expression darkened, he smiled. "No, it's not what you're thinking, I promise. You've been reading the newspaper? And you've read about the raid down on Whiskey Island?"

"Seen it in the paper, yes, and heard the gunfire myself."

"You were at the saloon?"

"Yes, helping your father and mother with a banquet."

He wasn't surprised the gunfire had been audible, since there had been a fierce battle on the waterfront. He was only surprised no one had died in the raid. "Clare's father lost everything. It's just a matter of time before he insists she marry one of his accomplices. He borrowed money, and he thinks that is the way to make certain he has time to pay his debt."

"What kind of father does such a thing?"

"A particularly bad one. I love Clare. I want to marry her and take her away from here. That's the only chance she'll have for escape. And it has to be tonight, before things get worse at home. While she still has a chance to get away."

"She's asked you for this?"

"No. She wouldn't ask anybody for anything. I've wanted to marry her for weeks now. I'd rather not do it this way, but we don't have a choice."

"I trust you. I know the kind of man you've become. Where and when, exactly?"

"Tonight at dusk. *Mamó*, will you encourage Father McSweeney to do the ceremony without proper notice? At the saloon tonight? He knows the story. I want my family there. It may be the last time you see me for a very long time."

"I don't have a *very* long time on this earth. Don't tell me that."

"We'll come back the moment it's safe. I promise."

"There's the matter of a license."

"I think I can see to that without Clare. I have friends at the courthouse."

"If I'll see to Father McSweeney...and your parents?"

"Please, it's a difficult time. I'm sorry to ask so much, but I have to try to get my whole life in order today."

"You'll need money."

"I've lived frugally and saved. Clare has some, as well."

"You'll have more this evening."

Glen knew better than to argue. Nobody argued with *Mamó*. He stood and kissed her cheek. "I'll miss you most of all."

"That's akin to my saying that you're my favorite grandson. My dearest lad, I know you. Losing us will be like losing a limb. You'll miss us all, each and every one."

chapter 31

Clare put on a demure lavender dress with a pique collar and pearl shell buttons. She thought the dress made her look young and virginal, too young, she hoped, to get married right away. The morning was taut with tension. Even with her bedroom door closed, she could hear her father shouting at the men who worked for him. She wasn't able to piece together much, since she wanted to stay out of his way. But she thought Tim was demanding that they go over, once again, exactly what they had seen and heard on the night of the raid. She knew that a great deal of money had disappeared. She wondered if her father believed that one of his own men had taken it.

When he left the house, she crept downstairs for lunch. She considered going directly to Whiskey Island Saloon before Niall Cassidy arrived, but she found her guardian sitting at the bottom of the stairs. This man was kinder than the others, she thought, but perhaps that was only sentimentality. Perhaps she believed this of him because he was from Ireland and she found his accent so charming.

"My father has gone?" she asked.

"That he has. And you're not planning a trip yourself, are you, Miss McNulty?"

"I'm planning lunch. Will you join me?"

"I doubt your father would approve, but I'll sit with you."

She doubted he was offering his presence for company. The dining room windows were low to the ground and easily opened.

He followed her to the kitchen, where she spoke to the cook, who promised soup and sandwiches. Then Clare made herself some tea and carried the pot and two cups into the dining room. She put the pot on the table, waiting for the tea to finish steeping.

"So, things are not what they should be around here," she said casually. "Were you, perhaps, on Whiskey Island two nights ago?"

"Whiskey Island?" He looked pensive. "I'm still so new to your country, Miss, that I haven't yet learned where everything is. But Whiskey Island sounds like a place worth knowing."

"We both know what I'm talking about."

"Not me." He shook his head.

She supposed if she were in his shoes she wouldn't be talking about this, either. "I think we're expecting company this afternoon. A man named Niall Cassidy?"

"I've heard the name."

She decided the tea had steeped long enough, and she poured two cups. "Your name is Liam, correct? How do you take it, Liam?"

"Not at all."

She added sugar and cream and pushed it toward him. He sighed and lifted the cup to his lips.

"I know, it doesn't make good sense to be friends with the boss's daughter," she said. "Particularly when your job is to make her life as unhappy as possible."

"It's sorry I am to be doing that, Miss."

"Do you have a wife and children?"

"Does it matter?"

"No, but a man who loves his wife usually likes other women well enough and often feels protective of them."

"My job is to protect you."

"Your job is to protect me from myself and any instincts I might have that go against my father's. Instincts like not marrying Niall Cassidy."

"I'd know nothing about that."

"Well, I'll fill you in. I think my father has lost everything except the hair on his head, Liam. And in order to make certain he's not killed outright for his debts, he needs time to pay back money he borrowed. He believes if I agree to marry Mr. Cassidy, that will buy him some time. Do you follow so far?"

"This is no concern of mine."

"Oh, but it is. Because you're the one who follows me everywhere, and you know it's not Cassidy I love."

Liam was silent.

She lowered her voice. "I don't know you well enough to ask favors, but I must, because I have no other choice. Today, will you please stay nearby when Mr. Cassidy comes? I don't...I don't trust him. Do you understand? I don't want to be left alone with him."

"You're going to tell the man no?"

She shook her head sadly. "No, I'm going to tell him yes, and that will encourage him toward things I want no part of."

"They come with marriage."

She stiffened. "Yes, well, if I have my way, we won't be married for a very long time."

Liam considered. She thought she could see the struggle in his eyes. Self-interest versus good instincts. She was sure the good instincts were there—her own good instincts were at work.

"I'll stay nearby," he promised. "Any sign of trouble and I'll get you out of there."

"Oh, thank you." She felt genuinely relieved. The cook arrived with two bowls of soup and a platter of sandwiches. "Please, join me. It will make me feel better about asking for your help."

Liam seemed to know that accepting her hospitality bound him even closer to her. He sighed, but he took a sandwich and finished it in one hungry bite.

From the moment the two men had been introduced, Liam hadn't liked Niall Cassidy. Cassidy was a man who had no room in his own little world for anyone but himself. Liam suspected the man did not love Clare McNulty; he loved instead the things her beauty, intelligence and poise might do for his future. Liam was also afraid that Cassidy might be one of those all-too-common ruffians who enjoyed destroying anything of beauty. As a boy, Cassidy had probably torn off the wings of butterflies or thrown newborn kittens into the lake for amusement.

It wasn't Liam's job to like or dislike the men with whom Tim McNulty did business. Why should he like *them* when he disliked McNulty himself? Unfortunately, he did like Clare, who reminded him of Brenna. The circumstances of their lives were different, but neither woman had received the love she deserved. Now Brenna had Liam, but what did Clare have? The promise of a miserable marriage to a miserable man?

He didn't want to care, but he did.

On the night of the raid, Liam had been lucky to escape Whiskey Island. He had waited for hours, stealing away undetected just before dawn. Jerry had not been so fortunate, but he was out on bail now. Together they had listened to McNulty rave maniacally about fate and incompetence. Had they been quicker, smarter or safer, McNulty insisted, they would never have been caught. The liquor would be in speakeasy cellars and the profits in McNulty's pockets. To a man they were lucky he didn't strangle them with his bare hands.

Liam was surprised that McNulty would entrust such a bumbler to watch over his daughter, but McNulty had taken Liam aside that morning and told him not to let Clare out of his sight, at least not until Cassidy showed up. Then Liam was to turn a blind eye and deaf ear to whatever occurred.

By the time Cassidy arrived at the front door, Liam was still hoping that his promise to Clare and his job would not conflict. One glance at the cocky set of Cassidy's shoulders and his dismissive wave when Liam followed him into the parlor, and Liam knew that conflict was inevitable.

"Miss McNulty, may I get you anything?" Liam asked, ignoring Cassidy's attempt at expulsion.

She looked grateful. "Some water would be lovely, Liam. But bring it a bit later, would you?"

Cassidy might think she wanted to be alone with him, but Liam knew she was inventing a reason for him to intrude if things got rough. He nodded and departed, but he didn't go far. After he got the water he sat in the hall and listened intently as the ice melted in the glass.

"You like the flowers I got you?" Niall asked her.

Liam had noticed the flowers, a gaudy, exotic collection of blooms that belonged in a whorehouse parlor. Any sensible man would know that a modest woman like Clare preferred roses or maybe a small nosegay of violets.

"They'll light up any room I put them in," she said.

In the hallway, Liam smiled at her tact and at the slight pinprick hidden within it.

"You been thinking of me?"

"You're never far from my mind," Clare said sweetly.

Liam smiled again. Two hits for the young lady, two strikes for Cassidy, who was too stupid to know it.

"I brought you something else."

"One gift a visit is already so generous."

"Yeah? Well, this ain't a gift. Not exactly. It's like a contract."

There was silence. Liam could picture Niall Cassidy pulling something out of his pocket. He hoped that despite his own humble background he had been more sophisticated than this when proposing to Brenna.

"You like it?"

Clare was silent for a moment, then said, "I really don't know what to say."

"It's a beauty, hardly got a flaw. I know this guy on the North Side, and he gave me a deal. I told him I wanted big. He gave me big."

"Yes, he certainly did. That ring could sprain a finger."

"You don't like it?" Cassidy no longer sounded as pleasant or proud.

"Oh, it's truly a remarkable ring. I've just never seen one quite so..."

"Large?"

"Yes. Large."

Liam tried to picture the rock in question and decided that for Clare to sound this way, the setting must be on a par with the flowers.

Cassidy sounded happier. "Try it on, why don't you? See if I got the size right."

"Mr. Cassidy...Niall, it's too generous. I can't take something like...ummm...this."

"How else you gonna let people know we're getting married?"

"Married?"

"Sure, it's an engagement ring. You and me. What did you think it was for?"

"Well, you didn't exactly ask me to marry you."

Liam was trying not to laugh.

"It's a sure thing, right?" Cassidy demanded.

"I don't know. We haven't really talked about it."

"Well, I want you to marry me. Soon. You ain't going to be happy staying around here, that's for sure. People I work for ain't real happy with your father right now, and it's gonna be no fun living here. You're lucky I still want to marry you. *He's* lucky."

"Really? Is that so?"

"Yeah, he looks like a bungler, and nobody where I come from likes bunglers. A bungler's daughter?" Liam could almost hear him shrug. "A bungler's daughter ain't in high demand, either," Cassidy finished.

"I would hate to saddle you with a bungler's daughter."

"Hey, listen, that stuff'll blow over after we're married. I can make sure it does. Your father will have to listen to me, though. No mistake about that. I'll own him."

"Well, good luck there. He's not much of a listener."

"So, you want to set a date now?"

There was a long pause. Liam could almost read the poor young woman's mind. She was caught in a trap she had tried to avoid, but it had been thrust in her path, and now she was being forced to step into it.

"I'll marry you...Niall, but not right away." Her voice grew softer, as if she was moving away from the door, and probably Niall. "Until a few months ago I thought I had a vocation. I was going to become a nun. And now I'm going to be a married woman. Can you see? I need a little time to adjust."

"How much time?" He did not sound happy.

"Just enough to enjoy being a bride-to-be for a little while. Surely you won't deny me the excitement of planning a wedding, choosing a dress, coming to Chicago to meet your friends?"

"What kind of wedding? Tim's not going to be able to do much for you."

"Oh, small and simple, but the details have to be just right. I want to be married in my own church, with my friends around me. I want you to be proud of me, and I want our life together to start off well. Maybe I'm superstitious, but I feel strongly that a good marriage starts off with a good wedding. And we need to get to know each other a little more. I want to know how to please you."

"Oh, I can show you how to do that now. But put the ring, on first."

Liam leaned forward in his chair. There was silence, then Clare gave a little cry. "Oh, I'm sorry, Niall, but it's much too large. If I wear it now it will fall right off my finger."

"We'll take care of that tomorrow. I'll take you downtown and get it fixed. Nice and tight."

"Yes, well, okay..." There was a pause. "Niall, I don't—"

"Come on. Don't you think I deserve a kiss for that? A kiss for the flowers and one for the ring, and maybe one 'cause we're getting married." He didn't sound happy. Clearly Niall Cassidy normally chose women he didn't have to ask.

There was silence, and Liam got to his feet. But he didn't go into the parlor. Not yet. There was no use making a fuss if one wasn't needed, and a kiss, even three kisses, didn't warrant an interruption.

"That's enough, Niall." Clare sounded breathless and definite. "Remember, we're not married yet."

"Yeah, well, we oughta be. I don't know why we should wait, unless you're trying to stall. I know a hundred girls who would marry me like that."

Liam waited for Clare to advise Niall to seek them out, but obviously she knew better. "What kind of a wife do you want, Niall? The kind who throws herself at men?"

"Nah, I'll settle for one who throws herself at me." Something scraped across the floor, and Liam's hand flew to the glass of water. "You got some things to learn. Might as well learn 'em now."

Liam threw the door open so hard that it banged. "Here's your water, Miss—" She was pressed against the wall with Cassidy's body holding her in place and her head turned away from his. Liam felt rage rising inside him. The man was an animal and didn't deserve a woman like this one.

"Just a minute," Liam said. "I'm Miss McNulty's bodyguard. You're getting a little carried away."

"Get out!" Cassidy shouted. "Or *your* body will need embalming!"

Liam didn't want a fight. "I know a taste of the clover makes a thief of the cow, friend, but let's not move too fast. Let's just take it nice and easy. A pretty woman can do things to a man. I know—"

Cassidy rushed him before the rest of the sentence was out. Just before Cassidy reached him, Liam tossed the glass of water in his face. From the corner of his eye, he watched Clare scurry toward the door into the dining room.

Cassidy sputtered as the water sloshed over him, but he kept coming, snorting like a bull. Liam wondered which institution had been a better teacher? The streets of Chicago's North Side or a Christian Brothers orphanage?

He leaped to one side and stuck his leg out. As he'd expected, Cassidy went sprawling, but he took Liam with him, so that they were on the floor rolling over and over together before Liam could tell which side was up.

A fist smashed into his cheek. Liam wrapped his hands around Cassidy's neck and squeezed. Cassidy smashed at him again, but Liam squeezed harder. Finally Cassidy was forced to grab Liam's hands and try to pull them free. Liam rolled over again, and this time he was on top. He thumped Cassidy's head against the floor as he choked him. Once, twice, until Cassidy managed to pry his hands loose. He grabbed Cassidy's wrists as they rolled over again, but it was all he could do to hold them away from him.

Cassidy was grinning like a madman. Clearly he had the upper position, and in a moment he expected to have the upper hand. There was a crash, and the grin died slowly. He slumped and fell over, freeing Liam, who still held tightly to his forearms.

Clare stood above them. The remaining shards of a large crystal vase fell from her hands.

Liam stared up at her.

"Too bad, isn't it?" she said faintly. "This vase was the only one large enough for those hideous flowers he brought me."

Liam was momentarily tongue-tied. Part of him wanted to

laugh. The other part, the part that saw the repercussions of her action, was frozen in disbelief.

"Be careful when you get up," she warned.

He pushed Cassidy farther to one side and sat up. "You know what you've done, don't you?"

"I think I might have saved your life." She was very pale. He was fearful she might not remain on her feet.

"I would have been jim-dandy without you," he said, his pride wounded.

"Maybe. Maybe not." She stepped back and leaned against the arm of a chair. "What are we going to do?"

Liam didn't know. He couldn't dump Cassidy on the front lawn, although there was no one—particularly the unconscious Cassidy—to stop him. McNulty was going to be furious. And clearly the deal was off now. When Cassidy regained consciousness, he would figure out what had happened to him. No matter how strenuously Clare protested that someone else had broken the vase over his head, Cassidy would know.

"I'm not going to pretend it wasn't me," Clare said, as if she had read his thoughts. "Enough of lying to the man."

"What are you going to do?"

"I'm leaving." She held up a hand. "And don't tell me you're going to stop me. Do you think you have a place here after this? Besides, there's no job now, Liam. My father is out of business. He'll be lucky to survive. He certainly can't pay you anymore." She swallowed hard.

"Are you packed?"

"Yes."

"I'll make sure you get wherever you plan to go."

"You don't have to—" she began.

"Get your things right now. He'll wake up, and all hell's going to break out the moment he does."

She turned and fled the room, returning with a good-sized valise. Liam was on his feet by then. He had successfully picked his way through the glass and was waiting for her in the hall. Cassidy was just beginning to groan.

"Follow me," he said. "We're going out the back way. Be thinking about where you want to hide."

"I know where I'm going. The Whiskey Island Saloon."

She was escaping to *his* family. He knew better than to spend even a moment savoring the irony.

chapter 32

Clare looked around to be sure she hadn't been detected; then she grasped the door of the Whiskey Island Saloon and pushed. The door was locked.

For a moment panic filled her. Niall would be awake now, and he wasn't a man to slink away. He would look for her, and it was only a matter of time before her father became involved. Tim would notice immediately that Liam was gone, too. What if Liam had mentioned her picnic with Glen to anyone, anyone at all? Would they then put the facts together and think to look here?

She rattled the door this time, hoping she'd been mistaken, that it was simply stuck. But the door was locked tight.

She could go to Glen's apartment, but what if he wasn't there? They were leaving town tonight. Surely his day had been filled with arrangements. Still, what were her choices? The few friends she'd been allowed to cultivate might shelter her, but those were the first places her father would look. She thought of the church, but she didn't know if St. Brigid's priest would believe her story. Her father gave large sums of money to help the parish poor.

With little choice, she turned to head to Glen's apartment. When she was several steps away, she heard the door open behind her, and she spun around. "Oh, I thought no one was here."

"We're closed for the day. There's a...an event tonight."

Clare smiled in relief. "Oh, I think I'm invited to that."

The woman frowned. She was middle-aged, with a rectangular face and heavy lidded green eyes. "Do we know you?"

"Not yet. I'm Clare McNulty. Are you Mrs. Donaghue?"

"Clare..." The woman studied her; then she smiled a little. "Well, I can see what the fuss is about. Come in. You're a bit early, aren't you?"

"I had to be." Clare wondered how much to tell her. She wanted to warn everyone that there might be trouble if her father found her, but she really didn't want her future mother-in-law to know that she had just attacked a man with heirloom Waterford crystal.

The smile disappeared, and with one strong tug, Glen's mother ushered her inside. "You're not safe, are you?"

"Not exactly, no."

"Does anyone know you're here?"

"I really hope not, at least nobody who would hurt me." Clare was suffused with guilt. "I'm so sorry. I don't want to put anyone else in danger. Maybe I should go. Maybe we can think of a place where Glen can meet me. We could be married once we're settled."

"In a pig's eye. I'm Glen's mother, Fenola. You may call me Mother." Fenola turned and gave a sharp whistle. In a moment they were surrounded. "This is Glen's wife-to-be," Fenola announced once the din had settled. Clare's cheeks were bright with embarrassment. "Someone take her upstairs and help her unpack and hang out her dress. Maryedith, that will be you."

A young woman who looked very much like Glen stepped forward. "I hope you know what you're doing. Heaven help you if you ever want to have a conversation when the World Series is on the radio. And I hope you like meat loaf and mashed potatoes, because from what I can tell, Glen eats it for every meal."

"That will do, Maryedith," Fenola said. "You can educate the poor girl later. Right now she needs a few minutes to recover from meeting us. Then she can come downstairs and learn all our names."

With one chop of Fenola's hand the family parted like wheat falling to the thresher, and Maryedith led Clare toward a door that apparently led upstairs.

Clare turned around and gazed back at all of them. No one had moved.

"I hope someday I can learn everything about you. Every one of you." She turned back and followed Maryedith up a set of steps. Behind her, she heard Fenola.

"So what are you gawking at? She's lovely, she has good manners, and Glen's in love with her. What more do you need to know?"

Liam knew his days in Cleveland were numbered now. Even though it was McNulty's own daughter he'd rescued, he knew that McNulty would not understand. The man's whole future was at stake. His daughter's virtue was of lesser importance.

Despite that, Liam thought he had less to fear from McNulty than from Cassidy. McNulty was not a man to get his own hands dirty, and his employees had little reason for loyalty. Soon enough McNulty would be out of business for good. Liam was well liked, and he doubted McNulty could entice anyone to kill him for the pleasure of it. Cassidy, though, was a man who would seek revenge on his own terms. He would find Liam, or even his family, and the rest didn't bear thinking about.

Liam dropped Clare off at the Whiskey Island Saloon, then he headed for home. The moment he arrived he shouted for Brenna, and when she came down the stairs with Irene trailing behind, his throat nearly closed with sorrow.

"Brenna..."

She searched his face; then she nodded. "Where shall we go?"

He had thought of nothing else on the trip home. "I want you to take a train to Toledo. I'll meet you there as soon as I can."

"No."

"Brenna —"

She held up her hand to stop him. "I won't leave town, not until I know you're safe."

"You have Irene to think about."

"I won't do it."

He tried to think of another solution, but she thought of one first. "The old ladies, the ones I worked for. They'll take me in. No one will trace me there. You can call me, even if you can't see me. Promise you will."

The plan was sound enough. The ladies lived across town, and most likely nobody in the Tierneys' new neighborhood knew that Brenna had ever worked as a housekeeper, much less for whom. Even if Cassidy found his way to their old neighborhood, it was unlikely that anyone would remember the details of her employment.

"I'll take you there, but you have to hurry."

"I have clothes packed, and toys for Irene."

"How did you know?"

"I can read, Liam. Don't you think I figured out you were involved in that raid on Whiskey Island? Don't you think I've been worried sick about you?" She fled back upstairs, and he let her go. For the moment he let her believe that it was only the police they had to fear.

By the time twilight had deepened and Glen reached the family saloon, he didn't know what to expect. He certainly didn't expect the air of excitement that greeted him, or the smell of his grandmother's special dishes scenting the air. His mother took him aside and lectured him for not coming to her or his father first. His father, Terry, a tall handsome man who stooped a little these days and worried about losing his hair, took him aside and accused him of trying to break his mother's heart.

His grandmother bustled out of the kitchen and told him that Clare had arrived hours ago.

"She did?" Glen was stunned and immediately worried. He had expected Clare to sneak out at dusk, so that her father wouldn't discover her absence until morning. By then they would be long gone.

"I'll tell her to go home. You don't sound glad she's here," Lena said. She wore her best Sunday dress and marcasite combs to hold her hair in place.

"I'm thrilled beyond measure that she's here. I don't like to think what it might have taken to escape in broad daylight."

"She's a bit the worse for wear, but she's alive and well."

He intended to keep her that way. "I'm going up to see her."

"Think again, boy," his father said. "The women will claw out your eyes if you try to see her before the wedding."

He and Clare had so much to discuss and plan for, but he knew his father was right. They needed the semblance of normality, if only in such a simple tradition as that one. "Is Father McSweeney here?"

"Not yet. But he's on his way," Lena said.

Glen wondered how wise it had been to ask the old priest to preside. Had McNulty figured out by now that Clare was in love with another man or that she would try to marry her lover tonight? Liam, the bodyguard, certainly knew and would probably have no compunctions about reporting it. And surely a number of people had seen him with her at St. Brigid's, where they'd first met. Might the priest be followed to the saloon? That was a long shot, of course, but Glen wished now that they had thought of another, less obvious, way to get the old man here.

He decided he was being overly suspicious. If anything, her father only knew that she had left home. With any luck he would not immediately link her disappearance to a man but to a desire to escape Cassidy.

"You were able to get the license?" Lena asked.

"With a little finagling, yes."

"And a ring?"

"There wasn't time. I'll buy her one when we settle down."

"No, I have one for you." Lena reached inside the pocket

of her dress and pulled out a tiny cardboard box. "This was mine, from my first marriage to Terence, your grandfather. I put it away when I married Rowan. It belonged to Terence's mother. It's a poor ring, worn and scratched, but it's part of your history. And having met Clare, I believe she will treasure it."

He was touched. He kissed her cheek. "She *will* treasure it. Thank you from the bottom of my heart."

Lena smiled. "You've the gift of knowing how to make a woman feel good. Terence had it, too."

"What should I do now?"

"Sit and worry, which is what you'll do no matter what I say."

A Donaghue cousin—a particularly beefy one—was standing guard at the door. As Glen watched, he opened it a crack to usher in Father McSweeney. Glen went to pay his respects, his grandmother trailing behind.

"You do us all a great service, Father," she said, after Glen had thanked him.

The priest looked tired from the trip, even though St. Brigid's was not far away and a driver had brought him. "It will be good to get these two married and out of the city."

Lena ushered the priest to a comfortable chair. Glen's father pulled him aside to find out what plans he had made.

"I turned in my badge this morning, and I bought train tickets to Los Angeles. My boss thinks he can put in a good word for me there with the local police force." He paused. "And he let me keep my gun until I get settled, even though it's against policy."

Terry chose not to comment on that. "Los Angeles is too far away."

Glen was afraid it might not be far enough, but it was their best chance. His friend at the courthouse had promised to "lose" all records of the wedding for six months, so if either Cassidy or McNulty thought to check for such a thing, they would be stymied.

"I want you to have this," his father said. He handed Glen a package wrapped in white paper. "Open it now."

Glen did. Inside he found his grandfather Rowan's watch.

"He would have wanted *you* to have it," Terry said. "You're the only grandchild in law enforcement. He would have been so proud."

Glen wondered if one of Rowan's biological grandchildren should have this heirloom, but clearly Rowan had given it to Terry, his son by adoption. There had never been any favoritism in the family.

"I'll treasure it," Glen said.

"And take this." Terry pulled an envelope from his pocket. "It's from all of us. To help you get started. You'll stay in touch?"

Glen had already made arrangements to write to the family in care of a friend who would give them the letters. Too many precautions, perhaps, but better than too few.

He took the envelope and flipped through the bills. "Thank you. This is very generous of all of you."

A hush was falling over the saloon. Glen looked up and saw that everyone was watching him.

"Your bride is coming," Terry said. "Go to the front and stand by the priest, son."

Clare wondered how her mother had looked in this dress. It was ivory satin covered with layers of beautifully embroidered tulle and had a silhouette that was delightfully out of fashion in this era of the boyish figure. The neck was high, but the bodice above her breasts was sheer. The sleeves were sheer, too, but what she loved most was the train of delicate lace that hung from the shoulders. She felt like an angel with wings.

"Your mother is gone?" Fenola asked.

Clare already liked Glen's mother. She was down-to-earth, and she didn't hesitate to say what she felt. She was also fair, and Clare sensed that, under the no-nonsense facade, she was kind.

"She died when I was eight. I still miss her."

"Well, she would be weeping with joy to see what a beautiful bride you are."

Impulsively Clare took Fenola's hands. "I will take such good care of him, Mother. And I'll love him until the day I die."

"I can sense that. You won't blame us for worrying a bit, though, will you?"

"Of course not. And I promise, as soon as we safely can, we'll come back. I won't keep him from you."

"We'll come to see you if we can. When you're settled and when we're sure no one is watching."

Clare knew how hard that might be on their income. Surely Prohibition had cut into their family business, but these were people who would sacrifice everything they had for their children.

"Do you feel ready?" Fenola asked.

Clare looked down at her dress. Her hands were trembling, but not from fear. "I gave up hope of real happiness a long time ago." There was no self-pity in her voice, only joy. "I am the luckiest woman in the world to be marrying Glen."

"Yes, well, before I cry right here and now, let's go downstairs so I'll have company. I'll go first and open the door." Fenola leaned forward and planted a kiss on Clare's cheek. "He's lucky to be marrying you, too." She left the room.

Clare waited a full minute before she followed. She descended the stairs slowly, although she really wanted to run straight into Glen's arms. There was no music and no flowers; nobody had found the time to arrange anything appropriate. But the silence pleased her. She could not remember when she had been the center of so much attention, and she was not ashamed to enjoy it.

She reached the bottom of the steps and came through the door. There was an audible intake of breath, but she couldn't glance at the several dozen people standing on each side of a makeshift aisle. She searched for her husband-to-be, and she found him standing in front of Father McSweeney, turned so that he could watch her walk toward him. He grinned broadly.

She walked as if to music, and when she reached his side, he grabbed her hand. Father McSweeney beamed proudly at them both and began to speak.

Clare wanted to listen. She would only be married once, God willing, and she wanted to savor every word. But she could think of nothing except Glen, of how much she loved him and how unlikely it had been from the beginning that their love would end in marriage. She felt as if she were floating far above the ceremony, far above the gathered family and the priest, far above the saloon. She felt light and ethereal, the embodiment of joy.

Shots rang out. Glass shattered, and women screamed. Clare found herself on the floor, Glen's body half covering hers.

"Cassidy." He uttered the word like an oath. "Stay here."

She grabbed his arm. "Glen, no!"

"I have to stop him." He pulled away and got to his feet. As she tried to rise, too, he drew a gun from a holster under his jacket.

She hadn't known he was armed. "Glen!"

He looked down at her, as if to tell her everything would be all right; then he took off for the front door. Clare tried to follow, but Father McSweeney gripped her arm. "Stay here."

Someone was already on the telephone to the police; someone else was herding the others to the back of the saloon. Father McSweeney dragged her along. From the corner of her eye she saw that several of the men were on their way to the front. She saw that one, at least, was armed.

"Glen..." She tried to lag behind, but for a frail old man, Father McSweeney was surprisingly strong.

"He's safer out there without you, Clare," the priest said.

She knew it wasn't true. Cassidy was a madman, and first and foremost, he wanted Clare. His prime mission was to kill her, and that was why he had come. Instead, other innocents were going to die. All because she had fallen in love with Glen.

"Downstairs," Terry shouted.

With the others, Clare was herded into the kitchen, then down into a stairway to what she supposed was a basement. At the bottom, though, she saw that there was much more. What looked like an ordinary wall was a doorway leading into a narrow passageway lit only by the occasional lightbulb. She knew immediately what it must be used for.

"Where does this lead?" Father McSweeney was behind her now, but she addressed the question to one of Glen's younger cousins, who was hurrying along beside her.

"The hill and the road going over to Whiskey Island."

She wondered how much of her own father's liquor had made its way through this passage. There was no time to consider the irony of Tim's most precious assets entering and exiting through the tunnel. His liquor *and* the flesh and blood that he had been only too willing to sell. She did not want to be angry, not at this moment, when the man she loved was facing a maniac's bullets. She wanted to pray, to beseech God to spare Glen's life. But there was no time for anything more than crossing herself and a quickly muttered, fervent plea as she ran.

They stopped near the end of the tunnel. Terence had put himself in charge, and he held up his hand for silence.

Clare saw the door at the end, barred from the inside. She realized they were not going to escape but were going to hover here until the police arrived. Glen and the others were outside fighting for their lives and hers, and she was trapped with his family.

They stood in total silence. Clare could feel the thunderous beat of her heart, the trembling of her hands. She was terrified and resigned, and mutely, she prayed.

Footsteps sounded at the end of the tunnel by the stairs. Two men stepped in front of her to shield her.

"It's okay," a man shouted. "It looks like we scared them off. The guy who was shooting got nicked, we think, and lit out. They're making sure, but it looks like you can come back up in a few minutes."

The others began to talk quietly among themselves. Clare felt a hand on her arm. In the dim light of the bare bulb hanging just above their heads, she saw Fenola.

"It's my fault," Clare said. "All my fault."

"None of that, girl. It's the fault of those men up there, who don't know how to take no for an answer. And it's okay. Didn't you hear? Everyone came through it. We'll finish the wedding, then we'll get you out of here. Both of you. And not a moment too soon."

"But now you're all in danger."

"There's nothing for you to worry about there. The Donaghues have friends. We'll take care of ourselves, don't you worry."

But Clare *was* worried. These people had taken her in, befriended her even though she was stealing their beloved only son. And now she had put them at terrible risk. Because once she was gone, on whom would Niall Cassidy vent his rage? Her father? Yes, most certainly Tim, because Clare had earned Cassidy's wrath. But it was likely that Niall would seek vengeance on the Donaghues, as well.

The man who had joined them spoke a few minutes later. "I think we can start back. I'll go upstairs and check for sure. Don't come up until I've given the final signal."

In groups of two or three, they started back down the tunnel toward the saloon. Clare held back, and Fenola stayed beside her. "Are you all right?" she asked Clare.

"It's just been too much shock, I think. I feel a little dizzy." Clare wasn't lying, although she could easily have walked back.

"I'll stay with you until you feel better."

"No, I think I need a few moments alone. Please…"

Fenola nodded. "All right. But if you're not up in a few minutes, I'll send someone back to help you."

"Yes. Thanks." Clare leaned against the wall and closed her eyes. She heard the others making their way down the tunnel, the slow drag of Fenola's footsteps as she lingered, unwilling to abandon her daughter-in-law-to-be.

Clare wasn't clear about what to do. She knew only that she had to think. How could she marry Glen when it put so many people in danger? Was her personal happiness more important? She and Glen would be far away and safe, but these people would be forced to stay behind and answer for her decision.

She pictured Glen's face, Glen's dear face. She wanted nothing more than to be his wife and the mother of his children. She closed her eyes and prayed again, hoping for an answer.

It came in the form of gunfire, only this time near the tunnel door that opened on to the road. She heard shouts, and more bullets, and she knew what she had to do.

At the door she clawed at the bar, lifting it with great effort and swinging it left so that it was no longer an impediment. The key was in the lock, and it screeched as she turned it. Night rushed in, the very last moments of twilight. At first, as her eyes adjusted, she could see very little; then she saw two men. She recognized one of them as Liam.

The other was Niall.

"Stop!" She stepped outside, as clear about what she had to do now as she was about who and what she loved most. Niall turned, and for a moment she was looking directly into his eyes. He swung his gun around and aimed at her. She didn't flinch.

"You're going to die, Cassidy," Liam shouted. Then there was gunfire, three quick shots.

She had not realized what a good friend Liam had become to her. He had stayed behind to protect her, suspecting that Cassidy might find them. For the barest fraction of a moment she felt gratitude.

Then she felt nothing. Not pain, not surprise. Just the slow crumpling of her legs as she fell to the ground.

"Clare!"

She heard more gunfire, but it seemed as if it was coming from a different universe. She heard running, and shouting, and then Glen's voice. "Clare. Clare!"

She drifted until she felt him lift her in his arms. With all the strength left to her, she opened her eyes. "Glen..."

"We'll get a doctor. We'll save you. Hold on."

She felt another set of arms beneath her and with great effort moved her eyes to see Liam helping Glen. For a moment they seemed bound together, closer than brothers, united. It didn't seem strange to her. Good men, both of them.

"Niall?" she whispered.

"I'll find him. He won't get away with this."

She was beginning to realize how little that mattered. Niall had gotten what he came for. He would turn his attentions to other things now.

They were moving through the tunnel, but when she gave a soft cry, they lowered her to the floor, still yards from the door. She could not feel the ground beneath her, but she could see Glen's face.

"Marry—"

"Don't talk. I'll marry you just as soon as you're well and the doctors say we can."

"No, marry...another."

He was crying. This was something she had never expected to see. She wanted to tell him not to be sad, that he had given her more love in their brief moments together than she had ever hoped for. He had given her a family, too. She had belonged here. Too short... But right.

"Don't go, Clare." He was chafing her hands. She heard Liam retreating up the stairs, shouting as he went.

"I...love you. Don't be sad," she whispered.

It was odd. She was wearing her mother's wedding gown, but as her eyes closed she thought she saw her mother, dressed as she had been on the day she was married.

Clare smiled to welcome her.

chapter 33

Only rarely did Peggy rise before Nora's arrival. This morning she got up before the sun, and slipped on jeans and a sweatshirt to greet the day alone. Megan was sleeping soundly on the other side of the double bed, and Kieran was making soft little mewing noises, as if dreaming of something that pleased him.

What did please her son? She was no closer to knowing that than she had been on their arrival. In the most important ways, Kieran was a stranger. She had not unlocked the doors behind which he hid from the world. She had not solved the mysteries of how best to reach him. She could count improvements on the fingers of one hand. Now some of the time he ate with a spoon and recognized colors. He had formed an attachment of sorts to Bridie. Like a fiddler crab, he scurried sideways out of his own private hole, making forays in Bridie's direction, getting ever closer before he scurried home again.

In just a few more weeks Kieran would have his second birthday. His delays were still easy enough to pass off, his odd behavior might be the natural idiosyncracies of a sensitive child. But what would happen when he turned three, then four? The more he fell behind and refused to interact, the more he rocked or followed his hand or sat enraptured as light flickered on the wall, the more he would become an outcast.

She had not expected the Irish fairies to kidnap Kieran and leave a changeling in his crib. She had expected progress to be slow, but she had hoped that someday, with enough intervention, Kieran might attend a regular class in public school, join a Cub Scout pack, sing in a church choir. She no longer understood what it meant to be "normal," but she knew she wanted for her son what other mothers took for granted. The simplest things that might well be denied him.

Outside, a soft rain fell. She had seen entirely too much rain during her stay here, too much wind, too many dark skies. Yet she loved the way the morning mist drifted over Clare Island, the way the vistas changed with each blink, the cool, fresh feel of the air, the way Irish rain melted into her skin. The west of Ireland was not green. It was infinite shades of brown and gray, jutting rocks and tossing waves, a wild place.

She took the path that ran farther up the hillside, where Clare Island was visible and the neighbor's sheep could be counted. She thought that if she really lived here, she would raise sheep, too, not for food but for wool. She would learn to spin and dye, and when she wasn't prescribing antibiotics or performing minor surgery...

She crossed her arms over her chest and stared out at Clare, the sight of which must be like salt in the wound that was Finn's battered heart. Dreams died hard. His had perished in a storm. Surely with grace and with courage she could let go of her own childhood dream of becoming a doctor. She didn't know where Kieran's future lay, but she knew that she had to be right there, walking beside him. Not from duty, but from a mother's love.

Megan showered and dressed. Kieran was still sleeping restlessly, and she tiptoed out of the bedroom and into the kitchen, where Nora was making coffee. She said her good morning, then asked the obvious question. "Peggy's out?"

"I saw her walking up the hill when I arrived."

"Isn't it raining?"

Nora looked puzzled, as if that connection was difficult to establish. "Yes, I suppose it is."

"She's walking in the rain?"

Nora shook her head. "And you say you're a hundred percent Irish?"

"Make that ninety-nine percent. The one percent that's something else likes to be warm and dry."

"A pity. It's a particularly soft rain, and the views through the mist are perfect. Like peeking through to heaven."

Megan wondered if her sister wanted company. There was rain gear on pegs in what passed for a mudroom.

"I'll listen for the lad," Nora said. "If you can gather your courage."

Megan knew Kieran would probably sleep at least another half hour. "You're sure you don't need some help?" Megan said.

"I'm sure I don't."

"Then I'll go find her."

Megan donned a slicker and hat, but forsook the Wellingtons that looked to be her size. Her sneakers were up to the task.

Outside, she had to admit that Nora was right. And it wasn't as if she had never walked in the rain. Cleveland wasn't known as the Sunshine City. She thrived on gloom, and she would put Cleveland rain up against Irish rain any day. Niccolo, with his own roots planted deeply in soggy Western Pennsylvania, often said that their children would toddle on webbed feet and breathe through gills. Niccolo, who she missed the way she would miss the beating of her heart.

By now Peggy had started back down the hill, and Megan started up to meet her. Megan saw that her sister wasn't even wearing a jacket. She would be wet, and oblivious to it. Megan had spent her adolescence trying to keep little Peggy dry.

Peggy got within shouting distance. "This isn't like you, Megan. Have you noticed it's wet out here?"

Megan waited until her sister was closer. "I was afraid you'd slide right down that hill on your butt. I'm here to catch you."

"Come up and see the view."

Reluctantly, Megan climbed. She could not understand why people hiked or climbed for the fun of it. She was on her feet all day at the Whiskey Island Saloon, and "fun" seemed a contradiction in terms.

"Okay, what am I supposed to see?" she grumbled, when she reached Peggy's side.

"Look out there." Peggy pointed to Clare Island. As they watched, the mist off the water and the clouds above seemed to change places, weaving, dodging, entwining like lovers. "I could never grow tired of this view."

"You've got it bad. Irish fever. This is the third day in a row that it's rained, and you're soaking wet. That would cure most people."

"Aren't you having a good time?"

She wasn't, but that wasn't Ireland's fault. She was pleased to have met Irene, glad to have seen the village and country-side where her ancestors had lived, humbled to sleep in their cottage—although a far different cottage it was these days. But as glad as she was to be spending time with her youngest sister and nephew, she was all too aware that Niccolo should be here, too. They should be sharing these experiences, mak-ing memories, compiling stories to tell their own children on snowy winter nights.

She had left Cleveland, but she had not left her problems behind.

"You miss him, don't you?" Peggy continued to stare at the ocean and give her sister a semblance of privacy.

"I miss him." Megan was sorry she did.

"You've only told me a little about what's wrong. Did you actually fight?"

Megan had not told Peggy many details. Now, standing in the rain, she tried. "In a way. I told you he was gone too many nights, and even when he was home, he wasn't really there. I called him on it. It wasn't very pretty, but he's probably already forgotten. I wonder if he even notices I'm gone."

"What's the problem really about? Do you know?"

Megan was glad Peggy hadn't tried to defend or explain Niccolo's behavior. "I'm not sure. He loves me. He claims he's glad we're married."

"He is glad." Peggy sounded sure.

"Have you noticed that men are confusing, frustrating creatures?"

"I've noticed."

"Take your Finn, for instance."

Peggy turned to look at her sister. "My, that was quick."

"Quick?"

"A real hit-and-run. Here's my problem, now let's talk about you, Peggy."

Megan chewed her bottom lip. "I don't know what to say. I came to sort things out, only I feel a little like Kieran with his shape box."

"Come again?"

"I was working with him yesterday. That little devil's really bright, Peggy, I know he is, but he just can't get everything working together to put the shapes in the right places."

"In other words, you have the pieces you need to put your relationship with Nick in perspective, but you can't be sure where they go."

"You got it."

"When Kieran gets tired, he starts trying to stuff shapes in the wrong places, just to get rid of them."

"He did that yesterday."

"And that's like you, too, isn't it? Even when you know where the pieces of your life with Nick should go, you're too frustrated to put them where they belong. You just want them out of the way."

Peggy had taken the metaphor a step further than Megan had planned. She stopped chewing her lip and frowned. "I don't know about that."

"Are any pieces missing?"

"Well, he dreams he's a priest again." Megan forged on. "I want him to dream about me."

"Sure you do."

Admitting her selfishness, her neediness, had been hard. That Peggy had understood and automatically accepted it as natural and right was a relief. "You think?"

"I *know*. Megan, you have every right to want to be first. You just got married, and Nick's busy with everything and everybody except you. It has to be frustrating. What happens when you tell him how you feel?"

"When I get angry with him?"

"Are you angry?"

"Yes."

"And that's all you feel?" Peggy waited, brow cocked in question.

After a moment Megan sighed. "I feel hurt and rejected. Like I'm not good enough somehow to keep his attention. Like I've failed before I could even start."

"And you've told him this?"

"Not in so many words."

"Is this something he should just figure out, do you think?"

"I'd like it if he would."

"Wouldn't that be a perfect world."

Once again Megan was aware of a major role reversal. Peggy no longer needed an older sister to keep her dry or pick her up when she fell, but Megan needed a friend. And here was one all ready-made. What a system.

Megan decided to venture a step further into intimacy. "I'm afraid if I tell him how I'm feeling, he'll blow that off the way he's blown off everything else I've said since the wedding. If I tell him and he ignores me, that's not something I could live with."

"So by not talking to him, you're trying to save your marriage?"

"Peggy, you're making this sound easy."

"Trust me, I know from personal experience how hard it is

to talk about the things that really matter with the man you love."

"And you're not talking about Phil."

Peggy looked back out to Clare. "Not Phil. Never Phil."

"Finn?"

"There are so many wonderful things about him that you haven't seen."

"Just tell me this. Do you want to love him? Or do you want to save him?"

"Megan, don't you think I have my hands full already? I'm not looking for another project."

"But he is a project, isn't he? He's still mourning what he lost. Is he ready to find a new love?"

"Love just happens sometimes, even when the timing is wrong. We didn't want to find each other, but somehow we did."

"And the future?"

Peggy turned back to her. "Megan, I'm lucky to get through one day at a time, and so is he. We have that much in common."

"You'll want more someday, Peggy. Do you want it with a temperamental Irishman who is punishing himself for something he couldn't help?"

"No, I don't. But I might want Finn O'Malley. Only time will tell."

Kieran awoke with rosy cheeks and bright eyes, but Peggy, with a mother's instincts, suspected more than good spirits. She felt his forehead as she lifted him from his crib. He was warm, and he slumped against her, letting her cuddle him, which was a sign in itself that something was wrong.

She took his temperature as she changed his diaper and wasn't surprised when it registered just over 100 degrees. His nose was stopped up, and his eyes red, although he hadn't been crying. She wondered if he'd caught the cold that Tippy's daughter Maeve had been incubating at their play date last week.

In the kitchen he refused everything but apple juice and sat lethargically in his high chair as the others breakfasted.

"He's certainly not himself," Irene said. "We can actually hear each other's chatter this morning."

"I hope it's only a cold," Peggy said. "But I'm going to check his throat after breakfast, if Megan will hold him for me."

"Perhaps Finn will have a look at him."

Peggy wondered if he would. She wasn't overly worried. Colds and fevers were commonplace, and Kieran would certainly have his share. Still, she wouldn't mind a consultation, particularly if his throat turned out to be infected.

It was red, as she discovered after breakfast, and even in the hour since she had taken his temperature, his fever seemed to have climbed. She gave him acetaminophen and additional juice; then she sat with him in her lap and rocked while he lay dazed against her.

By the time Finn arrived to see Irene, she was growing concerned. He stopped by to say hello and frowned when he saw her rocking Kieran.

"That's not a sight I've seen often," he said.

"He's sick." Peggy helped the little boy turn. "His throat is red and swollen, and the last time I took his temperature it was 102."

"That would be high for an adult, but not so bad for a baby."

She was annoyed that he was placating her. "I know that, but I'm afraid he has an infection he'll need an antibiotic for. And before you tell me that doctors don't prescribe antibiotics for every little sniffle anymore, I know that."

"Good."

He didn't volunteer to look at Kieran, and she sighed. "Finn, would you mind just taking a peek at him?"

He was silent so long that she knew what his answer would be. "I don't practice medicine anymore, Peggy. You know that."

"You see Irene. You still have a license to practice. You even have a medical practice you haven't sold. I'm not asking you to do major surgery. Just to look at his throat and prescribe something if he needs it."

"You need to take him to see Beck. I can give you the number. He's in his surgery in Westport today, but if you let his nurse know that I told you to take Kieran to him, I'm fairly certain he'll see him."

She thought about the long drive into Westport with a sick child, and not just any sick child but an autistic child for whom new experiences were excruciating. She wouldn't have given it a thought if Finn hadn't been standing right here. But he *was* here, and he had the knowledge and the license to prescribe. He just didn't have the courage.

She bit off her reply. "That's what I'll do, then."

He didn't say anything more, didn't wish her well or encourage her. He went in search of Irene, and Peggy didn't see him again.

Megan accompanied them to Westport, and between them they got Kieran into the reception area to wait for Dr. Beck. Then, while Megan went off to explore the city's cheerful streets and shops, Peggy waited.

Kieran was frantic with exhaustion when the doctor finally got to him, two hours later. Dr. Beck was a young man, harried, condescending and dismissive. He gave her a prescription for a decongestant and cough syrup, then gazed with icy amusement over rimless glasses when she asked for an antibiotic.

"Prescribing medication is *my* job, Miss Donaghue."

She told herself to remain calm. "I certainly understand that, and I appreciate your caution. But he's *my* son, and I think this is more than a simple cold. Will you do a throat culture, just to be sure?"

"I think I know the difference between a serious infection and a little virus." He stood to usher her out of the room. "I've seen this same thing over and over for the past two weeks. It's nothing to worry about."

"I know how busy you are. You have too many patients and too little time. I understand that. But please—"

He shook his head and left the room ahead of her.

Megan was in the waiting room when Peggy returned, fuming silently. By now Kieran was so tired and so feverish that he fell asleep in Peggy's arms as she carried him to Megan's rental car.

By the time they got to Irene's, Peggy's anger had intensified. She had tried and failed to understand Finn's side of this. Kieran wasn't just any child; Kieran was the child of his lover. Surely Finn knew the sentence he had imposed by his refusal to look at Kieran himself. He knew Beck. He knew the man was seriously overworked and seriously lacking in bedside manner. Beck had completely dismissed Kieran's autism, even hinted that the child was simply spoiled and needed discipline. Only innate good manners and good sense had stopped her from telling him exactly what she thought of him. And Finn had known what she would be up against.

She was alone in the kitchen when Finn came for his nightly visit. Megan had driven into town to buy ice cream in hopes that Kieran could be tempted to eat some for supper. Irene was in her room resting and reading, and Kieran was sound asleep.

"Did you take Kieran to see Beck today?"

She was washing glasses for supper, and she didn't turn to speak to him. "I did, for all the good it did."

"He's a good enough doctor."

"Maybe that's true when he's not being an arrogant son of a bitch, or when he's not so overworked that a throat culture might be the straw that breaks the camel's back. But for all the good that trip did, I could have kept poor Kieran here and bought medicine over the counter at the pharmacy."

"You're angry."

"Damned tooting." This time she did turn. "You could have looked at him. You could have saved the poor little guy hours of waiting in a strange office. You could have saved me from dealing with Doctor God. But you couldn't see your way to that, could you?"

"No."

She was exhausted, and she felt something snapping inside her that could not be repaired. "When does this fear of making mistakes step over the line into self-pity, Finn? Are you afraid, or just too sorry for yourself to move on? This village needs its own doctor. And not just anybody. They need Finn O'Malley. Kieran is just one child who had to make the trip to Westport or Castlebar or God knows where to be treated by God knows who. And you're laying pipe or hammering boards or installing stoves, whatever the heck it is you do. And all those years of training and all that raw talent are lying fallow."

"You've finished?"

She stared at him for a long moment. "Yes, I'm afraid I have."

"This is beginning to sound like it's about more than my decision not to be a doctor."

"Maybe it is. Maybe it's about whether you're ever going to let go of the past and embrace the future."

"Not any future, though, am I right? The one you have planned for me."

"What does that mean?"

"You want me whole. You want the man I was before I drowned my wife and children."

"No, I want the man who can move beyond mourning an accident that wasn't his fault, the man who sees that his future can hold more than self-loathing and despair if he'll just stop punishing himself."

She had gone too far, and she knew it. She wasn't surprised when he left the kitchen without another word.

Somewhere between the cottage and Shanmullin, Megan realized that she had to go home. Someday she wanted a real tour of Ireland, but for now, she needed to be with Niccolo. Peggy was right. She had let fear stop her from telling him what she really needed. Niccolo loved her—distance had clarified that for her—but he didn't know how to be a husband any more than she knew how to be a wife. That was so easy to see now. She had to risk being honest with him, and in return, she had to really listen to his side of things.

So simple, but so difficult. She wasn't sure how the human race had survived for so many thousands of years.

By the time she was on her way back to Irene's with vanilla ice cream and more fruit juice, she was ready to call the airlines and book a flight.

As she pulled up to the cottage, she noted a strange car parked beside the door, the bumper sporting a sticker from the same company that had rented hers. For one ecstatic moment she wondered if her husband had come to Ireland to claim her. But she was nearly as happy when she saw Casey standing in the doorway.

"Case!" It wasn't like she hadn't seen her recently, but Megan hurried up the walkway to give her sister a hug. "What on earth?"

"I decided you two were having all the fun here, and that's not fair. So I hopped a plane."

Megan's plans to return to Ohio vanished. She couldn't leave right away, not when this had become a Donaghue sister reunion. Her emotions were decidedly mixed.

"I'm not here for long," Casey warned, before Megan could respond. "But I plan to pack plenty into a couple of days."

Megan hoped her relief wasn't apparent. She could leave for home when Casey did, and she would actually have company on the trip. "Next you'll tell me that Rooney and Aunt Dee are on their way, and all that's left of the Tierney family of Shanmullin will be under one roof."

"I don't think we'll ever get Rooney in an airplane, but Aunt Dee's planning to visit Peggy in the fall. Which is good timing, since I don't think this incredible cottage would hold us all at once."

"It held our ancestors, who knows how many at one time?"

Peggy joined them. She was clearly thrilled to have Casey with them, but she looked exhausted. The day had been frustrating and difficult. "Kieran's just waking up. Let's see if we can get some more juice in him and a little ice cream. Then we can catch up."

* * *

They caught up around a turf fire, more for effect than warmth. Irene had refused to go to bed before they did, and she joined them to hear what Casey had learned on the airplane from the newest batch of Maura McSweeney's letters. First they told Casey about Liam's involvement with the IRA and his hopes that Tim McNulty would contribute to their coffers.

"But McNulty lost everything during a Prohibition raid on Whiskey Island," Megan finished. "So there was nothing left to donate to anybody. And Liam was nearly caught and jailed."

Casey settled herself more comfortably against the cushions of Irene's sofa. "There are a lot of letters. I have the copies with me. I've had to piece this together, a little here, a little there. But it seems as if our grandfather Glen fell in love with McNulty's daughter and she with him. McNulty had other ideas for her, particularly after his bootlegging empire came crashing down around him. He wanted Clare, the daughter, to marry another bootlegger. Instead she sneaked away to marry Grandfather. And guess where?"

Megan looked at Irene, who refused to give anything away. "You *know*, don't you? This is something else you've kept to yourself."

Irene's eyes widened innocently. "I'm an old woman. I know so much, I can't remember where I've filed it all."

Megan knew better, but she didn't challenge her. "Where?" she asked Casey.

"At the saloon. At *our* saloon. Father McSweeney himself was performing the ceremony when the other bootlegger, some guy named Cassidy, started firing through the front windows. They escaped into—" She paused and smiled sadly. "Guess where?"

Peggy answered. "There's only one place to escape. We found that out ourselves. The tunnel?"

"Exactly. When they thought it was safe they went upstairs again, but Clare stayed behind, claiming she needed a moment to recover. In the meantime, Glen was outside trying to find Cassidy. She heard gunfire. No one knows exactly why she went outside. Maybe to find Glen and bring him in through the tunnel? Maybe to offer herself as a sacrifice? No one's sure. But Cassidy killed her. And guess what?"

Casey turned to Irene before they could guess. "*Your* father was there. Liam helped Clare escape her father's house and brought her to the saloon. And apparently he stayed behind to be sure she was safe. Together he and Glen were trying to stop Cassidy when she was killed. They brought Clare inside the tunnel. Together. But she died in Glen's arms."

They fell silent. On the hearth, the turf crackled audibly.

Finally Peggy spoke. "That's probably the saddest story I've ever heard. And I can't figure out why I never heard it before. This was our grandfather, and I thought I'd heard every family story at least a hundred times."

"I can make a guess," Megan said. "Grandfather must have been devastated. He married late, remember? And when he did, and found happiness at last with our grandmother, no one wanted to remind him of the tragedy of his youth. As a family, we're as good at keeping important secrets as we are at blathering forever about anything that's not."

"But he's been dead a long time."

"I imagine the story just disappeared, out of respect for our grandmother. And those who lived it are gone now. No one talks about Prohibition, either, or the speakeasy upstairs that wasn't supposed to be there. Different times, times to keep silent about."

"Was there anything more, Casey?" Peggy asked. "Irene still doesn't know how her father died."

Irene spoke before Casey could. "As a matter of fact, dear, I do."

Peggy didn't look surprised. She rose and found an afghan on the back of a chair and took it to Irene, tucking it around her legs. "Then I think we'd better make you nice and comfortable, because this may be a long night. Why don't you start with why you've been telling us one story when another is obviously true? If you've known the way your father died all along, then you've been misrepresenting more than I thought. And don't use that excuse about wanting to find out what kind of women we are. You already have that figured out."

"And there's no better way to discover a person's character than to ask for help," Irene confirmed. "But there's a bit more to it than that. I'll let the rest of the story come out on its own, I think. It's time now. In fact, the timing couldn't be better with Casey here." She beamed at Casey. The two had hit it off immediately.

"Is this going to be it?" Megan pulled her legs beneath her and rested the back of her head against the sofa. "Because I do have to go home someday, you know. We all do."

"Oh yes, you do have to go home, dear. You'd need to, even if there was no other reason than to discover the end of this story."

"I thought you were going to tell us the ending."

"Well, very nearly. Just be patient. You'll see what I mean."

Megan closed her eyes and thought of Niccolo, waiting for her in Cleveland. "I'll hold you to that."

1925
Castlebar, County Mayo

My dearest Patrick,

How dear is family and how lightly we dismiss it when we are young. I have many friends and neighbors, but in my final hours, it will be you I see, standing at my bedside as I stood by yours so many hours when you were a young lad suffering from one illness or another.

Your care fell to me because our mother had the work of four women before her each day and she could not falter. Still, I don't regret the many hours I spent caring for you, Patrick. In later years I had no sons or daughters of my own, but I had memories of sharing your childhood. If this is the last letter that I ever write you, please know that your love, and the love of our sisters, has made me the woman I am. I am happy to be that woman, and I will die thinking of all of you.

Your loving sister,
Maura McSweeney

chapter 34

Liam found no joy in waking early. Dawn held no romance. As a child, it had been his chore to milk the family cow, and if he lay abed longer than his mother deemed necessary, he suffered a beating for it. His days with the Christian Brothers had started before sunrise, too. Gathering eggs from chickens well about their business, Mass before a porridge breakfast so meager that boys routinely fainted from hunger before and after. He found no joy in brightening skies or the songs of birds. Today, however, he greeted both with some enthusiasm. He had hidden himself for three days, and this was his first foray outside.

After Clare McNulty's death, Liam had vanished into the bowels of Cleveland, but he had learned from the newspaper that in the hours after the fatal shot, Cassidy had skipped town. Liam was certain that Cassidy would never willingly show his weasel face in the city again and equally certain that Chicago's wheels of justice would not turn energetically enough to spit him back in this direction. Cassidy was gone for good.

McNulty was not. His one opportunity to garner favor with the North Side gang had died in a tunnel. Perhaps he mourned his daughter for more than this, but Liam was in no position to find out. His job had been to guard Clare, then disappear when Cassidy arrived on the scene. Instead, he had spirited her from the house to marry another man. If McNulty knew the truth—and surely he had guessed some of it—McNulty would never forgive him. It was past time for Liam to take his family and leave Cleveland.

Except for one detail.

As the sky lightened gradually, that detail lay nearly within his reach. He lay on his belly in Whiskey Island scrub, remembering the night of the raid and the path of the Canadian captain through these woods. His memories had been forged in darkness, but even in the chaos, he had tried to notice landmarks. He thought he was close to the place where the captain had stooped, nearly disappearing from Liam's view for the moments it had taken him to accomplish some task. Liam had a fair idea what the man had done. Now he had only to find the spot and undo it.

He had been listening intently for long minutes, but the only sounds he had heard were those of a lone tug out on the river, the squirm and rustle of birds and small animals, the shrill whistle of a train. He crept forward now, another ten yards, waited, then resumed his journey.

At last he came to the spot where he planned to begin his search. This was as close as his memory could peg it. He rose to a squat and began to filter leaves and soil through his fingers. He searched for holes in the soil, for rocks he could dislodge, for crevices in stumps or dead branches. He inched along, taking time every minute or two to listen intently for intruders.

Ten minutes passed, then ten more. Frustration gnawed at him, although he'd expected this. He knew his search might be futile. Others could have been here before him. Surely even in captivity the captain had been able to communicate with someone. McNulty himself had probably searched these woods with Jerry. Worst of all, perhaps Liam had been wrong from the beginning and misinterpreted what he had seen that night.

He inched to the right and continued to dig and sift. A half hour passed as he made a circle, then another hour as the circle widened. Now he doubted he was in the right area. He thought he had been the only witness to the captain's flight, but the storm and darkness might well have played havoc with his sense of direction.

The sun was about to break over the horizon. He knew he had to leave. He was on foot these days, his beloved Model T abandoned on a side street, in case someone was looking for it—and him. He could continue tomorrow, but that meant another day in Cleveland. Brenna and Irene were still hidden with her former employers, but the longer they stayed there, the more likely McNulty would be to discover them. And McNulty would use Liam's family to get back at him. That was one thing Liam knew for certain.

He scooted right and decided to search one additional area. He lifted a rock and found nothing, drove his fingers between the wide roots of a tree and found nothing. Just as he was about to give up for the morning, he noticed a rotten limb lying to one side of him. It had been there for years, he thought, the family home of carpenter ants and beetles who had set about its destruction with single-minded purpose. They had yet to accomplish their goal, but the limb disintegrated beneath his fingers as he lifted it. He knew as he did that he had not been the first to do so. Sawdust and bark lay in untidy piles underneath it, as if the limb had been recently disturbed.

At first nothing caught his eye; then he saw an indentation in the ground. Not deep, and nearly hidden by more of the decomposing bark. He swept the bark away with his foot to find the prize he had sought.

The wad of bills astounded him. He had expected fewer, had been sure that McNulty had paid the rumrunners most of their money up front. Now he understood why his former boss was so determined to locate what the captain had reaped at the end of the transaction. Surely there was enough money here to pay back much of what McNulty had borrowed. With what he could sell quickly and with whatever clout he could still muster, McNulty would be saved. But not now. Not when the money was in Liam's hands and not his.

That thought gave Liam great pleasure.

As he pocketed the money, he looked around once more. The birds were louder now, and the trumpeting of frogs had ended. The day was beginning in earnest, and soon he would be clearly visible. Crouching, he found his way deeper into the forest, along the path he had plotted earlier for his escape.

When he was able to straighten, he found he was no longer alone. Under the sheltering branches of a tree, Glen Donaghue was watching him.

"When I was a boy," Glen said, "there were stories of bodies buried here. The famine Irish were too poor for funerals and consecrated ground, so when our own died, we buried them ourselves. Then, if a priest was generous enough of soul, he might take a walk along the right path to say a few prayers and sprinkle the grave with holy water."

Liam thought of Clare, who had died not far away and would be buried in the McNulty family plot tomorrow. "It's a haunted place," he agreed.

"In many, many ways." Glen pushed away from the tree trunk. There were new lines in his boyish face, battle-scars. There was no light in his eyes. "So why would a superstitious Irishman like yourself choose the hour just before dawn to stroll here? Spirits and fairies are still about. In the dark hours the *pooka* might well come crashing through these woods looking for people of evil intent."

"Should *I* be afraid?"

"You have blots on your record, Liam. You were on McNulty's payroll."

"They say the devil will have his own."

"Yet you went against him to protect Clare."

Liam waited. He was certain Glen knew why he had come here and what he had found. He felt like a mouse under the shrewd gaze of a farmer's wife. He was armed, but he would never use a weapon against this man. Glen didn't know that, of course, but that only made the situation more dangerous.

"You've been following me," Liam said at last.

"Not easily. I'll say that much for you."

"What do you want from me?"

"To see what's in your pocket."

"And what has that to do with you?"

"Show me, and we'll see."

So far Glen had not brandished a gun. But what did that matter? Liam wasn't going to fight him, and he wasn't going to tell him why. He was at an impasse. He thought of Brenna and Irene. He hoped that once the money was in Glen's possession, he would let Liam go without arresting him. Glen was an honorable man, but perhaps he could be persuaded that Liam had done nothing more than search for and find the money.

"Take it," Liam said, holding his arms out from his sides. "I have a gun. I don't plan to use it on you."

"Why not?" Glen stepped forward and reached inside the pocket of Liam's jacket.

"Because I have no quarrel with *you*."

Glen pulled out the wad of bills. His weight was on the balls of his feet, his body tense. Clearly he was ready for anything Liam might try. When Liam simply stood there, Glen stepped back. He held the bills where he could see both them and Liam. He whistled softly.

"More than I've seen at one time." Liam smiled. "Of course I only stumbled on it when I was taking my morning constitutional."

"That so?"

"I've no idea how it got here."

"That would be a story for the police to sort out."

"I was hoping it wouldn't come to that. I was hoping that for the sake of friendship you might just say you found it yourself when you turn it into the authorities."

"Friendship?"

"My friendship with Clare. Yours with Clare. She was a good woman. I'm sorry...." Liam shook his head.

"And you think because you tried to help her at the end, I should let you go?"

Liam wasn't certain where this conversation was heading. Glen's voice betrayed nothing. He might well be planning to kill Liam for revenge against everyone ever connected to McNulty or Cassidy. Or he might be planning to become a local hero, the man who turned in the money that sank McNulty's bootlegging empire once and for all.

"I don't think anything," Liam said at last. "The only thing in life I've ever counted on is surprise."

"Why did you work for him?"

"In my wife's words, it takes a dirty hand to make a clean hearth. I have a family to support."

Glen held up the wad of bills. "This would have more than done it, huh? Sink it all into the stock market, and you might become a millionaire?"

"No, I had other uses for it, as well."

"I've done a bit of research. Your immigration records show that your full name is William Francis Tierney, come here by way of Canada. Oddly enough, a man your age and description with the name of Liam Patrick Tierney is wanted by the authorities in Ireland. He shot a man just a month before you showed up here."

"Is that so? And how many other Irishmen came to this country at the same time I did?"

Glen ignored that. "He was an IRA man. The IRA wouldn't be that other *use* you have for this money, would it?"

"As I told you, I stumbled on the money by accident. I've had little time to consider exactly how best to use it."

Glen rippled the bills with his thumb. "And would one of those ways have been McNulty himself?"

"McNulty? I've no loyalty or affection for the man. He forced his only daughter to flee. He was going to give her to a man who is everything he should have shielded her from. He's a thief and a liar, and if he ever got a penny of this, it would have been off my cold, dead body." Liam was surprised at the ferocity in his own voice. With an effort, he softened his tone. "I would rather the police have the money, since it's come to that."

"If the police or the Treasury Department takes it, what do you suppose that will do for McNulty's case?"

Liam didn't understand. "His case?"

"With the men in Chicago who loaned him the money in the first place?"

Liam wasn't surprised Glen knew about that. At this point he imagined there was little loyalty left in McNulty's organization. Surely people were talking to the authorities in exchange for their own freedom. "I don't know what it would do for McNulty. What do *you* think?"

"I think if those Chicago boys knew that the money truly did disappear that night, the way McNulty said, and that the police had it now, they'd be less inclined to blow McNulty away. They'd take whatever he could scrape together as payment. They might kill him as a warning to others, but then again, they might not. It's a gamble."

Liam understood. "But if they believe McNulty might still have the money, or that he didn't do enough to find it, then they'll kill him for sure?"

"Incompetence is one thing. Fate can intervene in even the best-laid plans, and they're smart enough to know it. But disloyalty or treating the North Siders like fools is another."

Liam wasn't certain where Glen was heading with this. He waited to see.

Glen continued. "Do you know that I turned in my badge the day I was to marry Clare? They let me keep my gun, although they shouldn't have, but they knew we were in danger. I was to return the gun later."

"Do you think I care if you're armed? Unless you're planning to point the gun at me."

"I was surprised that your last name is Tierney. There are Tierneys in my family. Did you know that?"

"How would I?"

"All dead. And even I don't carry the family name. Tell me, because I can't remember from your records. You have a son?"

"A daughter."

Glen nodded. "Yes, that's right. No one to carry on your family name, either."

"I hope to remedy that someday. Of course, if you turn me in and somehow the authorities confuse me with this other man from Ireland and send me back, I'll be hanging from a rope in Dublin."

"I'll take back my badge, you know. In a week or a month. After the funeral, and after I've had some time to myself."

Again Liam waited.

Glen rippled the bills once more. "But for now, I'm just a normal citizen, no longer sworn to uphold any laws, either good or bad. Prohibition's a foolish law, because it breeds men like McNulty and Cassidy and puts honest distillers and distributors and too many honest saloon keepers like my own parents out of business. But we've created a new breed of criminal now, and someone has to catch the bootleggers. It might as well be me. And now that Clare is dead, I have a greater stake than most."

"I'm sorry you do."

Glen looked at the money in his hand; then he looked at Liam. He stepped forward and held the bills out to him. "There's been enough death and destruction in Ireland, don't you think...Liam Patrick Tierney? There's more than enough money in my hand for you to start a new life for yourself and build lives for others."

"You're giving it back to me?"

"Use it well, so that McNulty can make no use of it at all." Glen shoved his hands in his pockets, turned his back on Liam and walked away. In a few moments he had vanished into the woods.

chapter 35

By the time Liam left Whiskey Island, the city was coming to life. He had hoped to get to Brenna and Irene while it was still dark. He didn't know exactly what Tim McNulty knew about his part in Clare's escape and death, but surely, at the least, McNulty believed Liam hadn't watched her carefully, and that was sin enough. It seemed unlikely that McNulty would spare any of his dwindling supporters to search for Liam instead of the money, but Liam couldn't be too careful.

He wondered where to spend the hours until evening. He hadn't been home since the night Clare died. He needed a bath and a change of clothing, and he wanted a few things Brenna had left behind. In their one brief phone call she'd lamented forgetting several small keepsakes. He wanted to retrieve them, gratitude for all she was giving up. It was too dangerous now, but he wondered if it would be safe that evening? Clare's wake would begin about sunset, most likely at

McNulty's house. Everyone who had ever known her, everyone who had ever done business with her father, would be there.

If McNulty's cohorts were at the wake, Liam's chances of creeping back into his own house unnoticed would be better. Then, under cover of darkness, he would make his way to Brenna and Irene, and by morning the Tierney family could be safely on their way west. Liam wasn't certain where they would go, Colorado or Wyoming, perhaps, away from city life and temptation. But once the Tierneys were out of Cleveland, they would have time to decide where and how to spend the rest of their lives.

He decided that the best place to spend the day was in one of the empty houses at the end of his block. From that vantage point his own house would be plainly visible, and he could watch to be sure no one came calling. On foot, he made his way to his neighborhood through the back streets, making certain not to call attention to himself. He arrived without incident and let himself in through a back window. Except for cabinets and trim, the house was nearly finished. On one of his neighborhood strolls he'd learned that the carpenters would begin the final stages of construction next week.

He made himself as comfortable as he could. He was still hungry, although he had bought rolls and milk on the walk and devoured them. Hunger was an old friend and would help him stay awake. He sat far enough back from the front bedroom windows that he could not be seen, and close enough that he had a good view of his neighborhood. Then he began his wait.

The day was blessedly uneventful. He dozed twice as afternoon lengthened, waking up with a start to look out on an unchanged street. Activity was reduced to a mother pushing a pram and the occasional promenade of neighborhood dogs. By the time the skies had darkened again and the men were home from work, he was famished and out of patience. He left the house the way he had come and carefully made his way to his own.

He had locked all the doors and windows on the day he left

the house and most of what he owned behind. Now the back door was ajar. He drew the Colt .45 McNulty had so thoughtfully supplied and listened carefully before he entered. The house was silent. Once inside, he saw that it had been turned upside down. Someone had demolished most of the contents. Brenna had lavished such care on the house and its furnishings, his Brenna who had begun life with nothing and seemed to have nothing of worth all these years later.

This had not been an act of vandalism. Someone had systematically gone through the house looking for something. And what did Liam have of real worth?

Nothing that wasn't burning a hole in his pants pocket.

There was only one explanation. McNulty suspected that Liam had found the rumrunners' money. If McNulty's men had come here simply to find him, they would not have searched the house so thoroughly. No, in his quest to find the money and pay back the North Side gang, McNulty was leaving no stone unturned.

Liam wondered if he was a pebble or a boulder in McNulty's suspicions. Had this search been routine or narrowly targeted? And if the latter was true, what were the chances that Liam could leave the house again without being seen? If McNulty truly suspected him and could summon the manpower, he would have left someone behind to watch the house. Someone could be watching now.

He debated looking for Brenna's missing keepsakes. A curl from Irene's first haircut, a bow from the dress Brenna had worn on their wedding day, a photograph of a childhood friend who had died of influenza. She had so little, yet she wanted only these simple things. He knew where they had been kept and decided to take the chance. He was armed, and it would take only moments.

He took the steps two at a time. In his bedroom he found Brenna's heirlooms on the floor under the overturned cigar box where she had kept them. He scooped them up, wrapped them in a clean handkerchief he found on the floor and placed them in the pockets of his trousers. There was no time for a bath, but he recovered a fresh shirt and changed into it, combed his hair, wiped his shoes on the shredded bed linen and carefully rolled clean socks into a ball and stuffed them on top of the keepsakes. It was time to go.

Unfortunately, an old friend thought otherwise.

"Thought you'd come back," said a familiar voice.

Liam whirled to find Jerry blocking the doorway. He was only surprised that a man so large could climb the stairs without noise. All Liam's senses had been finely tuned.

Jerry shrugged, as if he knew he had to clear up that question. "Don't worry. You couldn't have heard me. I been waiting in your little girl's room. I guess I fell asleep."

"For how long?"

"Not so long. I got here just before dark."

Liam cursed his own naps. "Is this *your* handiwork?"

"You can put the gun away. I didn't come here to shoot you." Jerry held out empty hands. "See? I wanted you, I'd have shot you before you knew I was here."

"What are you doing here then?"

"This wasn't me." Jerry gestured to the mess. Even the mattress had been ripped to shreds, along with the fan quilt made from scraps of Brenna and Irene's dresses.

"I can guess what they were looking for," Liam said.

"Didn't find nothing, neither. I told 'em you didn't steal the money. You were running that night like all of us, only you were lucky not to get caught."

Liam knew this was no ordinary social call. "Why aren't you at the wake?"

"Why aren't *you?*"

"A man who sends thugs to destroy my house isn't a man who wants me to pay respects to his daughter."

"You're right about that. No matter what I say, Mr. McNulty thinks you got the money."

"And what makes him think so?"

"Because you weren't there to stop Miss Clare from running away the day she was killed. You were supposed to be at the house watching her. Why else would you take off and leave her alone unless you didn't need your job no more?"

For just a moment Liam was taken aback. McNulty believed he had abandoned Clare and that was the reason she had escaped to the Whiskey Island Saloon? "How does he know I wasn't there?"

"Because both you and Miss Clare were gone when Cassidy got to the house."

"He's spoken to Cassidy? The very man who murdered his daughter?"

"Cassidy sent him word, after, well, you know. Says when he got to the house that day he found a note from Clare to her father saying she was running away. Cassidy just tried to find her and stop her, that's all. She got in the way of a bullet meant for the new boyfriend."

The way that Jerry put it, Cassidy had been a man trying to right a wrong and stop a woman's impulsive act, a hero of sorts. Suddenly the murder was an accident, and the two men who were really at fault were Liam and Glen Donaghue—now known as the new boyfriend.

Obviously Cassidy hadn't wanted anyone to know that Clare had broken a vase over his head, nor that Liam himself had been there to thwart Cassidy's advances and help her escape. Liam wondered why the housekeeper hadn't reported the truth, as she'd undoubtedly heard it from the kitchen. He guessed that after he and Clare left the house, she had taken one peek at the prostrate Cassidy, gathered her things and fled the McNulty house for good.

Liam felt his way through an explanation. "So McNulty believes I found the money? He has a reason?"

"That captain, the Canadian guy, got word to him that he hid the money on Whiskey Island before they caught him."

"Even if that's true, why would he tell McNulty?"

"'Cause they're sending him home, and he'll never be able to come back here to get it."

That didn't surprise Liam. The captain thought it was better for McNulty to find the money than to have it disintegrate under a dead limb. Maybe McNulty had offered him a deal, or maybe the captain thought it was a small price to pay for his own safety. If McNulty got his money, revenge was one less thing the captain had to worry about.

"That still doesn't explain why he thinks *I* have it," Liam said.

"Couple of people saw you and the captain disappearing in the same direction. They think maybe you saw where he hid it."

"Maybe we left the same way, but I never saw the man again. You know how dark it was and how many paths lead out of there. I was worried about getting caught and nothing else."

"You know, this would be a good time to turn your pockets inside out, just to show me, okay?"

"Show you what?"

"That you're not carrying the money. We know it's not in the house."

"Jerry, if I had it, do you think I'd be carrying it around with me?"

"It's not here. You do this, then I can tell McNulty one more time that I don't think you took it."

"If I did find the money, it could be hidden anywhere."

"Just show me, okay?"

Liam was the one who had the drawn gun, but he suspected that Jerry was armed, even if he wasn't brandishing a weapon. He wanted to avoid a confrontation. The other man was as big as a bull and unlikely to be stopped by a single bullet. At least, not quickly enough.

Liam placed his own gun on the windowsill, then took out the socks, waved them for Jerry to see and placed them on the sill, too. He took out the handkerchief with its carefully wrapped treasure and unwrapped it. That, too, was placed on the windowsill.

Then, slowly, he turned his pockets inside out. A key fell to the floor, some coins, and nothing else. "Satisfied?"

"Take off your shoes, too, okay?"

Liam laughed. "You won't like the smell."

"Just do it for me."

Liam did, holding them out so that Jerry could see they were empty; then he pulled his shirt free of his trousers and shook them to show that nothing was hidden under his pants legs.

"Why did you stay around town after Clare was killed?" Jerry asked.

"A good question. First, if I found the money *before* Clare died, do you think I would have stayed around Cleveland? No, I stayed because I had a job here, and I thought McNulty would recover from his losses."

"And after?"

Liam told the story he'd fabricated in case McNulty caught up with him. "After Clare was killed, I knew McNulty would hold me responsible, but it takes time to make arrangements to leave town. I didn't have a lot of money sitting around. I had to sell a few things, figure out where to go, make sure my family was safe...."

"Maybe that makes sense, but you left Miss Clare alone. Where were you when you were supposed to be watching her?"

"Cassidy's a liar. When he arrived I *was* there, and so was she. He got rough with her, and I tried to stop him. He was out cold on the floor when we left the house."

"And you let her go running off to some other man?"

Liam prayed that Jerry had some trace of romance in his soul. "Yeah, I did, and I knew McNulty would never forgive me for it. I knew I had to get out of here."

"So you came back and moved your family."

"And I'm about to move myself. If you'll let me."

"You could go to McNulty, tell him the truth."

"What, that I helped his daughter escape the man McNulty had chosen for her? He's not going to believe Cassidy attacked Clare, because it doesn't suit him to believe it. You know how little regard he had for her. Maybe he's playing the grieving father tonight, but we both know the truth."

Jerry frowned. "Yeah, okay. You're dead here. I guess you're right."

"Would it serve any purpose to make sure I'm really dead?"

Jerry lifted one massive shoulder. "I remember that day at

Squeaky Frank's place. You got me out of there when you could've left me for the booze agents."

"I just want to start over someplace else, Jerry. That's all."

"I guess you don't have the money. I guess you can leave."

Liam felt the beginnings of relief.

"That Donaghue fellow won't be so lucky, though," Jerry said. "Mr. McNulty's gonna make sure he don't live too long."

"And what would be the point of that?"

"Weren't for him, Miss Clare would be engaged to Cassidy by now."

"Lucky Clare, huh?"

"You ever thought about who turned us in the night of the raid?"

"I assume the boats were spotted off shore, that's all."

"Those Canadians were good. The best until now. They'd never been caught. No, Mr. McNulty thinks Miss Clare got wind of the shipment somehow. She lived in his house, after all, and she had ears. She hears about it, tells the new boyfriend, Donaghue sets up the raid." Another heave of Jerry's shoulders. "Donaghue's gotta die. Weren't for him, Mr. McNulty wouldn't be in this trouble, would he? Miss Clare wouldn't be dead."

"I imagine Donaghue will take his chances. McNulty's not a man with much muscle these days."

"Maybe not, but he's got an ace in the hole. Miss Clare's grave. Donaghue really loved her, he'll go and visit her there. Mr. McNulty will have him picked off like a crow on a farmer's fence post."

"I doubt this Donaghue fellow's that stupid. He won't go to the funeral."

"Who said anything about the funeral?" Jerry smiled a little. "I'm going now. You be careful. Do what you gotta do tonight and get out of here. I won't say I seen you. But that's all I can do for you." He turned and squeezed back through the doorway.

"Jerry?"

"Yeah?"

"Thanks."

One more lumberjack heave and Jerry was gone.

Liam waited until he was sure he was alone before he returned Brenna's keepsakes to his pocket and topped them with the socks that held a bootlegger's treasure rolled up inside.

Had Glen been anyone else, Liam would silently have wished him well and forgotten about him. He would have gone for his family, told the old ladies where to find his car, traded car keys and driven to Toledo to catch a train west. As it was, he was fairly certain that Glen was too smart to visit Clare's grave. But grief did strange things to a man. Defenses were lowered. Impulses took control. When Glen turned his back on the rumrunners' money, he turned his back on his own stern ideals. Understandable, yes, but risky, too. And what else would he risk while the memory of Clare's death was so fresh?

Liam couldn't take a chance of someday learning that a simple message to stay away from the grave and watch his back might have saved his cousin's life.

Liam knew more about Glen than he rightfully should have. He knew where Glen lived, the Chinese restaurant where he sometimes ate dinner, his barber shop and favorite newsstand. He had kept an eye on his cousin, partly because of Glen's relationship with Clare, partly because Liam had wanted to be closer to his own flesh and blood. Now the details he'd learned served him well. He made the rounds of Glen's neighborhood, keeping to shadows, checking over his shoulder. Despite Jerry's assurances, Liam didn't trust his colleague completely. Jerry's first loyalty was always to McNulty.

He visited Glen's apartment, but Glen wasn't home. A note might have sufficed, but he had no paper, and even a clean shirt hadn't improved his appearance or aroma enough to borrow anything from Glen's neighbors. When an old woman across the hall opened her door and peered warily at him, he decided he'd better search elsewhere before she called the police.

He had checked St. Brigid's, but he checked again. Two

women in opposing pews were busy with rosaries, and at the front, near the altar, a man in overalls polished brass. The rectory and Father McSweeney were close at hand. He could leave a message with the old priest and know it would be delivered, but when he passed by the house, every light was off. If he knocked and made a fuss, he would draw too much attention to himself.

There was one more place to try. He headed for the Whiskey Island Saloon.

He was known there now. Not as family, but as the man who had tried to help Glen save Clare's life. Out of respect for her, the establishment had been closed since the night of her death, but tonight there were lights inside. As he had from the beginning of his search, he checked his surroundings carefully before he tried the door. It was locked, but from somewhere behind it a man called out that they were closed until the following week.

Liam went around the back to the kitchen, knocked again, and kept knocking until that door opened. Glen's father stood on the other side.

"You," Terry Donaghue said.

"May I come in?"

Donaghue stepped aside. "You're looking the worse for wear."

"I'm looking for your son. Have you seen him tonight?"

"He's not at the wake, that's for certain."

Liam had a feeling that Terry knew where Glen was but wasn't ready to tell him. "I have to see him." He considered how much to say. "I need to warn him."

"About what?"

Liam gnawed his bottom lip. Terry was his first cousin—although the older man would never know it. He wished the circumstances were different, that he could tell Terry everything and enlist his help. The need for family, good solid family, was an ache he had only just admitted to. Now family was an arm's length away, and what could he tell this man that would bring Terry anything except shame? Liam was a rebel, a murderer, a bootlegger. And Terry, so far removed from Ireland's troubles, wouldn't understand any of it.

"I'm not going to tell you where he is unless I know why," Terry prompted.

Liam knew his credibility was seeping away with every silent second. "I was waylaid by one of McNulty's men tonight," he said before credibility disappeared forever.

"You used to work for McNulty."

Liam figured Glen had told his father that much. "Used to. Now he's after me for helping Clare." He turned his palms up in supplication. "I need to find your son. He's in danger, too."

"From McNulty?"

"McNulty blames Glen for Clare's death. He's going to stake out the cemetery, keep a man there in hopes that Glen visits the grave."

"And you came here to tell him at your own risk?"

"He's not thinking so clearly, is he now?"

Terry's expression was answer enough. "I'll tell him what you said."

That should have been enough. Liam was free now to make his escape. Except that there was something in Terry's expression that concerned him. Terry believed him, but he believed even more in his son's good sense. He would get the message to Glen, but perhaps not until tomorrow. Terry was sure that Glen would not risk a visit to Clare's grave until days after the funeral, if at all.

"I'm not sure I made this clear enough," Liam said. "It's not just a matter of the cemetery. He's in danger anywhere he goes, at least for a while. For all I know, they're hunting for him right now."

"Glen's careful and smart."

"McNulty has no men to spare, but he's going to post someone at the cemetery. That's a clear indication he's serious."

"Glen was going to his grandmother's house."

"Then I'll—"

Terry held up his hand. "Then he was going to a friend's. That's probably where he is now."

Liam knew where Glen's grandmother lived. He had walked by the house once just to see it, a hopelessly maudlin gesture. "Tell me where to go, and I'll find him."

Terry frowned, clearly torn. "The two houses are on opposite sides of town."

Liam could feel the night slipping away. "Do they have telephones, then?"

"My mother does, yes, but she won't answer it after dark. She claims there's no news that can't wait until the morning, good or bad. And his friend doesn't have one at all."

"Then don't waste another minute. Tell me where to go. I've no car, but if I'm lucky, the streetcars will be running."

"No, I'll do it. I can drive. I'll try his friend first, since that's more likely, then my mother's."

"And if you don't find him?"

"Then I'll go by his apartment and leave a note to call me."

Liam had done what he could. "I'll be leaving, then. There's one thing, though, that you could do for me."

Terry cocked his head in question.

"Let me out through the tunnel where Clare died."

"Why's that?"

"Because if I was followed here, they'll most likely be watching the front door."

"Followed?"

"I've been careful. You be careful, too."

Terry crossed the kitchen and opened the door that led downstairs. "You can find your way?"

"I can."

"Don't turn on the lights, or you might be seen going out. There are candles by the door going down. Take one and blow it out as you leave."

"That's exactly what I'll do." Liam held out his hand once the door was open. "Don't take this lightly, Mr. Donaghue. McNulty's a desperate man, and sometimes all that's left to desperate men is revenge."

"Glen will be careful. It's in his nature."

Liam stared at him for a moment and saw what he most feared. Terry trusted his son to the point of blindness. Worse, he believed that goodness would prevail. He had already forgotten the lesson taught by Clare McNulty's death.

They shook hands, and Liam descended the stairs. The door closed as soon as his candle was lit.

Liam almost left for the East Side. There was still time to get Brenna and Irene and leave for Toledo. He had done what he could to protect Glen, and now it was time to protect himself.

Instead, he stood outside Lena Donaghue's house and wondered why he had put Glen's safety first once again. Was it fear that Terry's faith in his son would dilute the warning? Or was it one last opportunity to see his cousin face-to-face? He'd been sure he had escaped the Irish curse of sentimentality, but he was afraid now that he'd fallen prey at last. Glen was probably across town, yet here Liam stood, gazing up at Lena Donaghue's house, the house of the aunt he had never known.

The house was larger than he'd expected, but still small for a growing family. He could picture the Donaghue children spilling out to the wide front porch on summer mornings, wrestling on the grass, rolling hoops down the tree-lined street. He wondered what it might have been like to grow up here. He had seen the outcome of this life in the expression on Terry Donaghue's face when he talked of his son. Love, respect, faith. Elements missing in his own childhood and Brenna's, but present in Irene's, he hoped.

A lamp shone on a hallway table, and somewhere in the back of the house another was lit. He debated how best to make his presence known. He didn't want to frighten Lena Donaghue, but neither did he want to wait and watch the house in hopes Glen might appear. He had seen a dog behind the neighbor's fence, and he knew that if he tried to reach the back door to peer inside, the canine alarm would sound throughout the neighborhood.

He climbed the porch steps and rapped softly on the door. After a moment he heard footsteps and the door opened. Glen stood on the threshold. "What are you doing here?" He kept his voice low.

"Looking for you."

Glen's gaze flicked past Liam to the street beyond. "What for?"

"May I come in?"

"My grandmother's not feeling well. She's still upset about Clare. She just got to sleep, and I don't want to disturb her."

Liam wished they could go indoors, where it was safer. There were a hundred things Liam wanted to say to him. How sorry he was about Clare, who had deserved all the good things life could offer. How glad he was to know that he'd come from good people after all, even if the ones who had raised him had been less than perfect.

He said none of them. He had no words, no opportunity, and no desire to see Glen's expression when he learned that Liam was his cousin. He shoved his hands in his pockets, hunching his shoulders. He spoke quickly.

"McNulty's after you. He thinks the raid was your fault, that you found out about the delivery from Clare herself. Between that and you trying to run away with her, he's gunning for you. Don't go to the cemetery. He'll have someone watching Clare's grave from now on. Stay alert and watch your back, at least until Moran and his boys take care of him once and for all. Then you'll be safe."

"I thought after this morning you'd be leaving town."

"I couldn't leave without warning you."

"Why? You don't owe me anything."

"There's been enough violence, hasn't there? I didn't like thinking there might be more once I was gone."

"Okay." Glen paused; then he held out his hand. "Thanks." Liam took it, and they shook. "You'll be careful?"

"I don't want to bring my grandmother more heartache."

Liam dropped Glen's hand; then he turned and hurried down the steps.

"Liam?"

He turned. "Yeah?"

"You need a ride?"

Liam hesitated. A ride would make escape tonight possible. If he went by car, he could be with Bronna and Irene in less than an hour, then on the road to Toledo.

Glen must have seen how tempted he was. "I'll get my keys." He closed the door behind him before Liam could object.

Liam looked up and down the street, but nothing seemed out of the ordinary. He had been careful since leaving his house, and so far his luck had held. Glen knew how to be careful, too. Surely a drive wouldn't put either of them in more danger.

Nevertheless, he melted into the shadow of the house, disappearing against the trunk of an ancient oak. Above his head, a treehouse nestled between branches. He pictured Irene playing there with her cousins.

He forced himself to concentrate on other things, on the car that drove past before unloading several girls in front of a neighbor's house. On the dog at the street's end who began a mournful howl until a porch light came on and an angry masculine voice commanded it to be silent.

He listened for footsteps, for car engines, for lowered voices. He heard nothing else except his own heartbeat and finally the creak of Lena Donaghue's front door. As he watched, Glen paused in the doorway, examining the street, listening, stepping forward and starting all over again. Clearly he had taken Liam's warning seriously.

Glen glanced at Liam, who was still flattened against the tree and nodded toward the street. He started for a blue Ford that was parked in front of a neighbor's house, and Liam trailed behind. Halfway there, he heard the screeching of tires and the gunning of an engine as a car pulled out of a parking space down the street and roared toward them. He knew that despite great care, he had led McNulty's men straight to Glen, the thing he had most feared.

He was still half hidden by a hedge, but Glen was out in the open. Liam drew his gun, but from his protected position there were no good shots. In the split second when a choice was still left, he thought of Irene and Brenna, who deserved so much more than they had gotten.

He raced out into the open, planting himself between Glen and the approaching car, and fired in the driver's direction. For a moment he was blinded by headlights. He heard Glen shouting, then the blast of shotguns. He spun under the impact and saw Glen dive for cover behind the door of his car.

Liam died without knowing that his body had blocked the worst of the bullets and saved his cousin's life.

chapter 36

No one had added turf to the fire. No one had fixed tea. The sisters listened carefully and questioned Irene when details were hazy, but they didn't interrupt beyond that. Now the only sound in the room was the snoring of one old dog who'd crept in earlier in the evening, withstood eviction and now slept contentedly at Irene's feet.

"I've auditioned a dozen responses," Peggy said at last. "But I still haven't come up with one that does the trick. I guess 'I'm sorry' says it best."

Megan's own reaction was similar. "If your father hadn't protected him, our grandfather would have died that night, and we wouldn't be here."

"I'm *glad* you're here," Irene said. "There's no reason to be sorry you're alive. My da made his choice, didn't he? He didn't want to die. I'm certain he hoped he wouldn't. But he stood up for a man he admired, perhaps even loved. That's not a bad way to leave this world. So many people leave it without ever having done one unselfish thing."

Casey's eyelids were drooping as jet lag deepened its hold. "Irene, how do you know so much? Your father didn't live to tell this story. Who did?"

"Glen Donaghue tracked down my mother after my father died. He was in the hospital himself for a day, injured in the shootout, although not critically, but when they released him, he went looking for Mam and me. By then she had claimed my father's body and wasn't hard to find. He told her what my father had done, and he helped her bury him."

Megan had to know. "Did our grandfather ever—"

"Ever know that Liam was his cousin?" Irene shook her head. "My mother didn't tell him. She thought that was the way my father would have wanted it."

"And she brought you back to Ireland? Here to this cottage?"

"Mam didn't want to stay in the town where Da had died. There was little enough waiting for her here, but it seemed better than remaining in America. Life was difficult, but in Mayo she was among people who understood her. And there were people here who remembered that my father had fought for Ireland's freedom, and they were willing to help her with whatever they could. She got by, and eventually she married a man who was both good and wealthy, at least by the standards of the day. Her later years were happy."

"Got by..." Megan waited, but Irene didn't take the bait. "What about the money?" she asked directly. "The rumrunners' money? You said that Liam had it rolled in a sock. Did the police find it on your father's body and figure out where it had come from? Is that why they didn't give it to her? Or did the bootleggers get it back?"

"I can answer that, I think," Casey said. "At least part of it. McNulty never got his money back, did he, Irene? Because he disappeared one night a month or so after the Whiskey Island raid, and nobody ever heard from him again. Jon did some research and told me that much. At first the police thought Tim had taken off for parts unknown, but that fall a fisherman found an expensive man's shoe, of the type McNulty had specially imported from New York, not far from the lakeshore, and they discovered a bloodstained shirt they were almost certain had belonged to him, as well. His tailor swore to it."

"And if he'd found the money, he would have paid off the gang in Chicago," Megan said. "It's unlikely they'd have killed him."

Peggy spoke for all of them. "It sounds like he got what he deserved."

"Cassidy got his, as well," Casey said. "You've heard of the St. Valentine's Day Massacre?"

"You're kidding." Megan poked her sister in the shoulder. "Cassidy?"

"One of the casualties. Gone and forgotten."

"Back to the money," Megan said. "Irene, do you know what happened to it? It's the final piece of the puzzle, isn't it?"

"Well, they didn't find it on my father's body," Irene said. "I can assure you of that."

"Then you don't know what happened to it?"

"I didn't say that." Irene seemed to be enjoying herself, now that recounting her father's death was behind her. She didn't look tired, although she should have been, after such an emotionally wrenching tale. But the story was new to *them*, not to her. She had said goodbye to Liam Tierney many years before.

"My mother spoke by telephone to my father just an hour before he died," Irene said. "He told her he'd hidden the money, and he told her where, in case something happened to him. She didn't want to hear that, of course, but he made her listen."

"He hid it?" Casey asked.

"He was afraid he might be caught if he went looking for Glen, no matter how careful he was. So he hid the money, then went to find him. I'm sure his intention was to go back and get the money once he'd delivered his message, that he would have asked Glen to make that detour on the way to get us. But he'd learned to exercise caution in the IRA. And it served him well, I'm afraid."

"He told your mother where he'd hidden it?" Megan was beginning to think her job in this conversation was to make everyone else focus. "Did she *find* it?"

"She never even looked." Irene was nodding as if she understood her mother's decision perfectly. "It was blood money, don't you see? In her mind, my father died because of it. No matter how badly we needed money, she wouldn't have any part of it. So we sailed for Ireland as poor as we'd arrived on Cleveland's shores and as soon as she could buy the tickets."

"And she never told anyone." Megan paused. "Except you, of course."

"Oh, she did try to tell someone, as far as that goes." Irene took a deep breath, purely for effect, Megan thought. She was a pro when it came to heightening suspense.

"She tried to tell your grandfather," Irene finished.

The sisters sat in silence, waiting.

"On the day they buried my father, my mother took your grandfather aside and told him that the money was his. She offered to tell him where to find it."

"And he turned her down," Megan said, as certain of that as she was that Irene was finally about to end her story once and for all.

"So that McNulty would look guilty," Casey took up the story. "And in the end, that was probably his death sentence. That was why Grandfather let Liam keep the money in the first place."

"It must have been a real moral dilemma." Megan tried to imagine it. "He was a straight arrow, but he was also a man who'd seen his bride gunned down. So he acted against McNulty by not acting. I can understand it."

"Grandfather went on to serve under Eliot Ness after Prohibition," Casey told Irene. "He had a long and distinguished career in law enforcement. And I remember Aunt Dee telling us that the day liquor was legal again, he was the first one at the saloon waiting for his drink."

"And that would be the whole story," Irene said. "Told to me on my mother's deathbed. She wanted me to know my father was more than a bootlegger and an IRA gunman. Your grandfather and my father, good people gone, and those left behind picking up the pieces of their lives. My mother found happiness, your grandfather married, and now you're here because of it."

"Grandfather had a good marriage, too," Casey said. "I've been told Grandmother and Grandfather were very much in love."

"Irene, did you instigate this reunion because you want us to look for the money for you?" Peggy asked. "Was that your purpose at the beginning? Do you need it?"

"Do I look like I need it, dear? I have everything I've ever wanted. And now I have you, all of you, the family I've always hoped for."

"Then you've told us just because it's part of our history?"

"I know you're good women, and I know you'll never tell anyone about my father's part in the theft, although it was so long ago, I suppose it doesn't really matter anymore, does it?"

Megan looked straight at Irene. "But that's not the *whole* story, is it, Irene? You've left out something, haven't you?"

"And what would that be?"

"The whereabouts of the money."

Irene's eyes twinkled. "Oh, I've told you where it is. Didn't you listen closely enough? I've told you because I want you to have it, you know. You're good women, and you'll do good things with it. And that's what I hoped for."

"I'd rather hear the location directly from your lips." Megan leaned forward and spaced her words. "Exactly where did your father hide the money?"

"Now, do you think I've left out something? I've told you where he was just before he was killed." Irene paused for effect one final time; then she smiled. "The truth is as plain as brown bread, dear, as plain as cabbage and mashed potatoes. Da hid it in the next to the last place he went to look for your grandfather. The money is hidden at the Whiskey Island Saloon."

chapter 37

Megan and Casey hadn't been gone for an hour on Tuesday morning before Peggy began to miss them.

On their final afternoon together, and after some telephone sleuthing, the sisters had driven to a small parish cemetery near Castlebar to visit the grave of Maura McSweeney. They'd gazed at the grave with its plain chiseled headstone, each silently thanking the woman whose letters had helped them piece to-gether the puzzle of their pasts. Then they had laid a bouquet of daisies there and gone off to lunch for one final conversation.

This morning, Peggy had been tempted to go back to Cleve-land on their flight. The list of her failures in Ireland was al-ready too long. She knew she had accomplished so little with Kieran that there was almost no point in continuing the pro-gram she had so carefully set up. Now she questioned every decision she had made for him.

She questioned, too, her relationship with Finn. What had possessed her to become involved with a man who was so immersed in his past that there was no possibility of a future to-gether? She hadn't set out to fall in love with Finn O'Malley. She had struggled against it, knowing that he was not ready to love again and might never be. But her struggles had drawn the emotions that bound them tighter and tighter.

Perhaps she'd seen qualities in Finn that weren't really there. Perhaps the healer inside her had been drawn to his wounded soul. Whatever she had fallen prey to, on the evening he refused to help Kieran, she had been struck by a greater truth. Finn cared less for her and for Kieran than he did for his own guilt and shame. She should be glad she had finally seen the truth.

She wasn't glad at all.

She remained in Ireland, of course, despite the temptation to go home. She had agreed to be Irene's companion for a year, and Irene had taken such care in the arrangements, never complaining about Kieran's behavior, his crying or tantrums. Peggy owed her too much to leave.

In the short run, there had been no chance of leaving with her sisters anyway. Kieran was still sick and in no condition to fly. He had been listless since his trip to see the doctor in Westport, with a low-grade fever and loss of appetite. And sound sleep, which had once been his salvation, eluded him.

"He's not feeling better yet, is he?" Irene, leaning on a cane, stood in the doorway as Peggy rocked her son, who had awakened moments ago from his morning nap.

"Whatever it is, he just can't seem to shake it completely."

"He's so pliable when he's sick. Almost snuggly."

Peggy was not glad her son was ill, but she was taking ad-vantage of this very rare opportunity to hold him close and com-fort him. In fact, the only silver lining to his illness was the way he seemed content at last to be part of the general human race.

"I'd take him back to the doctor if I thought it would do any good," Peggy said.

"You might give him a call and tell him Kieran's no better."

Peggy had tried that already, but her call had been inter-cepted by a snippy nurse who relayed the doctor's opinion that the virus simply hadn't run its course. Peggy hadn't told Irene about the call, but now her expression did.

"You could speak to Finn again," Irene said.

"Finn made his decision perfectly clear. I'm not sure he'd treat Kieran if the poor kid was convulsing at his feet."

"You sound bitter."

Peggy hadn't meant to. Irene and Finn had been friends long before Peggy entered the picture. "I'm sorry, I know he's been good to you. It's just such a shame that he refuses to help anyone else."

"Even you."

"Especially me." Peggy looked up from smoothing Kieran's hair away from his hot little forehead. "I shouldn't be surprised. He's never lied about the way he feels. I guess I just thought we were special enough that he would make an exception."

"You're very special to him. I'm sure of it."

"But not special enough for him to take a risk with his heart."

"He's a complex soul, our Finn."

"Not *our* Finn, I'm afraid."

Irene looked sad. "I'd hoped for something better between you than resentment."

"It's not something you should be worrying about, Irene. There are some things that even the kindest, most well-intentioned soul can't change. I know you sent Finn to pick me up at the airport hoping that the long trip here would be the beginning of a romance."

"How can you believe such a thing of me?"

Irene's words lacked conviction. Peggy tried to smile. "Because it's true. And who knows, maybe if things had been different, if he had been able to put his past behind him, you might have ignited a bonfire. As it is, whatever flickered between us?" She shrugged, hesitant to put it into words.

"Extinguished?" Irene asked.

Peggy shrugged again.

"I think perhaps he's not as easy to put behind you as you're pretending."

"It's not easy at all." Peggy looked down at Kieran, and her eyes filled with tears. "But it's necessary."

She arranged to be elsewhere when Finn came to see Irene that evening. She had avoided his early morning visit, too, pretending she was too caught up helping her sisters pack to peek out and say hello. This time, though, she left the house, strolling with Kieran along the path overlooking the beach. He was still feverish, despite a recent dose of the third fever reducer she had tried. She hoped the ocean breeze would cool him a little. He didn't fuss or try to climb out of the stroller. He leaned forward, propping himself on his arms, and sat perfectly still in that position, an inert lump of humanity who seemed to be giving up on the world around him.

By the time they returned, Finn had come and gone again. She fixed Kieran applesauce and cereal, which he refused, and warmed up Irene's dinner, which she picked at without much success. Peggy ate a little, then prepared another cool bath for her son, hoping it would bring his temperature down far enough that he could finally sleep comfortably.

By the time she put him to bed his temperature was only a bit above normal and she had coaxed him to drink some juice. He went without protest, closing his eyes from exhaustion before she covered him with a light blanket. He coughed, babbled something in a hoarse voice, then, as she stood beside his bed, fell into a restless sleep.

She played cards with Irene for a little while, one ear tuned for sounds from her bedroom. Irene tired quickly, and Peggy helped her get ready for bed.

Irene apologized. "Too many late nights with your sisters. I'm afraid I'm done in."

"You sleep well tonight, and stay in bed in the morning. The house won't rock on its foundations."

"It was such fun having them here, like a houseful of daughters."

"I was afraid it was a bit much for you."

"It did me a world of good. I've wanted you, all of you, to know about my father for a very long time."

Peggy, in the midst of hanging up Irene's housedress, turned. "Then you knew about us? Before you contacted us, I mean? *Well* before?"

"I knew from some digging long ago that your grandfather married and had two children late in his life. I've known about you and your sisters for..." She paused, as if counting. "Six years. You see, I hired a man in the U.S. to find out what he could. A private investigator."

"And you didn't get in touch with us then?"

"I wasn't sure what to do. I didn't want you to feel burdened by the presence of an old woman you didn't know. I thought I might just put the story in a letter to be delivered at my death. Eventually I realized you might feel as cheated by that as I did. So once I had a computer, I decided to contact you."

Peggy took her hands. "I'm so glad you did. We all are, Irene. And you know it has nothing to do with the money. Who knows if Megan will ever find it?"

"I have great confidence in your sister. Once she sets her mind to something, she comes through. Isn't that so?"

Peggy had to admit it was true. "Don't forget, though, they've torn the saloon from stem to stern in this latest renovation, and if anyone found anything of value, we certainly didn't hear about it."

"My mother knew exactly where in the saloon my father hid that money, but she didn't tell me the location, of course. She wanted no part of it and wanted me to have no part of it, either. She only wanted me to know that he was a good man with a good heart, and that she didn't profit from his mistakes in judgment. She was fond of simple lessons, a good mother until the moment of her death."

Peggy fluffed Irene's pillows and helped her swing her legs under the duvet. "Sleep well. You've given the Donaghue sisters a new mystery to solve. We'll enjoy every minute."

Irene wished her good-night and closed her eyes.

In the living room again, Peggy wandered aimlessly,

straightening sofa pillows and newspapers, sweeping Banjax's fur off the hearth. She wasn't ready to go to sleep. There was too much to think about.

The telephone rang, and she dove for it, afraid it might bother Irene. The voice on the other end was familiarly deep.

"Peggy?"

She lowered herself to the chair beside the desk. "Hello, Finn."

"You sound out of breath."

"Irene just went to bed. I didn't want the phone to wake her."

"It's a bit early for sleep. Is she all right?"

"Just tired from so many visitors."

"How's Kieran?"

She was almost surprised he had asked. Certainly it opened up a topic he would not want to discuss. "No better." Her tone was uncontrollably curt. "Thanks to the Irish medical establishment."

"I see. You don't have overworked, impatient doctors in the U.S.?"

"Of course we do. But in the U.S. I also have friends who would gladly have looked at my son in an emergency and helped me get him the best treatment."

There was a long silence. Peggy wondered if it was time to hang up. Then Finn spoke.

"I'm not the best person for that, Peggy."

"I know you *think* so, yes. That's not the same thing at all. And I'm afraid I've figured out something else. Kieran and I don't matter to you, Finn. If we did, you would have helped us. I deserve a man who can be a real partner and a father to my son. For some reason it's taken me this long to realize it, but I'm not selling myself short anymore."

"Well, that's concise."

"Be glad it's concise. Don't ask for the unabridged version. You wouldn't like it nearly as well."

"The part about me being a selfish bastard?"

Anger shot through her, anger she had tried to control. Her voice choked with tears. "No, the part about you being afraid to live again. The part that says you believe you're God Almighty and that you and *only* you held the lives and destiny of your family in your hands that day. The part that thinks every decision you make is so important that the world stops on its axis whenever you falter!"

"I'm hanging up now."

"You should have hung up sooner." Peggy slammed the receiver back on the cradle and dropped her head in her hands.

She heard a noise, but she didn't look up. She knew who it was, and that her own voice had awakened her. She felt Irene's hand on her shoulder. "Go ahead and cry it out, dear," Irene said.

"I'm in love with him. That's why this hurts so much." Peggy was as astounded as she was sorry. The love she felt for her family was effortless. The love she felt for Kieran had rushed forth at the instant of his birth as if it had grown with him in her womb. As difficult and heartbreaking as his autism could be, it had only made her love her son more.

But this...this was something different, something that defied all logic or attempts to eradicate it. She had not considered a life with Finn. Now, considering one without him was agonizing.

"I have to get out now," she said through her tears. "Before I'm in too deep to try."

"He's everything you want him to be and more. How could you not fall in love with him? You saw the real man, not the shell."

"He has everything invested in not being that man anymore."

"And you're young and impatient."

"I'm young and logical. And I know when I'm up against something I can't change. He treats you, Irene, because he loves you too much not to. But not treating Kieran—"

"That's because Kieran reminds him of his sons, Peggy. Can't you see that? I'm an old woman, and I'm dying. Even Finn knows that no matter how much magic he pulls out of his black bag, he can't manage eternal life. He can live with those odds now, can't he, knowing that his job is only to make my ending comfortable, perhaps to stave it off a bit? But your son has a long life ahead, just as his own sons did. And he can't help but make that connection."

"He has to help it!" Peggy wiped her eyes on the hem of her T-shirt. "You can't love if you can't act. Love *is* action, not words or thoughts. And it's a lot bigger than some sexual impulse that comes and goes at the sight of a young woman's breasts or lips. It's intentional and definite, and the way you show it is by acting for the good of each other and for the relationship."

"You've given this some thought, I see."

"No, I've been trying *not* to think about it. I think I knew if I *did* think about it, everything would be finished between us. Then this hit me smack between the eyes and I couldn't *not* think about it anymore."

"You're worried about Kieran, too, that's part of it."

"Of course." Peggy reached for a tissue on the other end of the desk. "If he's not better when he wakes up tomorrow morning, I'm going to take him into the emergency room in Castlebar. I'll sit there all day if I have to, but somebody has to treat my son."

"A very good plan. We'll have Nora drive you. She won't—"

A wail interrupted Irene. Peggy jumped to her feet. "There he is. I woke him."

"No, you weren't that loud, dear."

Peggy was already halfway across the room. She was afraid that Irene was right. Kieran's wail did not sound like that of an annoyed child awakened from a sound sleep. It was a thin wail, and it spurted unevenly, as if he was struggling for breath.

She found him sitting up and forward, leaning on his hands. She lifted him from his crib and was shocked at how hot he was. She didn't need a thermometer to know that his temperature had risen again, this time to a dangerous level. And he was drooling, as if swallowing was too painful to attempt. "Kieran?"

He stared at her as he so often had, as if he wasn't certain who this demanding woman was. But this was not autism looking back at her. Kieran's gaze was fixed and his breathing so shallow that for one terrible moment, she wasn't certain he was breathing at all.

She had made a terrible mistake. She had not followed her own good instincts and taken her son elsewhere for a second opinion. She'd allowed herself to be bullied by a nurse she had never seen and a physician so overwhelmed that he had taken every shortcut when examining her son. Kieran's life was at risk now because of it.

Irene came to the doorway. "How is he?"

"Irene, call Nora. Please. I have to get him to Castlebar this instant. There's no time to wait."

"Mother Mary..." She clumped away, but by then Peggy was frantically reviewing what she could do to aid her son until Nora arrived. His breathing was labored, but he wasn't coughing. It might be pneumonia. She also knew something about croup, about the sudden onset after a drawn-out illness, about the struggle to breathe. It was common enough, and usually responded to—

"Steam..." She wrapped him in a thin blanket and ran toward the bathroom, closing the door behind her. Then she turned on the tap, tearfully grateful when hot water poured forth. Without a heater that kept water at a constant temperature, hot water at this hour was never guaranteed.

She turned on the shower and stepped inside the tub, pulling the curtain around them and aiming the showerhead directly into the drain so they wouldn't be splashed. It seemed like forever before steam began to fill the enclosure. She turned her son away from her shoulder and toward the showerhead, praying that the steam would ease his breathing. Kieran was too sick to struggle.

Minutes passed, and as she'd known it would, the steam began to wane as the last of the day's hot water drained away. She turned off the tap but continued to stand there, hoping the remaining wisps would help.

"Peggy..."

"Come in." Peggy heard a door open and close.

"Any better?"

Kieran was still sucking in air as if it was coming to him through a narrow reed. "No. Did you get Nora?"

"Finn's coming."

For a moment Peggy thought she hadn't heard her right. "I asked you to call Nora."

"But Nora's not a doctor, is she? Finn will take you to the hospital. He's on his way."

Peggy could imagine that conversation, but she didn't care. Whatever Irene had said to Finn had done the trick. He was coming, although she was sure this was the last place he wanted to be. And Finn would drive faster than Nora, who nourished a distrust of anything with an engine.

Peggy stepped out of the tub. Kieran's hair lay in wet curls against his scalp, and his cheeks were bright from steam and fever. Each labored breath was audible, and his little heart beat frantically against his mother's chest.

"They might admit him," Peggy said. "I've got to get a bag together."

"Tell me what to pack."

"A change of clothing for the trip home." Peggy hoped there would be such a thing. She was nearly frantic with worry.

"And clothes for you, as well. A toothbrush..." Irene hurried away, moving faster than Peggy had ever seen her.

Peggy followed when the last of the steam was gone, finding her purse and tucking it under her arm, lifting an extra blanket to stuff into the diaper bag, a picture book Kieran had shown a little interest in yesterday. Just yesterday her son had sat on her lap, letting her turn the pages and point to the figures on each page. As sick as he'd felt, he had tried to croak out dog. She had been sure of it.

Her eyes filled with tears, and she clutched him tighter.

The front door closed with authority. She heard footsteps coming toward her room and Finn appeared.

"Let me look at him."

She was not so foolish as to refuse. She lowered herself to her bed with Kieran on her lap, and Finn stooped in front of them. She saw that he'd brought his medical bag and already taken out his stethoscope to warm against his palm. He asked her to take off Kieran's pajama shirt, then sat and watched the little boy breathe. "How long has he been struggling like this?" he asked after what seemed like forever.

"Just since he woke up."

"Tell me what else you've noticed. Fever, appetite, abdominal distress?"

She told him everything she had observed, then detailed her phone call to Beck's office.

He spoke softly to the unresponsive little boy as he placed the stethoscope against his chest and listened. Not satisfied, he placed a hand against Kieran's chest and pushed gently at the end of several breaths. Kieran jerked once, but didn't move away, absolute proof he was very ill.

Peggy held her breath and sat still as Finn listened. He sat back on his heels and pulled out the earpieces. "No crackles, but he's having trouble getting air."

"Aren't you going to check his throat?" She started to tilt his head back so that Finn could look inside.

"Absolutely do not do that."

She dropped her hand, surprised at his tone. "Why not?"

"Has he been immunized for Hemophilus influenza? Type B?"

"He got the first shot, but he had a pretty severe reaction, and I decided not to continue. My doctor was ambivalent, but I thought he was probably allergic to something in the vaccine. I—"

"Peggy, listen to me." He spoke calmly and smiled gently at Kieran. "The most important thing right now is not to upset Kieran. Do you understand? We're going to move slowly, and you're going to be very reassuring with him. We don't want to do anything to make it harder to breathe. If he's upset, it could cause laryngospasms."

"What's wrong with him?"

He glanced at her. "I'm not sure, but probably epiglottitis. We have to get him to the hospital stat."

She'd only had one year of med school, but she knew that epiglottitis had nearly been wiped out by the Hemophilus influenza vaccine. The same vaccine she had chosen not to continue with. "Then this is *my* fault."

"Don't think about that now. More important is that you realized this was something more than a cold and set out to do something about it."

It was not the time for recriminations, but she was devastated. How much better to have been wrong, to have Finn tell her that this was only a nuisance virus, that her son's lungs were clear and once the fever broke he would be on the road to recovery.

"Peggy, can you manage him? He's better off with you. He trusts you." Finn grabbed the diaper bag off the floor and took the other bag that Irene handed him.

"Yes." She pulled her son's shirt back over his head, then got carefully to her feet and started after him, holding Kieran gently against her.

"I called Nora," Finn said. "She's coming to stay with you." He addressed this to Irene as he headed for the door ahead of Peggy.

"You'll call? The moment you know something?"

"We'll call. Beck's going to meet us there."

Peggy knew better than to upset Kieran further. She kept her voice low. "I don't want him anywhere near my son."

"He's a good doctor, Peggy, and for that matter, he was probably right. This may well have started as a virus that's unrelated to the epiglottitis. Unfortunately, he should have listened to you when you called back today."

She was too angry and too worried to reply.

He had the car door open and the engine running by the time she and Kieran got there. She slid in and waited while he reached across her to fasten her seat belt. "He doesn't sound good," Finn said. "I don't want to lie to you. I'd call EMS if I thought they would get here quickly enough, but out here in the country, sometimes the wait's too long. At this point our worry is additional respiratory distress. Your job is to keep him breathing while I drive. As long as he's conscious, he'll be all right. But if he passes out, we have to worry about his airway. Help him sit forward with his chin extended." He demonstrated. "Like this."

She nodded, and Finn pulled the car into the lane leading to the main road. She listened as Kieran struggled to breathe. He began to flail weakly, fighting the lethargy of fever and the panic of not getting sufficient air. She spoke soothingly but knew better than to try to comfort him by smoothing his hair as most mothers would have. Kieran's world was so different and mysterious, and the fact that he was allowing her to hold him at all was miracle enough.

They were out on the main road, close to Shanmullin, when he flailed once, twice, then jerked and fell forward. Panicked, she listened for breath sounds.

"Finn, I don't think he's breathing."

He didn't question her. "Push him farther forward and extend his chin gently."

She jostled him a little as she did, but she still couldn't hear the gasps that had characterized each breath. "He's not breathing! And he's unconscious. Oh God."

Finn didn't stop. He pressed down on the accelerator and sped toward the village. "Just hold on," he said. "Hold on."

"But he won't make it to the hospital."

"No." He drove even faster and made a turn onto a side street. She knew then where they were going. Finn's office.

The moment he could get his keys out of the ignition, he was out and running for her door. It flew open, and he helped her out; then he left her to make the short journey with the unconscious Kieran and ran ahead to unlock the door and turn on the lights.

"In here."

She saw him in the doorway of an examining room off the reception area. The office was spotless. He might have abandoned it, but she knew in that moment that despite everything he'd told himself, he had never abandoned hope that one day he would come back.

"Put him on the table, face up." Finn was rummaging through boxes.

"What are you going to do?"

"We have to establish an airway, and we have to do it now. We can't wait for Castlebar."

She laid Kieran on the table. He was no longer flushed with fever. She recognized cyanosis. Her son was turning blue.

She had worked in an emergency room during college, and the doctors had taken her under their respective wings, explaining, demonstrating. And she had been a med student for one incredible year.

Her son was going to die.

"He's going to go into cardiac arrest!" She bent over Kieran, slapping his cheeks and calling his name.

"Not if I can help it." He pushed her aside and stood over Kieran. She recognized the oropharyngeal airway in his hand, but she'd never seen one so small. "I've done this before, Peggy. We practice emergency medicine out in the country, more than we'd like. We'll get an airway, then oxygen."

"You have oxygen?"

"We'll bag him." Finn was tight-lipped, concentrating. "Use the phone in the front and call EMS. The number's on the wall above the phone. Call now."

She was torn. Finn had turned Kieran to his side and was beginning to work the plastic tubing into his mouth.

He didn't look up. "Go, Peggy."

She ran into reception, and found the telephone and the number where Finn had said they would be. Once someone answered, she explained what she could. The man on the other end told her someone would be at Finn's office as soon as possible.

"They're coming." She stopped short of the table. Finn was removing the tube. "What's happening? Why are you—"

"The epiglottis is too swollen. There's no way around that obstruction. We're going to have to do a tracheostomy."

"Here?" She knew that a tracheostomy, which involved making an incision in the throat and inserting an endotracheal tube, was not a simple matter. She had seen it done more than once. Each time an anaesthesiologist had performed the surgery, and an endoscopist had been on call in case of difficulties. The procedure had been done under sterile conditions, with anaesthesia.

"We have no choice, Peggy. Give me your permission."

She was sobbing now. *She* had done this to her son. She had not continued the vaccinations, and, more recently, she had not followed her own instincts and insisted that someone see Kieran again. If Kieran died, she would be responsible.

"Say yes," Finn demanded. "Damn it, Peggy, this is not the time to falter. Say yes!"

"It's different with children. I remember that. You've done this with a child?"

"Yes, Peggy. Just say yes."

A child's physiology was different. A child's needs were different. How could he possibly have the right equipment here?

Somehow, though, he did. She saw him pick up Kieran's hand and measure her son's pinky against several tubes he had already placed beside him.

She didn't know what to say or do. She was faint with anxiety. "Yes," she croaked. "Go ahead." It seemed like the wrong choice, but it was the only choice Kieran had. Without oxygen, his heart would fail. Her son would die right here.

He made the incision with lightning speed, and in what seemed like a moment he was threading the tube between her son's vocal cords. "Got it," he said. "In the top drawer over there you should find tape. Bring it now."

She couldn't move. She was so frightened that her body had shut down.

"Peggy!"

She put one foot in front of the other, sobbing again. She found the tape and brought it to him. He was holding the corner of Kieran's mouth and the tube together. She tore off pieces and he taped it quickly so that the tube was stable and could not be moved, then he stepped one pace back, examining Kieran's chest. "He's breathing. But we'll bag him for the trip."

The Parting Glass   475

"He's breathing?"

"Now that he can, yes."

She leaned over and saw that Finn was correct. Kieran's skin was still tinged with blue, but even during the moments that she watched, his color seemed to improve.

She stifled another sob. "What will they do at the hospital?"

"We'll run an IV and start a drip in the ambulance. We'll do blood work in hospital, X rays. We'll probably ventilate him temporarily, definitely start antibiotics. Most likely the edema will resolve itself in the next forty-eight hours. If it's Hemophilus, we might do a lumbar puncture to be sure there's no meningitis."

"Meningitis?"

"It's the same organism."

The front door opened, and two men arrived. "Lucky for you," the first man said, "we were just on our way back from another call."

"And lucky for the boy that the doctor didn't wait," said the other, grimacing with sympathy at the limp little body. "Good job, there. That's more than we could have done for him."

While one man draped a blanket around Peggy's trembling shoulders, Finn had a terse conversation with them. Then, with Finn carefully carrying the still unconscious Kieran, they started toward the ambulance.

chapter 38

The sight of her tiny son on a ventilator in intensive care should have been the saddest sight of Peggy's life. But a far sadder sight would have been her child at his wake. She had come so close to that, within minutes or even less, perhaps.

If Finn had not acted decisively, she knew that Kieran would have died of respiratory failure because of decisions that *she* had made.

"A closer call and he'd be with the angels," said the nurse who was monitoring Kieran's vital signs. "And what have you done in this life, Miss Donaghue, to entitle you to a miracle?"

Peggy tried to smile. Alice, the nurse, a matronly woman with a steel wool perm and startlingly bushy eyebrows, had tried for the past half hour to help her put Kieran's condition in perspective. She needn't have bothered. Peggy knew a miracle when she saw one, and she was not unacquainted with Irish angels. She had witnessed one in action little more than an hour ago.

She reached for another tissue. "Finn saved his life."

"It's good to have the doctor back, you know. Dr. O'Malley was a favorite. Never impulsive or condescending, and his decisions were never questioned by the staff. As they say in your country, you've the luck of the Irish to have him at your side."

"Kieran still looks so sick." But even Peggy, with a mother's natural fear and doubt, could see that Kieran was improving. He was getting oxygen, fluids and antibiotics. He had been sedated enough to keep him comfortable and, so far, asleep. And as soon as the swelling in his epiglottis dissipated, the doctors would surely extubate him. With more luck, she and her son would be home in a matter of days.

"Well, he is ill, poor little lad, but he'll pull through. And here's the doctor to tell you so."

The room wasn't private, and people had streamed in and out since their arrival, but not Finn. Now Peggy turned expectantly, but Finn wasn't behind her. Dr. Beck stared back at her. Blond, with regular features, he might normally pass for good-looking, but tonight he was rumpled, and the eyes behind his glasses were red-rimmed, as if he had pulled himself from a sound sleep to make the hospital trip.

His voice was a careful monotone. "I've gone over the work-up. Everything that should have been done has been. Your son had a close call, but he'll recover."

She waited for an apology, for a statement, even a hint that he had been negligent, but he shrugged as he spoke. "Epiglottitis is known for its sudden onset. It's rare these days, and of course there's no way to predict it. There was certainly no swelling of any magnitude when I examined him. You were clever to get him to the hospital at the first real symptoms."

"No, I brought him to *you* at the first real symptoms, and that wasn't clever at all."

"I sincerely doubt the two infections are related." He overrode her attempt at reply. "But most likely we will be able to tell once the test results are in."

"Even if the lab tests come back with neon arrows pointing right at you, I'll be astounded if you admit you could have done more for my son."

"That's uncalled for."

"No, it's part of my education. You've gone a long way toward teaching me what kind of doctor I don't want to be." She turned away from him and moved closer to Kieran's bedside. A nurse and lab technician passed by on their way to another bed.

Beck lowered his voice. "I welcome you to put yourself in my shoes, Miss Donaghue. Try treating fifty percent more patients than you ought to and see how endearing they find you. I try to settle for quality and speed. It's not what I went to medical school for, but it gets the job done."

"Except tonight. Tonight my son got caught in your speed trap."

"That remains to be seen." He picked up Kieran's chart and scribbled something on it, handing it to Alice, who had bustled around the bed during Peggy and Beck's exchange as if she was too busy to notice any of it.

"Why are *you* writing on my son's chart?" Peggy demanded.

"I'm his doctor."

"No, Finn O'Malley's his doctor. Kieran wouldn't much need a doctor right now if it weren't for Finn."

"Dr. O'Malley asked me to take charge."

Peggy couldn't believe it. She looked to Alice for confirmation, but the nurse only shrugged and said, "Sorry, but I have no information except what it says here." She turned Kieran's chart so that Peggy could see it. Dr. Beck was listed as Kieran's doctor.

"Where's Finn?" Peggy wanted to shout the words, but there had already been too many angry exchanges in this room. Kieran, even deeply asleep, needed calm around him and gentle, loving voices.

"Miss Donaghue, it's not my job to figure out what Finn O'Malley is thinking or where he's intent on going. When I arrived, he caught me up on what occurred with your son, then he left the hospital."

"Left?" Peggy couldn't believe it. Finn had saved Kieran's

life, then simply abandoned him to the care of a man Peggy despised?

"Perhaps he's on his way home. I'm sure he knew you intended to stay with your son tonight."

She wasn't certain, but she thought that Beck might actually be trying to cover for Finn, to ease the shock of Finn's desertion and change it into something understandable, even sensible. It was the most accommodating and human response she had seen from the man. And it didn't help one bit.

"I see." She bit her lip. Tears sprang to her eyes, but she would not give him the satisfaction of witnessing them. "Then I'm allowed to stay with Kieran tonight?"

"We encourage it. It's best for him to wake up and find you here. We need to keep him as calm as we can. We'll make you as comfortable as possible." He gave a weary and not convincing smile. "Which is not all that possible, I'm afraid."

He left the room.

"He's no Finn O'Malley," Alice said, "but he's competent enough. Don't you worry, now. He'll be certain the boy's well taken care of. Under the circumstances, you might get better treatment than normal."

Peggy wanted Finn. Beck, even a Beck who was trying to prove himself, wasn't good enough. Where had Finn gone, and why? The first question couldn't be answered, but the second answer was all too easy.

Finn had retreated one last time. He was gone from her life and Kieran's as surely as if he had never been there.

She didn't know she was crying until Alice came over and patted her shoulder. "Now, now, Miss Donaghue. Let me find you a comfortable chair. You need something to drink, and then some sleep. Things will look better in the morning. You have everything to be glad about."

Finn knew he had saved Kieran Donaghue's life. He had acted decisively, certain at each point along the way that he knew exactly what he had to do. The instruments had belonged in his hands; the examining room had welcomed him home. From one moment to the next he had ceased being Finn O'Malley, glorified day laborer, and resumed the identity of Finn O'Malley, physician, honors graduate of the medical school at National University, Galway, survivor of a coveted, rugged internship at St. James hospital in Dublin.

Husband to Sheila, father to Bridie, Mark and Brian.

The young woman who was cleaning off nearby tables at The Castle Bar stopped by his, although he was so far off in a corner he was surprised to be noticed. "Like another?" She pointed to his glass.

He held it out in answer, and she took it, returning a short time later with a Guinness filled to the brim. He handed her some Euros and she nodded. She was pretty enough, curly blondish hair pulled casually on top of her head, pink cheeks, breasts large enough to be remarked on by men who had drunk slightly more than he had. She ventured a tentative smile, pausing longer than she needed to. When he didn't smile back, she moved on.

He hadn't been in this pub for a number of years. When his practice had flourished, he had come to The Castle Bar with colleagues for brief consultations over lunch or a quick drink after rounds in the evening before he headed for home. After the accident, he had done his drinking *at* home, after Bridie was in bed for the night. In the mornings he would wake up early, before she did, still fully clothed, cheek pillowed on a kitchen table littered with bottles. He'd had no desire for conversation as he drank himself into a stupor.

Finn didn't think he was a genuine alcoholic. He craved oblivion, not alcohol. In the years of total abstinence he had not awakened at night yearning for the complex roar of whiskey or the clean slice of vodka. He had yearned to forget, and he suspected that if he could forget, he would be perfectly able to stop at one drink or two and go home unimpaired to his daughter.

But forget he could not.

He held up the brimming glass in silent toast to the little

boy who had brought it all back again. Not that the deaths of his wife and sons were ever far from his thoughts. But he had learned how to tamp down the worst parts, how to avoid situations that brought back the memories, how not to challenge his fragile stability. Tonight, everything he had learned had been for naught. He had been thrust back into the world he had so skillfully avoided to save the life of someone else's child.

He had not been able to save his own sons, but he had saved Peggy's.

He wasn't sorry he had saved Kieran. God no, he wasn't sorry. The infant Kieran had arrived in an alien, frightening world, and now the little boy deserved every good thing the residents of it could do for him. And Kieran had been so brave, so resigned. In the grip of a nearly fatal illness, he had not behaved as a child, particularly an autistic child, might have been expected to. He had not thrashed or fought. Finn had looked into the child's fevered blue eyes and seen not hostility or fear, but a simple, poignant resignation.

Faced with Kieran's death, Finn had been honor bound, even desperate, to save him. But what terrible twist of fate had let him save Peggy's son and doom his own to death?

He could still make emergency decisions, even life-and-death decisions. Tonight's revelation had been both surprising and bitter. He had learned that he *could* act when compelled to, take complicated, even desperate, measures to save a life. His judgment was no longer impaired by fear and grief; perhaps it hadn't been for some time. If he wanted to practice medicine again, he was able to. He might need a colleague's support and guidance until his confidence was completely restored, but his skills were still sharp. There were no lies or facades to hide behind now.

"Finished already?" The young woman who'd refilled his glass was back again. He was surprised enough to glance down at the table where the glass, empty of everything but a bit of foam, sat waiting to be refilled.

How many had he had?

"Closing time before long." She smiled at him. "You might not have another chance."

Closing time was often a figment of some local official's imagination, but he didn't want to take a chance that in this pub it was rigidly enforced. He nodded, and she removed his glass and left him to stare at the wet spot where it had been.

A new man wobbled up to the bar not far from the corner where Finn sat and leaned both elbows on it. "Can't have any more, Sean," he addressed the bartender. "Had one too many, as it is. I won't be walking a straight line on the way back home tonight."

Finn tried to ignore him, but the man's voice was boisterous and high-pitched, and soon enough it was answered by Sean the bartender, whose voice was nearly as loud.

"You won't be walking a'tall unless you eat a bit," Sean said. He had the long, narrow face of a Dickens character and the soulful-eyed demeanor to go with it. "You'd best have something before you go. Crisps or biscuits. Which will it be?"

"Poisoning me, are you?"

"Trying to soak up the poison is more like it."

"Well, one biscuit or two, and you won't want me here."

"Who says I want you here anyway?"

"I'm al—allergic to grains, I am, and there's no getting around it. Wheat's as good to me as arsenic, don't you know?"

"And what happens when you eat it?"

"I'm a wild man." He beat both fists on his chest. "My stomach feels like a horse kicked it. Why do you think I drink rum instead of good Irish whiskey? Made from grain, isn't it now?"

"Wild man?" The bartender laughed.

The man seemed to sober. "Tried to kill myself when it got too bad. Couldn't keep a thought in my head but that one. All that went away the moment I got a new diet."

Sean didn't seem convinced, but he reached for a packet of crisps and waved away the man's attempts to pay for them. "I don't want any wild men in here."

The man grinned and wobbled back down the bar, where a group of friends made room for him.

Finn's entertainment had ended and a new Guinness had appeared in front of him. He paid for it and again didn't encourage conversation. The young woman left permanently for greener pastures.

"Cel...iac disease." Finn stared at the full glass in front of him. He'd diagnosed it himself more than once, and he remembered the startling changes in one patient, a young man who was virtually wasting away because he experienced so much abdominal pain after eating. Some researchers called it the "Irish disease" and believed that as many as one in fifty Irish men and women were affected by it, although most estimates were lower.

He hadn't thought about that for a long time, of the young man who had gone on to marry and father children once his health was restored, of the others he had helped. He had not wanted to think of them, to feel responsible for their continued health or for patients just like them who needed his skills. He had abandoned Shanmullin and all the people who had counted on him to care for them.

He still did not want to care for them.

"Wild man." The words sounded fuzzy to his own ears. The pub was a raucous enough place, but it wasn't the noise surrounding him that distorted his words. He was sorry he didn't have a collection of glasses on the table to help him remember how much he'd had to drink. More than three, for certain. Many more.

"Wild child." He didn't know where that connection came from. He couldn't seem to stop thinking about Kieran, whose own neurological peculiarities would make his life a difficult one. From the beginning, Finn had admired Peggy for her patience in the face of Kieran's rebellions, for her obvious love for the boy even when he seemed incapable of returning it.

He'd seen other autistic children in his practice. It was a mysterious phenomenon, with conflicting research and opinions. Peggy had ingested them all with the dual talents of a scientist and a mother, creating her own program from the most promising leads. She was to be admired for that, as well as so many other things.

He could almost see Kieran now, the way the child—no more than a baby, really—had stared at him tonight as if saying, "It's been a tough ride, and it's going to end, isn't it?"

And it very nearly had.

Something tugged at him, something he couldn't quite grasp hold of—although that was no surprise, considering where he was and what he'd done for the past two hours. Kieran had been different tonight, not just because he had been so terribly ill, but because he had seemed to "be" there. So many other times the child had seemed absent, uninvolved, in a private, miserable locked cell of his own. But tonight, despite being so very sick...

"Wild child..."

No, he hadn't been wild tonight. And something was familiar about that. Finn had seen Kieran that way once before. He tried to remember, but his brain was working in slow motion. He had seen it once before....

When Kieran was cutting a tooth. He remembered now. The child had been fussy, the way his own children had been fussy when undergoing the same experience, but he had also been more willing to be held, more accommodating, more... "there."

He'd said the word out loud, but he didn't care. Why should he care about that or anything else? He lifted his glass to that, toasting the air again. So what if Kieran had seemed more focused tonight and in that one isolated moment in his past? Both times he had been sick, one much worse than the other, of course. But obviously the illness had drained away his energy, and the rest was an illusion. People saw what they wanted, even former doctors who prided themselves on logic and observation.

But was it an illusion?

Finn couldn't seem to let go of it. Yes, possibly Kieran's illness was the reason he'd seemed different, but wasn't it more likely that illness would only have intensified his usual behavior? That instead of letting Peggy hold and comfort him, he would have been frantic to get away from her?

He was sorry his thoughts were so muddled. A lump formed in his throat, and for a moment he thought he was going to cry on cue, like any stereotypical drunk. Next he would belt out a chorus of "Danny Boy."

"What else...could it be?"

His words were slurring even worse now, but he didn't really care. He was like a dog gnawing an old bone. There was nothing of interest left, but he couldn't give it up. What else? What else?

Kieran had been sick. Kieran had been feverish.... He discarded that as the cause. Teething produced a slight fever only, if that. Kieran had been in pain.... That went out with the mental rubbish, too. Pain did not make children more loving, more aware.

Both times Kieran had gotten little enough sleep, but surely that had nothing to do with it? Perhaps fatigue had blurred the edges of his autism, but it was unlikely.

He hadn't eaten.

Finn stared at the table as the pieces fell into place. Now he understood why the man's celiac disease had interested him, and why somehow his belabored brain had made the connection between the man and baby Kieran.

He scrambled to remember an article he had read last year in one of his medical journals. He had not stopped his subscriptions to the journals, just as he had not abandoned his office. He had received them, and in the darkest hours of night, he had paged through them, reading some articles, skimming others. He was a fraud and a liar, a man who could not make up his mind to be anything else, except perhaps a murderer of the people he loved most.

The article...

He tried to remember the research, the syndrome. Something about wheat, something akin to celiac disease in autistic children. But there was more.

He rested his head in his hands, trying hard to remember. It seemed imperative to remember it now, not later, when he could go home and find the article.

"Think!"

Not just wheat, but *milk,* as well. Grains and milk. A diet free of all gluten found in wheat and most other grains, and casein, the phosphoprotein found in dairy products. The anecdotal evidence from parents was extremely positive, although too little hard research had been done. The diet didn't help every child and certainly didn't cure autism, but it did seem to affect some children to the point that eventually they began functioning in a normal range.

Even some children for whom the diagnosis of autism was completely dropped later in their lives.

"Kieran...not eating."

He looked up, and the room swam. The noise and the crush seemed to poke at him in waves, but he didn't care. Kieran's appetite had vanished when he cut his tooth and more recently when he fell so ill. He'd had juice to drink and little more. Peggy had remarked on it.

"Gluten and cas—casein."

Peggy had conducted a trial of this yet unproven theory, and she hadn't even known she was doing it. Kieran's diet had changed temporarily. Kieran's behavior had changed temporarily, too.

Even drunk—and he *was* drunk, "stocious" as his father would have said, blootered, plastered—he was too good a scientist to believe it was that easy. But he saw the window of opportunity. The child was in hospital now, and the hospital could restrict his diet while he remained. Peggy could continue a diet free of most grains and dairy when she took him home. They could monitor his behavior, see if anything improved. There were many dietary substitutions that could be made, and the child's nutrition wouldn't suffer. Peggy was the sort of mother to follow through religiously if she thought her son would improve.

Had the symptoms of Kieran's autism begun when Peggy introduced him to solid food, when, perhaps, she had gone off to medical school and stopped nursing him?

Finn wanted to know. He wanted to know more than he

wanted to remain here and drink his pint, where he was safe, where nobody asked anything of him except money. Here, where he could drink enough to forget that he was a shell of the man he had been.

He got to his feet, and the room spun. He was not surprised. He had consumed so much in such a short time that he ought to be out on his feet. He fought a wave of nausea, gripping the edge of the table until it passed.

What if he forgot? What if he found a place to spend the night and in the morning his revelation was gone for all time? Worse, what if he remembered in the morning and discovered this was a drunk's revelation, filled with nothing but hot air and hyperbole? For a moment he weighed the two alternatives.

There was a third. He could write himself a note; then, in the morning, over a cup of coffee and a raging hangover, he could evaluate it.

And leave Peggy alone tonight, wondering where he had disappeared to and why. Wondering how she could ever have seen something in him that clearly wasn't there.

He hung his head, and the room spun. Shame spiraled through him, and dizziness followed in its wake. "God..." He was praying, not cursing. What had he become that he could let his private misery overcome his need to help her through this?

He loved Peggy Donaghue, and he loved her son. And this, more than anything he had done tonight, had sent him to this terrible, bleak place inside himself and to this pub filled with strangers. He was afraid, so very, very afraid, to love again.

He stumbled outside. The hospital wasn't far away. He had walked here, relishing each step that added distance between them. Ten minutes and he'd arrived at the pub. If he made it back, it would take far more than ten now.

He struggled to stay on the sidewalk. Each step was a puzzle to solve. Staying upright took a gymnast's concentration. Minutes passed. He turned a corner, hoping he knew where he was going. Castlebar, which once upon a time had been as familiar as Shanmullin, was now strange and menacing, and the streets were a maze to untangle.

The night air did little to clear his head, but by the time he finally arrived at the hospital, he thought he was steadier. He straightened his jacket, made sure the zipper on his trousers was up. He ran hands through his hair, and he prayed.

Inside, the hospital was a rabbit warren of corridors and rooms. He paused in the lobby and swayed on his feet. The lift wasn't far away, and he made the trip with only a gallon of false dignity holding him erect. Luckily he was alone inside, and still alone when he reached the floor he wanted. He stumbled stepping off the lift, and nearly fell. Humiliation filled him, but he started down a corridor, bumping against one wall when he had to avoid a cart in the middle of the hallway. Luckily it was late, and the hospital was nearly empty.

Except for one too familiar man walking toward him.

"O'Malley? I thought you'd gone." Joe Beck stopped just in front of him and frowned. He examined Finn; then his expression turned to disgust. "You're stinking drunk, aren't you?" Beck looked around, and, seeing no one else, he pulled Finn into the nearest room, which happened to be a linen supply closet.

Finn went without protest. He was too unsteady on his feet to make a stand.

"Look at you." Beck shook his head. "We've got to get you out of here before somebody else sees what I see."

"I'm going to see—Peggy."

Finn made a grab for the door, but Beck stepped in front of it. "Don't act the maggot. You think they'll let you practice here ever again if somebody reports you? In case you've forgotten, drunks don't make good doctors."

"Kieran Donaghue—"

"Is *my* patient. I'm the doctor of record, and you aren't going anywhere near him the way you are now."

Finn tried to shove him away, but Beck shoved him back. Finn fell against a shelf, which tipped, starting a landslide of towels onto the floor.

"Listen to me!" Beck said urgently. "I'm trying to help you."

"Kie—Kieran Donaghue has—" Finn couldn't get his

tongue around the more convincing scientific explanation. Nor did he have the ability to explain his reasoning. "Just listen—" It came out as "lis-shun." He was not drunk enough to escape embarrassment at his own slurred speech.

Beck interrupted. "Kieran Donaghue is fine now. You did a good thing tonight. You always were the best. Did you know you had a gift the rest of us envied? I wanted to be as good as you. Now? Now you're a stumbling, drunken fool. You're wasting the talents God gave you. You're a disgrace to the profession. You make me sick."

"Kie—ran may be 'lergic to grains and milk." Finn was proud that he had formulated the sentence. "'S'autism, it might—"

"Go home, Finn!" Beck lowered his voice, and suddenly the anger was gone. "It's gibberish. Don't you know that? Your brain isn't working like it ought to. You pickled it tonight. Kieran's on a ventilator. What matter is it if he's allergic to anything right now?"

"Have to...tell Peggy."

"Do you really want her to see you this way?"

Finn hung his head. What had he done? He had the most promising of news for Peggy, yet he had destroyed his chance of delivering it. And why had he come? Beck was right, of course. By coming, Finn had put his future here at risk. He didn't know if he even wanted a future, but he wanted the option. Damn it, he wanted the option.

"Look." Beck put his hand on Finn's shoulder. "I'm going to find an orderly, then we're going to get you out of here without anybody else having to see you. I know a place where you can sleep this off. Nobody has to know."

Finn looked up. Even now, he could see that Beck was actually trying to help him. "Why?"

Beck stared at him. "Because I made a mistake with that boy, and you had to clean up my mess. I should have done a culture, like Miss Donaghue asked. Epiglottitis can be a casualty of strep. Not often, but often enough. If I'd caught it then..."

Finn shook his head, a bad idea under the circumstances. For a moment he thought he might pass out. "You wouldn't make a different decision...Beck. Even if you had it to do over again. You did—you did what you thought was right."

His own words pierced through the alcoholic haze. He might as well have been speaking of himself. In that moment it was as clear to him as it should have been before he fell off the wagon, as it should have been if years of regret and shame hadn't dulled his spirit. Like Beck, he would not, could not, have made a different decision.

If he was in the water with his two little boys right now, even now, knowing what he knew about the outcome, he would still do what he'd done that day two years ago. He would try to save them both. What else could any father do? What other choice could he have lived with?

"I did think it was right," Beck said. "But maybe I was wrong."

"Next time...you'll listen."

"It's going to haunt me until I know."

"You can't go back in time." Finn heard his own words, and he knew that, drunk or not, he had never said—and would never again say—anything more profound. It was a simple, unavoidable truth.

"You can't go back." He looked up at Beck. "That's all I've thought... That's all I've wanted since the accident, you know. To go back..."

Beck, an unemotional man, a man who rarely saw people as anything except flesh to heal, swallowed hard. His eyes misted. "I know, Finn. We all know, and we're so sorry."

chapter 39

Finn had never cried for his family. He'd nearly been dead when rescuers found him after the accident, and afterward he had fought for his life. Then there had been funeral arrange ments, Bridie's emotional state to think of, selling the house he could no longer abide living in, trying to resume his prac tice and later giving it up.

And finally, hours and hours of drinking to ease the pain. He had never cried. He had never allowed himself to cry.

On the morning after he saved Kieran's life, Finn looked into a strange mirror at a man he was only beginning to know. Last night Joe Beck had persuaded a spinster aunt to give Finn her guest room. She was a tight-lipped woman with an overly tidy house and a blessedly underdeveloped need for gossip. She put him to bed and told him where clean towels were kept. Then she left him alone in a room in which he could com fortably have done surgery.

Despite his drunken state, he had not gone to sleep immediately. By the time Miss Beck closed the guest room door, he was sobbing. He thought of everything he had lost; then, one by one, he laid them all to rest. His beautiful, ethereal Sheila. Little Mark. Baby Brian. The life they had led together. The man he had once been. All gone and never, never, to return.

He could never go back.

He awoke to a world he didn't know, sitting up in a strange, antiseptic bedroom and feeling as if he lived in a stranger's body. How would he live now? Since the accident, each morning had started with regret. Regret had been his breakfast companion. He had lunched with it, and allowed it to sit between himself and his beloved daughter each night at dinner. He had survived the accident, but he hadn't been glad to. With the magical thinking of a child, he had wished for what he had lost, bargained at times, held on tightly to every memory to punish himself, as if by doing so he might wake up one day and find it had all been a terrible dream.

And now he had to start this morning as a new and different man. A man with another life, yes, but a man with the right to another round of happiness. He could never bring back what he had lost, but he could move forward.

He stared at the man in the bathroom mirror. Eyes redrimmed, cheeks flushed, a day's growth of beard. He saw that his hostess had been there before him. A disposable razor, a fresh toothbrush, a new bar of soap.

He almost smiled. He had needed a place to begin. And it was this simple. First things first. He said a silent prayer of thanksgiving.

Peggy felt better after taking a brief shower down the hall from her son's room and changing into the clean clothes she had brought with her. The nurses had been more than kind. They had taken care of her as if she were a patient, too. And they had taken marvelous care of her son.

Now she stood by her son's bed and gazed down at him.

She was alone with him for once, the other occupants of the room in X ray or being moved to less restrictive quarters.

Every time she gazed at Kieran, he looked better. His color had improved immensely. Dr. Beck had stopped by at seven to examine him and say that if the swelling continued to decrease Kieran would be extubated by nightfall. She hadn't asked about Finn again. What would be the point? He had made his decision and made it clear.

She had so much to be thankful for. Finn had saved Kieran's life. Eventually, perhaps in fifty years, that would be the only thing she remembered about him.

"He looks good."

She whirled at the sound of Finn's voice. She was as astonished at his presence as she had been at his absence last night.

Finn strode to the bedside and lifted her son's chart, paging through it, checking what test results had come in and which were still out. He nodded. "Exactly what I hoped to see." He looked up. "And Kieran's mother looks better, too. Did you get some sleep?"

"What are you doing here?"

He didn't answer immediately. He reached for the pen in his shirt pocket and uncapped it. Then he made a notation in Kieran's chart. He held it out to her. He had crossed out Dr. Joseph Beck as the physician of record and substituted his own name.

"The chart should reflect that I'm Kieran's doctor."

She was angry, frustrated, and terribly, terribly confused. "Finn, I can't take much more of this." Tears filled her eyes. She was tired of crying, but there were the tears anyway, proof that crying oneself dry was a fallacy.

"Just say you'll have me as his doctor," Finn said.

She nodded, because talking had become temporarily impossible.

"I left here last night and got stinking drunk," he said. "And in that state, something occurred to me."

"You've started—" she drew a deep breath "—drinking again."

"No. I fell off the wagon last night. Tonight I go to AA. Tomorrow I see my priest. It's about time, isn't it?"

"Priest?"

"To help me deal with whatever I still need to deal with. I—I don't think I wanted to feel better until now. Now I know that I do."

She didn't know what to say. He didn't look steady on his feet. Conversely, he looked better than she'd ever seen him. More relaxed, and at the same time, more determined.

"About Kieran," he said. "Going to the pub was good for one thing, at least. I overheard a snatch of conversation, and it started me thinking. Peggy, have you heard of the gluten- and casein-free diet for autistic children?"

She was having problems concentrating. Finn, a different Finn, was back in her life after she had bade him goodbye twice before. She was thrown off balance yet again.

"There's a theory," he went on, "a fairly complicated one that we can explore thoroughly later, that the incomplete digestion of certain proteins creates elevated levels of peptides. The theory goes that these peptides are biologically active, and in some individuals may even cause the symptoms of autism."

Now she was mentally paging through the thousands and thousands of documents she'd read after Kieran's diagnosis. "That's familiar, but I discounted it. I decided to put him on a diet with no additives instead. The wheat- and milk-free diet seems unhealthy, and most allergy studies didn't corroborate it, did they?"

"That's because the problem is more toxological than allergic in nature. More a poison to the system than a sensitivity. And the unfortunate result is like hallucinogens to the brain."

"What are you saying, Finn?"

"I'm saying that Kieran's behavior improved markedly both times he was ill recently. First when he was teething, and second when this occurred." He nodded toward the bed. "Both times he stopped eating. He was drinking juice or water and little else. Am I right?"

She tried to remember. She thought that perhaps he was. "But couldn't that simply be the illness? Or even a coincidence?"

"Let's find out. Put him on a wheat-free, dairy-free diet for three months, Peggy. That's the suggested time to see if the diet's working. I'll help you come up with foods he can eat. We'll watch his behavior and see if the new regime has any effect. I'm not saying I believe it will, and certainly not that it will cure him. I'm just saying that it might help, that we have some evidence already that it *has* helped, even when we didn't make the connection. And anything that helps, even a little, anything that makes it easier for you to work with him and easier for him to participate, is worth almost any trial. Are you willing?"

Her mind was buzzing, her heart lifting with hope, as it would in the future every time she heard about something new that might help her son.

But her ears heard one word she hadn't expected to hear again.

"We? *We'll* watch his behavior? *We'll* put him on a diet and come up with foods he'll eat? What is this *we*?"

He set the chart down and came to stand in front of her. His eyes were sad, and he didn't smile.

"I'm not much of a bargain. I've got a lot of work to do before I'm out of the emotional woods. But for the first time my feet are on the path, and I'm heading in the right direction."

He reached for her hands and grasped them in his. "The last time I fell in love, I lost almost everything. But like other decisions I made, I wouldn't, couldn't, change that one, either. Not even with all the pain it brought at the end."

"Last time, Finn?"

Now he smiled. "Let me get my life straightened out. Let me come to you whole."

"Come to me?"

"To say all the things I shouldn't say right now. I want you to hear them when you're sure of me."

She was sure of him now. She supposed she had nearly always been sure of him, even though the past few days had been a particular trial. Sure that the Finn everyone else had known would be back one day. Sure that he was the man she had waited to love.

And she was sure, too, that he was right. He needed to find his way back to himself without obstacles. He needed to be certain he was ready to love again.

She thought she might be able to wait as long as he needed.

"But you'll be around?" She squeezed his hands. "Around to help me with Kieran's diet?"

"I'll be around as much as you let me, Peggy-o. There's no place else I want to be."

She kissed him then. It was the natural thing to do, and for the first time it felt completely right. He clung to her, pulling her against him as if he'd feared that he had lost *her,* too. She felt the warmth of his body, both the strength and gentleness in his grasp.

Peggy guessed that she would not have to wait much longer after all.

chapter 40

Megan let herself into the house on Hunter Street and from the hallway gazed through open doors at the rooms beyond. She hadn't been sure what she would find with three generations suddenly free of the woman in their lives, but the house looked the way it always did. Clean, orderly...home. She was more than grateful.

"Niccolo?" She hadn't called to tell him she was coming back, which had been a wise decision, considering her trip had been painfully extended due to bad weather and airline labor disputes. Now her voice echoed through empty rooms.

Niccolo wasn't home. She indulged in one cynical moment culminating in "Of course he's not, he's never home," before she caught herself. He'd had no way of knowing she would arrive today. Even she had given up hope that she might. So why should she expect him to be here waiting with open arms?

She left her suitcase in the hall and wandered into the kitchen. In Ireland it was midnight, but her appetite was back in Cleveland and shouting for dinner. She opened the fridge and pulled out what looked like fresh leftovers. Nothing Niccolo cooked stayed around long. Rooney had been known to eat Nick's pesto tortellini right out of the Tupperware.

She found spaghetti with clam sauce and plopped a portion into a bowl for the microwave. Another container yielded salad, and that went into another bowl for a dollop of dressing.

At the table she stared at her lonely meal and felt a twinge of annoyance. She had so much to tell her husband, and he wasn't here to hear it. She wondered if this was the way he had felt when she abandoned him. Nobody to talk to, no chance of fixing what was wrong.

The front door opened, and footsteps sounded in the hall. She peered around the doorway, hoping to see Nick.

Rooney appeared instead, dressed in clean but wrinkled trousers and a green polo shirt he favored. She suspected it reminded him of the saloon, where green polo shirts were the standard dress for staff.

His face lit up in a smile when he saw her. Since she was never quite sure how she would be greeted, she felt warmly welcomed.

"Back..." He nodded.

She was pleased he remembered that she'd been gone. "How are you, Rooney?"

"Doin' okay."

She motioned to a seat at the table and got up to fix him the same dinner she'd made for herself. "You're hungry?"

He wrinkled his forehead in concentration. Sometimes even the simplest things were a stretch for him. "Guess so."

"Well, I'll get you dinner. Have a seat." She got the same containers out of the refrigerator and fetched a can of cola to go with the food, pouring it over ice as the spaghetti warmed.

"Do you know where Josh is?" She handed him the cola, then went back to the counter to dress his salad. "Or Nick?" she asked as casually as she could.

"Josh..." He took two big sips. He often forgot to drink as his day progressed, and one of Megan's jobs was to keep him hydrated. "Camping." He smiled, glad to have the answer available.

She snapped her fingers. "Oh, that's right." Josh had just started his senior year, and the senior class began with a week-long camping trip at a state park. She was sorry she hadn't been here to help him get ready. She hoped Niccolo had taken up the slack.

"Got a new sleeping bag," Rooney added. "Soft. Says it's warm."

It sounded as if Niccolo had made certain Josh was all set. She was glad to hear it.

"And Nick? Do you know where he is?" she repeated.

"Missed you."

She looked up from dressing Rooney's salad. "What did you say?"

"Missed you. Moped like a lovesick teenager."

She stared at her father. Rooney was so much better, but this kind of observation was rare. His strange private world was too often the only one he lived in. "Did he? I'm glad to hear it."

"I missed your mother."

She went to the table. "Oh, and you remember that?"

He looked puzzled, as if that was the silliest question he'd ever heard. "Still miss her." He took the salad from her hand. "You think it goes away? Missing people?"

Her eyes filled with tears. "No, of course not. I'm sorry I sounded surprised. I miss her, too, you know."

"You're like her. I'm glad." He started in on his salad.

Megan took her seat again. "Rooney, you had a good marriage, didn't you? Even with the troubles you had?"

"Not easy for her. I know that. Something's wrong with me. Loved me anyway."

Megan covered his hand with hers. "Yes, she did. And so do we."

"Missed her every day. Hard to get up in the morning."

Megan wondered why none of them had given Rooney credit for these deep feelings. Sometimes he wasn't able to articulate them; sometimes he probably wasn't aware of them.

But Kathleen Donaghue's absence was as much a part of his life as the air he breathed. She was filled with a renewed wave of love for the man who had fathered her.

"What made your marriage good? Do you know?" The microwave sounded, and she got up to get his dish, wiping her eyes on a napkin as she did.

He laughed, as he sometimes did when a question seemed foolish. "Love."

"Well, sure. I know that part. But it takes more than that, doesn't it? You can love someone and still not be able to understand them, can't you?" She set the spaghetti in front of him, and he abandoned the salad to dive into it as she seated herself again.

He was halfway through before he answered. "You talk, she listens. She talks, you listen." He looked up, clam sauce on his chin. "Nothing hard about that."

She wondered if it could be that easy. She and Niccolo hadn't quite met those standards. He had talked, but had she really listened to what he said? Or had she listened for the things she was sure she would hear?

And how could he have heard what was really bothering her when she had never found the courage to tell him?

"Very wise." She looked down at her plate. Her appetite had fled. Rooney, on the other hand, was finishing quickly. He rose a few minutes later and took his dishes to the sink. The gesture touched her. This was definitely Rooney at his most lucid, and she loved every second of it.

"Peggy called." He started from the room.

She had planned to call her sister as soon as it was 7:00 in Ireland. Now she was sorry she hadn't called right away. Peggy was probably wondering why Megan wasn't home yet. She hoped her sister had talked to Jon, because Casey had kept him up to date every hour of their delay.

"Kieran was sick, but he's better." Rooney left the room.

Megan stared after him, mystified. She suspected, though, that she wasn't going to learn any more from Rooney.

She had already learned the things she really needed to know, anyway.

The doorway filled again. She hadn't heard the front door close, but now Niccolo stood there. As she watched, he opened his arms.

She jumped to her feet and ran to them, circling his waist with hers.

"You were gone too long," he said into her hair. "And I missed you from the moment you left."

"Oh, I missed you, too. More than I can say."

"You could try."

"Damn you, Nick, what's marriage done to me? When we're not together, I feel like something major is gone."

He set her away so he could see her face. "Me, too."

"I know why we were having problems."

"So do I."

"Me first, okay? Rooney just set me straight."

"Rooney?"

She feasted on his face. He looked tired, but wonderful. She imagined he had worked nonstop since her departure.

"In a nutshell, he said the secret to a good marriage is that when one person talks, the other one listens. I realized that neither of us knew how to do that. Me, I just solve problems. Period. I listen to myself, and only myself because for a long time I was the only one available."

He smiled and stroked her hair. "Megan, it pains me to say this, but there were *always* other people for you to listen to. You just never wanted to."

She winced. "Okay, maybe so. But I think we'll both agree that independence was more important for me than for girls raised in a more normal family."

"I'd definitely agree with that."

"And you, Nick. You were taught to listen to one voice only."

"God's. Yes." He nodded. "Listening to a wife was definitely not one of the classes they taught at the seminary."

"I'm sorry," she said. "I thought I was listening, but all I heard was that you were more interested in your job and showing people through the tunnel than you were in me. I never listened to your reasons, and I never told you I was taking it very personally. Not in so many words."

"Megan..." He touched her cheek. "I'd fall at your feet if you'd let me. And I was doing all that work out of some misguided belief that that's what husbands do. They provide for their wives, even if their wives don't need providing for. I was treating our marriage like I'd treated my church, trying to do everything in sight to make it run properly. I'm sorry, too."

She grabbed him by his shirt and hauled him closer. Then she kissed him. Hard. Even though that much effort took all her energy.

She stepped away at last. "We need a time every week when we concentrate on us. Just us. Dinner out, maybe, where nobody can disturb us and we can talk about what's really important. And I promise I'll tell you what I'm feeling, really feeling. Then, even if you're swamped the rest of the week—"

"I won't be swamped."

"Why not?"

"I've decided to stop pursuing funding for Brick. I'm downsizing. We'll make do with what we have and whatever comes our way from St. Brigid's or local fund-raisers. When the right situation comes along without strings and without requiring me to give up my married life and my wife, then maybe we'll expand. Meantime, I'm going to be satisfied with things the way they are."

She thought about all the kids who needed Brick who wouldn't have access to it now. She started to protest, but he silenced her with a kiss.

"I've given this a lot of thought. Brick won't be any good for anyone if the director is exhausted and lonely, Megan. That's the way it is."

She wondered what she could do in return, and the answer came quickly. "Maybe you *should* stop this endless search for funding, at least for a while. But I don't want you to stop the tunnel tours. I'm sorry I was such a bad sport about that. I was so afraid you still wanted to be a priest that I couldn't see you just needed to be a pastor. Helping people glimpse God is what you're all about. You don't need to wear a collar to do it, or have a church filled with people, but you do need to be free to act when the spirit moves you."

His eyes showed his pleasure. He picked up her hands and squeezed them. "Thank you."

There was so much more she wanted to tell him, but first things first. "Would you like to go upstairs with me? I'm going to take a shower and climb into bed. I'd like it if you'd climb in with me."

He brought her hands to his lips. "More than you know, but there's something I'd like you to see first. Do you have the energy for a short drive?"

She wasn't sure if she should be excited or disappointed. "Sure, if you think it's important."

"I think you'll be glad we went."

"Let me wash up a little first."

Five minutes later they were in Niccolo's new Ford Focus, the replacement for the Honda that hadn't survived the pre-tornado winds. The moment he made his first turn, she knew exactly where they were going.

"Did you finish the renovations?" She leaned slightly forward, as if that might get them there faster.

"You'll see."

"Surprises annoy me."

He shot her a grin. "I'll have to remember that *next* time."

"You're not going to say another word, are you?"

"How much sleep have you had in the past twenty-four hours?"

"Okay, okay..." She leaned back and closed her eyes.

He parked where the maple tree had once stood. The spot was clearly marked by a sign with her name on it. There was room for only one car.

"Way cool," she said. "My own spot? Never had one before."

"I know, and that was a mistake. Now you do."

"Thank you." She got out and noted new landscaping, small but flourishing green shrubs, and tall terra cotta pots filled with blooming chrysanthemums in shades of bronze and rust. It was a huge leap from parking beside a rusting Dumpster. Another universe. "Nobody will ever see this but me, Nick."

"And your point?"

"You did this just for me?"

"I told you I'd fall at your feet if you let me."

"I like this a lot better, thanks." She gave him a quick hug. "Come in and see the rest."

She followed, waiting as he unlocked the kitchen door. The kitchen had been finished before she left, but now she saw the newest touches. Brightly framed pages from early twentieth-century ladies' magazines took up every extra inch of wall space, recipes and colorful advertisements. One was a step-by-step lesson on corning beef.

"Oh, where did you get them? They're perfect."

"I saw the magazines at a shop on Lorain. I bought a dozen."

"You're so good to me."

"Come see the rest of it."

She noted other additions to the kitchen. A bright red enamel jug to hold scrub brushes, a cobalt blue dishrack on the shining stainless steel sink. Her hands twitched. She was ready to cook for a hundred people, but that reminded her of another decision she had made.

"Nick, are we going to be able to open next week, or the week after at the latest? As soon as I get stocked and publicize it?"

"I don't see why not. With a christening party."

"As soon as I can afford to, I'm hiring more help. If you're cutting back on your hours, then so am I."

"You've given that some thought?"

"I don't see why I have to be at the saloon at night anymore. I think I was spending all that time here because I was lonely. Now it's time to let go of all those details and find good people who can take care of them for me."

"I like the sound of that. Are you coming?"

"Yep." She followed him into the saloon proper and

stopped. It was spectacular, better than she could have imagined. The layout had been subtly altered from the tried and true. The gleaming walnut bar curved where it hadn't before, giving better access through the front door. More shelves lined the original mirror, each just tall enough for a bottle. Built-in booths flanked one corner, giving twice as much seating in an area that had only held two tables. Elisha's quiet nook was a reality, and the idealized mural of Ireland, the Brick kids' own creation, was nearly finished.

There were other new features, too, but she didn't take the time to note them all. She hugged him hard. "It's done?"

"It's done. Every last nail."

Family photographs they had salvaged were back on the walls, along with new photographs of more recent Donaghue family members. The green walls were a slightly different hue, mellower, she thought, and more contemporary. The wood wasn't as dark as the original, and the lighter wood, along with brass chandeliers, gave the room a warmer glow.

"It's perfect." She couldn't believe it, but it was. After everything they had been through, it was perfect.

She walked to a wall and gazed at a family portrait she had seen a million times, but it held new meaning for her now. She pointed at one man, blond-haired, serious, dressed in a perfectly pressed suit. "My grandfather, Glen Donaghue."

"I know. Your aunt told me when we were putting them on the wall."

She thought about Glen and Clare, about Liam and the money that was hidden somewhere inside this building. "Have I got a story for you."

"And I have one for you. But I don't want to tell mine here. Can you stand one more trip?"

She was fighting true exhaustion, but she nodded. "One quick trip. Then home to bed."

"That's incentive enough. Come on." He took her by the hand and led her back into the kitchen. He opened the door into the basement and flicked on the light. "Ready?"

"I don't know. Am I?"

They didn't stop in the basement, which had yet to be renovated. They continued through to the tunnel. Somehow she had known that was where they were going.

"I've run some more lights down here. I think we need to think long and hard about how to use this space in the future."

"What about the image?"

He switched on the lights, and the tunnel glowed softly. "See for yourself."

She followed him, flashlight in hand, just in case. They stopped where the image had been, where she had found him on their wedding day, alive and miraculously unhurt.

Only the remnants of the image were visible. She was surprised to hear her own moan. She felt curiously choked up at the sight. "No..."

"It began to fade when we ran the new pipes."

"So it *was* caused by a pinpoint leak in the old ones?"

"Or poorly sealed joints, condensation..." He shrugged. "We'll never know for sure. But it's almost gone now. With all the new ventilation we installed upstairs, it will be completely dry by the end of the week."

"No more miracle." She was sadder than she would have imagined.

"Well, that depends on the way you look at it."

He put his hand on her shoulder and pointed above the fading outline. "What do you see up there?"

She saw a wall and a ceiling. The ceiling was beamed, and in some places the plastered walls rose only as high as the bottoms of the beams. There was a space between ceiling and wall here, as there was in other parts of the tunnel.

"It doesn't look any different than the rest of the tunnel," she said.

"It might have looked different to Liam Tierney. I'm sure he found some way to mark it."

"You know?"

He nodded. "Casey told Jon the whole story of Liam and Glen in one of her phone calls from Shanmullin. He told me."

She narrowed her eyes. "Darn them. I was scooped!"

"You can tell me your version later. Okay?"

"Why did Jon tell you?"

"I'll show you."

For the first time she noticed a stepladder leaning against the opposite wall. Niccolo dragged it across the corridor and set it up in front of the image. Then he climbed to the top step and reached inside the crack. He pulled out a tall cannister, narrow, but large enough to hold spices, perhaps, or coffee.

Megan didn't need to be told what was inside.

He rejoined her on the floor. "On the night that Liam died, he came here looking for Glen. He must have gone out this way."

"He did. I remember Irene saying so. He claimed he didn't want to be spotted by McNulty's goons."

"He came down here. He must have looked hard for a place to hide the money. It probably wasn't difficult to find a tin to hide it in. Even then, the basement area was used for storage. He emptied a can, or found an empty one, and put the money in it. Then he looked for a place to hide it."

"Why the wall?"

"I guess we'll never know. Maybe there was a ladder in use nearby and it was easy to climb up and drop it inside. It was a perfect little hiding place. There are boards running between the joists. This was resting on the top one, nice as you please. He'd wrapped a chain around it. I think the very end of the chain might have dangled just at the top of the wall, not so anyone else would notice it, but so that he could spot it if he came back. It probably fell inside at some point."

"If he came back?"

"Doesn't it strike you as odd that he'd hide it here? I think he did it because he didn't really expect to come out of the situation alive. Either he had a premonition of his own death, or he just knew McNulty's men too well. Whichever it was, he knew that if he died and Glen didn't, Glen would help his wife."

"And before he died, he told Brenna in a phone call where to look for the money." Megan thought for a moment. "Or maybe Liam thought that even if he died and Brenna didn't retrieve it, at least the money would be found by family someday. His family."

"The leak dripped against the tin. A drop here, another there. The tin was placed in such a way that the water dripped off of it on both ends, down the plaster, eventually to the floor, leaving a trail each time. The ends of the cannister sat right where the Virgin's eyes were supposed to be. Depending on how often the water was used each day, the leak dripped off the tin at different speeds and angles, making her look like she was crying. Eventually the plaster below it was soaked."

"Like an ink blot. The plaster absorbed it the way paper absorbs ink." She took the tin from his hands. "How much, Nick?"

"Open it and see. I put it back so you'd have the pleasure of treasure hunting, just the way I did."

She struggled to pry off the top, rusted now, and not happy to give up its wares. If Niccolo hadn't already removed the top once, it wouldn't have yielded for her smaller hands at all.

It came off after one exasperated tug. She stared inside before she reached for the money. The tin fell to her feet. She was astounded at the number of bills. "Lord, what a haul!"

"There are one hundred of them."

They were thousand-dollar bills. One hundred thousand dollars. She gazed up at him. "I can't believe it. It's so much."

"I guess we know why McNulty wanted his money back so badly. It's a lot of money now. Then it was a fortune."

"All these years. Just sitting there, Nick. Here all this time."

"Sitting there, channeling water against the plaster, creating its own sort of miracle."

She thumbed through the bills. She couldn't believe how many there were. Then she knew exactly what she wanted to do with them.

"When Jon told you the story, did he tell you about Liam's childhood?" she asked.

"I know a little, from things I heard along the way."

"It was fairly miserable. He never had any help or guidance. Everything he became he became entirely on his own.

If someone had just reached out a hand to him along the way, he probably never would have died the way he did."

"What are you thinking?"

She looked up from the money that had caused nothing but death and destruction. It was time to change that now. Past time. "This belongs to Peggy and Casey, too, Nick, I can't do anything without their permission. But I'm pretty sure they'll agree. We'll put some aside for Kieran's therapy and education. That's easy. But the rest should go to Brick. A memorial for Liam Tierney."

"I can't let you do that."

"Of course you can. Don't you see? You're helping the Brick kids on to the right path in life. If someone had helped Liam, think what he might have become. We can't enjoy this money, and none of us would want to. It's a different sort of money laundering, Nick. We'll make something good from something bad, and we'll honor Liam as we do it."

He didn't reply, but gratitude shone in his eyes.

She smiled and touched his cheek with the hand that wasn't filled with a new start for Brick. "What made you investigate? How did you find it? Was it just curiosity when the image started to fade?"

"No, it was more than that. When the Virgin began to disappear, I thought the time had come to do some checking. I hadn't wanted to probe too closely before. I didn't want to be the man who destroyed a miracle, even if I didn't really believe that's what it was. Too many people would have been outraged."

"And when it began to disappear?"

"I came down here one afternoon on a break, and I stared at the fading image. It's hard to explain, but I felt such sadness that the image was evaporating. I wanted to check out the wall behind it, but at the same time I didn't want to. I guess I wanted to believe in the possibility of the divine as long as I could."

"Then what happened?"

"I was standing here, just staring at it, and I felt a hand on my shoulder. Just the faintest touch, like the soft hand of a woman. When I turned, there was no one there. But all my apprehension was gone. I knew it was time to see what had caused the image."

She stared at him, her heart brimming with love. "Who touched you? The Virgin? Or Clare McNulty?"

He leaned over and kissed her before he spoke, a lingering promise of a kiss. "It will always be a mystery, Megan. There are some things we just aren't supposed to know."

epilogue

Spring had arrived again in Ireland. Yellow primroses bloomed in ditches, lambs frolicked in gorse dotted pastures, clouds rolled over Clare Island and showered the coast at inconvenient times. But the rain was soft and warm, and the chilly nights were perfect for fragrant turf fires.

This evening Peggy had laid a fire after supper, hoping that Irene would be able to enjoy it. But the old woman had taken to her bed that afternoon and hadn't wanted to leave it. She spent longer hours in bed each day, sleeping more and more. Peggy knew that one day she would go to check on her and find Irene had slipped away. Gone in her own bed, her own cottage, with the people she loved nearby. Not such a terrible thing, but one that would leave a space in everyone's lives.

But since it falls unto my lot
That I should go and you should not,

> I'll gently rise and softly call,
> Good night and joy be with you all.

The front door opened, and Finn and Bridie stepped inside. Bridie removed her raincoat and hung it on a peg, and Finn closed his umbrella. Banjax greeted them with a thump of his tail. He divided his time between Irene's bedside and the fire, and now he lay in front of it, soaking up all the heat.

Finn leaned down and kissed Peggy lightly on the lips. Bridie had beat her father there to steal a hug, and now she was off to look for Kieran. A moment ago he had been in his schoolroom building towers from blocks. Peggy had tried to coax him away with the offer of a rice cake and homemade peanut butter, but he had screwed up his little face and told her to "Go 'way!"

And of course she had, smiling as she did. In this rebellion, as in so many other things now, he was a normal two-year-old.

"How's she done today?" Finn asked.

"No better, no worse. She seems comfortable enough, and her dreams are good ones. Today she dreamed her mother came to introduce her to her father."

"She's eating?"

She nodded. "And drinking."

"And how's the little king?"

Truly, Kieran deserved the title. The household ran around him. No child had ever received more loving attention, not even genuine royalty. "Good moments and bad. I'm still learning what to look for on labels. I gave him a dairy-free hot dog, then discovered it had modified food starch in it. I called the manufacturer and unfortunately it was wheat. Kieran was at his worst for about twelve hours afterwards."

Finn didn't quibble. He had seen Kieran in action after dietary slip-ups himself. The little boy had made significant strides since Peggy changed his diet. Most of the foods she'd so lovingly prepared for him before, whole grain breads, the natural cheeses and fresh milk, were forbidden now. He hadn't been happy about the changes, but he had favorites among the new foods he was allowed.

Kieran was talking, even putting words together into short sentences. In the classroom, his attention span was considerably longer, and he enjoyed many of the things he had once found so frustrating. He would sit on Peggy's lap when she read to him, even point to objects without being asked to and label them. Recently they had begun work on toilet training, and it looked as if he might be successful soon. There were flashes of eye contact now, and he seemed to understand the purpose of names, although he didn't yet use them. There were still miles to go, and no one was using the word *cure*, but Kieran was making strides. Someday the simple things Peggy most wished for him might all come true.

"Casey called this morning, after you left," Peggy told Finn.

"And how's little Jon?"

Peggy tried to picture the baby she hadn't yet seen. "In danger of being called Little Jon for the rest of his life."

He laughed, winding a lock of her hair around his index finger to reel her closer. "Over the colic, is he?"

"He's better. Casey says he's a big healthy guy, he just likes to cry."

"And I bet she never puts him down."

"Between Casey and Megan and the rest of the family, he's in somebody's arms all the time. But that's not why Casey called. There's more news." Peggy's eyes were shining. "There's going to be another family member about Christmas time."

"Megan and Nick?"

"Isn't it wonderful? But we're not supposed to know. The news just slipped out, so act surprised if you answer the phone and Megan tells you."

He wrapped his arms around her. "You'll have to go back to see them when the baby's born, you know."

"I know. I miss them all so much."

She didn't say the rest, that by Christmas Irene would no longer be with them, and Peggy wouldn't be needed as her companion.

"And will you come back to Ireland afterwards?" He held her away so he could see her face. "Or will I have to come there and steal you back?"

She pretended to be perplexed. "Don't I have a date in Shanmullin? A medical practice we're going to share, Drs. Finn and Margaret O'Malley, general practice and pediatrics?"

"There's the small matter of finishing your education."

"I have that appointment in Galway next week, to talk to the administrator of the Medical School. Could I live here, do you think, and go to school there? I'd have to take a room near the university during the week and find a school in Galway for Kieran once he's ready, but—"

"You could do it. You know we'd all help."

"Finn, Irene told me something this morning...."

He waited, brow cocked.

"She's leaving me Tierney Cottage. She wants us to live here once we're married, with the natural understanding that Megan and Casey and their families are welcome any time."

His gaze was indulgent. "I've known that for some time."

"You have?"

"Who else but you, Peggy-o? That was all part of meeting you, you know, of luring you here. Not just the hidden money, but knowing you and your sisters were the sort of women who would look after Tierney Cottage properly."

Her eyes filled with tears. "I don't want her to go."

"She's very nearly ready." He gripped her hands and brought them to his lips.

Finn had come so far. He had resumed his practice, part-time at first, but more than full-time now. The village had warmly welcomed him, and so had the other physicians within driving distance, who saw a helpful drop in their own case-loads. He had visited a counselor for several months at the advice of his priest, and talking honestly about his grief had been the final step on his journey out of despair. He and Peggy had resumed their relationship slowly and carefully, but it had quickly assumed a momentum of its own. Now, months later, they were sure of each other and ready to make a final commitment when the time was right.

Bridie appeared with Kieran in her arms. For once he wasn't fighting to get down. "Hello, hello," he called.

"Hello, lad, and how are you today?" Finn asked.

Kieran covered his face with his hands, and Finn laughed. "That bad, huh?"

"Is Granny 'rene awake?" Bridie asked.

"Let's check." Reluctantly, Peggy moved away from Finn. As wonderful as their children were, she did lament the absence of time alone with him. They had learned to steal moments whenever they could.

She opened Irene's door and peeked inside. The old woman was sitting up. She often slept that way, since it was easier for her to breathe, but now she was awake, and she looked ready for company.

"Finn's here," Peggy said. "And Bridie."

"Show them in." Irene smiled. "By all means, show them in."

Peggy pushed the door wide. Bridie put Kieran on the floor and went to greet Irene, perching on the edge of her bed. Finn watched from the doorway, his arm around Peggy's shoulders.

Peggy felt something brush against her jeans; then her son dashed around her and into the room.

Peggy watched to see what Kieran would do next. He was still fascinated by Bridie, but most often he ignored Irene. As Peggy and Finn watched, breaths held, he approached the bed.

One step, two. Bridie fell silent and so did Irene. Peggy felt her breath catch in her chest as Finn's arm tightened around her. She knew that Finn felt exactly the way she did, a special connection with this child he had come to love, and, more important, a premonition.

One step more, then another. And as Peggy watched, Kieran climbed on the bed. He gazed at Irene for a moment, then he lay down carefully beside her and pillowed his head on her shoulder.

* * * * *

*Turn the page for
a sneak peek at*

WEDDING RING

*the new MIRA hardcover from
bestselling author*

Emilie Richards

*available in
July 2004
wherever books are sold.*

1

After she surrendered to the inevitable and gave up trying to make her grandmother open the front door, Tessa MacRae resigned herself to spending the rest of the sweltering morning in what passed for shade on the front porch. The time wasn't completely wasted. From the vantage point of a creaking old swing, she could observe almost everything she needed to know about her grandmother's world.

First, in an area renowned for its natural splendor, this drought-ridden little corner of the Shenandoah Valley was not holding up its end.

The evaluation was interrupted by the screech of a window being wrenched open just above her.

"You still down there, missy?" Helen Henry asked. "I didn't ask you to come, you know, and I sure didn't ask for these!"

Suddenly the air was filled not with much-needed rain, but with balls of paper sliding off the tin roof to the ground below. Tessa tried to count them as they fell. A dozen, at least. Then, after a sustained pause, half a dozen more.

The window above the porch slammed shut again.

Tessa got to her feet, picked up and smoothed a wad that had landed on the front steps. Two women and a man, with broad smiles and glowing silver hair, stared back at her from a golf course fairway.

"'Green Springs Retirement Community,'" she read out loud. "'Because today is the first day of the rest of your life.'" Crumpling the page in her fist, she wondered how many similar brochures her mother had sent Helen during the past weeks. She returned to the swing, drew her knees up to her chin and got on with her assessment.

The drought that had affected the entire area had been particularly bad here. Corn was *not* going to be knee-high by the Fourth of July, which was only three days away. Only the dandelions seemed to be holding their own.

Then there was the heat. Virginia was no one's idea of a summertime oasis, but Tessa, a native, couldn't remember a hotter July. While waiting for her grandmother to reconsider her options, Tessa had probably sweated away an entire quart of bottled spring water.

The window screeched again. "And take these, while you're at it!" Helen shouted. "You think I need your fancy presents?"

The nightgown, then the robe, that Tessa had bought her grandmother on her last birthday floated to the rambling rose that sprawled uncontrolled along the trellis and porch railing. They blomed there in soft shades of violet and pink, as close to real blossoms as the rose had produced in years.

"Or your mother's!" Helen added.

Tessa hoped her mother hadn't given Helen a piano or a safe. She was glad when the only thing to flutter past was a garnet-red sweater on its way to the holly bush beside the rose.

"And don't forget this!" Helen said.

If the first paper blitz had resembled hailstones, this one resembled snow. Pastel-colored snow. One of the tiny shredded pieces drifted to the porch floor. Tessa could see it was the corner of a check, most likely one of the many her mother had sent—one of the many Helen Henry had never cashed.

She waited for the window to slam once more. When it did, she tied up her conclusions.

Helen was not taking care of the farm. The Old Stoneburner Place—as it would be called until doomsday—had never been a showplace. It was a working farm, the product of German immigrants who had crosscut timber to build their first dogtrot cabin, cleared fields with the help of mules and multitudes of sons, shivered through mountain-shadowed nights and shuddered under summer skies.

Helen, a Stoneburner by birth, had worked the farm without help from family for years. Somehow she had eked out a living and held on to the land despite rising property taxes, managing somehow. Clearly she was not managing anymore.

The farmyard looked neglected. On the way up to the house, Tessa had been forced to maneuver ruts in the driveway as deep as the drainage ditches lining it. The daylilies and peonies that had multiplied decades ago were being choked out by weeds and waist-high saplings; the fence around the vegetable garden was sagging and torn.

The house looked neglected, too. There were a thousand farmhouses like it in rural Virginia. Long, deep front porch, tin roof, white clapboard siding always in need of touching up. A screen door stood between an open heavier door and the world outside, welcoming breezes and neighbors.

Today it was a typical farmhouse fast declining. Problems with the exterior were almost too extensive to catalog. And inside? The interior was a mystery, a black hole of gruesome possibilities.

So now Tessa waited, poised for her mother to arrive and the fun to begin. She was being forced to spend the remainder of her summer vacation caught between two women who regarded each other like boxers in a ring. On top of that, if the inside of the house was anything like the outside, she would be painting and patching for all of July and August.

But what did it really matter? What was waiting for her at home in Fairfax? *Who* was waiting for her?

Tessa turned her head to watch a cloud of dust move toward her along the road. In the center was a black sedan, her mother Nancy's sleek Mercedes. Nancy was going too fast when she turned into the driveway. She narrowly avoided the northern ditch, overcompensated, and straightened just in time to avoid the southern.

Tessa didn't move. She felt the remainder of the summer closing in on her. *Life* was closing in on her. She was not strong enough for this, might never be strong enough again. Yet here she was, dutiful daughter, solicitous granddaughter, peacekeeper. Tessa MacRae, high school English teacher, wife of a successful attorney, survivor. She had already been through the worst that life could throw at her. She reminded herself there was nothing that could happen here to rival it.

She tried to gain comfort from that and failed. She waited until Nancy's door slammed and her mother was halfway up the overgrown path before she rose to her feet.

 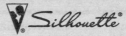

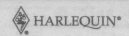 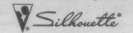

Carnival Elation
7-Day Exotic Western Caribbean Itinerary

DAY	PORT	ARRIVE	DEPART
Sun	Galveston		4:00 P.M.
Mon	"Fun Day" at Sea		
Tue	Progreso/Mérida	8:00 A.M.	4:00 P.M.
Wed	Cozumel	9:00 A.M.	5:00 P.M.
Thu	Belize	8:00 A.M.	6:00 P.M.
Fri	"Fun Day" at Sea		
Sat	"Fun Day" at Sea		
Sun	Galveston	8:00 A.M.	

TERMS AND CONDITIONS

PAYMENT SCHEDULE:
50% due upon booking. Full and final payment due by July 26, 2004.
Acceptable forms of payment are Visa, MasterCard, American Express, Discover and checks. The cardholder must be one of the passengers traveling. A fee of $25 will apply for all returned checks. Check payments must be made payable to **Advantage International, LLC** and sent to: **Advantage International, LLC, 195 North Harbor Drive, Suite 4206, Chicago, IL 60601.**

CHANGE/CANCELLATION:
Notice of change/cancellation must be made in writing to Advantage International, LLC.

Change:
Changes in cabin category may be requested and can result in increased rate and penalties. A name change is permitted 60 days or more prior to departure and will incur a penalty of $50 per name change. Deviation from the group schedule and package is a cancellation.

Cancellation:

181 days or more prior to departure	$250 per person
121—180 days or more prior to departure	50% of the package price
120—61 days prior to departure	75% of the package price
60 days or less prior to departure	100% of the package price (nonrefundable)

U.S. and Canadian citizens are required to present a valid passport or the original birth certificate and state issued photo ID (driver's license). All other nationalities must contact the consulate of the various ports that are visited for verification of documentation.

We strongly recommend trip cancellation insurance!

For further details call 1-877-ADV-NTGE or visit www.GetCaughtReadingatSea.com

----

For booking form and complete information
go to www.getcaughtreadingatsea.com
or call 1-877-ADV-NTGE

Complete coupon and booking form and mail both to:
Advantage International, LLC
195 North Harbor Drive, Suite 4206, Chicago, IL 60601

Harlequin Enterprises Ltd. is a paid participant in this promotion.

THE FUN SHIPS, CARNIVAL DESIGN, CARNIVAL AND THE MOST POPULAR CRUISE LINE IN THE WORLD ARE TRADEMARKS OF CARNIVAL CORPORATION. ALL OTHER TRADEMARKS ARE TRADEMARKS OF HARLEQUIN ENTERPRISES LTD. OR ITS AFFILIATED COMPANIES, USED UNDER LICENSE.

Visit us at www.eHarlequin.com

GCRSEA2

If you enjoyed what you just read,
then we've got an offer you can't resist!

Take 2
bestselling novels FREE!
Plus get a FREE surprise gift!

Clip this page and mail it to The Best of the Best™

IN U.S.A.	IN CANADA
3010 Walden Ave.	P.O. Box 609
P.O. Box 1867	Fort Erie, Ontario
Buffalo, N.Y. 14240-1867	L2A 5X3

YES! Please send me 2 free Best of the Best™ novels and my free surprise gift. After receiving them, if I don't wish to receive anymore, I can return the shipping statement marked cancel. If I don't cancel, I will receive 4 brand-new novels every month, before they're available in stores! In the U.S.A., bill me at the bargain price of $4.74 plus 25¢ shipping and handling per book and applicable sales tax, if any*. In Canada, bill me at the bargain price of $5.24 plus 25¢ shipping and handling per book and applicable taxes**. That's the complete price and a savings of over 20% off the cover prices—what a great deal! I understand that accepting the 2 free books and gift places me under no obligation ever to buy any books. I can always return a shipment and cancel at any time. Even if I never buy another The Best of the Best™ book, the 2 free books and gift are mine to keep forever.

185 MDN DNWF
385 MDN DNWG

Name	(PLEASE PRINT)	
Address	Apt.#	
City	State/Prov.	Zip/Postal Code

* Terms and prices subject to change without notice. Sales tax applicable in N.Y.
** Canadian residents will be charged applicable provincial taxes and GST.
   All orders subject to approval. Offer limited to one per household and not valid to
   current The Best of the Best™ subscribers.
   ® are registered trademarks of Harlequin Enterprises Limited.

BOB02-R   ©1998 Harlequin Enterprises Limited

EMILIE RICHARDS

66888	RISING TIDES	___ $9.99 U.S.	___ $11.99 CAN.
66862	IRON LACE	___ $9.99 U.S.	___ $11.99 CAN.
66693	PROSPECT STREET	___ $6.99 U.S.	___ $8.50 CAN.

(limited quantities available)

TOTAL AMOUNT $_____
POSTAGE & HANDLING $_____
($1.00 for one book; 50¢ for each additional)
APPLICABLE TAXES* $_____
<u>TOTAL PAYABLE</u> $_____
(check or money order—please do not send cash)

To order, complete this form and send it, along with a check
or money order for the total above, payable to MIRA Books,
to: **In the U.S.:** 3010 Walden Avenue, P.O. Box 9077, Buffalo,
NY 14269-9077; **In Canada:** P.O. Box 636, Fort Erie, Ontario
L2A 5X3.

Name:_____
Address:_____ City:_____
State/Prov.:_____ Zip/Postal Code:_____
Account Number (if applicable):_____
075 CSAS

*New York residents remit applicable sales taxes.
 Canadian residents remit applicable GST and provincial taxes.

MIRA®